THE WIFE WHO KNEW TOO MUCH

Michele Campbell

ST. MARTIN'S GRIFFIN
NEW YORK

This is a work of fiction. All of the characters, organizations, and events portrayed in this novel are either products of the author's imagination or are used fictitiously.

Published in the United States by St. Martin's Griffin,
an imprint of St. Martin's Publishing Group

www.stmartins.com

The Library of Congress has cataloged the hardcover edition as follows:

Names: Campbell, Michele, 1962– author.
Title: The wife who knew too much / Michele Campbell.
Description: First edition. | New York, NY: St. Martin's Press, 2020.
Identifiers: LCCN 2020006773 | ISBN 9781250202550 (hardcover) | ISBN 9781250202567 (ebook) | ISBN 9781250272898 (international, sold outside the U.S., subject to rights availability)
Subjects: GSAFD: Suspense fiction.
Classification: LCC PS3613.A78648 W54 2020 | DDC 813/.6—dc23
LC record available at https://lccn.loc.gov/2020006773

ISBN 978-1-250-31334-8 (trade paperback)

First St. Martin's Griffin Edition: 2021

10 9 8 7 6 5 4 3 2 1

Praise for *The Wife Who Knew Too Much*

One of "20 Must-Read Fiction and Nonfiction Books of the Summer"
—*Newsweek*

One of "The 20 Most Anticipated Books" —*Parade*

One of "The Betches Summer Reading List" picks —Betches

One of "14 of Our Favorite Authors Share Their Picks for Summer Beach Reads" picks —*Glamour*

One of the "Most Anticipated Reads Of" —*Working Mother*

One of the "Great Fiction Book Releases to Look Forward To"
—The Nerd Daily

One of the "Most Anticipated Thrillers" —She Reads

One of "Twelve Heart-Pounding Thrillers for Your TBR" —Bookstr

One of the "15 Best Books of Summer" —Books, Brunches & Booze

One of the "20 Most Anticipated Mystery and Thriller Books"
—Comet Readings

One of the "Top Ten Books for Your Book Club in Summer"
—Book Club Chat

One of "15 Summer Releases for Your TBR Pile" —Ms. Career Girl

One of the "20 Best New Books to Read This Summer" —SheKnows

"Taut, unpredictable, and sensual, Campbell's writing provides the perfect escape." —*Newsweek*

"This page-turner is poolside ready." —*Publishers Weekly*

"Cleverly revealed subterfuge and a genuine aura of danger and confusion make this a fast and exciting read." —*Booklist*

Also by Michele Campbell

It's Always the Husband

She Was the Quiet One

A Stranger on the Beach

For Jennifer Enderlin

Acknowledgments

This book is dedicated to my editor, Jennifer Enderlin, who inspires me to do my best work. Every book is different, and the writing process for some goes more smoothly than for others. For whatever reason, this one was more of a heavy lift, requiring a lot of work to get right. Jen's unerring editorial judgment, her creativity, and her honesty enabled me to see it through. I am incredibly fortunate to collaborate with her, and a much better writer because of her.

I am indebted to the amazing team at St. Martin's Press for publishing, marketing, and publicizing my work so brilliantly. Thanks especially to Jordan Hanley, Brant Janeway, Sallie Lotz, Kerry Nordling, Erica Martirano, Lisa Senz, Jessica Preeg, and Jessica Zimmerman.

As always, the guidance, support, and friendship of my agent, Meg Ruley, not only makes it possible for me to do my job, but makes it fun. I am grateful to the wonderful team at Jane Rotrosen Agency, and especially to Rebecca Scherer and Chris Prestia for their hard work on my behalf.

Special thanks to Crystal Patriarche and her team at BookSparks, who are just so good at publicizing books in the digital age and have brought my work to the attention of countless new readers.

Finally, as always, I'm profoundly grateful to my family for their love, especially to my husband for his enduring support of my work.

When you run with the wolves, don't trip.

—Proverb

1

NINA'S DIARY

July 4

I'm writing this to raise an alarm in the event of my untimely death. This is hard to admit, even to myself, let alone to the world. My husband is planning to kill me. For obvious reasons. He's in love with someone else. And he wants my money.

I'm sitting in my office in the tower room at Windswept as I write. I look out over the ocean. The waves pound the beach as dark clouds sweep in from the east. A storm is coming. This house belonged to my first husband, Edward. On the day we met, I was twenty-three, working in an art gallery, barely scraping by. Edward was fifty and one of the wealthiest men in New York. People said I was a gold-digger. But they were wrong. Edward might not have been the perfect husband, but I loved him. When he got sick, I nursed him. When he died, I grieved him. A year later, I met someone else and fell in love. And I married again.

That was Connor, my second husband. On the night we met, he was thirty. I was fifty and one of the wealthiest women in New York. Connor didn't have a penny. People took that to mean he could only be after my money. I didn't see it that way. People had been wrong about me. I assumed they were wrong about him, too.

But they were right.

I just finished meeting with the private investigator, and I'm writing this with tears in my eyes. A photograph sits before me on the desk, incontrovertible proof that the two of them are together—and have been for a very long time. I don't know how far it goes, or what they're capable of, but I fear the worst. As Connor well knows, we have an airtight prenup. The prenup says he gets nothing if he cheats. I can divorce him and throw him out on the street. Everything I gave him—the cars, the clothes, the expensive watches, that boat he loves so much, the jet—I can take away. And I will. He knows I will. How far would he go to prevent that from happening? I hope I'm being alarmist, but I fear he'd go to extremes.

I'd throw him out right this minute, but I'm expecting three hundred guests. I'll be holding my annual Fourth of July gala tonight, here at Windswept. It was at that very same party two years ago that I first saw Connor. Infatuation at first sight. I should have slept with him and left it at that, but I'm too much of a romantic. Or just a fool. Well, I won't be foolish tonight. I'll be extremely careful. As soon as my guests leave, as the fireworks fade from the sky over the ocean, I'll confront him. I'll tell him it's over and kick him off my property. I won't do it alone. I'll take precautions. I'll have security with me, because I fear what Connor might do if he knows he's about to lose everything. I'll be careful. I'll do it cleanly, quickly. And this marriage will be done.

It's going to be so hard, though. I still love him. I love him so much that I have to fight the urge to give him another chance. To ask him to explain the things the investigator found. I can't do that. It would be a terrible mistake. It could even put my life at risk. I don't trust myself with him. That's why I'm leaving this diary where it's sure to be found. If something goes wrong, I want an autopsy. If I die unexpectedly, it was foul play, and Connor was behind it. Connor—and *her.*

2

SOUTHAMPTON, New York, July 5—Noted businesswoman and philanthropist Nina Levitt was found dead early this morning. She was 52.

Mrs. Levitt was discovered unresponsive, floating in the swimming pool at Windswept, her mansion in Southampton, where she had just thrown a lavish party attended by hundreds of guests. She was rushed by ambulance to Stony Brook Southampton Hospital, where she was pronounced dead upon arrival. Cause of death is believed to be drowning, to be confirmed by an autopsy, results of which are pending.

Mrs. Levitt was best known as the widow of real-estate tycoon Edward M. Levitt, the founder of Levitt Global Enterprises, Inc., which maintains offices in New York, Hong Kong, and Dubai. Mrs. Levitt served in various capacities at Levitt Global, including most recently as chairwoman of the board.

During Edward Levitt's lifetime, the couple were fixtures on the social scene in New York and Southampton. Mrs. Levitt was famous for her lavish parties and fashion sense, and appeared frequently in publications such as *Vogue, Town and Country*, and *Avenue.* Her ethereal beauty—she was known for her pale skin and red hair—made her a favorite subject of fashion photographers.

The Levitts' accomplishments as developers of commercial real estate in the United States and abroad, and as collectors and donors of late-twentieth-century contemporary art, were often overshadowed by scandal. The couple were frequent subjects of tabloid stories concerning Mr. Levitt's extramarital affairs. In the years since Mr. Levitt's death, Mrs. Levitt was believed to have found happiness with her second husband, Connor Ford. Mr. Ford is currently an executive at Levitt Global, having enjoyed a meteoric rise within the company since his marriage to Mrs. Levitt.

Mr. Ford did not respond to repeated requests for comment in regard to this story.

3

TABITHA

Memorial Day weekend

The night Connor Ford walked back into my life, I was waitressing, just trying to make ends meet.

I was standing by the bar at the Baldwin Grill, waiting to pick up drink orders for my tables, when I happened to glance out the window. A sexy black sports car with New York plates was just pulling into the parking lot, and I remember thinking, *That guy must be lost.* We don't rate the jet set, and that car screamed money. Don't get me wrong. The Grill is right on Baldwin Lake, one of the prettiest spots in New Hampshire. This area used to be ritzy back in the day. But not anymore. We draw a rowdy crowd in the summertime, folks from Mass., New York, and Jersey who can't afford the shore. Partiers and big drinkers. They come for the local microbrews scrawled on the chalkboard and the big-screen TV tuned to the game. But they're not the rich and famous, no way.

As I watched, a man got out. A tall, gorgeous man. And it was *him.* He glanced at the restaurant with an air of purpose and started walking toward the entrance. I couldn't believe it. My heart was pounding. I started to sweat.

Connor and I were together for just one summer, back when I was seventeen. It was a tumultuous summer for us both. We fell into each other's arms and stayed there, clinging for dear life, until they pried us apart. To this day, nobody has ever reached me like he did. I'd been married and divorced, in and out of my share of half-assed relationships. But I'd never gotten over him.

Now, there he was, looking cool and gorgeous in dark jeans and a crisp white shirt. And here I was, pushing thirty, makeup melting off my face, my clothes smelling like food, as the love of my life walked through the door ten feet from where I stood. What did I do? I panicked. I backed into a customer, knocking his half-empty beer out of his hand and onto the floor, where it rolled around and splattered people's shoes.

"Oh my gosh, I'm so sorry. Let me take care of that," I said.

In the ensuing chaos, as I raced to get paper towels, mop up the mess, and replace the poor man's drink, I lost track of Connor in the crowd. On this Friday before Memorial Day, the Baldwin Grill was jammed to capacity. You couldn't turn around without bumping into some beefy, red-faced guy who was sloppy drunk. Which made me wonder—what the hell was Connor doing here, anyway? His family sold their lake house years ago, after his grandmother died. The lake had gone downhill since then, while Connor had only come up in the world. He'd married a woman who was rich and famous, and their pictures were constantly in the tabloids. Shouldn't he be on a yacht somewhere with Nina Levitt, instead of at a second-rate sports bar, rubbing elbows with the common people?

Unless.

Could he possibly be looking for me?

"Hey, Tabitha, I just sat a hot guy in your section," the hostess called out as I passed by with my tray of drinks.

And I knew it was him.

I almost turned around and told her to give him to somebody

else so he wouldn't see me like this. Let's face it, even if I wasn't waitressing, I'm not what I was at seventeen. Who is? But we were fully booked tonight, and short-staffed. There was nobody to cover my table. I'd have to face him, whether I liked it or not.

Out on the terrace, it was a party scene. The sun hadn't yet set, but everybody had their buzz on. Music blasted from the speakers. Motorboats raced across the water, and somebody was shooting off Roman candles from the dock. I saw Connor out of the corner of my eye. He was seated at a table along the railing, facing the restaurant, his back to the lake, scanning the crowd like he was looking for somebody. A woman, presumably. His famous wife must be joining him, and he'd saved her the chair with the view. A gentleman, as always. That gave my heart a wrench.

It took a while before I could get to him. I had two tables waiting for drinks, three ready to order, two with food sitting in the kitchen that I needed to get out, and two others ready to pay. I was glad for the delay, which gave me time to collect myself. I'd dreamed of this moment so often. Sometimes it ended with us in each other's arms. Sometimes with me telling him off for letting his family come between us. Never once did it involve me taking his drink order.

When I couldn't avoid it any longer, I grabbed a pitcher of water and headed for his table. And found myself looking right into his eyes. Those hazel eyes I'd loved so well the summer I was seventeen.

4

TABITHA

Thirteen years before

The first time I saw Connor Ford, he was standing by the pool at the Baldwin Lake Country Club, in swim trunks and Ray-Bans, surrounded by a gaggle of girls. I was working as a pool girl, setting up beach chairs, collecting soggy towels, fetching burgers and shakes from the grill window. The moms would sit tanning and day-drinking while the kids screamed and splashed and threw food, and the dads hit on me. But I liked spending my days in the sun, and I enjoyed the party atmosphere, even if it wasn't meant for me.

Connor was nineteen and gorgeous, and Nell Ford's grandson besides. Mrs. Ford, a prima donna with a deep tan and a Brahmin accent, who wore pearls with her golf clothes, owned the biggest house on the lake. Though even back then, Baldwin Lake wasn't what it had once been. That sense of coming down in the world probably had something to do with Nell Ford's snobbish attitude. According to my grandma Jean, she'd take the smallest lapse in service as a personal slight and wouldn't rest until some poor slob paid with their job. Grandma Jean, who'd worked at the country club for years, had gotten me the pool-girl gig that summer. The one piece of advice she gave me when I started was to steer clear of Nell Ford and her family. Right—easier said than done. Ford grandchildren were everywhere I turned. They were spoiled and bratty—private-school kids from New York and Connecticut, who ran wild and made tons of noise and mess. I spent my days fetching food for them, cleaning up after them, and feeling put-upon by them. Until Connor arrived, and everything changed.

For the first week or so, I watched him from the corner of my eye as I went about my duties, too intimidated to speak to him. One hot afternoon in early July, I discovered he'd been watching me, too.

I don't know where everyone had disappeared to. Connor was alone, lounging on his usual chair with his sunglasses on, his skin all delicious and tan and gleaming, looking like he must smell of coconuts.

"Hey, Tabby, c'mere," he said, like we were old friends.

I'd been collecting dirty dishes that were baking in the sun. I had to look around to make sure he was talking to me.

"Yeah, you," he said, grinning.

I shouldn't've been surprised. I was seventeen that summer, fit and tan, my hair bright from the sun. My uniform was itty-bitty short shorts, Keds, and a polo with the club crest. Plenty of men stared. Even so, I had assumed Connor was out of my league.

As I walked over to him, he took off the Ray-Bans. His eyes were a hazel I've never seen the equal of, green and gold and gray all at once, with long sooty lashes.

"I wasn't sure."

"You're the only Tabby around here, aren't you?"

I wore a name tag for the job, but most club members didn't bother to look at it. They waved a hand or said "Hey" to summon me. His grandmother, Mrs. Ford, actually snapped her fingers—that's just how she rolled. So, I was surprised that Connor even knew my name, let alone that he'd use it. I put the dishes down and walked over to him.

"It's Tabitha. Nobody calls me Tabby."

"I do."

I nodded, trying to play it cool, when really I wanted to whoop and turn a cartwheel because Connor Ford had a pet name for me.

"So, listen. My cousin Robbie and I have this band. We're playing in the clubhouse at nine tonight, in the TV room off the dining hall. You should come."

"You want me to come hear your band?"

"Why not? You got someplace better to go?"

"Staff isn't allowed at club events. There's a policy against it."

"Well, look, this isn't an actual club event. It's just some kids jamming. So, that rule doesn't apply."

"I don't know."

"Just say I invited you. It's a stupid rule, anyway. Nobody's gonna care."

Nobody except your grandmother, I wanted to say.

"I can't. Thanks for asking, though. That's nice of you."

He looked at me steadily. I felt dizzy, staring into those eyes.

"Well, if you change your mind, no tickets required. I'll even dedicate a song to you."

I laughed. "I'll think about it."

"You do that."

I walked away, beaming. For the rest of that day, I floated through my chores, slowly convincing myself not only that I could pull it off, but that I had to. A guy I had an awful crush on had asked me to come hear his band play. Why shouldn't I go? He was right. The rule was stupid. Yet, sneaking out wouldn't be easy. My grandparents' house was tiny, and if Grandma Jean caught me, she'd be upset.

I'd been living with my grandparents for years at that point, and though I loved them to pieces, I longed to escape. I'd grown up an army brat, moving every year. When I was ten, my mom died. At the funeral, her parents, Grandma Jean and Grandpa Ray, convinced my dad to let me spend the summer with them. When summer ended, everyone agreed I should stay on. Everyone but me. Nobody asked me what I wanted. My grandparents became my legal guardians. To this day, I don't know which was harder—my mother dying, or my father letting me go so easily. At least Mom wanted me. Dad eventually remarried and moved to Texas with his new wife and kids. I was not invited to join them.

Every time I went near the pool that afternoon, Connor made an excuse to talk to me. He ordered a milkshake and three Cokes in a three-hour period, brushing his fingers against mine when I handed him something, making me flush and stutter.

The pool closed at six. At ten of, I was collecting ketchup squeeze bottles from the grill area when Connor came up behind me. He put his hands on my waist and spun me around to face him. He was so tall. I could smell the suntan lotion, warm on his skin.

"Tell me I'm gonna see you later, Tabby. Please?" he said.

"I want to."

"Then, what's the problem?"

"Besides that I could get fired? I'd have to sneak out."

"I sneak out all the time. And it's just a job, right?"

Connor could afford to think that way. I couldn't. But his smile sent a thrill right through me.

"All right. I'll be there."

"That's my girl," he said, and I loved the sound of that.

That night at supper in the cramped kitchen, things seemed particularly grim. Grandpa Ray was suffering from his emphysema, and Grandma Jean had had a bad day at work.

"This damn recession," she said, her face gaunt, her eyes tired behind her glasses. "They're talking layoffs."

"Not you, Grandma Jean. They couldn't get along without you."

"You're sweet, honey."

"You guys go watch TV. I'll clean up."

I washed the dishes by hand, since the dishwasher had broken last year and never been fixed. We sat on the sofa for a while and watched the History Channel. Time dragged. I could feel life happening outside the walls without me. I wondered what Connor was doing right then.

By eight-thirty, Grandpa was snoring loudly, and Grandma was nodding. A loud commercial came on, and her head jerked up.

"I think maybe we'll turn in. Help me get Grandpa to bed, Tabitha."

My grandfather leaned on my arm, wheezing, as we walked down the narrow hallway, Grandma Jean wheeling his oxygen tank alongside us. He hadn't worked in years because of his condition, so money was always tight. We lived in a tiny ranch-style house in Baldwin, one town over from Lakeside, where the country club was located. The lake and the big houses were all in Lakeside. Baldwin was where the working folks lived. Our house had two bedrooms side by side with a paper-thin wall in between. If I wanted to leave the house, I'd have to walk right by my grandparents' door.

I spent some time picking my outfit and doing my makeup, then tiptoed to their bedroom door and listened. Loud snores from Grandpa Ray. Nothing from Grandma Jean, but that didn't mean she was sleeping. I went around the house turning off lights like I was closing up, then returned to my room, shutting the door with an intentionally loud thud. I sat on the bed and listened to the silence. At five to nine, I was done waiting. I crept out of my room, down the hall to the front door.

Outside, the night air smelled sweet, and light still glowed in the northern sky. I felt like I was taking my life in my hands for the first time, and that it had been a long time coming. I wheeled my bike down the driveway and set off. Twenty minutes later, I was at the club, hurrying past the kitchen and dining hall on my way to the TV room, praying that nobody I knew was working late.

The TV room was jammed with kids lounging on the rug. They'd taken the chairs out, pushed the sofas back against the wall. The lights were dimmed. Connor and three other guys stood on the carpeted riser that passed for a stage. They were in the middle of a song—a cover of "Desperado," by the Eagles. He had a guitar slung across his chest, and he looked even taller and more perfect in the spotlight than he did in the sunshine by the pool. I plowed through the crowd to a spot right up front, sinking down cross-legged on the floor.

The band was called Big Summer, and they were pretty good. Connor sang in a soulful, quavering voice that was all the rage among indie singers then. I ate it up. *These things that are pleasing you will hurt you somehow.* I should have paid more attention to those words, but I was too busy worrying that he hadn't noticed me come in because the spotlight was shining in his eyes. I'd risked everything to get here. What if he didn't even see me? But I needn't have worried. Toward the end, there was a pause in the music as he consulted with his bandmates. He walked back to the microphone and looked right down at me.

"This is for Tabby in the front row, with the long blond hair," he said, and the band broke into a cover of "Wonderful Tonight." As he sang of the girl brushing her long, blond hair, I trembled and wiped away tears. My heart felt like it would explode. When he'd finished playing, all his friends whooped and hollered, but he didn't pay them any mind. He came right up to me—the pool girl in the front row, Cinderella at the ball.

"Told you I'd dedicate a song to you. Are you glad you came?"

"Totally."

People saw us. I didn't care. He took my hand. We went out on the golf course and made out under the stars. And that was just the beginning.

5

After that first night, as far as I was concerned, any moment not spent with Connor wasn't worth living. Most nights, I'd sneak out of the house and ride my bike to the golf course. We'd lie together on a blanket in the moonlight, the sweet smell of the grass all around us, kissing, whispering, laughing, our hands slipping beneath each other's clothes. I'd never known anyone like him. He was good-looking as a prince, but that wasn't what got to me. It was the things he said, how he carried himself, everything he knew. At work during the day, I'd take the long way back to the kitchen, stopping by the tennis courts just to watch him play. When he was out on the lake water-skiing, I'd drop what I was doing to gawk. The talent, the grace—I couldn't take my eyes off him. He'd been to private school, read great books, been to Paris and Hawaii. He was in college now, real college—not some certificate program to get a dull job that you'd spend your life doing, just to die. The boys I'd dated at Baldwin High had no ambition beyond this sorry town. And no interest in me, beyond that I was a pretty girl who might sleep with them. Connor paid attention to me. He listened. He confided in me. He sought my advice. He was as head-over-heels as I was. He didn't ask for sex until I was ready (which, okay, happened within a week of when we started dating). He said *I love you* first. He made me feel worthy, like we were equals.

We had more in common than I ever would've guessed. The year before, his father had left his mother for a younger woman and now had an infant son. Connor's parents' divorce wasn't yet final. His father was hiding assets and screwing them over on support payments. In the meantime, Connor, his mother, and his siblings were financially dependent on his grandmother. Nell Ford paid for their schools, the divorce lawyer, the mortgage on their house, but her generosity came with strings. His whole family did whatever she said, for fear that she'd cut them off.

People at the club knew there was something between us. How could they not? We'd spend all morning circling each other, hands brushing, heads together, giggling at our inside jokes. At noon sharp, I'd take my lunch break, grabbing a vanilla shake from the grill and heading to the boathouse, where he'd be waiting. It was cool inside after the glaring midday sun, with the sound of water lapping, and dark except for the shimmer of light around the boat launch. Connor would step out from behind the rows of stacked canoes and kayaks. He'd kiss me and lead me up the stairs to the storage loft. We'd lie back against piles of moldy life jackets, sipping the milkshake, kissing. To this day, the taste of a vanilla milkshake evokes the feel of his mouth on mine.

One day toward the end of summer, we were up in the loft when I heard the door open below.

"Tabitha? I know you're up there," my boss, Gil, called from the bottom of the stairs. "I need you at the counter. *Now.*"

We hurriedly arranged our clothes and came down blushing. Gil was my dad's age, balding and paunchy—not a bad guy, but a stickler. There was nothing he could do to Connor except tell him to get lost. But I was a different story. Once Connor was gone, Gil put me on probation, which meant I'd be fired if I did the slightest thing wrong.

"I'm going to hold off on telling the general manager about the misuse of club facilities. But Jean's a friend of mine—"

"Oh, no. Please, Gil. Don't tell her."

"Of course I'm gonna tell her. I should've told her a long time ago. It's been obvious something was going on, and now it's gotten out of hand. This is for your own good."

In the car on the way home that evening, the air was thick as thunderclouds.

"Grandma Jean, Gil said he was going to speak to you. I can explain—"

"Honestly, Tabitha, I can't discuss this when I'm driving. I'm too upset."

Grandma Jean's eyes were red. Had she been crying? I looked out the window, stomach sinking, my eyes prickling, too.

Later that night, I was up to my elbows in soapy water, washing the supper dishes, when she came up beside me. She looked crumpled and soft—wearing a printed housedress and plastic sandals, her iron-gray hair frizzing around her forehead in the humid kitchen.

"Come into the living room. I don't want Grandpa overhearing this. His heart can't take it."

As I dried my hands on a dish towel and followed her, my guilt flowered into resentment. I hadn't done anything wrong. Having a boyfriend wasn't a crime. I didn't need a lecture. But, as she sat down on the sofa and patted the space beside her, the disappointment in her eyes tugged at me.

"Don't be upset, Grandma. I know what I'm doing. I've had health class since middle school."

Her jaw clenched with determination.

"This isn't about the facts of life, Tabitha. It's about the Fords. I know that family, and they're bad news. You can't trust them."

"Connor's not like the rest of them."

"My guess is, when push comes to shove, he is. Exactly like them."

"You don't know him. You think he's some kind of entitled, spoiled brat. But you couldn't be more wrong. He's not taking advantage of me. He's wonderful to me. I *love* him."

Her faded blue eyes went wide behind her glasses. "Oh, gosh. This is worse than I thought."

"It is not. It's the best thing that's ever happened to me. Why can't you just be happy for me?"

"Because I'm worried about you. I know Nell Ford. She won't tolerate her family mixing with the likes of us. And she rules those kids with an iron fist."

"I don't care what his grandmother is like. I've barely said two words to her all summer."

"Okay, now. Doesn't that tell you something, that he won't introduce you to his family?"

That brought me up short.

"He does introduce me. I know his sisters and all his cousins."

"Know them as friends? Or because you fetch their food and clean up their messes?"

I looked away, flushing. She was right, of course. At six, when the pool closed, the Ford kids would pile into cousin Robbie's Jeep or cousin Hope's Land Rover and take off God knows where. I wasn't invited. That hurt, because wherever they were going—into town, or to the mall, or just home for supper—was sure to be more exciting than anywhere I'd ever been or ever would go. Sometimes I'd pick up extra hours serving dinner in the dining hall. On those nights, I'd look across the lake, see the glow of their firepit and feel the call of everything I was missing. Marshmallow roasts. Beers and joints getting passed around if their grandmother wasn't at home. Connor and Robbie strumming their guitars. The girl cousins in their cutoffs and

Birkenstocks and fishermen sweaters, flipping their broom-straight hair and laughing throaty laughs at the boys' jokes. The boy cousins deigned to talk to me now that I had something going with Connor. But the girl cousins pretended I didn't exist.

"They're not your friends, are they?" Grandma Jean said.

It was easier to be mad at her than at Connor. I got to my feet, full of righteous indignation.

"I'm almost eighteen, and this is *my* life."

"Honey, I know it's hard, living here with the old folks. It's hard for me, too. I'm sure we both wish your mom was around to deal with this situation, but she's not."

"Grandma, I don't know how else to put this. My love life is none of your business."

"I've raised you since you were a girl. I've earned the right to speak my mind. As for my business, the club is literally my business. It's my livelihood. Don't you think it affects me—Gil catching my granddaughter, who I asked him to hire, half-naked in the boathouse?"

"He never saw me half-naked. That's a lie."

"Maybe he didn't see, but he sure as heck knew. I'm not a prude, Tabitha, and I'm not trying to control you. But that's not nice. It's disrespectful to the job, to your boss, to me. To yourself."

As she spoke, and her words sank in, I began to feel smaller, until I wished I could sink into the sofa and disappear. She was right. I'd been selfish. I hadn't stopped to think how my behavior would affect her. This was my grandma, who'd taken me in, who'd raised me. She deserved better than how I'd behaved.

"You're right," I said. "That *was* wrong of me, Grandma. I see that now. I apologize. I won't do it again, promise. Forgive me?"

The relief on her face broke my heart.

"I forgive you."

"I love you, Grandma Jean."

"I love you, too."

We hugged, tears in our eyes.

"Now, that was exhausting. Time for bed."

I pecked her soft cheek and watched her walk heavily down the hall, my heart full of love for her. That was at eight o'clock.

By ten, I was jonesing for Connor so bad that I couldn't see straight. The need to touch him, kiss him, feel his skin against mine, overwhelmed my guilt and my better judgment. I'd promised Grandma not to mess around at the club. And I would keep that promise. But I never said I'd stop seeing him. As long as we didn't go to the boathouse—or the golf course, which was club property—then I wouldn't be breaking my word.

I put on a cute sundress, lip gloss, and mascara. I fluffed my hair and spritzed on perfume. I tiptoed out the door.

Outside, the night air was velvety and redolent of summer. I hurried down the block to where Connor was waiting for me in Robbie's old Jeep, top down, open to the indigo sky. A yellow moon sat low on the horizon, surrounded by a haze of humidity. I climbed up into the passenger seat. Connor grabbed me and kissed me breathless.

"Something bad happened," I said, pulling away. "Gil told my grandmother about finding us in the boathouse. I almost didn't come out tonight."

"Shit. Are you okay?"

"Yes, but she's upset. I promised her we wouldn't hook up at the club anymore."

"Don't say that. I can't go all day without a fix of you, you know that."

He slipped the strap of my dress from my shoulder, nuzzling my neck, his hand sliding up my thigh. My breath got faster. But I twisted away, worried the neighbors might see.

"Not here. I want to keep my promise to her."

"Okay."

He turned the car on.

"We can't go to the golf course, either."

"Why not? It's totally deserted at night. Nobody will ever know."

"I can't take the risk. I'd be breaking my word."

"So where we gonna go? I need to be alone with you, like now."

We kissed some more. His hand slipped inside my panties. It took willpower, but I moved it away.

"I need you, too. Just not here, and not at the club. *Think.*"

"Okay. We could park in the woods near the Bear Creek trailhead," he said.

"That's so creepy at night. Anywhere outdoors—I don't know. What about your grandmother's house? Can we go there?"

"It's risky. I'd have to sneak you up the back stairs, so my grandmother doesn't find out. You don't want her recognizing you from the club."

That rankled. It reminded me of what Grandma had said earlier—about Connor not wanting to introduce me to his family.

"I don't? Or you don't?"

He gave me a look. "What's that supposed to mean?"

"Are you ashamed of me?"

"I'm ashamed of *her.* She's a massive snob. If she recognized you, she'd throw a fit, just because you work at the club."

"So what if she does throw a fit? Are you afraid she'd cut you off?"

He got defensive. "I mean, sure, but that's not the reason. I don't want to subject you to her temper tantrums, that's all."

"I'll take my chances."

"You sure?"

"Yes."

"Okay. Don't say I didn't warn you."

We raced across town, music blasting, the wind in our hair. He didn't speak. His expression said he was worried, maybe even angry with me. So far gone was I with crazy love that I spent the drive admiring how his eyebrows drew together, the way his jaw clenched, his perfect bone structure.

When we got to the road that wound around the lake, Connor slowed down and shut the music off. As we approached the Ford house, my armpits felt damp and my chest felt tight. I didn't want to meet his grandmother. She scared me senseless. I just wanted him to want to introduce us. He'd proved he was willing to. Now I wished we could go somewhere else. But I'd made enough of a fuss that I couldn't back down.

We turned in to the driveway. The rambling, shingled house was mostly dark, except for a couple of lights on upstairs.

"Are they sleeping?" I said.

"My grandmother goes to bed by ten. Mom's in Connecticut for a court date, and my aunt and uncle went back to the city."

I breathed out in relief.

We picked our way down the driveway, which was parked up with cars and littered with fallen bikes and sports equipment. He took me in the back way, through the screen porch. Viewed from across the lake, Nell Ford's house sparkled. Up close was a different story. The screen door sagged on its hinges. The porch was crammed with musty old furniture. We stepped through the door into a large kitchen, its appliances decades out of date. A tang of garbage hung in the air, just like in any old house.

Connor led me up the creaky back stairs to the third floor, where he pushed open a bedroom door. The room was narrow and dark, with two sets of bunk beds and clothing strewn across the floor. Robbie lounged on a bottom bunk, talking on his flip phone. Two other Ford kids were on the bed above, staring at a Nintendo screen, their gangly legs hanging off. Their names were Tyler and Caleb, though they were called Punk and Boo. They were brothers, maybe twelve or thirteen. They gawked as I entered.

"You guys know Tabby," Connor said.

"Tabby, *what uuup,*" Robbie said, slurring as he closed his phone. He sounded drunk, or high.

"I need the room," Connor said.

Robbie got up, yanking on Punk's leg where it hung off the bed. "You heard the man. Move it, dudes," he said.

The younger boys followed Robbie out, poking each other and grinning. Connor shut the door and took me by the hands, drawing me down onto the lower bunk on the opposite side of the room. It must be his bed. It was narrow and lumpy, with a green wool blanket that felt scratchy against my skin as he undressed me. But I loved being in the place he slept each night, and I adored the way he looked at me.

"Your body is unreal. I'm crazy for you, you know that, right?" he said.

The bed squeaked like crazy as we made love. I heard giggling coming from the other side of the door.

We didn't get caught that night. Therefore, naturally—despite the obvious dangers of hooking up in his grandmother's house—we did it again the next night, and the night after that, until it became a habit. Three or four nights a week, I'd sneak out. Connor would pick me up at the end of my street. We'd get to his house late, when it was dark and quiet, and sneak up the back stairs. I never ran into Nell Ford.

Never—until I did.

All the Ford kids knew about our rendezvous, and I'd been worried that someone would snitch. Connor claimed that could never happen. All the cousins were guilty of something. Knowing each other's secrets created mutual assured destruction. But we hadn't reckoned with the effect of Connor's feud with his middle sister, Chloe. What had gone wrong between them, I didn't fully understand, though I knew it had something to do with the parents' divorce. One night, out of the blue, Chloe decided to tell.

We were lying under the scratchy blanket when Mrs. Ford pounded on the bedroom door.

"Connor, open up. Have you got a girl in there?"

"*Shit,* it's my grandmother," he said, under his breath.

We jumped up and pulled our clothes on. I started to speak, but he shook his head and put a finger to his lips, nodding toward the door.

"Coming right out, Grandmother. One second."

Nell Ford couldn't wait. She threw the door open and caught us half-dressed. I had my shorts and bra on but not my top. Connor was just stepping into his jeans. He stumbled and nearly toppled over.

"Wait a minute, Grandmother. Stay out."

"Don't tell me what to do. This is my house. So. You're Jean Parker's granddaughter? What does your grandmother think of your behavior?"

Connor looked stricken. "Tabby is my friend."

She looked me up and down, her face puckering with distaste. "Apparently, quite a close friend."

"I'll take her home."

"She can get herself home. You and I need to talk, young man."

"But—"

"*Sit down.* And you, please leave my house. Now."

I looked at Connor. He wouldn't meet my eyes. He sat down on the bed and hung his head. I walked out, past the grandmother, down the stairs. Robbie was sitting on the screen porch. I borrowed his phone to call Grandma Jean to come get me.

When she pulled up fifteen minutes later, I was sitting on the front steps, dry-eyed in the dark. Connor hadn't come looking for me. But Nell Ford must've been watching from the window. As I walked down the driveway, the front door flew open, and she rushed past me, bearing down on my poor grandmother.

"Jean Parker, I need a word with you."

Grandma Jean got out of the car and met her with shoulders squared. They had it out right there on the front lawn, loud enough to wake the neighbors. Grandma Jean stood up for me, and told Mrs. Ford to look after her grandchildren, who everybody knew ran wild all over town. It was hardly a fair fight. The next day, I was let go from the club. Grandma Jean got an official reprimand in her file for inappropriate conduct toward a member. Later that year, when layoffs came, the blot on her record gave them an excuse to fire her. As for Connor, he called the next day to apologize. When I wouldn't come to the phone, he kept calling, until he gave up and wrote me a letter. When I didn't answer that, he wrote again. I burned the letters unopened. Eventually, he stopped writing.

I didn't see him again until he walked into the Baldwin Grill on Memorial Day weekend, thirteen years later.

6

TABITHA

Memorial Day weekend, present day

Those eyes.

I felt dizzy. I had to grab the back of the empty chair across from him to steady myself. I took a breath. Connor looked shocked. Then he looked transported. His cheeks flushed, his eyes widened, he shook his head slightly. He broke into a huge grin. That sparkling, ravishing smile that I'd never managed to forget, hard as I tried.

"*Tabby.* It's you, right? How incredible to find you here," he said, and laughed out loud.

Connor's smile was as beautiful and carefree as I remembered—white teeth, crinkles around the eyes, a dimple in his cheek. He had the sort of smile that makes a young girl fall in love. Or a grown woman. All I know is, my stomach fluttered the way it had the very first time I saw him. Which scared me. Every time I saw his picture online, it threw me for days. What would a real-life encounter do to me?

I was speechless, and my silence confused him.

"Wait, you do remember me?" he said, looking worried.

"I'm just—*shocked.*"

"You scared me there for a minute. I thought maybe you forgot."

"Never."

The silence lengthened as we gazed at each other.

"You look amazing," he said.

"You look even better. Marriage agrees with you, I guess."

"You know about that?"

"The whole world knows, Connor. You're famous."

"*She's* famous. I'm just Mr. Nina Levitt."

I nodded at the empty seat across the table from his. "Would you prefer to wait for her to place your drink order?"

"Huh?"

Only then did his gaze take in my white shirt and black pants—the typical waitstaff uniform—and the pitcher of water in my hand.

"You *work* here."

"I do," I said, in as cool a tone as I could muster.

My cheeks felt hot as I filled his water glass. We'd never been equals. But now the gap between us was wider than ever.

"Can I start you with a cocktail? Or, would you prefer to wait for your wife?"

It was his turn to flush. "She's not coming. This is a solo trip."

"All right, then. What can I get you to drink?"

"Uh, Hendrick's and tonic?"

"Certainly."

"Hey, no, wait. Can we start over? Please, sit down for a few minutes. I'd love to catch up."

"I'm sorry, that's not possible when I'm working."

"Quickly, then—give me the basics."

He touched the empty spot on my left ring finger where my hand clutched the chair back.

"You're not married, I see," he said.

The way my body reacted to his touch—that unnerved me. I took a step back.

"I was. I'm divorced."

"Children?"

"No."

"Me, neither. It's funny, whenever I think about you—"

He paused. My heart skipped a beat.

"You think about me?"

"I envision you with a minivan full of kids. You always wanted a big family."

"I was an only, remember? I wanted what I never had. Your family seemed so jolly."

"Jolly, no. We were crazy."

"Hah, you said it, not me. Still, I was jealous. I remember you wanted kids, too."

We'd talked about that, once, lying in the grass out on the golf course under a sky full of stars. Not how many kids we each wanted, but how many we would have together. Boys, girls, what we'd name them.

"I'm so glad you're still here at Baldwin Lake," he said.

"That makes one of us."

"Otherwise, I never would have found you."

He gazed up at me intently. The moment seemed to stretch out in time. Back to the past, off to the future, like we were picking up where we'd left off. But that wasn't possible.

"I, um. I have tables waiting. I'll be back with your cocktail."

I turned and walked away, hurrying to the bar where my friend Matt was on duty.

Matt looked like a biker, with a shaved head, a bushy beard, and sleeve tattoos, but he was the kindest soul I knew. He noticed me and came over.

"It's crazy out there tonight. Holding up okay?" he asked.

"Ugh. An ex showed up and knocked the wind out of me."

"Not Derek?" Matt asked, looking alarmed. "I thought you said he moved to Florida."

Derek was my ex-husband.

"He did, thank God. No, this is someone I dated years ago."

"Is he bothering you?"

"Just making me sad. I was crazy about him, and it didn't end well. Now he's rich as God, and I'm old and pathetic."

"Old? What are you, like, twenty-two?" he said.

I noticed he didn't dispute the second half of my statement.

Matt slapped a shot glass down in front of me and poured out a finger of expensive tequila. "This is good for what ails you."

I wasn't a big drinker, but if I didn't take the edge off my feelings, I wouldn't get through the night. I knocked the shot back.

"Another."

He raised an eyebrow. "You sure?"

"This guy broke my heart, Matt."

He refilled the glass. The second shot did the trick. A comforting layer of gauze dropped over the room. I placed the drink order and went off to the kitchen to collect waiting entrees.

By the time I got around to delivering Connor's drink, I was surprised to see that a woman had joined him at his table. She was pretty, with shiny dark hair, wearing a flowy dress. They leaned toward each other, talking intently. She definitely was not his wife, whose picture I'd seen many times. Nina Levitt was older than this woman and had famously red hair. The flame-haired Nina Levitt, or "Titian-haired," they said in the press. Titian was an artist who liked to paint pictures of women with red hair. I knew this because I'd looked it up. He was before Nina's time or else I'm sure he would've painted her.

I was too busy to dwell on this mystery woman, however, and too proud to admit that I cared. I took their order like I didn't even know him. Other than shooting me an intense look, he didn't acknowledge me, either, or attempt to introduce me to her. The evening passed in a blur, helped along by the tequila. I was back and forth to Connor's table in between serving other customers. Before I knew it, two hours had passed, and he was alone. I brought him the check, and he handed me one of those Amex black cards. Titanium, cool to the touch. I'd never seen one before. They were like an urban legend. No credit limit, and you couldn't apply for one. Amex had to decide you were worthy.

"Is this for real? I thought only, like, Beyoncé and Saudi princes had these."

"It's real."

"I didn't think you had room to come up in the world, Connor Ford, but I was wrong."

He gave a harsh laugh.

When I came back ten minutes later with the slip for him to sign, the woman hadn't reappeared.

"What happened to your girlfriend?"

A worried look came into his eyes. "Not a girlfriend. Just a business associate."

"Guess I won't sell her picture to the tabloids, then."

My tone was light enough to convey that I was just razzing him. But Connor didn't get the joke. He went deathly pale and grabbed my wrist.

"Tell me you didn't take any photos tonight."

"*Hey.*"

I jerked my hand away.

"I'm sorry," he said, "but this is important."

"I was teasing, because you're famous now. It was a joke, okay? Jeez."

I rubbed my wrist.

"You don't understand. I'm under a lot of pressure. If you took a photo—"

"I said I didn't."

"Can you just— I know this sounds crazy, but can I see your phone? Just to check."

"Seriously?"

He stared back at me, looking almost ill. He wasn't joking.

"Fine. Here. Go through my photos if that'll make you feel better."

I took my phone from my pocket and opened my photos. Connor grabbed the phone from my hand and scrolled frantically. After a minute, he breathed out, handing the phone back to me.

"Okay?" I said.

"Thank you. I'm sorry to be such a jackass. If you knew my situation—"

"I get it. You have people taking advantage of you on a daily basis. You and I haven't seen each other in years, so for all you know, I could be the type who'd make a buck selling your picture. I'm not. Please, accept my apology, and allow me to comp your drinks."

"That's not necessary."

"I insist."

"No, Tabby, really. I'm sorry, I overreacted. I don't want it to be like that between us."

"Like what?"

"Like we're strangers. A waitress and a customer."

He was looking at me with those eyes, and I felt their power. I needed to put a stop to this before he broke my heart all over again. Given the presence of the attractive brunette, he was probably already cheating. A player, despite his protestations.

"Listen, it was nice seeing you. I'll get out of your hair now. Enjoy the rest of your evening."

"Wait. No."

He sounded almost desperate.

"Let me make it up to you. Buy you a drink?"

"I'm working."

"Afterwards, then."

"It's dead around the lake at night. By the time I get off work, everything will be closed."

"I know somewhere we can go, just to talk. Please, give me a chance to redeem myself. It's a gift to run into you out of the blue. I can't let it end with me blowing it like this."

His eyes were pleading. It was unnerving how upset he'd gotten over a dumb joke. But on the other hand, he was Connor, and he was right. It *was* a miracle, running into each other after all these years. In a sense, the damage was already done. He'd wormed his way into my head, my heart, all over again. If I passed up the chance to have a drink with him, I'd regret it.

Besides, it was just a drink. Right?

"Please, Tabby," he said.

Nobody else ever called me that, before or since. I looked into his eyes. I put my hand momentarily on his shoulder. I didn't have the willpower to refuse.

"Just one drink?" I said.

"If that's all you have time for."

"Okay. I get off at eleven."

His smile lit the room.

"I'll be waiting outside when you're done."

7

I finished my shift at eleven and stepped out into the darkness of the parking lot. The only cars that remained belonged to me and my coworkers. No Connor.

Disappointment hit me like a slap. That's how messed up I was over him already. I should be glad that he'd decided not to show. After all, what good could possibly come of us having a drink together? Fighting tears, and mad at myself for it, I got out my keys and headed for my old Toyota. Just as I pointed the key fob at the door, that black sports car came roaring into the lot and screeched to a halt beside me. Connor lowered the window.

"I'm so sorry I'm late. I was worried you'd be gone."

I didn't ask where he'd been, since that was none of my business. He leaned over and pushed open the passenger door. The sports car was sleek and sinuous and low to the ground, like something Tom Cruise would drive in a spy movie. I looked back at my old rust bucket, then over at his car, and thought, *What's wrong with this picture*? What did he want with me after all these years? He was married to a famous beauty, a woman who traveled on helicopters and yachts, draped in diamonds. Was it because I'd seen him with that brunette? Maybe he wasn't satisfied that I'd been joking? Maybe he was even upset. The thought made me uneasy.

"Should we just talk here?" I said.

"In the parking lot? That's not a good idea. I'm staying at a friend's ski house. It's a ten-minute drive from here, with a great view. He stocks the best liquor. We can talk without worrying about who's watching."

Right. He was famous, and married, and I'd already rattled him by joking about selling a picture. He didn't need paparazzi photographing him with a woman. Not just the woman from the restaurant. Any woman. *Me.*

"It would mean so much to me to catch up. *Please,* Tabby?"

He leaned on the *please* so winningly. That dazzling grin, that honeyed voice, the square jaw, the beautiful eyes. I knew this was bad for me. But if I could spend an hour with him, just talking, catching up, I'd have memories that would last for years. I nodded, and Connor pushed open the passenger door.

Sinking into the fragrant leather seat, I gawked at the intricate instrument panel and the lovely grain of the wood on the dashboard.

"This car is awesome. What is it?"

"Lamborghini. A gift from my wife," he said, and his voice tightened when he mentioned her.

"I hope you wrote a nice thank-you note," I said.

He hit the gas, and the car leaped forward. We zoomed out of the lot onto the road that led away from the lake, racing past the old country club, the defunct golf course, the ski resort with its lodge and lifts shuttered for the off-season. Everything was closed, deserted, locked up tight. He turned onto the narrow road that wound up Baldwin Mountain.

"I have to confess," Connor said, his eyes on the road, "I was surprised to see you there tonight."

"*You* were surprised? Imagine my reaction. Connor Ford at frumpy old Baldwin Lake? The place has gone downhill, big-time. And your family sold their house ages ago."

"Yeah, after my grandmother died. How did you know?"

I know everything about you.

"Heard it through the grapevine. Why come back?"

"Business. The old golf-course land is on the market. I was thinking of buying it and trying to develop it into something."

"That's who the woman was?"

He gave me an uncomfortable look.

"We were discussing a project. Anyway, what about you? Why are *you* still here? You wanted to move to the big city. Become a journalist—a TV reporter, right?"

"That seems ridiculous now."

"Why? You had the looks for it. And the smarts."

"I decided to become a smart, good-looking waitress instead," I said.

The bitterness in my voice was palpable. He glanced over at me, sadness in his eyes.

"Sorry if that sounded condescending. There's nothing wrong with earning a living, as long as you're happy."

"Happy endings are for rich kids. You know that."

He looked stung.

"I'm sorry, that wasn't fair," I said.

"I can see why you might think that. If it makes you feel better, there was no happy ending in my family. We ended up broke and at each other's throats."

"Why would that make me feel better?"

"After the way my grandmother treated you, you'd be justified in hating her."

"I don't wish bad on anyone."

"You wouldn't. You're too good. Most people would say we got what was coming. We were living off my grandmother's money. My mom, my aunts and uncles, all the cousins. *Me.* The financial crisis wiped her out. She died not long after, and the battle for the estate was crows fighting over a corpse. It got ugly. Most of us still don't talk to each other."

"That's sad. You and your cousins seemed so close."

"It looked better from the outside than it actually was. Everybody was nuts."

He fell silent, concentrating on driving. The dark, narrow road switched back as it climbed, and he took the hairpin turns expertly, the Lamborghini cornering like the exquisite high-tech machine it was.

"This car is amazing."

"You like it?"

"*Love.*"

"Check this out."

Connor grinned and hit the gas. The car leaped, and I squealed as the g-forces slammed me into the seat.

At the top of the mountain, he jammed on the brakes, then swerved onto an unpaved road, kicking up dirt. We bumped along, hitting every rut and hole till my teeth clattered, and we arrived at an elaborate iron gate that slid open as the car approached.

"That was the most fun I've had in years," I said.

"Me, too."

He sounded sincere, but I couldn't help doubting. Wasn't his life normally full of fast cars, private jets, speedboats? The tabloids would have you think so.

We got out. Wind rustled in the pines. I hugged myself against the chill as I followed Connor toward the house. It loomed, enormous and dark at the edge of a precipice, with open air below. I looked up at an eerie yellow moon, hiding behind wispy clouds, then across the valley to the mountains of Vermont, fifty miles away. Involuntarily, I shivered.

"Your friend isn't home?" I asked.

"I'm borrowing the place. He doesn't use it in the summertime."

He unlocked the door and flipped on the lights. Inside, there was a musty chill, like the house had been closed up since last winter. We stood in a two-story great room dominated by an enormous stone fireplace. At the far end, tall windows faced the view. Against the dark of the night, they were black mirrors reflecting my image back at me, tiny and vulnerable in the towering space.

"I'll find us something to drink," Connor said, and disappeared.

I walked over to a big leather sectional that faced the fireplace and sat down gingerly. The house was beautifully crafted, with log walls, gleaming floors covered in Navajo rugs, and faux-rustic furniture straight out of a magazine. But you could tell it wasn't lived-in, and it had a sterile air about it. Connor came back with two crystal glasses and a bottle of scotch. He poured slugs for both of us, then leaned back on the sofa and pointed a remote at the fireplace. Blue flames sprang to life, doing nothing to banish the chill. We clinked glasses. He sighed and took a long pull of his scotch.

"It's so good to be here with you. I can't even tell you," he said.

I didn't reply. I was trying to decide whether to take him at his word. It meant a lot to me to be here, more than it ever could to him. Or so I thought. Was he playing with me? I had to be careful not to make this into more than it was. I took a sip of the scotch. It tasted smoky and rich.

"You didn't answer my question," he said.

"What question?"

"Why you stayed. This town always seemed too small for you. I remember, you were dying to get out and see the world."

"You made me think that was possible."

His eyes searched my face. It felt too intense. I looked down at my glass, swirling the scotch, trying to decide how honest to be, how vulnerable. But he wouldn't let me get away. He reached out and put a finger under my chin, tipping my face up so I was gazing into his eyes. With anyone else, it would've felt like a violation. With Connor, it was deep communion.

"But it wasn't? You can tell me the truth. Even if it's *You and your fucked-up family ruined my life.*"

I smiled. "All right, then, yeah. You and your fucked-up family ruined my life."

"Hah, I asked for that." His words had a bantering tone, yet he looked genuinely crushed.

"I'm joking," I said.

"No, you're not, and that's okay. I left you hanging. I have a lot of regrets in life, but that's one of the big ones."

"Well, you were in a tough spot. Your family was under your grandmother's thumb."

"I should have stood up to Nell, but I didn't have the guts. She terrified me till the day she died."

"She was a scary lady. That doesn't make my family's problems your fault. The recession hit. There were layoffs at the club. Grandma Jean was let go. But we didn't starve. We had her social security and Grandpa's disability. When there was no money for college, I went to work. Me, and millions of other kids. It wasn't a tragedy. Grandpa died. Grandma got sick. I was her only family. I stayed around to take care of her, and I was happy to do it. That's just life. I did get my associates degree eventually, after she died. I had a good job at the hospital. Things were good, until I went and married the wrong guy—but that was on me."

I stopped. Connor was watching my face.

"Tell me about your marriage," he said gently.

"I'd rather not talk about it. It's behind me, and I like to keep it there."

"Understood. Then, you'll relate. Marriage hasn't been easy for me, either," he said.

"From what I see in the magazines, you look happy enough," I said, and instantly regretted giving away the fact that I stalked him online. But he didn't seem to notice. Or if he did, he didn't mind.

"I must sound like an asshole," he said.

"You don't. I didn't mean to imply that at all."

I gazed at him, wanting to memorize him, not as he was at nineteen, but now, as a grown man. He put his hand around mine, where I was holding the glass. But I moved away. We were on dangerous ground.

"I'm just saying, my marriage is not the fairy tale it's made out to be. We got married too fast, before I really knew her. She was beautiful and rich and famous. She turned my head."

"That happens. I've seen her pictures. She is beautiful."

"It's not just her, it's the way she lives. You can't even imagine. The houses, the cars, the jet, the travel. She has people to do everything for her. Assistants and secretaries, housekeepers, a personal yoga instructor, a stylist, hair and makeup, a driver, chefs. I can't even count them all. She just has to think something, and it happens. She doesn't even *walk* on her own."

"Walk?"

"Like, she exits a building, and somebody guides her to her car, holding an umbrella if it's raining. She gets into an elevator, someone else pushes the button, and tells her what floor she's going to. Her feet don't touch the ground. She doesn't so much as flick a light switch. When I'm with her, they do all that for me, and I've gotten used to it. Do you understand? It's a terrible thing to admit. I feel like I sold my soul."

"Um—I don't know what to say. I see how that could be very seductive."

"But you. You were so real. That summer. You were just this—I don't know—this angel of my youth."

I laughed. "Angel?"

"Yeah. The long blond hair, the long legs. Always tan."

"Well, I worked outdoors."

"I don't mean to make it just about how you looked. It was so much more. I saw you tonight, and that whole time in my life came rushing back. How messed up I was. Hating my dad, which I still do, by the way. My mother on the verge of a breakdown. I remember, I'd go somewhere, alone with you, and everything would magically get better. Your voice, your laugh. You had magic powers. You could cure me, Tabby. It was so perfect, so simple, what we had. I never found that again. And this thing with Nina—it's twisted."

He shook his head, shuddering. I couldn't believe what I was hearing. I was afraid of the things he said, how they made me feel. I should have told him to stop. But I couldn't.

"Talking like this, I feel it again. Like we're still kids. Like I'm still in love for the first time," he said.

He was looking in my eyes as he said that, and I was sipping the scotch. I started to cough and couldn't stop. He patted my back.

"I'm okay," I managed, eyes watering.

"I'm sorry. It's not fair, unloading my regrets on you. It was my fault, the way things ended. I had no backbone. I wish I could have a do-over. Anything not to've hurt you."

"It was a long time ago."

"But I'm not over it. If I could recapture that feeling—well, I'd give a lot."

How could I stay strong when he said things like that? I went there.

"If you're so unhappy with your wife, why do you stay?"

He hesitated, sipping his drink, gazing into the fire.

"I'm afraid of what she'd do if I left. I don't know if you know much about Edward Levitt—"

"I know he was famous for his affairs."

"The way he treated her. He humiliated her publicly. It's like she has PTSD from it. She's insecure. Depressed. Suicidal, sometimes. With me, she can't help it, she's incapable of trusting. Like, to the point of being paranoid. She believes that I'm cheating on her, that I'm lying, that I'm trying to hurt her. I'm not doing any of those things. But she won't believe me. It's almost like she can't."

I decided not to mention that dark-haired woman at dinner. He'd claimed she was a business associate, and anyway, if Connor was having an affair, it was really none of my business. It did caution not taking what he said at face value, though.

"What about counseling?" I asked.

"I suggested couples' counseling. Nina's been in therapy for years, and the only thing she'd consider was having me see her analyst, separately. I tried. It was useless. He just sat there and said, 'Hmmm.'"

"What will you do?"

"I've tried to show her how devoted I am, to convince her that I'm not Edward, that I would never behave the way he did. But from the beginning, she couldn't let me breathe. She insisted on knowing where I was every second. She monitored my phone calls. She made me give her the passwords to all my accounts so she could read my emails. I should've said no, but I was trying to reassure her. I thought it would help, but it ended up making things worse. The more information she got, the more paranoid she became. Now we're down the rabbit hole. Every move I make is suspect."

"That sounds extreme."

"It is. It's gotten to the point where I don't know what to do, Tabby. I really don't."

He dropped his head to his hands. He looked so desperate that it got to me. I rubbed his shoulder.

"Hey," I said, shifting closer to him.

He looked up and our eyes met. As if in slow motion, he leaned toward me, and I thought, *Don't do this, you'll regret it.* But my lips parted.

A sudden crashing sound outside made us both sit up in a flash. We stared at the blankness beyond the tall windows.

"What was that?" I said.

Connor jumped to his feet, rushing over to press his face up against the glass of the window.

"It's too dark out there. I can't see a thing. I worry sometimes that Nina is having me followed."

My hand went to my throat. "Do you think someone followed us here?"

He turned from the window. "We'd probably have seen them on the road. But I'd better check. Stay here, I won't be long."

"Be careful."

Connor marched out the front door. I wrung my hands in my lap, listening to the wind howl. Up here on top of the mountain, it was like summer had never come. I stared into the blue flames and shivered. Did my phone even work up here? I dug for it in my handbag. No service. Figured. I got up and walked around the great room, looking for a landline telephone, but there was none. I didn't have the nerve to go search one out in the other rooms. I went back to the sofa and downed the rest of the scotch in one go. It warmed me up without calming me down. When the front door banged open suddenly, I jumped. But it was just Connor coming back. I heaved a sigh of relief and stood up to meet him.

"What was it?"

"There's a big tree branch down on that side of the house. It must've come down in the wind. I think that's what we heard. Come, sit down."

On the sofa, I drew my knees up to my chest. We sat closer together than before, turning toward each other. Connor picked up his glass and took a big gulp. He seemed tense. I wondered if he'd told me the whole story.

"You're worried. Your hands are shaking," I said.

"Honestly. That's from being around you."

"Don't say things like that."

"Even if they're true?"

"Shouldn't you go to the police?" I said, looking to change the subject.

"To say what?"

"That your wife is having you followed?"

"I have no proof. It's just a feeling."

"Then what are you going to do?"

"I don't know. But seeing you, I realize I have to do *something.* I don't want to go on like this."

His hazel eyes were so near that I saw my reflection in them. I loved the line of his mouth, so strong and yet so vulnerable. I wanted to kiss him, badly. But he was married, and troubled, and dangerous for me.

"Sometimes I wonder what my life would be like if I'd married you instead," he said.

I'd been waiting years to hear him say that. Now that it was happening, I wasn't sure I could handle it.

"Don't play with my feelings."

"I'm not. I really mean it. I should have come back here a long time ago. What we had was so pure. Those were the happiest days of my life. I'd give anything to feel that way again. Please, can I just—"

"No. It's not a good idea."

"Please. Let me."

He raised his hands and undid my hair. It came cascading down. He buried his face in it.

"I remember this," he said.

"We should stop, before it's too late," I whispered.

"It's already too late."

He leaned in to kiss me, and my lips parted like they remembered him. His mouth was the same, his taste as sweet as ever. My hands found their way to his shirt. The cotton was finer than what he'd worn in my memory, his body underneath my fingers subtly changed. I undid the buttons. Then he took off my shirt. We paused, taking each other in with our eyes, our hands moving over each other. He was sturdier, more solid, more defined than I remembered, but the texture of his skin under my fingers, the hollow at his collarbone, I remembered vividly. When he touched me, every man I'd been with in the intervening years faded away. They'd all been wrong. Every one. He knew how to touch me like nobody else did. My breath came in gasps. Our clothes were in piles on the floor. He was on top of me, his skin silken against mine, his body moving against me, his face filling my vision. He was all that I could see. All I ever wanted to see. *Please,* I thought, *let him stay with me this time. Let him never leave. I know this is wrong. But it feels so right. And I don't want it to end.*

8

Delicate morning light streamed through the tall windows of the ski house, illuminating Connor's face as he slept. We lay on the sofa, naked and tangled in each other's arms, partially covered by a cashmere throw. I was cold and stiff, and I needed to pee. But I held perfectly still, fearing that, the moment he woke, my time with him would come to an end.

He stirred, opening his eyes.

"Hi," he said, and kissed me lightly on the lips.

"Hi."

This was pretend. There was someplace else he ought to be, another woman he belonged to. He knew that better than I did. Anxiety flared in his eyes as reality set in. He sat up abruptly and grabbed his phone from the coffee table. The screen as he unlocked it was covered with the bubbles of multiple text messages. I watched him scroll through hurriedly, watched his shoulders slump, watched as he rushed to pull on his underwear. And I knew what it meant: He'd leave, and I wouldn't see him again.

"Was that your wife?"

He didn't reply.

"It's okay. I understand," I said, reaching for my clothes.

"No. Just—there are some things I should deal with."

"Sure."

"I wish it were different," he said.

"Yeah. Me, too."

I couldn't look him in the eye for fear I'd choke up and beg to stay. Or else, get angry, which I had no right to do, since I'd known what this was, and did it anyway.

We got dressed in silence.

Outside, the air was fresh and cool, smelling of pine and green leaves. I took a breath to banish my sadness, but the beauty of the day only magnified it. The house had lost its air of menace and looked like the glamorous millionaire's ski retreat it was, the kind of place I'd normally never get inside, unless I was catering a party. I wished we could stay longer, that we had the right to be there together. But we didn't. Our night together had been stolen from its rightful owner, Connor's wife. She was the one who belonged with him in places like this. He must feel that, too. He fell into a troubled silence that hung over us like a cloud all the way back to the Baldwin Grill, where I'd left my car.

The restaurant didn't open for hours, and the parking lot was empty. In the light of day, the restaurant looked shabby, in need of paint, the parking lot riddled with potholes from spring rains. This was my life, not that ski chalet. Connor pulled up next to my dented ten-year-old Corolla, the only car in the lot. I was fond of that car. She even had a name—Corrie. Yet the contrast between her and the sleek Lamborghini brought home a hard truth. He was rich. I wasn't. We were about to part ways, presumably forever. He'd return to his glamorous existence, his glamorous wife. I'd head back to the daily grind—alone.

I reached for the door handle. "I hope things get better for you. Goodbye, Connor."

"Wait. Don't go. This can't be the end."

I turned back, shrugging hopelessly. "What else can it be?"

"I have meetings all day today. But afterwards, the rest of the weekend, I'm free. Can I see you?"

There was nothing I wanted more in life than to see him again. But where would it lead?

"Connor, this isn't good for us. And it's not right."

He laid his hand against my cheek and looked deep into my eyes. "Last night with you was the first time in years that I felt like myself. The world made sense again. I know I have nothing to offer, no right to ask anything of you. But if you'd let me see you—if it's just a few hours, minutes, even—anything you'll give me, I'll take."

"Say we spend another night together. What happens then? You go back to your wife, right?"

"I won't lie to you. The answer to that is yes, for now. I want to leave her. But it's complicated, and I can't put a time frame on it."

"Thank you for being honest. I love you, Connor. I really do, I always have. But this—I just can't. I should go."

His face fell as I flung the door open.

I ran to my car, got in, turned on the engine. The Lamborghini hadn't budged. Connor sat there, staring at me through the glass, looking as devastated as I felt. I wanted to run back into his arms. I couldn't. I don't know how I managed, but I put the car in gear and drove away, second-guessing myself all the way home.

I was such a mess at work that night that everybody noticed. Not just Matt, the bartender, but my manager, Liz, whom I'd worked with at another restaurant before following her here. And the hostess, Hayley, who was a ditz, but a sweetheart. They all saw that something was wrong from the expression on my face and kept asking if I was okay. I said I was fine. But after I screwed up a couple of orders, Liz pulled me aside.

She was an ex-hippie, big-boned and apple-cheeked, with a bright blue streak in her graying hair.

"Something's wrong. What is it?" she asked.

"Nothing. I'm sorry. I'll try to focus."

"Is it the guy from last night? The ex with the sports car?"

"Matt told you about him?"

"Uh-huh. You went home with him?"

"Yeah. Stupid. Now I'm crazy for him again, and it's already over." I teared up.

"Aww, babe, don't cry. Why does it have to be over?"

I wiped my eyes, fighting back the tears.

"He's only in town for the weekend."

She shrugged. "A lot can happen in a weekend."

"*And*, he's married."

"Oh. Well, that sucks."

"Yup."

"You know, Bart was married when he and I first met."

Bart was her husband of twenty years. They had four children together.

"I didn't know that."

"I was with someone, too. But we were both miserable. And from the second we met, we knew it was meant to be. I'm just saying. You only live once."

She patted my arm.

I went back out on the floor, thinking about what Liz had said. What if Connor and I were destined to be together? What if we were true soul mates, who would never find happiness with anyone else? He was going to divorce Nina anyway, eventually. I'd sent him away without even exchanging phone numbers. What if he got single and couldn't find me? I might not stay at the restaurant forever. Maybe I'd missed my chance. Made a terrible mistake. As the shift dragged on, I got more anxious. The mistakes piled up. I served the wrong food to one table, knocked over a wineglass at another. An hour before my shift ended, I was standing at the coffee station, when I saw Liz heading my way, and geared up to beg her forgiveness.

"I clocked you out," she said. "I'll cover the rest of your shift."

"Look, I know I've been a klutz, but you don't need to—"

"He's here. Your friend with the fancy car. He's asking for you."

"Where?"

"At the bar. I said I'd send you over. Go. You're useless, anyway."

"I'll make it up to you."

"Yes, you will. You owe me, sister," she said, with a wink, and walked away.

I hurried to the bar, squeezing through a solid wall of customers as I craned my neck to spot him. He was wedged in at the bar, facing out, scanning the crowd for me. Our eyes met. He put down his beer and came right over.

"Don't be mad," he said, hands on my shoulders, looking down into my eyes intently, "but I had to come. There's something I need to tell you. Something I should have said—that I regret not saying."

"Okay."

"Can we go outside?"

I nodded.

In the parking lot, the air was cool and sweet after the heat of the restaurant. He started walking, but I stopped him with a hand on his arm.

"You said you have something to tell me?"

"I do. I'm just stalling. I'm afraid of scaring you off."

"Just say it."

"All right. Here it is." He took a breath. "I went to the restaurant last night on purpose, to find you."

I opened my mouth in confusion. "I don't understand."

"I'm just—I guess, I'm at a crossroads. In my life, my marriage. A few months ago, things were so dark, I—well, I started asking myself how I ended up like this, where I went wrong. And I kept coming back to our summer. How it ended. I didn't fight for you, Tabby. And nothing has been right since then."

"So, you purposely came looking for me? Is that what you're saying?"

"Sort of. I wanted to come back to this place. I didn't really imagine you'd still be here. But then I stopped for gas at the store in town, and that same guy still owns it. He told me I could find you there. I pumped the gas and got back in the car. I sat for a while, trying to decide what to do. I knew that if I found you, something big would happen. But then I came here. And it has."

"The real-estate deal, does that even exist?"

"Yes. I'd been thinking about you. About this place. I wanted to come back, but I didn't act on it. Maybe I didn't have the guts. But when I learned the land was for sale, it was like fate. I had to come up."

"Why tell me this now?"

He took my hands in his. His were hot, emotion coming through them like a wave.

"I couldn't leave without letting you know how I feel."

"You feel like your life went bad when we broke up. I get it. Things haven't been great for me, either. We all wish we could go back and fix our mistakes. But the question is, who are you now, Connor?"

"I'm the guy who never stopped loving you. I have until Tuesday morning, and I want to spend that time with you. Talk to you, touch you, eat a meal with you. Make love in front of the fire again. I don't care what happens after that. I don't care if the world ends. I need you now."

He leaned toward me, and the kiss was molten. I was done fighting this. I had no ballast—no husband, no kids, no prospects to hold me back. No reason to deny what my heart was feeling. We hurried, hand in hand, to his car. On the drive to the ski house, we couldn't stop touching, kissing. It was a miracle we made it up the mountain in one piece. At the house, he unlocked the door, and we tore off each other's clothes as soon as we were inside. He pulled me down the hall to a bedroom and threw me down on the bed without bothering to turn on the lights.

It was everything, and more.

In the morning, I texted Liz that I'd be out for the rest of the weekend. She wasn't happy. So, I repeated back to her the words of wisdom she'd had for me last night. The words I told myself when I opened my eyes in the darkness, feeling sick with guilt, looking at Connor sleeping beside me and knowing it wouldn't last. Knowing I'd pay a terrible price for feeling joy like this. *You only live once.*

9

That weekend was like our honeymoon. We spent hours in the massive bed, piled high with pillows, in a rustic-chic guest room straight out of a magazine. We made love by the glow of the fire in the gas fireplace, getting up occasionally to raid the gleaming Sub-Zero for delicacies or the wine tower for vintage wines. We soaked in the hot tub and watched the sun rise over the mountain from the wraparound deck. We talked of everything under the sun, from the most serious to the most inconsequential. Our families, what we wanted from life. What we'd been like as children. The personalities at the restaurant, the office where he worked, the places he'd traveled. I loved his voice, his sense of humor. I loved his eyes when he laughed and his face when he slept. We hid from reality, and by hiding, let ourselves get entangled, deeply.

But we couldn't hide forever.

On Tuesday morning, Nina sent the jet to collect him. He dropped me at my car on the way to the airport. In the parking lot, I clung to him, wetting the front of his shirt with tears. He took my face in his hands.

"In our hearts, we're always together. I need you to remember that," he said.

"What does that matter, when you're going back to her?"

He wiped my tears away with his fingers, then kissed my cheeks, my nose, my forehead. His mouth found mine. I knew the kiss would only prolong the torture, but I couldn't help myself. I kissed back.

"It matters. It means everything. It's you I love. I hate that we have to be apart," he said.

"You're not a prisoner. You could stay here if you wanted to."

He tangled his hands in my hair, looking at me, deeply, desperately.

"It's complicated."

"Complicated. Meaning, that's a lot of money to walk away from," I said, my voice raw with hurt.

"No."

"Why go back if not for the money? If you're going to tell me she's unstable—"

"She *is* unstable. She's threatened suicide before."

"That's not the real reason."

He sighed and looked away.

"Hey," I said, grabbing his arm. "Tell me the truth. I can take it. You say our love is so pure, that you're your best self with me. Well, be yourself. Not some fake version of you. I want the real thing."

"Even if it's not pretty? Even if I really haven't changed that much from when I was afraid to face life without my grandmother's money?"

"Even that."

He looked at me for a long time. Then he nodded, his hazel eyes glittering with resolve.

"All right, then. The truth is, there's a prenup. If Nina divorces me, I get ten million. If I leave her, or if she finds out I'm cheating and kicks me out because of it, I get nothing. Ten million, Tabby, versus nothing."

That took me aback. I'd never seen an exact estimate of Nina's wealth. I knew it was vast—so vast that I couldn't wrap my head around it. Ten million, though—that, I could understand. He was right. Ten million was a lot of money to leave on the table. Still, this didn't feel right.

"To Nina, ten million's chump change," Connor was saying. "She won't miss it. But I could live on that for the rest of my life. *We* could. Do you understand? I'm going to leave her. I just need to do it in a way that doesn't trigger the prenup."

"Is that even possible?"

"I have to make her think a divorce is her own idea."

"How?"

"I'll figure something out. Otherwise, you know what happens? I lose my job at Levitt Global, because she'd never let me keep working there. I signed a noncompete, which means I'd basically be blacklisted, unable to work in that industry. I'd have nothing."

"I don't care. I'll take you flat broke. It's how I live already."

"I appreciate that. But wouldn't you rather have me with ten million?"

That question sounded flip to me. I yanked my hand away. "This just feels wrong."

"You told me I could say anything."

"I don't feel right, being part of that kind of deception."

"You're not part of it. This is on me. It's my marriage. I'm the one who'll end it. I was going to, anyway. You just made me certain. Besides, it's not only for the money that I want it to end clean. I don't want to hurt her the way Edward did."

"How long will this take?"

"I don't know. A while."

"And during that time, we don't see each other. We don't talk."

"Hey," he said, leaning close, "I'm not okay with not talking to you. As for seeing each other, maybe—"

"*No.* You don't want her to know about me. If she has you followed, if she has the passwords to all your accounts, she would find out."

"Maybe. Yes. Okay, you're right."

"We can't see each other. We can't talk."

"You have to believe me, that I want to be with you," he said, sighing. "It's just complicated. There's a lot at stake."

His phone was buzzing with texts.

I looked away. "Your plane is waiting. You'd better go. So, don't call me, and I won't call you, I guess."

He put his hands on my shoulders and leaned in. "Tabby. Don't give up on me."

I tried to look away, but his eyes were mesmerizing.

"Wait for me? Please? I love you. I'm going to get free, and then we'll be together. It'll be worth the pain, I promise."

He wrapped me in his arms. I wanted to believe him. But I didn't.

"I love you," I said.

We kissed, and in my mind, I thought we were saying goodbye.

In the days after we parted, I was consumed. I couldn't eat. I couldn't sleep. I burned for him. I sleepwalked through my life not seeing what was in front of me, not hearing what people said. My senses were filled with him. His mouth, his hands, his skin, his hair, the way he smelled. It was like a low-level fever that I'd been able to manage until I saw him again in the flesh. Now the disease raged, and it ravaged me. Plus—the guilt, the shame, the humiliation. I'd slept with a married man, and he'd left me to go back to his wife. Grandma Jean didn't raise a fool, or a home-wrecker, yet there I was, both. I spent my days staring at my phone, willing it to ring, and staring at his number in my contacts, trying not to call. I was lost.

Weeks passed. The weather turned hot, and everywhere I looked, people went about their happy lives. Couples walking hand in hand. Moms at the grocery store, pushing chubby toddlers in shopping carts. I'd never known that peace, that contentment. And now I didn't even want it. I wanted to walk into the fire. After years of feeling numb, I was back where I started—obsessed with Connor, believing he was the one road to nirvana.

I threw myself into my work, looking for a distraction. I got a part-time job as a data-entry clerk in the billing department at a local insurance company. But typing payment codes into the computer left my mind free to wander. I sat there reliving every caress, until I could hardly see the screen. I took extra shifts at the restaurant so I wouldn't be alone in my apartment at night, tossing in my bed, touching myself like he was with me. But every time I passed the table where he'd sat, I stopped in my tracks, like I saw him there.

When I was alone, I gave in to the exquisite torture of searching photos of him online. Connor wasn't the newsworthy one. Nina was, so every picture of him was of the two of them together. And they *were* together—still. Connor and Nina at a charity gala in New York, a gorgeous couple in their finery, smiling for the cameras. Or on the terrace of a restaurant in the South of France, eating lunch with a famous film director and his actress wife. Connor in a white shirt and sunglasses, his arm slung casually across the back of Nina's chair. Frantically, I searched the dates. The photos were new. They didn't look like a couple headed for divorce. They looked content. Not madly in love, perhaps, but undeniably together. How was that possible, after the time Connor had spent with me? He'd seemed so in love. He said he was. And I'd believed him.

Had it all been a lie? Probably. After all, it's not like I hadn't shown poor judgment in men before. Derek. My ex-husband. Can't get much worse than that.

Derek Cassidy was a mechanic at the auto repair shop where I got my car serviced. He had clear blue eyes, amazing biceps, a leather jacket, a motorcycle, and a pickup truck. He was ex-military like my dad. His bad-boy aura should've been a warning, but we met not long after Grandma died, and I was feeling too alone in the world to listen to the voice of reason. All I saw were good looks, a steady paycheck, and the fact that he'd chosen me.

It was only after we were married that things got rocky. He was secretive. He had a temper. I'd threaten to leave, he'd promise to do better. And it would get better, for a while. Then, one night on a dark road, the cops pulled us over. And I learned that Derek had been dealing pills out of his truck. There was a hidden compartment underneath the floorboards. I knew nothing about it, but I was in the passenger seat, so they arrested me anyway. I could've had the charges dropped if I gave information. But Derek threatened me, and I knew him well enough by then to take him at his word. I pled guilty to a misdemeanor possession charge with a guarantee of no jail time because my lawyer said it was the best I could do. I got five years' probation and fired from my good job at the hospital because they couldn't have someone with drugs on her record.

That black mark is there to this day, holding me back from better things. Derek, on the other hand, I did manage to shake. He went away for five years, and I divorced him while he was in jail. He wasn't too happy about that.

Once burned, twice shy. I dated here and there after Derek, but I was always leery of getting serious. Nobody got through my armor until Connor came back. And he'd left me dragging through my days, feeling like the hollowness inside would never go away. That's why, after several weeks passed with no word from Connor, I let Hayley at the restaurant shame me into going on Tinder. She'd just gotten engaged to a guy she met on there. A nice guy, who owned a lawn-care company and went to church with her on Sundays. When I told her one time too many that I had no weekend plans, she grabbed my phone out of my hand and insisted on making me a profile. I don't know if I was reckless, or stupid, or just desperate. But I let her do it, figuring it couldn't do any harm. Wrong.

At home that night in the privacy of my apartment, out of curiosity I opened Tinder and started browsing eligible men in my geographical area. None of them could hold a candle to Connor, and I was about to give up when I found myself staring at a photo of my ex-husband. I couldn't believe it. What the hell was Derek doing on there? I'd set Tinder to show me profiles within a twenty-mile radius. He'd gotten out of jail a year ago and moved to Florida. I'd heard that from enough people to accept it as fact. Whenever I woke from a bad dream about Derek, the thought that he was a thousand miles away always comforted me. But if Tinder was showing me his profile, that could only mean one thing.

He was back.

If I'd seen his profile, had he seen mine? If he had, would he come looking for me? I jumped up and drew the blinds. I double-locked the door, looked in both closets, and pulled my shower curtain aside. Then I sat back down on the sofa, my breath coming in fast spurts. After he went to jail, I'd moved from the small house we'd rented together into this ground-floor studio in an apartment complex. My address was not listed anywhere online that I was aware of. On the other hand, Derek and I knew people in common who knew where I lived. My apartment faced the parking lot and had two large windows with flimsy locks. I knew my neighbors well enough to smile and exchange pleasantries, but none were friends I could turn to in a moment of need. If I screamed loudly, I was pretty sure they'd call 911, but that was small comfort. I took a butcher knife to bed with me that night, and barely slept.

The next day at the restaurant, I was constantly looking over my shoulder. I told everyone to be on the lookout for him, and even pulled up an old photo on my phone and showed it around. Matt tried to reassure me that, since I hadn't swiped right on Derek's profile, we hadn't *matched,* so it was unlikely that he'd seen mine. For all I knew, Derek had been back in this area for months without getting in touch, so maybe I had nothing to fear. Still, to be safe, I had Matt walk me to my car that night, and for several nights after.

A week passed with no sign of Derek. I let my guard down.

It was a Tuesday night. My shift had just ended at the restaurant and I was walking to my car through the dark parking lot when Derek came up from behind. I saw him from the corner of my eye, and the look of him shocked me. He'd always been a big guy, a gym rat, built. I'd liked that at first, until it scared me. Now he looked heavier, and not in a good way—puffy, unhealthy, with pasty skin. His hair was different, too, shaved into a fade that screamed jailhouse. I backed away, my chest tight with fear.

"Not so fast. Where do you think you're going?" he said.

"I don't want any trouble. Leave me alone."

"Why should I? You're my wife."

"Not anymore."

"Because of some bullshit piece of paper? I know you're mad over the drugs, but come on—divorce? I was just try'na make a buck for us, babe."

"Don't blame me for your arrest. I never asked you to break the law."

"Oh, right. You just wanted shit. A house, a new car—"

"I never said that. You decided to deal, without telling me."

"Whatever. I apologize, okay. Now, cut the bullshit, and come home to me. I see you on Tinder, giving yourself to strangers. I'm right here. I miss you."

He stepped toward me, into the light, and I got a look at his eyes.

The pupils were pinpricks in the light-blue irises. He was on something. I started walking. He grabbed my arm. I screamed, and he clamped his hand over my mouth.

"Shut up, you'll get me in trouble."

My whole body was shaking. Derek had never physically hurt me before, but he'd punched walls and broken things. When he got the divorce papers in the mail, he called from prison and said I'd regret it and I shouldn't make the mistake of thinking we were done.

I bit his hand. He yelped and let go.

"*What the fuck.*"

A rowdy group of customers exited the restaurant, shouting and laughing. Using them for cover, I ran for the door. He didn't follow. Inside, I told Matt in a trembling voice what had happened. He insisted on calling the police. By the time the officer showed up and searched the parking lot, Derek had gone. There was a piece of paper stuck under the windshield wiper of my car—a flyer from a pizza place with Derek's handwriting on the back.

"Nice to see you too," the note read, and I heard the words in Derek's bitter voice. "You dump me when I'm down & then your on Tinder looking all happy. You owe it to me to meet up. Call me." And he left his number.

The officer was an old guy with gray hair and a beer belly who refused to take the situation seriously.

"He's not here. Call if you see him again," he said.

"That might be too late. He's hostile. He's stalking me."

"He says right here, nice to see you."

"That's him being sarcastic. He grabbed me, I'm telling you."

"Any witnesses to that?"

"No."

"Then it's he said, she said, and you won't get far in court. If he was still loitering, I could do something, but."

"I thought the police were supposed to protect people from criminals. My ex-husband has a criminal record. He's on probation."

"There's your recourse, then. Call his parole officer and complain."

"What's the parole officer going to do?"

"With a domestic complaint like this—"

"It's not domestic. We're not married, not anymore."

"He can sit him down and give him a talking-to."

"*Talk?*"

"Yes."

Which would achieve nothing except to piss Derek off.

I spent the next two nights tossing and turning on Matt's couch. He and his husband, Justin, told me to stay as long as I liked. But they lived in a tiny house with one bathroom and two enormous rescue dogs. A third person in that space was a lot, and I couldn't impose forever.

I went back to my place. I wasn't sleeping much. I was thinking about buying a gun to protect myself. On top of everything, I seemed to have picked up some weird stomach bug that left me feeling queasy. I hated my life and couldn't imagine a scenario in which things would get better.

That's the frame of mind I was in when Connor finally called.

10

The buzzing of the phone woke me from a fitful sleep. Pink light glowed around the edges of the windows as I reached blearily toward my nightstand. A number I didn't recognize was flashing on my phone. It started with 917. New York. It was him.

I'd been telling myself that if Connor called, I'd decline. Instead, I frantically swiped Accept before the call rolled over to voicemail.

"Hello?"

"Did I wake you?" he said.

His voice on the phone was low and intimate. My blood raced just from the sound of it. I looked at the clock. It was a little before six.

"It's okay."

"I'm on a boat," he said.

"A boat?"

"In the Mediterranean."

Oh, that kind of boat. He meant a yacht.

"It's later here. I tried to wait, but I just had to talk to you."

"I'm so glad you called. I miss you, but I was afraid to. We said we wouldn't," I breathed.

"We shouldn't. I'm only calling because I have an important question. Did you send me a photo?"

"What?" I asked, sitting up in bed.

"Did you text me a photo just now?"

"No. We agreed not to communicate."

He paused. I heard static on the line.

"Right," he said, "that's what I was afraid of."

"What photo?"

"Of the two of us, from the first night at the ski house."

I gasped. "That's the night we heard the noise."

"I know. Someone was actually there. I don't know how. I went outside and searched, remember? And didn't see a thing."

"It's a picture of us? Taken through the window?"

His sigh echoed across the ocean. "No. From closer up."

A chill went through me. "You mean, somebody was *inside* the house?"

"From the looks of the picture, they were standing a few feet from us."

"How is that possible? We would have seen them."

"In the picture, we're sleeping."

I felt nauseous. "Oh, God. Are we . . . ?"

"Yeah, sleeping, naked, together. The whole deal."

"Jesus. That's creepy."

"It's a fucking disaster."

"Who would do that?"

"Someone who works for Nina, I imagine. The only thing I don't get is, why send it to me? Why not just give it to her directly?"

"Maybe they did already."

"I worry about that. She has the photo, and she's biding her time till she kicks me out."

"Isn't that what we want, though? For her to end it?"

"Not if she has proof of infidelity. That triggers the prenup, remember?"

How could I forget? He'd gone back for the money, that was the bottom line. I knew I should hate him for it, too. But love didn't work that way. The sound of his voice on the phone was making me itch to have him in bed beside me.

"Are you there?" he said.

"Do you miss me?" I said, hating that I needed to ask.

"Of course. I think of you constantly. I want to call. I want to be with you. But I have to handle things here. I don't know what this means."

"Whoever sent the photo—did they ask for money?" I said.

"No demand for money. No message, nothing."

"What are you going to do?"

"I don't know. This situation keeps getting worse. I'm sick of it. I just want us to be together."

I waited for him to say something more. Like, when that might happen, or what his plan was for achieving it. But he didn't.

"When will I see you?" I asked, a note of desperation in my voice.

"I'm working on it. We're on the boat the next couple of days, but we're flying home in time for the Fourth. Once we're back in Southampton and have some privacy, I'll talk to her."

"Talk to her? You mean, ask for a divorce?"

"That's the plan," he said, but he sounded vague. "It's tricky. I need to figure out how to finesse things. Under the terms of the agreement, I can't be the one who does the leaving."

I was silent.

"Tabitha, believe me, I wish I could see you."

"If wishes were horses . . ."

"I mean it. Talking to you is the only time I don't feel crazy."

There was a noise in the background.

"Shit, I have to go."

"Connor. *Wait.*"

"I'll call when I can. Don't call me, okay? It's too risky."

He dropped the call.

I sat there staring at the phone in my hand, feeling sick to my stomach. *Classic.* I'd become the thing I'd sworn I'd never be. A mistress, a side chick, stuck waiting for her married lover to call. I wasn't just ashamed. I was stupid. We were no closer to being together than we'd been the day he left. If anything, we were farther apart. I wanted to give up on him. But hard as I tried, I couldn't bring myself to do it.

11

You think things can't get worse, and then they do.

The same day that Connor called to tell me we'd been photographed naked, I was driving to work at the restaurant when I looked in the rearview mirror and noticed an ominous-looking SUV tailing me. It was a black Chevy Suburban with windows tinted so dark that I couldn't see the driver, following closely enough to rear-end me if I braked hard. I sped up. The driver sped up, too, and stayed behind me all the way to the restaurant, a solid fifteen minutes that included getting on and off the highway and making three separate turns. Each time he followed me through an intersection, I felt a sick jolt of fear. When I turned in to the restaurant parking lot, the Suburban slowed down momentarily to get a better look before speeding away.

Shaking, bathed in sweat, I wondered—who would *do* that? Derek? From what I knew, unless he was dealing again, he couldn't afford a brand-new, tricked-out Suburban like that one. And if Derek went to the trouble of stalking me, he wouldn't hide behind tinted windows. He'd get up in my face, so I knew it was him. Could it've been the same person who'd followed me and Connor to the ski house and photographed us sleeping? But why would they bother with me? I was a struggling waitress with a thin wallet, not worth blackmailing. The incident made no sense. I tried to calm down, to tell myself that I was overreacting. Some jerk just tailgated me, and that's all it was. Trying my best to believe that, I went to work.

The Baldwin Grill closed at ten on weeknights. At the end of the shift, as I walked to my car, the northern sky glowed with a delicate light, and a balmy breeze washed over me. The beauty of the night made me long for Connor. Who was with his wife, on a yacht, in the Mediterranean. What a fool I was.

Thoughts of him distracted me as I pulled out of the parking lot and headed home. As I merged onto the highway, I looked up and saw that Suburban on my tail again. The shock made me swerve into the next lane, which caused the driver coming up beside me to lean on his horn. I jerked my car back into place and stepped on the gas, surging ahead. When the Suburban kept pace, I broke into a cold sweat. Twice in one day? This was no coincidence. That SUV was definitely following me. I looked for a license plate number, but there was no front plate. As hard as I tried, I couldn't see in through the dark tints. Who was behind the wheel, and what the hell did he want?

If I continued on to my apartment, he'd see where I lived.

I couldn't go home.

Shit.

It was dark by now. There weren't many cars on the road. Most businesses were closed. I drove past my usual exit, hands tight on the wheel, with no idea what to do. I let a second exit go by, then a third. I was well past my town now, flying along at seventy-five, heading nowhere, with the Suburban right behind me. The gas light blinked on. *Shit.* A sign said NEXT SERVICES 17 MILES. Okay, if I could make it that far with what was left in the tank, I'd at least be in a populated area.

There was a big commercial strip with a Home Depot, a Walmart, a Pier 1. The stores would be closed by now. But there were service stations and fast-food joints. Something would be open, people would be around—if only I could make it there before I ran out of gas.

The next fifteen minutes felt like fifteen years. I white-knuckled it in my old Corolla, the Suburban lurking like some horror-movie creature behind me, until finally I glimpsed the exit in the distance, coming up fast. This was my chance to lose him. I was no stunt driver, but I'd have to pull a fast move if I wanted to get home tonight. Holding my breath, I pushed the pedal to the floor and barreled straight ahead, jerking the wheel at the last second and swerving sideways across the solid line onto the off-ramp. My car fishtailed, tires squealing, as an acrid smell filled the passenger compartment. But the Suburban shot past, missing the turn.

I'd lost him, for now.

As much as I wanted to disappear to some back road where he wouldn't find me, I needed gas ASAP. I pulled into a Sunoco station just past the exit ramp. I started the gas going, then reached into the glove compartment for the flyer where Derek had scrawled his phone number. He was the most logical suspect, and I refused to live in fear of my ex-con ex-husband. I'd call him up and confront him. The gas station was brightly lit. It had a convenience store with customers inside. I felt safe here for the moment—safe enough to demand answers.

The phone rang for a long time before he picked up.

"Who's this?" he muttered.

From the thickness of his voice, it sounded like I'd woken him. He couldn't be asleep at home and following me in a giant SUV at the same time. Unless he was pretending.

"It's Tabitha. Are you following me?"

"What?"

"Are you following my car, in a black Chevy Suburban?"

"Hah, right. You wish."

"So, you're not?"

"Why would I follow you?"

"Why did you jump me the other night? I can't explain how your brain works. I'm telling you right now, Derek, if it's you, I'm calling your parole officer."

"I didn't jump you. I wanted to talk, and you made a scene. And I'm not following you, okay? I don't own a Chevy Suburban. I don't even have a friggin' driver's license right now. They suspended it."

As plausible as that sounded, I didn't really believe him. How did he get to the restaurant the other night if he couldn't drive?

"Don't come near me, or we'll have a problem," I said.

He was in the middle of an angry reply when I dropped the call. He dialed right back. I hit Decline.

Derek was probably lying. I *hoped* he was lying, because if it wasn't him in the Suburban, then a stranger had followed me. And that would be a first. I had no enemies. I wasn't important. I didn't have enough cash to make it worth blackmailing me or shaking me down. *Although.* I was involved with a man who did. A married man. With a powerful, unstable wife.

Could that be some goon in the Suburban, hired by Nina Levitt?

A woman with white hair pulled up in a Volvo and got out to pump gas. Her golden retriever poked his head out the back window, tongue lolling. Oh, to be her, with a sweet dog, a normal life. To be anyone but me right now.

Enough. The Suburban hadn't found me yet. Better get the hell out of here before it came back.

At home, I double-locked the door, pulled the blinds, and turned down the lights. I had to talk to Connor—to tell him about being followed and ask if he had any news about the blackmailer. But he'd said not to call. Crap. I didn't know what to do. I started pacing. I was feeling sick. And strange, like my breasts hurt. Actually, they hurt a lot, come to think of it. With every step, the pressure of the bra made them ache. Maybe my period was coming.

Wait a minute, when did I last have it?

Crap. I was late.

I sank down onto the sofa and tried to remember the precautions we'd taken. I wasn't on the pill. I had sex so rarely that it didn't seem worth putting those hormones in my body on the off chance. Connor'd had condoms. We'd used them. But we'd had sex a lot, and maybe—

Shit.

Okay, calm down. Stress could make you late, right? Lord knows, between Derek coming after me, the Suburban following me, and the crazy emotions caused by my affair with Connor, I was under enormous pressure. That could explain it.

Or else I was pregnant.

Nausea overwhelmed me. I ran to the bathroom and threw up. That could only mean one thing. I needed to take a pregnancy test to be sure. It was after midnight, and the only open pharmacy was a fifteen-minute drive over dark, empty roads. I hadn't seen the Suburban since my stunt-driving maneuver on the highway an hour earlier. But it could still be out there. I hesitated, rinsing my mouth. When the cardboardy taste of the water in the Dixie cup made me gag, I knew this was urgent, and grabbed my keys. All the way to the pharmacy, I kept an eye on the rearview mirror, relieved when the hulking black SUV failed to materialize.

Back in my bathroom, I ripped open a foil packet, sat down on the toilet, and peed on the stick. One line in the window meant you weren't pregnant.

Two lines.

I did the second test in the box, hoping against hope. Two lines again.

Fuck.

I lay down on my bed and stared at the ceiling, dry-eyed. For the first time in my life, I was pregnant. That should bring me joy. Instead, I was terrified. I knew my options just like every woman did. But from the second I saw the two lines, I knew I wanted this baby.

His baby. I wanted to have a baby with Connor.

What if he'd lied? What if he had no intention of leaving his wife—and her millions?

Then I'd have to raise this child alone.

I knew what it was like to live through an unstable childhood, with absent parents. I wanted the baby, but not with upheaval, and insecurity, and lack of resources. I wanted this baby to have two parents, and a good home. I wanted it with Connor by my side.

He'd told me not to call.

Screw that.

I dialed his phone. It went straight to voicemail. I left a message saying I needed to speak to him right away, that it was extremely urgent. Then I waited. An hour passed with no word from him. Where did he say he was, again? I Googled the time zones of the Mediterranean. It was two here now, which meant it was eight there. Eight A.M. He could goddamn well answer. Another hour passed. Nothing. I made some herbal tea to settle my stomach, but the flowery smell of it just made me throw up again. There was nothing left in my stomach, and no word from Connor. I texted him—Please please please call, emergency.

Morning came, and I was late for work. I stared at the computer screen at the insurance company, billing codes blurring before my eyes as I struggled to concentrate. Dizzy with hunger, yet constantly nauseous, I managed to choke down a few saltine crackers. At the restaurant, working the dinner shift, the intense food smells made me gag. I was running to the bathroom so often that Liz eventually came looking for me. She found me standing at the sink, pale and wan, wiping my lips with a paper towel. After looking under the doors of the stalls to make sure we were alone, she demanded to know what was going on.

"Are you sick?" she said, sniffing the air.

"I might be coming down with a stomach bug."

Liz knew better. She'd borne four children, after all. She frowned at me skeptically. I couldn't meet her eyes. I wasn't ready to tell anyone—except this baby's father, who refused to return my calls.

"Go home," she said.

I didn't protest.

The road from Lakeside, where the restaurant was located, to my apartment in Baldwin had been widened in the years since I'd traveled it by bike. Still just two lanes with strips of grass and then woods on either side, it was now spacious and smooth, with a forty-mile-an-hour speed limit instead of twenty-five. It was around six, still full light outside on this pretty summer evening. I was driving on autopilot, caught up in my problems and ignoring the rearview mirror, when the Suburban suddenly emerged from my blind spot, hurtling at me like a demon. I braked to let the SUV pass faster. Instead of passing me, it slowed and veered toward me. He was going to run me off the road. I floored the Toyota, managing to slip out of the way a split second before the SUV sideswiped me.

Now he was behind me. In what felt like slow-motion, I pressed the pedal to the floor, my eyes on the mirror. My poor old Toyota was not up to the task of outrunning the Suburban. Stunned, I stayed on the gas as he rammed me from behind. Metal was grinding, sparks flying. I leaned on the horn, screaming uselessly at him.

"Stop! *Stop it!* Asshole!"

Cars came at us from the opposite direction, and the Suburban fell back. But the minute they'd passed, he was on me again. I heard the low roar as the SUV came up beside me, its dark bulk looming until it filled the driver's-side window. I strained to see my aggressor's face, but the tints were too dark. Who would *do* this? Holding the wheel steady, I refused to cede the road. But my Toyota was no match for that behemoth. The SUV sideswiped me once, with a screech of metal. Then it hit me again, and the second impact sent me hurtling onto the grassy shoulder. Bouncing forward, bones rattling, I fought to keep control of the car, finally managing to skid to a stop just short of the tree line. The airbag didn't deploy, thank God. Hyperventilating, I stumbled out onto the grass, my legs like rubber. The driver's-side door was crumpled and scratched.

A woman in a minivan had pulled off the road behind me. I could see kids in her car. She came toward me now, waving.

"Hey, are you okay?"

"Did you see that? Did you see what he did to me?"

"He ran you off the road. Do you need me call an ambulance?"

She had a phone in her hand.

"No. I'm not hurt."

"The cops, then?"

I leaned over, hands on my thighs, trying to catch my breath, and nodded.

"Yes. Thank you."

"It was a black SUV, right?" she asked.

"Yeah, a Suburban."

"With New York plates?"

"New York plates? Really? I didn't see."

"Orange and blue. That's New York, right?" she said.

"Yes."

New York plates. It couldn't be Derek, then. Deep down, I'd known that. Derek wanted me back. Not dead. Who else could it be? The obvious answer was someone who worked for Nina Levitt. Was Connor's wife trying to kill me? I couldn't believe that. Correction—I didn't *like* believing it. I hated that I'd done something bad enough to cause another person to want to kill me. But I had. I'd slept with her husband.

The police showed up and took a report. The woman in the minivan hadn't gotten a plate number, and the Suburban was long gone. The officer asked if I thought it had been a random act of road rage. Did anybody have a grudge against me? I *almost* told. I almost said, *Actually, the unstable woman who is married to the father of my unborn child has the means and the motive to hire someone to kill me. It had to be her.* But I didn't say that. Even thinking it, it sounded far-fetched. Instead, I mentioned Derek's name, while telling the officer I didn't believe it was him, because of the New York plates.

Once I was safe at home, I tried Connor's number. I had so much to tell him—things he needed to know. I was expecting his child. I was being followed. Someone had tried to kill me—possibly the same person who'd taken the photo of us, who, in all likelihood, worked for his wife. Yet, each time I called, the phone rang only once before rolling over to voicemail. I tried texting instead, but the texts showed as undelivered.

It was almost like he'd blocked me. But that couldn't be true. More likely, Nina was interfering with our calls. I wouldn't put it past her to tamper with his phone so that my number was blocked, and he didn't even know. There was only one way to get around that.

I had to drive down to New York and speak to him in person.

12

NINA

July 4

Nina closed her diary and stared at the photo the private investigator had given her. The one of Connor with *her.* She ought to be hardened to it. She knew the drill. Edward always had someone on the side, and it had never made sense. Nina was beautiful, witty, cultured, on every best-dressed list. What did these women have that she didn't? The answer was nothing, nothing at all. He just wanted something shiny and new. With Edward, she'd ignore it. Redecorate a house. Buy a painting. Pretend to be a Parisian who didn't care about fidelity. This was different. It cut, it burned. She'd wanted this love to be real.

She was angry with herself for getting so invested. She'd been warned about Connor, specifically. And though the source was untrustworthy—Hank, who had an obvious conflict of interest—she'd taken precautions, going so far as to hire a private detective to follow up on Hank's research. When the PI hadn't come back with anything conclusive, she'd gone ahead and married Connor, but with fingers crossed behind her back and an airtight prenup. What good was a prenup, though? The only thing it protected was your money.

A distant rumble of thunder made her look out the window of the tower room. To the east, the horizon was dark with clouds, and Connor was heading out for a swim. She raised the binoculars that she kept on her writing desk and watched as he stripped off his shirt, tossing it onto the lounge chair that the staff had set up for him. She appreciated his body as he waded into the surf and his elegant form as he struck out into the waves. Under different circumstances, she might've called from the window, or sent the housekeeper down to beg him to please not swim right now, the water was too rough. But she was angry. Let him drown out there. He wouldn't, of course. He was an accomplished swimmer. And like all narcissists, he led a charmed life. Born to be a man of leisure, a momentary bump when his family lost its money, saved by marrying into the Levitt fortune.

That was no accident. She'd been set up. The plan was a classic. Meet a rich, lonely widow. Romance her. Marry her. Then murder her and inherit her money. The only thing she didn't understand was, what was taking so long? Why hadn't he made his move yet? It should be easy enough. You fake a suicide, or an accident. By waiting, he'd given her time to uncover the truth. *They* had. She now knew everything about them—the two of them. Connor's girlfriend wasn't who she claimed to be. They'd known each other for years and been lovers in the past. They saw each other in secret, as recently as six weeks ago at Hank's ski place up north.

Nina didn't trust Hank, either. Not then, not now. She didn't trust Hank's ex-wife, Lauren. The fact was, if she was smart, she wouldn't trust anybody, including people who'd worked for her for years. It was impossible to know how far this conspiracy went, or where it ended. But she knew where it started—at her July Fourth party, two years ago tonight.

July 4—two years earlier

Nina stood with Hank Spears at the far end of the terrace. The party was in full swing—band playing under the stars, famous faces circulating in the crowd. The Fourth of July gala at Windswept was the event of the season in the Hamptons. They came by the hundreds to people-watch, to eat lavish food and drink vintage champagne. Most of all, they came for the house.

Windswept was a thirty-room brick-and-limestone Gatsby-era palace, set magnificently alone on a promontory that jutted into the sea. The grounds included ten acres of manicured lawns and gardens, an Olympic-size swimming pool, a pool house with bathrooms, and a glorious stretch of beach to roam in the moonlight. A security team had been brought in for the night, headed by Steve Kovacs, a private security consultant who'd worked for the Levitts regularly since Edward's time. Steve's team worked the perimeter, patrolling for crashers. Every year, people tried it. Paparazzi, nosy tourists, local hooligans on the prowl for free booze. Trespassers were turned over to the police.

Nina looked her best tonight. The Levitt emeralds glowed at her neck, setting off her black dress and porcelain skin. The sky was velvet, the fireworks an hour away. It should have been romantic. But, as Hank's arm snaked along the balustrade behind her and made contact with her bare back, she flinched.

"What's the matter? I did what you asked," he said, his mouth petulant.

Hank was accustomed to getting his way. He'd been Edward's right-hand man and was now CEO of Levitt Global, a position he'd long coveted and had ascended to on Edward's death. He and Edward were polar opposites. Edward had been a visionary—magnetic, mercurial, creative, with blazing blue eyes. Hank was a company man through and through. Trim and self-contained, graying at the temples, in a perfectly tailored suit. Shareholders found Hank a reassuring presence during this time of transition. Nina had found him a reassuring presence, too, through the long, difficult years of her marriage. At every dinner party, every conference or foreign trip or important event, at the very moment she'd feel the lowest, Hank would turn up at her side. When Edward's affairs hit the news, he'd claim the seat beside her at dinner and distract her with talk of the art world, or whatever topic came to mind. If Edward spoke harshly to her in front of other people, Hank would deflect the conversation, help her save face. She'd assumed that he did this for Edward's benefit—or, really, for Levitt Global's. Nina was a refined and sophisticated corporate first lady. She held up her end on charitable boards and in the art world. The Levitt marriage played well in the press. Any woman who came after her was unlikely to fit the job description, since Edward's tastes ran toward "models" who'd never held modeling jobs and were young enough to be his granddaughters. Not that Nina had any standing to complain. There'd been a first Mrs. Levitt at the time Nina and Edward met, who'd received a lavish settlement, happily remarried, and eventually died of cancer. Nina's guilt made her tolerant of Edward's transgressions. She knew what she was getting into and accepted it as just deserts.

The point was, Nina had misunderstood the nature of Hank's attentions. She thought he was looking out for the company, when actually he'd had feelings for her all along. She'd encouraged him more than she'd intended, just by leaning on him for support in her misery. She'd never dreamed he was seriously interested in her. Why would he be? Hank was married to Lauren Berman, the head of PR, who was not only a player in the company, but sultry and gorgeous—all dark hair, pouty lips, and curves.

After Edward died, Hank waited three months, then invited Nina to dinner. He told her that he was unhappy in his marriage and had loved her for years. She didn't want to hurt him. Not only was he a good friend, but they worked together regularly. So, she told him it was too soon. That was a mistake. Hank responded by arranging for them to be thrown together in ever more intimate settings, with work as a pretext. Six months ago, they'd been at a conference in Aspen together. And she slipped. She was feeling so low—old and alone, sad that she'd never had children. They got drunk and ended up spending the night together. Nina had been backpedaling from it ever since. She simply didn't have those feelings for him. After what Edward had done to her, she also felt legitimately guilty about sleeping with someone who was married, and leaned on that as her excuse. Hank took her at her word. Lauren and Hank were now in the middle of a bitter divorce battle, because Hank had left Lauren. For Nina. Without discussing it with Nina first. Which had made things extremely awkward at the office. Nina was now viewed as the other woman, a designation she loathed, and which was untrue. They had no ongoing romantic relationship. But nobody believed that—especially not Hank.

"Hank, I'm sorry. But I never asked you to leave Lauren. Never. You misunderstood me."

"You said we couldn't be together as long as I was married."

She took his hands and looked into his eyes and was gutted to see the pain there.

"I said I wouldn't get involved with a married man. I never said that I was ready for a relationship, or that I had those feelings for you."

Anger flashed across his face. "I divorced my wife for you."

He'd raised his voice. People were turning to look.

"You shouldn't've done that without talking to me first."

"You refused to talk about it while I was married."

"Can we discuss this another time, when we have more privacy?" Nina said.

"When? I never see you except at board meetings."

The fact was, Nina had been avoiding him.

"We'll find a time. Next week. Dinner in the city."

"You promise?"

"Yes."

She scanned the terrace, looking for any excuse to get away from Hank. A man stood by the stairs to the beach, talking to her personal assistant. Nina took him in in a dazzling flash. The way the breeze lifted the crisp waves of his hair. The perfect features, athletic frame, the ease of his gestures. He wore a blazer and jeans that would've seemed dull on another man, but on him, looked like he'd stepped off the deck of a yacht. He must have felt her gaze, because he turned and looked right at her. But his gaze traveled on, as if it had only rested on her unintentionally.

"Who is that with Juliet?"

Hank turned.

"Don't look," she said, too late. Now he'd know she'd been talking about him.

"That's Connor Ford. He works for Lauren in PR. I think they have a thing going, actually."

"Lauren—and *him*?"

He shrugged. "He's too young for her, right? I don't mind, if it gets her off my back, so I can focus on you."

Hank was simply a friend. She wanted to confront him, tell him off, for putting her in the middle of his divorce, but that would only lead him to declare his feelings yet again. She cared about him, but he was making it impossible for them to stay friends.

"Excuse me, I need to speak to Juliet about something."

"Hey, no. Wait."

He reached to stop her.

"Hank, this is too private a matter. I promise, next week in the city, we'll talk. Now, please."

He let her go.

Nina crossed the terrace. Juliet was talking intently. Seeing Nina coming, Connor very noticeably withdrew his attention from Juliet, following Nina with his eyes as she approached.

"Were your ears burning? We were just talking about you," Juliet said.

Juliet Davis was underdressed for the evening, in black pants and a silk top, her dark hair tucked into a neat chignon. That was her style—quiet, efficient, unflashy. Juliet had come to work for Nina shortly after Edward's death, and had become indispensable. Nina didn't make a move without her.

"Why?"

"Remember, I was going to put you in touch with Connor regarding that profile?"

Nina had no memory of that. But then, his name meant nothing to her before tonight.

Connor was watching her. Her face felt warm. Her voice came out fluttering.

"Which profile was that again?" she asked.

"About your yoga practice?"

Nina frowned. "Really? I don't recall."

"It was Dawn's idea—her yoga teacher," Juliet added hastily, nodding toward Connor.

"I was just telling Juliet, I think that's the wrong angle for you, Mrs. Levitt. Connor Ford, deputy director of PR."

He smiled into her eyes as he extended his hand. That first touch was like a jolt from the universe, powerful and cosmic.

"Wrong for me—why?"

"Too trendy. Lacks gravitas. It's not how you want the world to see you."

"I agree. Though Dawn can be very insistent about her pet projects."

"Ooh, touchy territory," Juliet said, smiling. "I have things to see to. I'll let you two hash it out."

Juliet melted into the crowd, leaving them alone together. Nina, who was used to being assertive—in boardrooms, on the red carpet—felt suddenly tongue-tied.

"I was about to get a drink. You want one?" he said.

She nodded, and he tucked her hand under his arm. As they headed to the bar, people turned to watch. Nina looked around for Hank, worried about what he'd think. But he was nowhere to be seen.

"People are wondering who you are," she said.

"No, they're looking at you in that dress."

The dress was black and beaded, with a dramatic low back.

"Is something wrong with my dress?"

"Something's very right. It fits you like a glove."

There was a long line at the bar, but people let them cut. It was Nina's party, after all, and her house. She was used to being stared at, but there was a new sense of excitement, with Connor's hand on the small of her back. The bartender asked for their drink order, and Nina's mind went blank. She looked at Connor, shrugging.

"Bourbon on the rocks for me and a Vesper for the lady," he said, smoothly.

"Vesper?" she asked.

"It's a type of martini."

"Gin, vodka, and Lillet, right?" the bartender asked.

"Yes, with a twist," Connor said, then turned back to her. "It's perfect for you. Ian Fleming made it famous. It was James Bond's martini recipe."

His physical closeness was distracting. She caught a faint whiff of sandalwood. Was he wearing cologne? It was so subtle that she wanted to lean in and sniff his neck, but there were too many eyes on them.

"Is that the image you have in mind for me? Bond girl?"

"Not a Bond girl. *Bond.*"

"Oh, I'm a spy?"

"An international assassin, with style."

"Who told you I'm an assassin? That didn't come from Lauren, did it? I know she's your boss. She's not very happy with me, these days."

"I don't listen to gossip."

But she could tell from his inflection that he'd heard all about it.

"Good, because what you'd hear is totally wrong," she said, then worried that that made her sound guilty, and started blathering, out of embarrassment. "Sometimes Levitt Global feels like a singles bar. At least, it did in Edward's time. Lucky for him, he died before #MeToo really hit, or God knows."

"That must've been difficult for you," he said. "And a good reason to reinvent yourself, for the post-Edward era."

"As a *spy.*"

He laughed. The sound was golden, his teeth perfectly white.

"Really, though. I don't want to be Lady Macbeth. I'm seen too much that way already."

"You're viewed as a powerful woman in your own right. People have trouble with powerful women. That's just misogyny. Personally, I admire you."

"Thank you. I wish the public felt that way. What can we do to change that? I think about Jackie O as a blueprint. A famous widow who went on with her life, but she was popular."

The crowd at the bar was closely packed. Connor put his hand on her waist and drew her closer, so they were touching from chest to thigh. There was an excuse for it—maybe. He was trying to protect her from the crowd.

"In a different era. And she may've been popular, but was she happy? Jackie lived in a gilded cage. Nina Levitt should be free."

"You don't think I'm free?"

"Are you?"

"Sir? Sir, excuse me? Your cocktails?"

The bartender was trying to get Connor's attention, but he was busy looking into Nina's eyes. She could feel her heart beating. He broke eye contact reluctantly, taking the drinks and passing the Vesper to Nina. She sipped it as they stepped away from the bar. It was clean and cold, with a kick as powerful as a hit of cocaine.

"Wow."

"You like it?"

"*Too* much."

"Good. I'm glad I got it right."

"I'm not sure I can handle it, though."

"I doubt there's anything on this planet you can't handle. Shall we?"

"What?"

"A walk on the beach? I don't know if you've noticed, but people are staring."

She felt breathless and nervous. Worried what people would think—what *Hank* would think, if he heard about this.

"Won't they stare more if I walk out of the party with some man I just met?"

"I'm not some man you just met."

"No? Who are you, then?"

"I'm your image consultant."

"What image will I project if I ditch my guests and leave with you?"

"That you're Nina Levitt, and you do as you please. The world can wait."

"Okay. I like the sound of that."

She took his arm.

13

On the beach that night, they kicked off their shoes. He took her hand to help her over some rocks, and it felt natural. They walked until the sound of the waves drowned out the band, and the glow of tiki torches faded to a smudge in the distance. The moonlight shimmered on the water, and the fresh, briny smell of the ocean filled her senses.

"So," she said breathlessly, "what's somebody like you doing working as an assistant in PR? Isn't that a bit lowly?"

"I'm a late bloomer. Misspent youth."

"I'd like to hear about that."

"It's a cliché, to be honest. I thought I could be a rock star. Dropped out of school to chase a record deal. Got close enough a few times that I kept at it longer than I should, probably."

"Well. Music's a tough racket."

"Especially for the undertalented."

"I'm sure that's not true."

"I could sing and play the guitar. I looked good onstage. But I was no songwriter. Eventually, I gave up. Went back to school. And was happy to get a job in a company that promotes from within. There are real prospects for me at Levitt Global. I've applied to the management program, so we'll see where that goes. And I'd love to work on retooling your image. If you'd like. I'd love to be helpful."

It was really the other way around—that Nina could be helpful to him. With a phone call, she could get him accepted to that training program, or have him promoted without jumping through any hoops at all. Connor knew that as well as she did.

They'd reached a beautiful, deserted stretch of beach. He took off his jacket and laid it on the sand for her. She perched gingerly on the edge of it, feeling adrift, out here all alone with him. Other than the Levitt Global connection, they had little in common, being from different generations and very different income brackets. But then he started talking, and it felt easy. They drifted from topic to topic—the company, PR, fashion, art, travel. He was charming and knowledgeable, from a background similar to her own.

The wind picked up. He rested his hand lightly on her bare back, and she shivered.

"Are you cold? You're shaking. C'mere."

He put his arm around her and drew her close. She thought he was making a move, but he just gave her a friendly squeeze.

"I've monopolized you long enough. I should get you back," he said.

She was surprised at how disappointed she felt. He helped her to her feet. When they got back to the party, she wasn't ready to let him go. She held on to his arm, taking him with her as she mingled, introducing him to people he wouldn't've gotten close to otherwise. A Pulitzer-winning novelist. A TV star with a huge Instagram following. The editor of a culturally significant magazine. She told everyone that Connor was her publicist, which had the virtue of being true, but was beside the point. Mingling with him on her arm had no official purpose. She wanted to show him what she could offer. Not just great wealth. Access. Connections.

The massive fireworks display had just ended. With the smell of sulfur hanging in the air, Nina bid her guests good night from the bandstand. People began making their way down the paths to the front of the house, where the valets waited to fetch their cars. She'd spent the past two hours with Connor by her side and hadn't gotten tired of him. Normally, after a party, she'd feel drained, and need to be alone. She felt the opposite—energized, reluctant to let him go.

"Stay a little longer. Are you hungry? The caterers left a feast in the kitchen," she said.

"I'd love to, but—"

He really had the most extraordinary eyes. She noticed them as he looked past her, across the terrace, to where Lauren stood watching them with a resentful look.

So, it was true.

"Lauren's waiting for you, I take it?"

"She's my ride. Living in the city, I don't own a car."

"Sure."

"That's all it is. You know Levitt Global has a nonfraternization policy."

Nina raised an eyebrow. "Which everybody follows to a T."

"Now who's listening to gossip?"

She had no right to be jealous, but she was. Lauren was around forty, closer in age to Connor than Nina was. A sultry brunette, she looked fabulous in her body-skimming red dress and sky-high heels. That's who Connor was going home with tonight. It wouldn't do for Nina to seem like she cared.

"Get in touch with Juliet. She'll set up a meeting to discuss your PR ideas. Have a great night, regards to Lauren," she said, pecking him on the cheek dismissively.

"You know what. I can Uber back to the city. Let me just tell her."

She watched him go over to Lauren, and saw the poisonous look on her face. Lauren would now believe Nina had stolen a second man from her. Though, Nina herself didn't know what would happen next. Maybe something, maybe nothing. She'd keep her driver standing by to take Connor home. It was three hours easy back to the city. Late at night on the Fourth, that Uber would be an expensive proposition for an assistant director of publicity. If he ended up going home at all.

Nina dismissed the housekeeper, and they sat at the island in the vast kitchen, eating cold lobster and drinking champagne. She told him funny stories about people he'd met at the party, including a well-known music producer, who'd seemed to take a liking to Connor.

"Too bad I didn't meet him a decade ago."

"Who knows? Maybe it's not too late. So, let's hear it. Sing me something," she said. But he just laughed.

"Seriously. You claim you were on the way to becoming a rock star. Show me. Sing me a song."

"Oh, come on."

"I mean it. Indulge me."

"Ah, all right. Let's see. How 'bout this? 'If I was a carpenter, and you were a lady—'"

His voice was pure and clear, and the words went straight to her heart. But there was a sly grin on his face, like the song was a joke to him.

"Don't laugh. It's beautiful. I love it."

"Ah, it's sappy. You're too easy on me."

She was easy on him. When he asked for a tour of the house, she was happy to oblige. They spent half an hour wandering the first floor, starting in the ballroom, where the food had been set up tonight. It had sixteen-foot ceilings and an abandoned air, with the caterer's tables gone and the rug still rolled up. They wandered through parlors, fingers grazing, laughing and talking intimately. She pointed out paintings and told him the provenance of the antiques.

He knew a surprising amount about art. In the wood-paneled library, he sat down beside her on a window seat. She was in the middle of a sentence when he leaned in and kissed her lingeringly on the lips. She closed her eyes. The kiss went to her head.

"Sorry. I didn't mean to interrupt. I've been working up my courage to kiss you, and finally got there," he said.

"Am I that scary?"

"Not scary. Exquisite, untouchable. Like a perfect marble statue come to life."

It bothered her that he'd chosen words frequently used to describe her in the press. Was that a coincidence, or had he been reading up on her?

"So cold? I promise, I'm not untouchable. See?"

She took his hand and put it on her chest, just above her heart. His eyes glazed as he stared at the neckline of her dress, inching his hand down to the curve of her breasts. It wasn't like her to go to bed with someone she'd just met. She was too private. But she wanted him enough to change her ways.

A noise in the hall startled them both. Connor yanked his hand away like he'd been burned.

"Who's there?" he asked.

"Just staff. It's okay."

He didn't look reassured.

"Let's go upstairs. We'll have more privacy," she said.

As he followed her through darkened rooms and up the sweeping staircase, he was visibly edgy, as if expecting someone to jump out from behind the drapes.

His hesitancy vanished the second the bedroom door closed behind them. The room was dark, lit only by the moonlight streaming through the tall windows. He grabbed her by the waist and kissed her greedily, then walked her backward till she hit the bed. Easing her down onto piles of silk cushions, he tugged the hem of her dress up over her hips. She was naked underneath, and the primitive sound he made when he saw that, the way his breathing sped up, made her quake. He knelt before her, nudging her legs apart. It had been a long time. Feeling self-conscious, she resisted.

"Do you want me to stop?"

"No."

Her heart was hammering.

"It'll be okay. Just relax."

She felt his fingers, then his tongue, and melted back against the silk duvet, writhing. He brought her to the edge, then stood up and unbuckled his belt, looking down at her. She watched as he pulled off his clothes. He was perfectly proportioned, luminous in the moonlight. She'd never seen a more beautiful man. He hovered over her, then pushed in. Her hands went around his back, then down to his butt as he moved. She gave herself up to the sensations, feeling the power of him, and the loss of control was exhilarating.

When they'd finished, he kissed her lightly, then rolled off. Their fingers intertwined, but they didn't speak. After a few minutes, she got up and went to her dressing room. She still wore the beaded gown. Her stylist had sewn and taped her into it earlier that night. She tore it off, and beads went skittering across the parquet floor. In the bathroom, she looked at herself in the mirror. The spots of color on her pale cheeks, her swollen lips, made her look young. She felt strange, unlike herself. She had all the power, and yet she had none. She could ask him to leave. She could even ghost him, and he would accede with no fuss, and never attempt to contact her again. They could pass each other in the halls at Levitt Global and he would say a polite hello, without acknowledging this encounter, because he wouldn't want to impose. She was confident of that. On the other hand, she could tell him to stay at Windswept—stay indefinitely, not go back to the city, to the office, to whatever he had going on with Lauren—and she was pretty sure he'd do that, too.

She should probably get rid of him. That would be the smart move.

She went back to the bedroom. He hadn't moved. He was lying back on the cushions, naked and perfect.

She told herself to stop overthinking things.

"Come to bed," he said.

She did. And didn't leave the house again for days.

14

A week later, Nina helicoptered into the city to attend the Levitt Global board meeting. The bird's-eye view of skyscrapers sparkling in the sun was lost on her, as her mind wrestled with knotty problems. Connor had gone back to the city a couple of days before, and she'd discovered she hated being apart from him. She didn't like that he had a job—working for Lauren, no less, whom he'd admitted to having a fling with. They say if you love someone, let them go, but she didn't want him out of her sight. They'd tried talking on the phone. It wasn't enough. He suggested they sext, but Nina refused. For a public figure like her, nudes could get you blackmailed. Besides, she didn't want a picture. She wanted the real thing.

They touched down at the heliport. She wondered how long it would be until she was alone with him. Would she have to wait until tonight at the apartment, or would he come to her office? She could lock the door.

The car pulled up to the Park Avenue office tower that housed Levitt Global. Juliet waited by the curb with an umbrella to shield Nina's delicate skin from the July sun. Juliet had been hired as a personal assistant shortly after Edward's death, when Nina was inundated with messages of condolence and had no patience for replying. The lie of it all. She wasn't sad, she was free. Juliet took the annoying bits off her hands. Small and dainty, in her customary uniform of black pantsuit and glasses, her dark hair pulled back, she had an air of bland efficiency that Nina found soothing. As Nina stepped into a bigger role at the company, Juliet came along, making the transition seamless. Now she was indispensable, a combination personal and executive assistant and paid companion. She traveled with Nina, and spent weeks on end at Windswept, overseeing the household staff when that responsibility felt like too much. Nina could disappear into her love affair with Connor, knowing Juliet would be there to pick up the slack.

They went over the day's schedule as they crossed the soaring marble lobby to the company's dedicated elevator bank.

"Board meeting in thirty minutes," Juliet said as they got on the elevator, "giving you time to review the packet I prepared. Hank canceled your dinner date—"

"He *canceled*?"

Hank must've heard the gossip about Nina and Connor. This could be touchy.

"Do you know why?" Nina asked.

Juliet shot a meaningful look upward to the top corner of the sleek chrome cab, where a shiny cylinder concealed a camera. They were being watched. That was expected at Levitt Global, and they were well-versed in the location of surveillance dead spots. They got out on the executive floor and Nina followed Juliet down the hallway to an overlooked corner behind a potted plant.

"My take on it is, he's upset about your relationship with Connor. You should know, he and Lauren are going after him," Juliet said.

"Going after Connor? How?"

"Complaining about his work on the Saudi deal. Levitt Global is getting trashed in the press. They're blaming Connor, saying he mishandled the roll-out."

"I warned Hank that deal would not be popular. Of course the press is bad. You can't spin shit into gold."

"He's leaning on Lauren to move up Connor's performance review. Since Connor's only been at the company for ten months, he's technically on probationary status. A negative performance review could lead to termination."

"This is personal, you know. Hank's jealous."

"I believe you." She shrugged and raised her eyebrows, as if to say, *What can you do?*

"I'm going to speak to him right now," Nina said.

"You're not in his calendar."

"You're telling me he's trying to ruin Connor's career. I won't sit still for that."

Juliet followed Nina down the hall. The corner suite occupied by Hank and his staff had once belonged to Edward. Nina had an office just across the elevator bank, the better to keep an eye on company business. She was an activist board chair, and Hank didn't like that. He didn't fancy being overseen by the founder's widow. Interesting that his aggressive push for a personal relationship with Nina coincided with her growing role as a check on his corporate ambitions. She wondered whether he truly cared, or just wanted to control her.

As Nina swept through the anteroom, Hank's two assistants popped up from their desks like Whac-A-Moles to intercept her. She waved them off. Juliet ran interference, stepping in to mollify them.

Hank looked up from his computer, his eyes mild behind his glasses.

"Ah, Nina. What a surprise."

But, was it? Hank would have known the second she entered the building, if not sooner. Knowing Hank, he had spies at the helipad.

She sat down in a leather chair across from his enormous glass desk. He'd had the office gutted and redone. It was sleekly contemporary now, where in Edward's day it had been all dark paneling, cigars, and power. The view behind the CEO was the same, however—the island of Manhattan laid at his feet.

Hank looked past her to his assistants, who stood at the door with worried expressions.

"Bring Mrs. Levitt her beverage of choice, please," he said.

They scurried off. Hank leaned back in his chair.

"Here to review the Saudi deal before the board meeting?"

There were other, more pressing concerns on her mind.

"Back off," she said.

He looked amused. "I beg your pardon?"

"You're screwing with Connor because you're jealous."

"Ah, right, got it now. Look, Nina, Lauren told me he put in a leave request for a ridiculous amount of vacation this summer—"

"Since when do you care about the inner workings of the PR department?"

"It affects the bottom line. Have you seen the press on this Saudi deal? It's scathing."

"Because we're getting in bed with a terrorist regime."

"Because somebody's not doing his job. Perhaps you're unable to see that because of who *you're* in bed with."

"You're proving my point. This is personal for you."

One of Hank's assistants tiptoed in with Nina's iced skim flat white in a crystal glass, set it on a coaster on Hank's desk, and tiptoed out. She took a sip. It was so perfect that she knew Juliet had made it.

Hank raised an eyebrow. "No, it's personal for *you.* I see you on the verge of making a big mistake, and I feel it's my duty to warn you."

"*Warn* me."

"Yes. I have to ask—how much do you actually know about this man?"

He swiveled in his chair and pulled a file from a cabinet, then slid it across the desk to her with a soft, white hand. A spark of fear shot through her.

"What is that?"

"Connor's approaching a year with the company. This next performance review will determine whether he's retained. Naturally, we've done a thorough background check."

"Something tells me that's not his HR file."

"Read it. I think you'll find it very interesting."

"I know what I need to know about him."

Nina was not naïve enough to believe that she knew everything about Connor. Yes, they'd talked for hours, and he'd told her enough ugly things to make him seem transparent. But nobody was completely honest, in her experience. There was always something held back.

"After a few days in bed? Come on. Read it. Unless you're afraid to find out what it says."

She picked up the file, her chest tight with nerves. Hank was the king of digging up dirt. He'd vetted *Nina* back in the day. When she and Edward met, she was fresh out of Barnard, working as a gallerina in SoHo, living in a fifth-floor walk-up in Alphabet City when that neighborhood was just rats and riots. Blue blood ran in her veins, and Edward liked that. But she was poor as a beggar, spending her days shilling art of questionable value and nights snorting whatever was on offer in the bathrooms at the Limelight. Everyone had their skeletons. Nina knew what Hank was capable of—and yes, she was afraid to read his dossier on Connor.

For the next ten minutes, she read in silence, doing her best to maintain a poker face, conscious of Hank's eyes on her the whole time. Finally, she closed the file and looked at him, smoothing her features into a bored expression.

"It's nothing I didn't know," she said.

He snorted. "Really? The part about the missing girl? You didn't know that."

"Someone he was once involved with, who went missing *years* after they broke up. Why should that trouble me?"

"You're in denial. There's evidence of his involvement."

Nina sighed. "I see what you're doing, Hank."

"I'm trying to inform you that the man you're involved with has a possible murder in his past."

She reached across the desk and touched his hand. "I'm sorry if things didn't work out how you hoped between us. But smearing Connor won't change that."

He pulled his hand away, coloring. "This has nothing to do with us. Whether we're together or not, I consider you a friend, and I don't want to see you hurt. I can only conclude that your grief over Edward's death has impaired your judgment. Or else you'd see this man for what he is."

"And what's that?"

"A con artist, who's after your money, and who might be dangerous."

"Because he couldn't possibly be interested in me for myself."

"You know I don't think that. You're beautiful and very desirable. That doesn't make his intentions honorable."

"I know you're trying to protect me, Hank, and I appreciate that very much. But it is what it is. My feelings are not going to change."

He took off his glasses and rubbed his eyes. "I'm sorry to hear that. I think you're making a grave mistake."

He leaned back in his chair and steepled his fingers. Hank was nothing if not a shrewd businessman. He'd lost, and he knew it. He wasn't going to give *her* any more trouble. But that didn't mean he'd drop his vendetta against Connor. Nina would have to offer a real incentive if she wanted to protect Connor from Hank.

"I have a proposal for how to handle this, going forward," she said. "Hear me out."

She told him she would drop her opposition to the Saudi contract in exchange for Hank backing off on Connor and agreeing that he should be reassigned. Connor would no longer work for Lauren in PR, but rather become special assistant to the chairwoman of the board—Nina herself. Once he worked for her, he could travel with her, and nobody would raise an eyebrow.

"What you're proposing would be an HR violation," Hank said.

"This company is hardly a model of compliance. You were married to someone in your chain of command for ten years. And Edward—how many female employees did he sleep with over the years?"

"Exactly. And the company's spent millions on payouts on sexual-harassment claims. I've learned my lesson. I don't want to face that again."

"You won't have to. This is entirely consensual."

"We'd have to get the lawyers involved, to review what you're suggesting."

"Are you saying you agree?"

"I don't have much choice. I need your vote on this project, and you're holding it for ransom."

Nina was flush with relief. "Thank you. And Hank, your friendship means so much to me."

He waved her off angrily.

"Enough bullshit, all right? You're no better than Edward, looking for some boy toy. You never cared about me. Well, you got what you wanted. Don't expect us to be friends going forward. I see you for who you are now. I have work to do. Get out of my office."

Nina got up and walked out with her cheeks burning.

"If you're stupid enough to marry him, you'll get what you deserve," Hank tossed after her.

15

She hadn't planned to marry Connor. Quite the opposite. In her mind, this was going to last the summer. She'd be bored with him by September and let him down easy. Buy him a car or an apartment. Get him to sign an NDA. That was how Edward used to handle his women, and it had worked without fail.

That day in the office, after Nina voted her shares in favor of the Saudi deal, Hank delivered on his end. Connor was transferred out of PR and reassigned as her special assistant, effective immediately. While Connor cleaned out his desk, Nina sent Juliet to his apartment to pack a suitcase. The jet was on standby at Westchester Airport. They boarded in time for a late dinner and woke up in Italy. For the rest of the summer, they wandered where the spirit took them. Mount Fuji at dawn. A palm-fringed slip of white sand in the South Pacific. The Isle of Skye, where dusk lingered till midnight. Day and night, they were glued together, intertwined, touching, kissing, holding hands, making love, drinking too much, sleeping, Jet Skiing, working out, tiring of a place, moving on to the next one.

It wasn't all play. That would've been tedious. She discovered that

Connor was smart about business, much smarter than she'd given him credit for. She found his advice helpful enough that she let him read the materials that were sent to her. Deal memos, agreements, confidential cables. Inch by inch, she took him into her confidence. It was easy to rationalize. He was her assistant, hired by the company. He'd signed the required noncompete and nondisclosure forms. What trouble could he get up to when he didn't even leave her sight? But now and then, even in bright sunshine, Nina would look at Connor and feel a chill.

Hank had a long history of smearing people, and the story of Connor's missing college girlfriend matched that MO perfectly. There was no actual evidence. There were only insinuations too vague to be refuted. It was perfect that way. This girl and Connor had broken up when he dropped out of college, years before she disappeared. Her body had never been found. She might not be dead at all. But there was just enough to leave a bad taste in the mouth. They were both living in New York at the time of her disappearance. She'd been seen with a man matching his description not long before she went missing. In short, there was enough to make Nina worry that this time, it was for real—that her young lover might actually be a murderer.

She had to find out the truth.

Nina had brought Hank's dossier on the trip, moving it from one safe to another, making sure Connor never laid eyes on it. She wanted to send it to her lawyer for follow-up, but the puzzle was how to do that securely. The information contained in the dossier was potentially damaging, not just to Connor but by association to Nina herself, and even to Levitt Global. She couldn't risk scanning and emailing it or sending it via courier service. It needed to be hand-carried by someone she trusted. A few key members of Nina's staff had accompanied her on this trip, keeping a discreet distance but there when she needed them. Juliet. Dawn Forest, her yoga instructor. And Steve Kovacs, her security consultant. Of the three, Juliet was most easily spared. Nina quietly dispatched Juliet back to the States to carry the dossier to her lawyer and instruct him to look into the allegations.

In the meantime, Nina and Connor continued with their travels. She was Nina Levitt, after all. If it pleased her to vagabond around the world with a gorgeous man who spoke French and Italian, knew wine, looked incredible in clothes and made love to her like a gigolo, then she'd do that. And it did please her, like nothing ever had.

In late August, Nina and Connor were lounging on the flybridge of Nina's boat anchored off Monte Carlo, sipping pisco sours and watching the sunset, when the tender pulled up, and Juliet stepped off. She was carrying one of those slouchy, no-name leather bags that millennials bought for a hundred bucks off the internet. Seeing the bag, Nina felt a stab of fear, because she knew that the completed investigator's report was inside. She looked at Connor, his handsome features bathed in golden light, and decided not to read it tonight. Juliet waved from the lower deck. Nina ignored her, burying her face in the warmth of Connor's neck. Tomorrow was soon enough to face reality.

But she couldn't sleep that night, worrying about what it might say. Connor slept like a rock, but Nina tossed and turned, anxiety weighing on her. What if he was a killer? Around four, unable to stand it any longer, she pulled on her red silk kimono and went knocking on the door of Juliet's cabin.

Juliet opened the door within thirty seconds, eyes widening when she saw Nina.

"Oh. Mrs. Levitt."

"Were you expecting someone else?" Nina asked.

Hair down, in a slip of a nightgown, Juliet looked pretty. You'd never know it, during the day.

"I wasn't expecting anybody, ma'am. Please, come in."

Juliet stepped back and let Nina into the cabin. While small compared with the lavish master suite that Nina and Connor occupied, it was elegantly decorated, with a king bed, a picture window hung with raw-silk drapes, and a small seating area with a single armchair and coffee table. Juliet gestured at the chair. Nina took a seat.

"Can I ring for coffee?"

"That's not necessary."

"I assume you'd like to review the materials Mr. Barbash sent?"

Mark Barbash was Nina's lawyer.

"Please."

Juliet touched a panel in the built-in dresser, which sprang open to reveal a hidden safe. She punched in a combination, retrieved an official-looking manila envelope, and brought it to Nina. The envelope was marked CONFIDENTIAL and sealed with tape, but was otherwise blank, with neither address nor sender noted.

"Have you read it?" Nina asked.

Juliet's mouth dropped into an O of surprise. "Uh—was I supposed to? It's sealed."

"Just checking."

Nina hesitated with her hand over the flap of the envelope, throwing Juliet a meaningful look. The assistant grabbed her bathrobe and phone.

"I'll give you some privacy. Text me when you'd like me to return."

Once alone, Nina opened the envelope. Her hands were shaking. There were two files inside, one labeled INVESTIGATIVE REPORT, the other PRENUPTIAL AGREEMENT. She opened the file containing the report.

The first page was a summary, stating that the investigator had verified Connor's involvement with a young woman named Lissa Davila during his first two years of college, and Lissa's subsequent disappearance under mysterious circumstances eight years after their relationship ended. No evidence was found linking Connor to her disappearance. While the police case remained open, and the NYPD considered it unsolved, the investigator had uncovered new evidence suggesting that Lissa Davila had moved overseas, meaning that her "disappearance" had an innocent explanation.

Nina breathed out in relief. Everything was fine. She could have stopped reading right then. But curiosity got the better of her.

The next item in the file was a transcript of an interview with Lissa's college roommate, Sharla Jenkins. Sharla described Lissa as brilliant but troubled. Lissa had grown up in foster homes and had finally been adopted in her teens. The adoptive mom had died, and Lissa had no other family that Sharla knew of. Sharla stated that Lissa and Connor had an "obsessive" and "unhealthy" relationship that interfered with Lissa's friendships and schoolwork. When Connor dropped out of school, Lissa attempted suicide. She was hospitalized and withdrew from school. Sharla tried to keep in touch, but Lissa cut off contact.

Further investigation indicated that, by the time Connor ended his leave of absence and returned to college, Lissa had dropped out. According to the college records office, Lissa never returned, and never filed the request for her transcript that would have been needed had she transferred elsewhere. The conclusion was that she had not finished college.

Eight years after she left college, Lissa was reported missing by her landlord in New York City. The investigator determined that Lissa had been living alone in a small studio in a large Manhattan apartment building. The date of birth and Social Security number matched—this was definitely the same girl who'd dated Connor in college. When Lissa failed to pay her rent, the real-estate company tried to contact her, but her cell phone was out of service. They inquired with the doorman, who said he hadn't seen her in weeks. The building super then entered her apartment with a master key, and what he found was eerie. It was as if Lissa had vanished into thin air. There was a coat of dust on the furniture, clothing hanging in the closet; Lissa's wallet and keys were on the kitchen table. The landlord contacted the police, who opened a missing-person case. The police followed up with the employer Lissa had listed on her rental application, an import-export firm called Protocol Shipping Solutions, with a Midtown address. But the address turned out to be a mail-drop, and there was no evidence that the company actually existed.

Lissa Davila was a ghost.

The police tried to find Lissa's family, without success. Her adoptive mother, who'd lived in Maryland, had died years earlier. And the Maryland Department of Human Services was unable to locate Lissa's file to provide a birth certificate or the names of any living biological relatives. The only lead was that the doorman reported seeing Lissa with a visitor shortly before she disappeared—a man, tall and good-looking, with dark hair. There was no security camera in the building, but the police were able to pull footage from a camera mounted on the exterior of the bank next door. They found one grainy surveillance photo that the doorman said looked to him like Lissa and her visitor. That photo was included in the file.

Nina stared at it.

The man and woman walked hand in hand. The woman's face was a white blur, visible only in profile. The man's face wasn't visible at all. She studied it for a long time, gazing at the man. At the set of his shoulders, the tilt of his head, the texture of his hair. It was quite like Connor. Enough that it could be him. She leafed through the rest of the folder looking for more photos. There were none, not even a yearbook photo of Lissa, or any photo that showed her face. That seemed like an omission. Then again, Hank's original smear dossier hadn't included a photo of Lissa, so maybe there just wasn't one. If there was, you'd think Hank would've come up with it. While it seemed odd in this day and age, the truth was, not everyone had a social media presence, or even a driver's license. Some people left very little trace.

The lack of a photo bothered Nina. So did the name of the import-export firm where Lissa had worked. *Protocol Shipping Solutions.* She'd heard that name somewhere before, she was certain. She pressed her fingers to her temples, chasing the memory, but it remained stubbornly out of reach.

Did it matter, so long as there was an innocent explanation? Nina turned to the final page of the report, bearing the heading "Lissa Davila Possibly Living Overseas." The page summarized the findings of a second private investigator, hired by Mark Barbash to follow up on the information in Hank's dossier. That investigator had discovered evidence of a woman with the name Lissa Davila, and the correct birth date and Social Security number, working as an office manager for a company in Dubai called Gulf Ex-Im as recently as two years ago. There was no explanation for how Lissa had ended up in Dubai, or how the investigator had found her. The investigator had attempted to reach out to Lissa at Gulf Ex-Im in order to establish conclusively that she was the same person, but was unable to make contact. The business appeared to have closed. Still, the investigator wrote, given the identical birth date and SS number, the evidence supported the conclusion that it was her, and that therefore, she'd been alive and well and living overseas *after* going missing from New York.

Well. If it was good enough for the PI, it was good enough for Nina. Connor wasn't a killer. That was just a Hank smear, designed to control her, and interfere with her happiness. And she *was* happy. Happy in a relationship for the first time in her life. Happy with things just how they were. So, why change anything? Why—specifically—get married?

After Edward died, Nina thought she'd never marry again. Not because she was so grief-stricken. Oh, she put on a show of grieving, but the fact was, Edward had treated her like shit for most of their marriage. She stayed—and stayed faithful—for the money. Her prenup said that if Edward left her, she got a hefty settlement. But if she left him, she got nothing.

She worried constantly that Connor would cheat on her, like Edward had. That worry was based more on her past experience than on anything Connor had actually done or said. And it was possible she was being unfair to him. Maybe Connor wasn't like Edward. There was no way to know for sure. This was early days. Connor was on his best behavior. And besides, they'd been together nonstop since meeting at her July Fourth party, so he'd had no opportunity.

But summer was coming to an end. In the fall, they'd return to New York. He'd go back to work at Levitt Global, where Lauren was still head of PR. Lauren, whose divorce from Hank was now final, and who had a vendetta against Nina. Lauren believed that Nina had stolen two men from her. That wasn't true, but truth didn't matter. Lauren believed it, and what better revenge could there be than luring Connor back?

Nina watched him around the women they'd interacted with in the past two months, trying to gauge how susceptible he was. With Juliet, he was polite and friendly. With Dawn, her yoga instructor, who traveled with them, and who for some reason had taken a dislike to him, he was distant. With Nina's friend Anna, whose castle they'd stayed at in Scotland, and who was a terrible flirt, he'd been flirtatious. In each instance, the woman's conduct seemed to determine Connor's response. That wasn't very reassuring.

After what she'd been through with Edward, Nina would lie awake at night, watching Connor sleep, imagining him in bed with other women. She told him that if he ever cheated, they were through. He claimed he never would, but all men said that. How could she keep him faithful? Her mind kept coming back to the prenup Edward held over Nina's head for years.

She opened the second file now and read what her lawyer had drafted. Upon divorce, each party took from the marriage only the assets they'd brought to it, with the following exceptions. If Nina divorced Connor for any reason within the first five years of marriage, he got a one-time ten-million-dollar payout. After five years, he received an additional five million dollars for each year they remained married up to ten years. After ten years, the marriage vested, and Connor would receive half of Nina's assets upon divorce by Nina. *But*—if Connor initiated the divorce, *or,* if Nina could prove that he'd been unfaithful, or lied about a relationship with another woman, he forfeited all payouts. He got *nothing.*

The prenup was much more persuasive than a mere threat to end the relationship. It contained incentives and disincentives. It attached numbers—a cost—to leaving, or cheating. It was one thing for him to think, *If I get caught doing this, she might kick me out.* Another entirely to say, *If I cheat, I lose* ten million dollars.

Yes. The prenup just might work. The only problem was, you only signed a prenup if you were getting married.

Nina texted Juliet to return to the stateroom. When she got there, Nina handed her the investigator's report.

"Destroy this. *Don't* read it."

"Yes, ma'am."

Nina went back to the master, where Connor lay tangled in the blankets, fast asleep. She threw off her kimono and got in beside him, her hands snaking under the covers to find his naked body. His eyes opened, and he smiled drowsily.

"Hey, gorgeous," he said.

She stroked him under the covers until he got hard. He grabbed her and pulled her underneath him. The sex was intense, like always, and she was sad when it ended. Life would feel empty if they weren't together. She relied on him—in her bed at night, walking into a crowded room, muting the phone on a conference call to make fun of something somebody said. Her long, difficult marriage had made her unsentimental about love. She didn't quite believe in it. Yet, here she was, in love with Connor.

"Hey," she said, nuzzling against his neck, breathing in his scent. "You remember that song you sang to me the night we met?"

He raised himself on his elbow, brow furrowed. He didn't remember. How was that possible?

"Oh, yes, right," he said, nodding.

He'd scared her there for a minute, but now he started to hum the tune into her ear.

"The one about the carpenter who asked the lady if she'd marry him? That one?"

"Yes. I love that song." She paused. "So, what do you think? Should we get married?"

16

July 4—two years later

Nina sat at her dressing table in a black silk robe as her beauty team prepped her for the party.

"You asked to see me, Mrs. Levitt?"

Steve Kovacs, her security consultant, stood in the doorway of the dressing room. He was a six-foot-four ex-marine, ex–NYPD officer with a flattened nose, who'd worked for her on and off for years. She expected three hundred guests tonight, so Steve had brought in five off-duty cops to work security. They'd check invitations and keep out trespassers, but now she had a more delicate assignment for Steve. She wasn't sure she trusted him with it, but she had no choice. She needed backup or she wouldn't feel safe.

"Take a break," she told her hairdresser and makeup artist.

When they'd gone, she got up and checked the adjacent bedroom. Connor had been avoiding her all day and was still nowhere to be seen. He must sense what was coming.

There was no one moment when Nina discovered that Connor was cheating—in violation of their prenup, and every promise he'd ever made to her. The knowledge of it filtered through her skin like osmosis. She knew him so intimately. Everything about him—his body, his turns of phrase, the way he made love. She didn't need to read his private emails or mistakenly receive a text meant for someone else. She noticed every subtle change. The faint whiff of a strange perfume as he took off his shirt. A new rhythm to his speech. An echo of another woman in the way he touched Nina's body. This other woman haunted Nina like a ghost. She had to run her to the ground.

Lauren was the obvious suspect. They had a history, and maybe it wasn't exactly over when Connor and Nina got together. Connor's current position as vice president for North American development for Levitt Global required regular consulting with the head of PR. His meetings with Lauren always seemed to get scheduled for late in the day—too late to travel back to Windswept, where Nina slept. He'd wind up staying at the apartment in the city. Did he think this was her first rodeo? Nina had to sell her old apartment to get rid of the stench from all the women Edward brought there, on nights when he supposedly worked too late to make it home to the East End. She'd bought a new apartment for herself, and she liked it enough that she made sure to put safeguards in place. The doormen and the housekeeper were paid to report on Connor, whenever he was there without her. So far, he hadn't brought anyone there. That didn't mean he was faithful, just that he was careful.

Maybe the other woman wasn't Lauren. Nina's attention had shifted to a second suspect, one who cut more deeply. *Dawn.* The person on earth to whom Nina felt closest, after Connor, based on years of practicing yoga together, which to Nina was something intimate and spiritual. Dawn was beautiful enough to turn any man's head. Willowy, long mahogany hair—she looked like a ballerina. Early on, Nina had worried that Connor and Dawn would like each other too much, but then it had been the complete opposite. They openly feuded and mistrusted each other. Connor claimed Dawn's schtick was just a bunch of woo-woo nonsense, that she was a bad influence, sucking Nina dry with a charlatan's efficiency. Dawn said even worse things about Connor—he was a fraud, after Nina's money. Was it just a cover? The investigator hadn't been able to substantiate anything between Connor and Dawn. That didn't mean it wasn't happening.

Unsatisfied with the answers she was getting, Nina fired that investigator and hired a new one to root out the truth, and it turned out to be more than she'd bargained for. The new person had proved much more effective than the one from two years ago who'd cleared Connor of involvement in his girlfriend's disappearance. That was either incompetence or a whitewash—probably the latter. There was a conspiracy underway against her. She didn't know how far it went, but it was going to end tonight.

"I know you have your hands full with the guests," she said to Steve as she shut the door. "But something has come up that I need your help with. It's confidential, and rather delicate."

"Any way I can be of service. Confidentiality is a given. If you don't want to take my word for it, I signed an NDA when I came to work for you."

"Right. What I'm about to share with you is covered by that, obviously."

"Of course."

She unlocked the top drawer of her dressing table and handed him the investigator's file.

"Read this. It'll give you the background."

He sat down on the bench and opened the folder. His face slackened with surprise as he read.

"This is true?" Steve said, looking up at Nina with shock in his eyes. "Jeez, you think you know people."

She looked away, not wanting him to see the shine of tears in her eyes.

"I thought so, too. But I've learned that a woman in my position can't trust anyone. Not even the people closest to her."

"But . . . why? What's their play?"

"The obvious. They want my money. They want me out of the picture."

"Tell me what you want me to do," Steve said.

"I'm initiating divorce proceedings against my husband, and I'm going to need your assistance with safely removing him from my property."

He got to his feet. "I'll go grab him now. Throw him out before the party starts."

"Just—hold on a minute. Let's not get ahead of ourselves."

The dressing-room window looked over the terrace, where a tent had been set up in case of rain. The band must've arrived already. Nina couldn't see them, but she could hear them tuning and doing mic checks. The guests would begin arriving any minute. Some were actual journalists. Others had big Twitter followings, or just big mouths. Nina had spent twenty-five long years getting humiliated in the press by Edward's infidelities. This split was going to happen on her terms, which meant *quietly.*

"The timing of the investigator's report is unfortunate," she said. "Now that I know, I have to take immediate action, and yet, I don't want a scene. I'd prefer to go through with the party like nothing is wrong. Once the guests have left, that's when I'll confront Connor, with you present. In the coming days, I'll have a publicist make a discreet announcement that we've separated."

"Due respect, ma'am, that's not smart. From what the report says, this has been going on for a very long time. They knew each other from way back—"

"Exactly. This has been going on for years, so why make a move tonight, with hundreds of people around, including you and your team? All I ask is that you keep an eye on him. As soon as the guests are gone, you escort him to my office. My lawyer gave me the divorce papers. I'll ask you to serve them, then you'll escort Connor off the property."

"If that's how you want to play it."

"It is."

Steve looked troubled.

"What's wrong?" she said.

"I need you to understand that it may not be possible to monitor him every second."

"He's not going to attack me in front of a crowd."

Steve shrugged. "My expert opinion is, people do crazy shit. But this is your call, ma'am."

"I'm not worried. I have everything under control."

17

The skies opened just as the guests arrived. Heavy winds shook the tent as Nina snaked through the crowd, greeting and air-kissing, grabbing mojitos from passing waiters. By eight-thirty, it was hot and soupy under there, and she was halfway to drunk. Rain pounded the canvas roof, and thunder rumbled loudly enough to drown out the band. With every thunderclap or gust of wind, guests would look up and laugh nervously, like the tent might lift off and blow away. There was an edge of hysteria to the party. Everyone felt it, not just her.

An hour in, Nina had downed two mojitos on top of a Xanax and needed something in her stomach to beat back the creeping wooziness. The food was set up in the ballroom. She was working her way through the crowd on a path to the raw bar when a man in front of her turned abruptly, nearly crashing into her. It was Hank. She was shocked to see him. She'd invited him only out of obligation, expecting that he'd decline. Hank had never forgiven her for marrying Connor, and nowadays, they rarely spoke unless business required it.

Nina couldn't deal with him tonight, not after what she'd read in the report. She turned on her heel and walked out, but he followed, buzzing around her like a fly.

"Oh, that's rich. *You* won't speak to *me*? I'm the one with the grievance. I've been hearing rumors that you're planning to move against me at the next board meeting," he said.

"That's a lie."

"It sounds pretty plausible to me. You want to replace me with your power-grubbing husband."

If she didn't need to keep it quiet, she would've told Hank then and there that she was divorcing Connor. That Hank had been right all along about Connor. Of course, he knew he was right. There were things he could've told her, and hadn't, that would've exposed this whole scam years ago.

"You mean your little protégé?" she said.

"Connor—my protégé? You know I can't stand him."

"Not him. I have three words for you, Hank. *Protocol Shipping Solutions.*"

He looked flummoxed. "What about it?"

"It's your company, isn't it?"

"No. It's an old shell company of Edward's."

Nina frowned. Was it possible the investigator had it wrong?

"But—you're on the board," she said.

"I was, years ago. On the paperwork. There wasn't a board, not in reality. The company itself barely existed as I recall. Why? What's that got to do with anything?"

"I—I think you know," she said, but she was no longer certain.

Hank threw up his hands. "You're talking in riddles. Don't change the subject. I know you're moving against me. Lauren is close with your husband, still. He tells her things. In a moment of pique, she threw it at me that he's taking my job. Well, I've got news for you. That's not gonna happen. Watch your back, Nina. If you try anything, you'll lose. Badly."

Hank walked away, leaving her stunned.

Lauren was probably lying about the whole thing. But it didn't matter. Nina and Connor would be separated by tomorrow, and Hank would know for certain that it wasn't true. Still, Hank was angry. And Hank angry could be dangerous.

The rain stopped. The party went on. Nina mingled with her guests.

She was talking to a balding hedge-fund tycoon and his pretty young wife when she caught a glimpse of Connor across the tent. It was the first time she'd seen him all night. He stood head and shoulders above the crowd, his handsome face bathed by spotlights from the bandstand. He must've felt her watching, because he turned to look at her, and she felt an aching twinge of déjà vu, thinking of the night they met—at this same party, two years earlier. As he moved toward her, the crowd parted, and everything seemed to happen in slow motion. Feeling dizzy, and unsafe, she looked around frantically for someone, anyone, from the security team. But in the mass of swaying bodies, there was no one to be found.

"Are you all right, Nina? You look like you saw a ghost," Mr. Hedge Fund said, touching her arm.

When the tabloids wrote the story of this night, she wanted them to say that Nina Levitt was serene and calm before separating from her second husband. But Connor was going to make that difficult. He strode up to them and grabbed her arm, a tense expression on his face.

"Can I talk to you, please?"

"Connor," she said, her voice shaky, "do you know my friends—?"

Crap. She couldn't recall Mr. Hedge Fund's name.

"Darren Walder, and my wife, Stacy. Pleased to meet you."

"Likewise," Connor said, in a perfunctory tone, trying to pull her away.

She resisted. She needed to keep this conversation going until a security guard turned up. Floundering for a topic, she glommed on to the first one that came to mind.

"Darren, you mentioned ghosts. Did you know Windswept used to be haunted?"

"Really?" Stacy said.

"Oh, yes. When my first husband, Edward, brought me here, Windswept was under renovation. The main parts of the house were finished, but others were closed off, full of mice and cobwebs. At night, the wind would howl, and sometimes . . ." She paused for dramatic effect. "Sometimes, I would hear the faint sound of a child crying in the distance, even though no child lived in the house."

"Oh my God, you just gave me a chill," the wife said, with a squeal.

"Honey, it's just a story," Mr. Hedge Fund said.

"No, this is true," Nina said. "Years ago, I used to hear a child crying in the night. I told Edward about the sound, but he didn't believe me. He said it was the wind, that I was imagining things. Then, one night, the cries woke me from a dead sleep. This happened the night of a big dinner party. I'd had a lot to drink, so it's possible my ears played tricks on me. I remember, I staggered out of bed and followed the sound to the west wing, on the opposite side of the house. The electricity was out there because of the renovations, and the only light was the moon pouring through the windows. It was so eerie. I tiptoed down the hallway, and I came to the door to the attic. The cries were coming from behind it."

"What happened next?" the wife asked, her mouth hanging open.

"I turned the knob, but the door was locked from the inside. I ran back to the bedroom to get Edward. He was passed out, and I couldn't rouse him. I did tell him about it the next day, but then we went to Asia for a trip that lasted six weeks. By the time we got back, the renovation of the west wing had been completed. And I never heard the crying again."

"You never told me that before," Connor said. He looked angry.

"Oh, it's just an old story."

"And you never followed up? What happened to the kid? Weren't you worried?" Connor said.

"I don't think the child existed. That's why I say the house was haunted."

"Is that really how it happened, or are you—"

"What? You think I made it up?"

"It's a great story whether it's true or not," the wife said. "We're going to hit the caviar bar. Wonderful party, Nina, thank you."

They double-cheek-kissed. When they were gone, she whirled on Connor.

"You embarrassed me in front of my guests."

"Come down to the beach with me. We need to talk."

He pulled her in the direction of the terrace steps, but she didn't want to go. Not with him. Not tonight. She dug her heels in.

"No."

"What's going on, Nina? Did I do something wrong? You're avoiding me, I can tell."

"There are three hundred people at this party. I lost you in the crowd, that's all."

"All night? The party's almost over, and you never once spoke to me."

"Is it really that late? I lost track of time. Excuse me, I need to go consult about the fireworks display."

She took a step in the direction of the bandstand. He blocked her way. She looked around for anyone from the security team. They were MIA when she needed them most.

"Did you tell security to follow me?" he demanded.

"There's nobody following you, Connor."

"Then how come every time I turn around, one of Steve Kovacs's goons is behind me?"

She swept her arm around the tent. "Where? I don't see anybody."

He didn't answer. She moved, and again, he blocked her.

"What are you doing? You're scaring me. Stop it, or I *will* call security," she said.

He backed off a step.

"I'm sorry. I apologize. I'm feeling hurt. If there's nothing wrong between us, show me. Come down to the beach. Or let's go upstairs. Sneak away, like the first time. I miss us."

That got to her. She tried to tell herself that it was an act, designed to get her to let her guard down. But when he leaned in to kiss her, she let him. The kiss was intense, full of anger and hurt and mistrust, and Nina thought, *This will be the last time.*

"You see?" she said. "Nothing's wrong. Let me go, darling. I need to deal with the fireworks. I'll look for you on the beach during the fireworks display."

His phone rang in his pocket. That seemed to distract him.

"You promise to meet me there?" he said, reaching for it.

"Yes, but if we don't find each other, meet me in my office when the party's done."

Me. And my bodyguard.

Connor nodded and walked away, answering his phone as he went. She felt a twinge, wondering who he was talking to. She'd have to let go of the jealousy. The next time she saw him would be to end their marriage. With security present, to ensure her safety.

To make sure of that, she texted Kovacs, letting him know that she was not happy to have been left vulnerable during the party, and that he'd better come find her on the terrace, ASAP.

The pyrotechnic consultant waited near the bandstand. He was a short, grizzled man in his sixties who'd been doing this for forty years.

They stepped out from under the tent to assess the weather. The storm had moved out to sea, but the surf still pounded wildly. The sky was an eerie yellow, full of clouds and backlit by a full moon. The fireworks would be muted, swallowed by clouds. The alternative was to cancel the display and pay for it anyway. After some discussion, Nina decided to go forward. She mingled with her guests, relieved for the distraction, until the consultant gave the signal that the fireworks display would begin.

Up on the bandstand, the lead singer handed her the microphone.

"Thank you for braving the storm to come out tonight," she said, looking out over the crowd. "I hope you got to eat, drink, and be merry. And now that the rain has stopped, I'm thrilled to announce that the show will go on. Down to the beach for fireworks!"

A roar of approval went up from the crowd. People began surging en masse toward the stairs. Nina stepped off the bandstand just as Steve Kovacs came up to her.

"Where have you been? Connor nearly dragged me off, with nobody from your team in sight. And what happened to your lip?"

He looked like he'd been slugged in the mouth.

"We've been dealing with trespassers all night. One of them gave me some real trouble, and he's still at large. He was with a woman who—"

"Leave them to the police. We have more important things to deal with."

"But, Mrs. Levitt—"

"*I don't care.* I asked for your help with my husband, and you disappeared. If you want to keep working for me, you need to learn to follow orders."

The crowd on the terrace was thinning as guests migrated to the beach, and Nina's raised voice attracted attention. People were turning to look. Kovacs's jaw clenched. Men hated being ordered around by a woman, especially in front of people. Well, too bad. She paid his salary, just like she supported Connor. They needed to learn who was in charge.

"Do you hear me?" she said.

"Loud and clear, ma'am."

"Good. Connor went down to the beach. As soon as the fireworks are done, find him and bring him to my office. Let's get this over with."

As Nina turned and walked toward the house, a round of percussive booms sounded, making her jump. She'd thought it was gunshots. But it was the start of the fireworks display. A sulfuric smell invaded the tent, and it seemed like the world was burning down around her, along with her marriage.

18

TABITHA

It was late afternoon on the Fourth of July, and I'd been driving all day. New Hampshire to the Hamptons on a holiday weekend was slow going—especially when you needed to pull into random gas stations at intervals to throw up in their bathrooms. The sleeve of saltines and two-liter bottle of water that I'd brought along for nourishment were long gone by the time I hit the outskirts of Southampton, and my whole body shook with fatigue. It wasn't safe to keep driving. I needed to find a place to stay. I'd take a nap, have something to eat, and gather my strength before I tried to find Connor.

I drove around for a long time. All the affordable motels had NO VACANCY signs, which shouldn't have come as a surprise. This trip had been doomed from the start. Dropping in on Connor unannounced on the Fourth of July was a terrible idea—one I never would've entertained had I not been desperate. I'd Googled "Windswept" and gotten his address—correction, *Nina's* address—but I had no real plan, other than walking up to the front door and knocking. Nina would probably sic the dogs on me. Hell, she probably knew I was coming. I had a sick feeling that I was being followed again, though not by the Suburban this time. I'd noticed the same nondescript brown Ford Fiesta with New Hampshire plates behind me at several points during the drive, though it wasn't there now. Maybe it was a coincidence. But the New Hampshire plates had me worried it might be Derek.

My body was stiff from hours of driving and I was on the verge of tears when I finally spotted a motel with a VACANCY sign. The Ocean Vista had a parking lot full of potholes and a sad-looking swimming pool that backed up to the road. There was zero view of the beach, but Google Maps said it was a twenty-minute drive to Nina's house, and I wasn't likely to do any better. I parked by the office and got out of the car. The air felt heavy and smelled of rain. Thunder rumbled in the distance. Inside the office, the humidity was thicker than outside. An air conditioner buzzed, unable to keep up with the oppressive heat. A man in a turban sat behind the counter talking on a cell phone in a language I didn't recognize. Finally, he hung up.

"I saw you have a vacancy. How much is a room for the night?" I asked.

"Two hundred and thirty-nine dollars."

"*Really?*"

I winced. That was nuts for this place.

He shrugged. "It's July Fourth. You're lucky I had a cancellation. You won't find another vacancy between here and Montauk."

He was probably right. Anyway, I didn't have the strength to keep looking. I handed over my debit card.

In the room, I collapsed on the bed and pulled scratchy covers over me that smelled faintly of cigarettes. Fatigued like nothing I'd ever known, I was asleep instantly. When I opened my eyes again, it was dark out. Feeling dazed, I went to the bathroom and splashed water on my face. At least I looked better than I felt. My eyes were bright, my hair was shiny, and spots of color burned in my cheeks.

I'd brought a duffel bag with a change of clothes. I traded my crumpled jeans and T-shirt for black pants and a sleeveless black top. They were basic, from Old Navy, but serious enough for this daunting venture. With flats and a swipe of lipstick, I was as ready as I'd ever be to find Connor and tell him my news.

Just my luck—the storm that had rumbled in the distance all afternoon reached the motel as I stepped out of my room. The first fat drops fell, splatting on my bare arms and making me shiver. As I ran to my car, the rain became a deluge. I dove headfirst into the Toyota, already soaked.

The car smelled rank after the long drive. So much water sluiced down the windshield that I could hardly see out. It was like driving through a car wash. As I turned the ignition, a crack of thunder exploded close by. In the glare of the headlights, the driveway was a boiling cauldron, drops hitting the ground with such ferocity that they bubbled back up. Rain pounded the roof. A bolt of lightning split the sky, followed by a loud clap. The orange light on the dashboard reminded me that I was nearly out of gas. I'd wind up stranded on the side of the road before I could even find a gas station. I couldn't go back into my room without getting drenched, and these were the only clothes I had. I turned off the car engine and waited.

Desperate as I was to talk to Connor, I didn't feel safe driving in this mess. After ten minutes passed with no letup, I called an Uber. Surge pricing was in effect, forty-six bucks for a twenty-minute ride, my food budget for a week. But if I didn't do this now, I'd chicken out, and go back to New Hampshire without ever telling Connor about the baby.

The Uber arrived, and I ran to it. The air-conditioning was on full-blast, giving me goose bumps in my damp clothes. The driver was an older guy with gray hair, wearing heavy cologne. The pregnancy had increased my sensitivity to smells, and the cologne combined with the pine-scented air freshener hanging from the rearview mirror made me gag.

"I took lot of people to this party tonight. Some I recognized from TV," the driver said.

"Party?" I asked.

"You're going to Windswept, right?" he said, gesturing at the destination on his phone. "To that celebrity party."

Shit. Nina Levitt's annual Fourth of July party. How could I forget? I'd been reading about it in the gossip columns for years. Since Connor hadn't mentioned holding it this year, it had slipped my mind. This was a freaking disaster. No. Wait. It was an opportunity. A stroke of luck. Hundreds of people got invited to this thing. I could slip into Windswept with the other guests and walk around unnoticed, looking for Connor.

I finally had a plan. For the first time since setting off on my journey, I felt hopeful, even glad that I'd come. I'd never been to the famous Hamptons before, and I craned my neck from the backseat of the SUV, ogling the ritzy surroundings. We were now ten minutes from Windswept, cruising through the downtown. The sidewalks ponded with rain. Red-white-and-blue bunting and American flags hung limp and sodden from every quaint storefront. But even in this weather, the town managed to look storybook gorgeous.

Then I noticed that the driver kept glancing in the rearview mirror.

"What are you looking at?"

"Same car behind us the last ten minutes, making all the turns," he said.

With a jolt of fear, I twisted around to see. It was that Ford Fiesta again. Its headlights glared at me, and its windshield was obscured by rain, so I couldn't see the driver. To spend several hours at my motel, get in an Uber, and find the same car behind me? No way that was a coincidence. Someone was following me.

"Is it the paparazzi? You're famous, right? An actress? Yeah, I recognize you," he said.

"I wish. Can we lose him?"

"Why? You know this guy?"

"I have no idea who that is. It's just creepy."

"Ah, he's probably just on the same Google Maps route as me. Happens all the time. The phone takes you a weird way, and everybody else goes that way, too. Look, he just turned off. Gone now."

True, the car was no longer behind us. I wanted to believe that meant it hadn't been following me, but that seemed unduly optimistic. I kept checking behind us, waiting for him to come back.

"Wait, I got it now. You're a model, right? To show up so late, you gotta be someone special," the driver said.

"I'm nobody. I'm late because of the rain."

"This late, they might not let you in. An hour ago, I took somebody else, and the front gate was already closed," he said.

"There's a gate?"

"Of course. And guards checking names off the list. High security for a party like this."

How could I not have reckoned with Nina Levitt having security? What if I got caught trying to crash? Connor might find out. He'd think I was trailer trash. I looked ahead, straining to see the houses. The rain was letting up, but the street was dark and parked up heavily with cars on both sides. Fabulous cars—Porsches and BMWs and Mercedes, every last one beautiful and new. I couldn't see the houses. On either side of the road, high walls blocked my view. When the Uber's headlights shined on them, they looked like they were made of leaves.

"Where are the houses? Are those—walls?" I asked the driver.

"Hedges. They got tall hedges around the houses out here, so nobody can see in."

"Windswept, too?"

"Part of it, yeah."

"If the gate's closed, and there are hedges, how will I get in?"

"Is there a number to call, on your invitation?"

"I forgot my invitation at the hotel."

He glanced at me suspiciously in the rearview mirror. "It's not a smart idea to crash."

"I'm *not* crashing," I said, but my voice sounded like a guilty child's, and the driver wasn't fooled.

"You crash, they'll arrest you for trespassing."

At that, I blanched. When he saw the look on my face, he stepped on the brake.

"You should get out here," he said.

"Please. Take me to Windswept. I'm paying for the ride. What happens after that is my problem."

"No, look, I was young once, too. I get it, you want to have a good time. You won't get in the front gate if you're not on the guest list. But the beach is right there."

He gestured. Between the parked cars lay a narrow, sand-covered path. As the moon broke through the clouds, I saw the wide swath of empty beach beyond.

"You can walk down the beach to Windswept. It's maybe five minutes on foot. Sneak into the party the back way," he said.

That was probably wise. Not only so the guards at the entrance wouldn't ask to see an invitation, but so Nina—who, I had to assume at this point, had seen a photo of me—wouldn't spot me.

"You're sure it'll work?" I asked.

"No. But it's worth a try. Anyway, you get caught, you didn't hear it from me."

I wasn't sure if I was supposed to tip, but as a waitress, I erred on the side of caution and thrust a ten at him.

"I promise. Thank you."

Hot, sticky air enveloped me as I stepped from the air-conditioned SUV, and I instantly started to sweat. The rain had subsided to a light drizzle, but the road was a mess, mired with standing water and dotted with potholes. At the entrance to the sandy path, I took off my shoes and carried them. My feet sank into the wet sand with every step, making it an effort to walk. The narrow track sloped downward to the beach, between two picturesque fences made of weathered wood. At the end of the path, I stepped out onto the beach, gasping at its eerie beauty. The grand sweep of sand ran for miles in either direction, suffused with a strange yellow light from the hidden moon. The rain had stopped, but the surf was high. Waves crashed onto the sand, the wind rushed, and gulls cawed overhead. The beach felt utterly wild, and yet at regular intervals stood fabulous mansions the likes of which I'd never seen. Shingled manors, embellished with turrets and gables, with lush lawns, pools, tennis courts, outbuildings. I stumbled along, drinking in the sights, unable to believe my eyes, or to comprehend that Connor *lived* here.

I heard Windswept before I saw it, in the low roar of conversation and laughter, the sound of dance music floating on the wind. Up ahead, the land arched out into the water. Following the beach around the bend, I came upon Windswept, and stopped in my tracks.

I knew it from photographs, of course. The house is famous. But to see it in real life was to understand its magnitude for the first time. It wasn't just a beautiful mansion, like the others along this stretch. It was a palace, fit for royalty, built of brick and stone made to last a thousand years. And it belonged to Connor's wife. How could I think he'd give her up for me, when that would mean giving up this kingdom?

Whether he would or not, we had a child coming. And he needed to know.

I walked on. A hundred feet ahead, people milled on the beach in front of Windswept. Guests from the party, presumably—beautifully dressed, holding cocktails, out for a stroll now that the rain had stopped. Above their heads, a sweeping stone terrace was surmounted by a tent large enough to hold a three-ring circus. Noise and music emanated from inside. That's where the party was, and where I'd find Connor.

A man in a dark suit stood by the terrace stairs. A couple of guests walked up to him. He stopped them and spoke to them briefly before letting them pass. This must be the security that the Uber driver had warned me about. As I walked toward the house, the man's head tilted in such a way that I knew he was looking in my direction. As an unaccompanied woman coming from the far end of the beach, I was a plausible candidate for a crasher. He stepped away from the stairs and looked up and down the shore, but the casual nature of the surveillance didn't fool me. He was checking me out while pretending not to. I didn't know what to do. If I tried to go up the stairs, he'd intercept me, like he'd done with the others.

The security guard was staring at me now. He left his post and started walking in my direction. My heart pounded. The Uber driver thought they might be arresting people for trespassing. Was I on private land here? I had to get away before the guard intercepted me. To my right, a brick footpath, narrower than the path I'd taken to access the beach, turned upward and ran alongside a manicured lawn. It must lead back to the street. I turned onto it and kept walking, afraid to look over my shoulder. There were footsteps behind me. I sped up. The footsteps did, too.

"Sir! Stop right there, you're trespassing," a man shouted.

Sir? Yes, it was dark, but with my long blond hair, it was odd that he'd mistake me for a man. A scuffle broke out behind me. What the hell?

"Let go of me, asshole! I'm with *her*."

At the sound of the second voice, the hair on the back of my neck stood up.

Derek.

I heard the soft thud of a punch, followed by a grunt, and whirled to see the security guard and Derek in a clinch. Derek stared past him, looking right at me. The rage in his eyes made my blood go cold. That must've been Derek in the Ford Fiesta. He'd followed me here from New Hampshire. It wasn't me who'd attracted the guard's attention on the beach a minute ago. It was Derek, with his jailhouse fade, clad in gym shorts and a tank top that showed off his bruiser body. He'd been right behind me as I walked toward Windswept. With the waves crashing, and the soft sand, I hadn't heard his footsteps.

And was that Derek all along, following me in the Suburban? Had he actually tried to kill me? Thank God for that guard. It was plain, dumb luck that he'd stopped Derek before he grabbed me. They were evenly matched. Gritting his teeth, the guard pushed Derek back into the bushes. Derek got his arms loose and started pummeling the guy's ribs. They grappled, toppling over into the grass.

I wasn't sticking around to find out how this ended. I ran.

19

I ran down the path and skidded onto the beach, panting. The stretch of sand was empty now, ghostly in the glow of the moonlight. The steps to the terrace had been left unguarded. Seeing Derek had scared me so much that I was tempted to get the hell out of there before he came looking for me. But this was the chance I'd been waiting for. The guard was occupied with Derek. I could sneak into the party, find Connor, and tell him my news. It was now or never.

Under the tent, the bodies were tightly packed, and the air was overheated and humid. A band played at one end, in front of a dance floor jammed with guests swaying to the music. I felt conspicuously underdressed amid the beautiful, lavishly turned out women. Surely, somebody would stop me and demand to know what I was doing here. But as I melted into the crowd, I realized that these people had been partying for hours, on somebody else's dime. They were drunk and happy and not the least bit interested in me. The bigger problem would be locating Connor in the vast sea of people.

I weaved my way across the terrace in one direction, then back in the other, several times with no luck. Just outside the tent, people came and went through French doors that led into the house. The party continued inside. Maybe Connor was in there. Nobody stopped me as I stepped into a spectacular ballroom with high ceilings and a glittering chandelier. It was less crowded inside than on the terrace, and a quick scan told me Connor wasn't here. I took a moment to appreciate the grandeur of the room. All along the walls, tables staffed by waiters in tuxedos groaned with beautiful food. I'd barely eaten in days, and suddenly, not only did I feel better—I was famished. I went from table to table, piling up my buffet plate high with slices of roast beef, perfect little roasted potatoes, mini-tacos, wedges of cheese—anything that caught my eye. I took my haul and skulked like a thief back to the tent, where I faded into the crowd, found a dark corner, and stood there, stuffing my face.

Naturally, that was the moment I spied Connor. He was with Nina and two other people. The surging crowd eddied around them, and the lights picked them out as if calling on me to pay attention. Seeing Connor took my breath away. Tall and tan in a white shirt and cream-colored blazer, he positively shined in the light. I wanted to be with him, touch him, feel his skin, taste his mouth, hear his voice. But as I watched, he pulled at Nina's arm, and she flinched away. Seeing them together—in real life, not just in the tabloids—shook me. He wanted her attention. She wouldn't give it. I felt sick with shame for getting involved with a married man, yet riven by jealousy, seeing him with his wife. He belonged to her. Not me. Coming here was a mistake. Unless—was I misunderstanding? Maybe she flinched because she was angry. Maybe she was angry because he'd told her he was leaving. If only I could talk to him and find out.

The couple they'd been speaking with walked away, leaving the two of them alone. They continued talking. Nina gestured angrily. I handed my plate to a passing waiter and took a step forward, then back, my eyes glued to them, unsure what to do. If only he would look over and see me. How could I get his attention? What if I called him, right now? If he had his phone on him, at least I could see whether it rang through, and I'd know if I was blocked, or if he was screening my calls. And if he answered, I could tell him to meet me down on the beach.

I pulled out my phone and swiped his number. From across the tent, I saw him pat his jacket, then pull out his phone. I wasn't blocked. My heart raced. He turned and walked away from Nina. Before he could answer, someone grabbed my arm from behind. The phone slipped from my fingers and crashed to the floor.

"Hey! What the—?"

It was the security guard. Up close, he was scary-big, with a nose that had been broken before, a freshly split lip, and angry eyes.

"Gotcha. You're coming with me, lady. *Now.*"

"My phone!"

The security guard grabbed it and forcibly escorted me toward the terrace stairs. I was hoping that we would catch up with Connor, but instead of turning onto the beach, he yanked me back toward the path where he and Derek had been fighting.

"Take your hands off me," I said, struggling. "I've done nothing wrong."

He wouldn't let go.

"Tell it to the police. They're waiting to arrest you for trespassing."

"I wasn't trespassing. I was running from my ex. You saw him. He's dangerous. He has a criminal record. He's been harassing me, and I was afraid."

"Yeah, right."

"I swear. Did you arrest him? Where is he now?"

"You tell me."

"He got away? Please, you have to find him. He wants to hurt me. I'm not safe with him on the loose."

He studied my face like he was trying to decide if I was credible.

"Tell me the truth. Were you two trying to rob the house?" the guard said.

"*No.* I wasn't *with* him. This has nothing to do with this house. Derek was following me. He's been stalking me."

"If that's true, why weren't you running?"

The reality was, I hadn't known Derek was behind me until I saw the two of them grappling on the path. And I *was* trying to crash the party. But if I told the guard that, he'd have me arrested.

"I—I *was* running, but, I mean—"

"You know what, lady? Tell it to the cops. Let's go," he said, and led me up the brick footpath.

To the left, Windswept loomed. To the right, I saw a paved motor court and a six-bay garage. Cars lined the motor court, parked closely together with numbered tags stuck beneath the windshield wipers. With a start, I noticed a black Chevy Suburban, parked nose-out in the line. It had tinted windows similar to the SUV that had run me off the road up north. It couldn't be the same one, could it? But, why not? My original theory was that Nina had me followed and had one of her goons run me off the road. If that was true, the Suburban could very well be parked at Windswept. It would have a New York plate on the back, and a damaged passenger door from sideswiping me. I couldn't tell from this distance. I'd have to examine the car, but the guard had no intention of letting me do that.

We continued on the path, crossing a wide lawn and turning onto a gravel driveway. Up ahead, lights flashed. A police cruiser was parked just inside the open front gates. The guard marched me up to it, and shook hands with the uniformed police officer, who was a tall, broad-shouldered woman with dark hair pulled back under her police cap. They nodded at each other like old acquaintances.

"What the hell happened to you?" the officer asked, tapping her lip in the same spot where his was split.

"Ah, friggin' mope jumped me."

The officer looked back and forth in disbelief from me to the hulking security guard.

"Not her. The guy she was with. He got the jump on me and ran off. I went looking for him, but no luck. I found her, though."

"You didn't find us together because I wasn't *with* him," I said. "Officer, please, I can explain. My ex-husband attacked this gentleman on the path—that much is true. But I wasn't with him. I was running from him. I didn't mean to crash the party. I just turned into the first place I saw to get away from him."

"Can I see some ID, please?"

I handed her my driver's license.

"My ex has a criminal record. I divorced him while he was in jail. He's really pissed about that. He followed me here tonight. I think he wants to hurt me."

"Were you a guest at this party?" the police officer asked.

"She was not," the guard said.

"Let her answer, please."

"No, like I said, I just ran into the party to get away from Derek. I came to the Hamptons for the weekend. I was—visiting a friend. I noticed a car following me at times, but I didn't know it was him until I saw him behind me on the beach. I ran up to the house to get away."

"Did you witness any of what she's saying?" the officer asked the guard.

The guard frowned. "I saw her walking down the beach with the guy behind her. Not running, though."

"He was *behind* her? Not with her?"

"Yes," the guard said grudgingly. "Then she turned up the path onto the Windswept grounds, and he followed. I went after them for trespassing. He turned around and sucker-punched me, and we fought. He got away."

"Well, if you saw him behind her, then maybe she's telling the truth." The officer turned to me. "Do you have a restraining order against this guy, or anything else that corroborates your story?"

"I don't, because the cops back home told me there wasn't enough evidence for one. Derek's been harassing me ever since he got out. Coming by my work, saying he wants me back. But he wasn't violent. Not until tonight, anyway, when he attacked this gentleman," I said.

"Wait one minute," the guard said. "I found you fifteen minutes later, hanging around at the party. If you were so scared, why not run while your husband was busy fighting me?"

"I did run. I ran into the party and tried to blend into the crowd. I thought I'd be safer with people around, instead of down on the beach all alone."

"Look, miss, give me his name and I'll check him for priors. Let's see if we can back up what you're saying," the officer said.

I gave her Derek's name. She got in the cruiser, where I saw her typing information into a screen on the dashboard. A few minutes later, she came back.

"Yup, checks out," she said. "Derek Cassidy, did five years for opioid distribution, released six months ago, currently on probation out of Manchester, New Hampshire. Steve, is this the guy who jumped you?"

She held out her phone, displaying Derek's mug shot.

"That's him."

"I say we let her go, and you and me search the grounds for this jerk," the officer said.

The guard's phone buzzed. He pulled it from his pocket and looked at it.

"I've got another situation I need to take care of," he said. "Anyways, I looked for him already. He's in the wind."

"He's on probation and he assaulted you. I'll look for the guy myself if you're too busy."

"Uniformed police in the house is not gonna make my employer happy, Beth."

"It's not about making Mrs. Levitt happy. It's about keeping the streets safe."

"How about this? You search the surrounding area. Forward me that mug shot. I'll give it to my team, and we'll look for him on the grounds."

"Okay."

They exchanged information. The security guard pointed at me.

"You, off the premises."

"Fine, I will. Give me my phone."

He handed it back to me and walked off. The officer was holding my driver's license. She took a photo of it.

"I'll put your name in the report," she said, "so you have a record that he was following you and assaulted the guard who tried to stop him. You can use that to request a restraining order. Hoping you won't need one, though. If I get him tonight, he'll be charged with assault for jumping Steve, and go right back to jail."

"You can do that? How long would he go away for?"

"A new assault charge, while on probation? A year, at least."

"That would be a huge relief. Thank you, Officer. I'm really grateful."

"You have a ride home?"

"I'll call an Uber."

She nodded. "Give me a ring tomorrow to request a copy of the police report. It's Officer Rossi, Southampton PD."

"Will do."

"Stay safe."

She got in the cruiser and drove off. I waited until she was out of sight, then checked to make sure nobody was watching. Near the gatehouse, a couple of valets in white jackets waited for guests to come request their cars. They paid no attention to me. I was free to leave.

Or not. I could go look for Connor, or I could address a more pressing concern—the black Suburban with tinted windows that I'd seen parked in the Windswept motor court just moments ago. It must still be there, since I hadn't seen it drive past me and out the gate. It had a tag on the windshield, like it had been valet parked. If that was true, then it belonged to someone who was legitimately present at Windswept tonight—a guest at the party, or perhaps one of Nina's employees. It might not be the same Suburban that had run me off the road. But it might, and I needed to know. The way to tell would be to examine it for possible damage to the passenger-side door caused by sideswiping another car.

I retraced my steps, down the driveway, across the lawn to the motor court. Windswept was crazy big, its motor court as large as a mini-mall parking lot. I threaded my way among the rows of vehicles, searching for the Suburban. Just as I saw it ahead of me, I heard footsteps behind, and dropped to the ground, terrified that it was Derek coming to find me. I waited, heart pounding. A car door opened. An engine started. And I pulled myself up, looking through the windows of the vehicle that had sheltered me to see one of the valets drive off in a guest's BMW.

Before I got interrupted again, I hurried to the black Chevy Suburban that I'd seen before, approaching it from the rear. It had deeply tinted windows, and now I saw that it also had a New York license plate. I took a photo of the plate with my phone, then flicked on the flashlight, kneeling down to examine the passenger-side door.

And there it was. A visible scratch, and a swath of paint in the same faded blue as my Toyota.

This was the same car, parked at Nina's house. Nina Levitt had tried to have me murdered. That security guard had my name. What if Nina found out I was here? I wouldn't be safe until I told Connor what she'd done, and that I was pregnant. He'd make her stop. He'd have to.

A streak of light soared toward the clouds, followed by a loud boom. The sky lit up with bursts of blue and red and gold, diffused by the haze of the atmosphere. I ran toward the beach, where I'd last seen Connor. But when I got there, it was no longer empty. The party had moved there, and hundreds of people now milled about, watching the fireworks. The ocean was rough from the storm, and massive waves pounded the sand. I walked up and down, searching for him in the crowd to no avail.

As the fireworks display reached its crescendo, the air filled with thunderous bangs and the smell of sulfur. Only after it ended, and the guests began to drift away, did I finally see Connor. He stood about a hundred feet away in the thinning crowd, but he wasn't alone. He was with the guard who'd stopped me earlier, and with Nina. The three of them conferred, silhouetted against a smoky, red sky—Connor, his wife, and the man they'd hired to keep out the people who didn't belong. The trespassers. Like me.

This whole trip had been a waste. There was no chance of speaking to Connor alone. The truth was, if he loved me as he claimed, he would have gotten in touch before now. He hadn't. Time to recognize this situation for what it was and admit defeat. Time to go home.

20

NINA

Two hours later

The confrontation had gone badly.

Nina sat alone at her desk, trying to write down everything she remembered. But her mind was foggy. She struggled to form words, to make her fingers obey her command. What had happened? Where was Kovacs? He was supposed to escort them out, but he'd disappeared at the critical moment. Called away. Breach of security. Something about a man from earlier tonight—*vagrant, burglar, criminal.* Urgent. He had to leave. Leave her alone with them. Was she remembering right? Did Kovacs do his job? Was Connor gone? She couldn't be sure. She was safe in here. Or was she? What about *her*? *That woman.* She couldn't even say her name. She'd write it, instead. Write it, underline it, point them in the right direction.

She threw down the pen. She was wasting precious time. She needed to call someone. A doctor. The police. She looked for her phone. Her vision had doubled. The phone was missing. Or maybe it was here, and she just couldn't see it. She felt around the desk, then got to her feet, holding on to the back of the chair. Feverish, breathing heavily.

Something was very wrong.

She got lost in time.

Things had started to go bad down on the beach, when they found Connor watching the fireworks display. He looked up and saw her, smiling like things were normal. Kovacs was acting strangely. *Lies.* Everyone was lying. Hank had lied about the shipping company. Hank must know. He knew everything. The fireworks disappeared into the clouds. A waste of money. A thick, noxious fog settled over the beach. The smell of smoke. Her eyes teared until she couldn't see. Couldn't breathe. Felt ill. That was when she first suspected that she'd been drugged. In the confusion of the night, she'd paid little attention to what she ate or drank. So long as it came from a waiter, or from the tables laid out for the guests, she'd assumed it was fine.

Stupid. She was so stupid.

She should have called a doctor right then, when she first suspected. But no, she had a plan and she would stick to it. She pushed the thought from her mind. Nina called them to her office. Connor. Kovacs. *Her.* Served the papers. Kicked him out. Banished. It was over. She'd *won won won won.*

Sounds echoed in her mind. They'd laughed. Or cried? She couldn't remember.

She bent over and threw up in the wastebasket.

She needed help.

She unlocked the door and stumbled down the stairs. Falling, getting up. She couldn't feel her extremities.

Who could she trust in this house?

"*Gloria? Dennis?*"

Her voice came out so weak that it didn't travel. They wouldn't hear. The room was spinning.

She was in the ballroom but didn't remember getting there. It was empty, the tables bare, the caterers gone. How much time had passed since Kovacs left? Why hadn't he come back? She doubled over, the pain in her stomach so bad that she moaned, holding her side. Dragged herself to the terrace. The tent was empty, the bandstand abandoned. Was this real? A dream? She fought her way through flapping canvas. Outside the tent, the winds had picked up. There were lights on in the pool house. Shapes moving. Someone was down there. They would help her.

Could she make it?

Down the path. Was someone behind her?

The light rain woke her up, like Dorothy in the snow. The aqua swimming pool glowed from within. It was luminous—so beautiful that she walked toward it, mesmerized. Heard footsteps behind her. Turned. Hands. Pushing. Falling. She was under the water. She struggled toward the light. Time slowed. Her limbs were heavy as lead. Her lungs burned. Finally, her head broke the surface, and she sucked in one sweet mouthful of air, before the hand pushed her under for good.

21

TABITHA

July 5, 6:00 P.M.

I wasn't doing right by this baby.

I'd driven through the night last night to get home from the Hamptons, terrified of seeing Derek in my rearview mirror, then slept for a couple of fitful hours before going to work. I couldn't afford to miss another shift. I needed the money. Last night, I'd finally admitted to myself that Connor had no intention of leaving his wife. I'd probably never see him again, which meant supporting the baby on my own. And the terror that induced made me push myself harder than I should. Lifting heavy trays. Running myself ragged and sneaking off to throw up in the bathroom. Liz, my manager, was a good person and a good friend. If I told her what was going on, she'd want to help. The problem was, I could imagine what she'd say upon finding out that I was pregnant. That I couldn't support this child alone, and I needed to sue Connor for paternity and child support.

I wasn't ready to face that harsh truth yet. I still loved him. I still hoped.

Halfway through the shift, Liz came and found me on the floor.

I'd been avoiding her all night, worried that she was going to take me aside and demand to know what was wrong. Then I'd have to tell her, because I hated to lie.

It wasn't what I was expecting.

"You've got a call in the office. Derek's probation officer," she said.

I hadn't told Liz about Derek following me to New York. I hadn't even told her that I went there. I'd called in sick. Why had I done that? Now I had to worry about getting caught in that lie.

"Why is he calling me?" I asked.

"I don't know. He didn't say."

"I'll be quick," I said.

In her office, as I reached for the phone, I was overwhelmed by dread. At the time I left Windswept last night, Derek was at large, and the police officer had gone off in search of him. I was afraid to find out what had happened since.

"Hello? This is Tabitha."

"Ms. Girard? Mike Mandel from the Probation Department. I just got off the phone with an Officer Rossi of the Southampton PD. She told me that you reported your ex-husband, Derek Cassidy, had traveled to Southampton last night because he was stalking you?"

"Uh. Yes."

"It seems he was arrested down there, for attempted burglary and assault. The officer wanted you to know."

"Wow. Thank you. That's a relief. The police were called last night, but Derek got away. I've been looking over my shoulder ever since. So, they found him?"

"Oh, they found him, all right. He was arrested and charged. Because he was on probation, he won't get bail. He'll probably go away for a year or two, at least."

"I'm very glad to hear that. He's been coming around my work, actually. It was pretty scary."

"I had no idea. I wish you'd contacted us. I could've intervened."

"I called the police. The guy acted like there was nothing he could do."

"Well, that's wrong. Anyway, you don't need to worry now."

"Thank you. I'm very glad to hear that."

"Hey, if you don't mind, can I ask you a couple of questions?"

"Sure, I guess so. About what?"

"It's just, I'm trying to understand what happened. The situation is strange to me."

"In what way?"

"Like, why would Derek—who's no angel, now, I know, but he stays in his lane—"

"Stays in his lane?"

"You know, he's a two-bit pusher. Local. Not a heavy hitter. Why would he try to crash this high-society party down in New York, where, as far as I know, he's never been in his life before? Can you enlighten me?"

I had the distinct feeling that this guy was suspicious of me. I wasn't guilty of anything, but that had never protected me from being implicated in Derek's crimes. I should say as little as possible and get off the phone.

"As I told the officer, Derek followed me there, and that's all I know," I said.

"I take it you're acquainted with the people whose house it was?"

Why was he being so nosy? I refused to drop Connor's name. What if it got back to him somehow? The last thing I needed was Connor finding out that the convicted drug dealer who'd been arrested for trespassing and beating up the security guard at Windswept was my ex-husband. That would be impossible to explain.

"I was trying to get away from Derek, and I ran into the first house I saw. Now, if you'll excuse me, Mr. Mandel, I'm at work, and my boss is calling me."

"It's just weird, because, you know, the woman died."

That got my attention.

"What woman?"

"The hostess of the party. Nina Levitt."

"Nina Levitt *died*? That can't be right."

My heart started hammering.

"It was on the news. She drowned. Her body was found early this morning in the swimming pool at her home. Look, I'm not saying they think Derek had anything to do with her death—"

"*Derek?* Oh my God."

The room was spinning.

"No, I'm *not* saying that. From what I understand, they're treating this as an accident, at least until an autopsy can establish cause of death. But you have to admit, it's a crazy coincidence. Normally, I'd think murder is outside Derek's wheelhouse. But then I come back to, what the hell was he doing there in the first place? I was hoping you could shed some light."

"I can't, sorry. Now I have to go."

I slammed the phone down and collapsed in the chair. I felt so faint that I had to put my head between my knees. Liz walked in. Seeing me, she ran to my side.

"Tabitha. Jesus, are you okay?"

"Derek got arrested."

"For what?"

"Assault. Down in New York."

"That's a good thing, right? He'll go back to jail."

I was hyperventilating.

"You're scaring me," Liz said. "Hold on. I'll get a paper bag."

Liz ran out, returning a minute later with a paper bag. She held it up and had me breathe in and out until I stabilized.

"I feel better," I said, after a few minutes. "Thank you. I always thought that was an old wives' tale."

"It works. Take it from this old wife. You're white as a sheet, though. Go home."

"I can't. I've missed too much work."

"Someone can cover for you."

"It's not that, Liz. I need the money."

She nodded, understanding in her eyes. "Fine. But when your shift's done, you're gonna come back here and tell me what's really going on with you."

"Deal."

I went back to work with my mind reeling. Mandel was right. Derek was just a small-time drug dealer. A fuckup, a lowlife, and—as far as I knew—no killer. But he *was* an opportunist and desperate for cash. Maybe he tried to rob her, and something went wrong. The more I thought about it, the more terrified I got. Derek had no connection to Nina, except through me, and my affair with her husband. If he was involved in her death, it was certain to come back on me.

I got so worked up about the possibility of being implicated in Nina's murder that I couldn't think of anything else. At the end of my shift, I sat on the bench outside Liz's office, waiting for her to close out the till. It was the first moment I'd had to myself all night. And it hit me.

Nina was dead. Connor was free.

I knew that was a selfish thing to think about, but I couldn't help it. He and I could finally be together. I had to get in touch with him, right away. I walked out of the restaurant, my hands shaking as I dialed my phone. He picked up on the first ring.

"You heard?" He spoke quietly.

"Yes. I'm so sorry. Are you all right?"

"Hang up. I'll call you from a different number."

I sat in my car, waiting. Liz came out and tapped on the glass. I lowered my window.

"I thought we were going to talk," she said.

"I'm not feeling up to it. Tomorrow, okay?"

My phone rang.

"I have to take this."

"Tabitha—"

"Sorry, Liz."

I put the window up. She looked annoyed.

"Hello?"

"Tabby," he said with a heavy sigh. "Things are so screwed up here. It's really good to hear your voice."

Liz was watching. I turned away, hunching over my phone.

"You didn't call," I said in a low tone.

"I couldn't. Tabitha, Nina's dead."

"Yes. What happened?"

"She killed herself."

Suicide? That wasn't what the probation officer had said. I had questions, but they would sound suspicious enough that I couldn't ask them with Liz standing right outside my car.

"Can you hold on?" I said into the phone, and lowered the window again.

"Liz, I'm sorry. I need some privacy."

She shook her head, turned, and walked away, and my heart sank. She was going to lose patience with me. But what could I do? I hadn't heard from Connor in weeks. Nina was dead. We had to talk. This was too important.

"I heard she drowned," I said to Connor, once Liz had gone. "What makes you think it was suicide? Did she leave a note?"

"No. We found an empty bottle of pills. She'd been despondent. The theory is, she took an overdose and threw herself in the swimming pool."

Guilt weighed on me. "Oh, no. Because you told her you were leaving her?"

"I never went through with that. The day we got back to the States, she saw her doctor. She was diagnosed with terminal cancer. I couldn't leave her when she was dying. I would've felt too bad about myself."

"*Cancer?*"

"Lung cancer. She was a heavy smoker when she was younger. She'd been feeling ill for a while. Chest pain, shortness of breath. She had the specialist lined up and went straight there from the airport. She told me it was clear on the X-ray, a big mass on her lung. She was so upset. That's why I couldn't return your calls. I needed to be there for her. I just never thought she'd do something like that. God, I feel so guilty."

"It's not your fault."

"I didn't want it to end like that."

"Of course not. Still, that's a relief."

"A *relief*?"

"I'm sorry, that came out sounding selfish. I just meant, I'm relieved that it had nothing to do with *us.* With you and me."

Or with Derek. Thank God.

"Right. But still. If anybody knew about us, they might think there was some connection. We should hang up. We can't talk. Not until things settle down."

I'd been imagining that now we could see each other. He didn't even want to talk?

"We're talking now. I don't understand. What's the problem?"

"I shouldn't have answered. But when I saw your number come up—well, I didn't think. All I knew was, I wanted to hear your voice."

"I want that, too. I want to see you, be with you."

"Me, too, Tabby. Believe me."

"I've missed you so much. I can't wait another minute. I know things are crazy for you. I can drive down there right now."

"No, you're not listening. It's not possible."

"I can help. I can be there for you."

"If anyone finds out about us, it would look terrible."

"We'll just say I'm your friend."

"Who's gonna believe that? It's too risky."

"I don't understand. You said her death was a suicide. If that's true, what is there to worry about?"

"There's been no ruling yet. The police are investigating. You know how cops are. They rush to judgment. It's always the husband, even in cases where there's not a lot of money at stake. Here, there's a *fortune.* If there was even the slightest hint that I had a motive—"

"A motive beyond the money? Like, another woman? Me?"

"Exactly. That's the classic scenario, right? If anyone found out about us, frankly, I'd be in deep shit."

"But if she really killed herself, won't the evidence show that?"

"I'm no expert. But my sense is, this is one of those murky situations. They can make it look bad for me."

"How long will the investigation take?"

"It's not just the investigation. There's the estate."

"Estate?"

"I'm trying to get a handle on it. I have a call in to her lawyer. I don't know if there was a will. I don't know what the story is. That could take a long time to resolve, and until it's settled, I need to lead an exemplary life."

"So, we have to sneak around?"

"Not sneak around. We can't see each other."

"For how long?"

"I don't know. A year, maybe more, maybe less."

"A *year*? No. Connor—no."

"Does it matter? I'm committed to you, Tabby. I found you again after so long. I'm finally sure of what I want in my life, and it's you. I know that in my heart. You need to know it, too. We can wait another year. What's one more year if we know we want to be together forever?"

"Connor, this won't be a normal year. I've been trying to get in touch for days. There's something you need to know, something important."

"What is it?"

I told him.

22

MRS. TABITHA FORD

October

It was dark and rainy as the plane came in for landing. I'd only flown a few times in my life, and never into New York City. Awestruck by its beauty, I craned my neck to see the skyline from my sumptuous seat in first class. The lights of the skyscrapers disappeared into the clouds, giving off a soft glow like a watercolor painting. Connor had an apartment in one of those towers. It wasn't officially his yet, but it would be, along with Nina's entire fortune, once the will was settled. Which meant that it would also be mine, since Connor and I were now married.

The baby had changed everything. Once Connor heard about it, he couldn't wait for us to be together. A month ago, the police had ruled Nina's death a suicide, and we thought we were out of the woods. He rushed up to New Hampshire to see me. Being together for the first time in months, knowing the baby was coming, we got carried away, and on the spur of the moment, we went down to Town Hall. It was a reckless thing to do given the crazy circumstances. But, when I thought about how close I'd come to never seeing Connor again, to missing out on true love, on the family I'd always dreamed of, well, the narrowness of my escape chilled me. My new life was a dream. I was too overwhelmed with joy to think about the consequences.

Until now.

The plane touched down. I leaned out into the aisle and called Connor's name, but he didn't hear me. He was seated one row behind, in his own pod, surrounded by a privacy screen. The first-class seats were a marvel of modern technology. They turned into beds at the touch of a button and were fitted out with an elaborate entertainment system. But they were lonely. Connor had spent most of the flight catching up on paperwork. He stayed glued to his seat, and the only time I saw him was during the meal service. I shouldn't complain; that meal had been epic. Each seat pod came with a guest chair and table that the flight attendant called up from the floor as if by magic, and set with a white tablecloth, silver, and crystal glasses. We'd enjoyed a five-course dinner, starting with Dom Perignon and caviar, then filet mignon, flourless chocolate cake with berries, and a cheese and fruit course, complete with wine pairings (which I'd skipped, except for one sip of the champagne, because of the baby). All this on an *airplane,* in flight from Rome to New York, somewhere over the Atlantic Ocean. I was Mrs. Tabitha Ford, a role I was so ill-prepared for that I felt sick with anxiety as we taxied to the terminal. But I shouldn't question my good fortune.

The FASTEN SEAT BELT sign turned off. Connor stayed seated, his phone to his ear. I started to get my carry-on down, but the flight attendant swooped in.

"Let me get that for you, Mrs. Ford."

"Thank you."

I stood in the aisle waiting for the doors to open. Finally, Connor hung up and joined me.

"That was the CEO. I've got to make a connecting flight to Washington to meet him. There's a problem with the Saudi deal, and we need to negotiate some new terms. I'll be down there for a few days, maybe a week."

"Connor. *No.* I can't go . . . I can't go to Windswept without you."

I'd almost said *back* to Windswept, but I'd caught myself in the nick of time. Connor didn't know I'd been to Windswept before. I'd never found the right moment to tell him about Derek, and the altercation with the guard on the night Nina died. He didn't know my ex-husband was a convicted felon, or that I myself had an arrest record from that time in my life. It was all so awkward that I hadn't found the courage to bring it up.

"It's okay, you'll be fine," he said, flinging his arm around my shoulders, kissing the top of my head.

"Please, let me come with you."

Before replying, Connor looked around to make sure nobody would overhear.

"It's not smart," he said, his voice low. "I'll be with the people who run the company. Hank Spears, the CEO. Lauren Berman, the head of PR. People who knew Nina well. When they hear I got married—well, let's just say it'll raise some eyebrows. You have to let me lay the groundwork. Spin the narrative. Like we agreed, okay?"

We'd agreed to lie—or *spin,* as Connor preferred to call it—to everyone, about everything important, until the estate was settled. We had to say that we met for the first time after Nina's death. We could never let it slip that we knew each other before. We had to keep the pregnancy secret until the last possible moment. When the baby came, we'd say he was premature. I had to remember to tell these lies to everyone I encountered. I could never, ever slip, or the consequences would be dire. Because something bad had happened while we were away on our honeymoon.

We'd thought we were in the clear when the police ruled that Nina's death was a suicide. But a new claimant to the estate had come out of the woodwork—Nina's older sister, whom Connor hadn't even known about because the siblings had been estranged. Nina died without a will. Connor's claim to her fortune should be ironclad. Under the law, where there was no will, the entire estate went to the surviving spouse. But Nina's long-lost sister, a sixty-year-old woman from North Carolina named Kara Baxter, had filed a lawsuit contesting Connor's claim to the inheritance. The only way she could win would be to invoke something called the "slayer rule," which said you shouldn't be able to profit from killing someone. In other words, Kara would have to prove that Nina's death was foul play, and that Connor was behind it. It was a recipe for muckraking and mud-slinging, and we were terrified.

"What about the doctor? I need you to come with me to the first visit," I said.

"I can't. Not with this lawsuit hanging over us. You need to go alone and use your maiden name."

"Don't say that. I hate that."

"So do I, Tabby, but we have no choice. This isn't just about the money. If that woman slings enough mud, who knows, the police could reopen the investigation. I could wind up in jail for something I didn't do."

That might've sounded overly dramatic, but not to me. I knew it was possible to get prosecuted for something you didn't do.

"You're scaring me. Please, tell me it'll be okay."

"I hope so. We have to be careful."

The airplane door opened, and we walked down the Jetway.

"I have to run, or I'll miss my connection," he said, looking at his watch. "I texted Nina's driver, Dennis, to meet you and take you to Windswept. The housekeeper, Gloria, will meet you when you arrive. The staff runs the place. You won't have to do a thing. Just rest, and keep a low profile, okay? Don't talk to anybody outside of the house."

"I understand."

"Chin up. I love you."

He kissed me and ran off before I had the chance to ask how long he'd be gone. It always hurt when we said goodbye. But going to Windswept without him under these crazy circumstances was worse than just a separation. It was dangerous.

As I stood in line at Immigration, fear preyed on me. According to the press reports, Nina had died alone. There were no witnesses, and that was bad for us, given that she'd left no suicide note. The medical examiner found that she drowned while under the influence of an overdose of a commonly available opioid painkiller. Nina's personal assistant testified at the inquiry that Nina was despondent over her cancer diagnosis. She had a prescription for the pills, from the doctor who was treating her cancer. Based on that very limited evidence, the ruling was death by misadventure, or possible suicide. That's where it was left, but it wasn't airtight. No witnesses had come forward to claim foul play. Nobody had been accused of killing her. Not Connor. Not Derek—whose presence at the house that night hadn't come to light during the death investigation. *Not yet.* All that could change now that Nina's sister was poking around, trying to manufacture evidence for her lawsuit.

As I exited Customs, I saw a woman in a corporate-looking black pantsuit holding a sign that read MRS. TABITHA FORD.

"That's me," I said, pointing at the sign and blushing. I wasn't used to the name yet.

The woman shook my hand. She looked to be around my age, with a pretty face, dark hair, and glasses.

"Pleased to meet you, Mrs. Ford. I'm Juliet Davis. I was Mrs. Levitt's executive assistant. Mr. Ford has asked me to stay on for the time being to assist in your transition."

"He didn't mention you. He said a driver would meet me."

"Yes, Dennis. He's waiting with the car. Hold on, I need to text him to bring it around," the woman said, taking out her phone.

Her manner was crisp to the point of being cold. All around us, families hugged and kissed. It was strange to be met so formally. But I guess that was just how professional staff behaved. I'd have to get used to it.

"He's coming now. I can take your luggage."

"That's not necessary."

"Please, it's my job. Where is it?" Juliet asked.

"Right here."

My hand rested on the Samsonite roller bag I'd borrowed from Matt for the honeymoon. Juliet's surprised look made me conscious of how battered the suitcase was. My jeans and hoodie were crumpled from the flight. Juliet was the assistant, but she was dressed better than I was. What must she think of me—the hick from New Hampshire, come to take the place of the glamorous Nina Levitt, who always wore couture.

I followed her through sliding glass doors. Outside, it was pouring rain. Juliet, who was already wheeling my luggage with one hand, deployed a large umbrella and held it over me with the other as we searched for the car among the many jostling for space at the curb. That seemed foolish since her clothes were nicer than mine.

"Ah, there's Dennis," Juliet said.

We headed toward a sleek Mercedes sedan. A gray-haired man in a chauffeur's cap jumped out and opened the back door. I slid across, expecting Juliet to get in beside me. But she handed him my luggage and went around to the front passenger seat. A glass partition separated the front and back. I was nervous and lonely, and wished I could tap on it and ask her to come sit with me. But it was better this way. If I didn't speak to anyone, I wouldn't have to lie.

I stayed silent, staring out the rain-streaked windows for the ninety-plus-minute drive to Windswept. As we drew closer to the house, the surroundings began to look familiar. We passed the quaint downtown, the streets where the tall hedges hid magnificent homes, the path to the beach that I'd taken at the Uber driver's urging. The events of that night came back to me in vivid detail, and I slumped under the weight of them. I couldn't bear to think about Nina dying. I wouldn't go near the swimming pool where it happened.

We pulled up to the gate. It swung open, and the Mercedes proceeded through to an elaborate circular drive. Windswept loomed ahead, dark and ominous in the rain, and I shivered. We pulled up to a covered portico. I got out, then saw that Dennis had been on his way to open my door for me.

"Luggage coming right up, ma'am," he said.

"You can call me Tabitha," I said, but he didn't reply, and I could tell he would never take me up on that.

Juliet was beside me. "I'm sure you're tired after your journey. I'll take you to your room. Follow me, please."

I hurried up the sweeping staircase after her. By the time we reached the top, I was out of breath. I was beginning to gain weight, though not so much that people who didn't know me would notice I was pregnant. The morning sickness had abated, but other symptoms—fatigue, bloating—had set in. I would have to make an effort to seem normal.

We stood in a gallery that overlooked the magnificent entry foyer. Hallways branched off to the left and right, into separate wings of the house. The gallery was hung with abstract paintings that I should probably recognize. In their strangeness, they screamed "important art." Eager to change the subject, I pointed to one that looked like a skeleton surrounded by squiggly lines.

"Interesting painting. Is that—?"

"Basquiat, yes," Juliet said, nodding.

I was about to say Picasso. I'd never heard of Basquiat. Whoever he was, he'd painted something that looked like the Grim Reaper.

"The art in this house is priceless," she said. "Warhols, Lichtensteins, Harings. There's an amazing Lucian Freud portrait of Mrs. Levitt in the master suite. Come, this way."

I would rather not see a portrait of Connor's dead wife. But that seemed like an inappropriate thing to confess to Juliet. I followed her down a long, dark hallway. The entire east wing of the house was shuttered, the doors to the rooms closed and blank.

"This section of the house hasn't been used much since Mrs. Levitt died," Juliet said, following my gaze. "Mr. Ford preferred to stay in the guest wing, but now that he's remarried, of course he'd want to use the master."

Did that mean I'd be sleeping in Nina's bed? The idea made me cringe.

"Did he say that? Because I'd be happy to stay in the guest wing if that's easier for you," I said.

"Mr. Ford texted this afternoon to let us know you were coming, and he asked us to make up the master, yes. To be honest, that's the first we heard of your marriage. It was quite sudden, wasn't it?"

Until I'd arrived here tonight, it hadn't occurred to me that I'd be living among people who'd known Nina well, worked for her, and presumably cared about her. The staff hadn't had time to adjust to the idea of Connor remarrying. To me, he was mine. But in the eyes of everyone at Windswept, he belonged to Nina. They all must see it that way. *Juliet* must. I had a terrible sense of unease, realizing that the face she showed me—a pleasant, helpful face—probably didn't represent her true feelings. My natural inclination was to be friendly, make conversation, answer any question I was asked. But I had to be careful. As much as I wanted to get to know Juliet, she might not be well-disposed toward me. I shouldn't discuss my marriage with her until I knew if I could trust her. I had to be disciplined about everything I said.

I nodded and remained silent.

"In any case, we didn't have a lot of time to get ready," Juliet said. "The housekeeper asked me to convey her apologies that things aren't in better order."

"I'm sure it's wonderful. Please, tell her not to worry about me."

"You can tell her yourself. You'll meet her in the morning. She lives in the staff quarters on the third floor. It just got kind of late for her. Gloria's older. She's been here forever. Set in her ways, but she's a fixture."

At the end of the hall, Juliet stopped at a set of heavy, ornate double doors, unlike anything I'd ever seen. Carved with images of angels and devils, they looked like the gates to hell.

"Florentine. Sixteenth century," she said, mistaking my horrified glance for awe.

As we stepped into the bedroom, a smell of dust and damp rose up. Juliet flicked on the lights. The room was vast, with high ceilings, an elaborate canopy bed, and a glittering chandelier. She moved over to the windows and threw open the drapes.

"I know it's dark out now, but the view's so great. I just love this room."

Powerful surf crashed on the sand below, reminding me of the last time I'd been here. I turned back in to the room, looked up, and gasped. Nina's portrait was chilling. If not for the fact that her eyes were open, the woman in the painting might have been a cadaver on a slab. She was completely nude, reclining at an odd angle on a bed, her pale-white skin dappled with green and gray shadows. Her limbs were twisted, her legs splayed as if in spasm. Her head tilted strangely backward, exposing her vulnerable throat. The overall effect was ghoulish, with the only sign of life her crimson hair, but even that looked daubed with blood.

"Exquisite, isn't she? Edward Levitt commissioned that painting in honor of Nina's twenty-fifth birthday. It's considered a masterpiece of Lucian Freud's late period. There used to be a Warhol of

Edward himself, facing her across the room. After Mrs. Levitt remarried, she moved it down to the library. She didn't like her first husband watching her in bed with her second, I guess."

As Juliet chuckled, I blanched, realizing that Nina would be watching *me* tonight as I slept. I wished I could ask Juliet to move the painting, but that felt like overstepping. What right did I have to make a change like that? This house didn't belong to me. I'd have to wait for Connor.

"I'm afraid we haven't had time to clear out Mrs. Levitt's dressing room. We'll get started first thing tomorrow. It's a complicated process, but we'll move as quickly as possible. When are your things arriving?"

"I don't own a lot of things. Just what's in my suitcase, and a couple of boxes that my friend will ship to me."

"Oh," Juliet said, looking taken aback. "Well, I suppose that gives us more time. It's quite a job. I'll show you."

We stepped into another enormous room, lined with shelves and hanging poles displaying an incredible array of clothes. There was a beautiful dressing table with a professionally lit mirror, and across from it, a three-tiered full-length mirror with a pedestal to stand on, like you'd see in a tailor's shop. There was elaborate floral wallpaper, a marble-topped packing dresser with crystal knobs, glittering sconces, and a crystal chandelier. The clothes were organized by color as well as category. There was an entire section of furs, another of woolen coats, one that held only black clothes, another only white. The most flamboyant section displayed evening gowns in every color of the rainbow, glittering with sequins and beads, embellished with feathers. Racks and racks of shoes and bags and hats, a safe in the wall that must contain precious jewels. It went on and on.

"Wow," I said.

"Everything was inventoried not long after her death," Juliet said. "We're in talks with a couple of auction houses. Rest assured, it's all being looked after properly. There's so much here. Hermès and Chanel bags. Vintage evening wear. Furs. The value is significant, and it belongs to the estate."

"Oh, of course—I wouldn't—I don't think any of it is *mine,*" I said.

Juliet gave me a strange look, and I saw that I'd misunderstood her, and said something foolish, though I didn't know exactly what. The prospect of spending days among strangers in this enormous, glamorous yet gloomy house, uncertain of how to behave, having to watch my every word, made me feel exhausted suddenly.

A knock sounded on the door, and Dennis wheeled in my suitcase.

"Is there anything else we can do for you, Mrs. Ford?" Juliet asked.

"No, I'm fine."

"If you need anything, I have a room on the third floor, next to the housekeeper. I'll be staying there for the next several days to help you settle in. And Dennis lives over the garage."

I nodded. "Thanks, but I'm used to fending for myself. I won't be any bother."

"No bother, ma'am," Dennis said. "That's our job."

"Thank you. If you'll excuse me, I'm very tired. Good night."

I rushed them out, closing the door behind them and collapsing against it, relieved to be alone. But that feeling lasted only a moment. I felt a prickling on the back of my neck and turned to see Nina staring at me from the wall, her grayish skin and haunted eyes redolent of the grave. I was an interloper here, she seemed to say, and shouldn't get too comfortable.

23

I got in bed and turned out the light. The bed itself was more luxurious than any I'd been in before—a fluffy duvet, acres of pillows, a feather topper that made the mattress soft and welcoming. But I couldn't relax. I lay in the dark with my eyes wide open, alert for any sound that stood out against the drone of wind and surf outside, exhausted yet utterly awake. I couldn't get over the fact that Nina had slept in this bed. Touched these sheets. Made love with Connor here. Despite the heavy duvet, I felt a chill in my bones that I couldn't shake.

Realizing that I wouldn't sleep tonight, I flipped the light back on and dialed Connor's phone. The call went to straight to voicemail.

"Hi, babe, it's me," I said. "Um, Juliet put me in the master. She said that's what you wanted. I don't mean to be squeamish, but it's a little freaky, sleeping in Nina's old room. I'm wondering, maybe if you could call her and ask her to move me somewhere else? Or, anyway just call. I miss you so much."

Hours passed. I left the lights on and slept only intermittently. It was one-thirty when he finally called back.

"I'm so glad to hear your voice," I said, huddled under the covers, my back to Nina's portrait. "It's strange being here without you."

"You said *Juliet* put you in the master?"

"Yes. She said that's what you asked for."

"I didn't ask *her.* Gloria should be handling everything."

"Gloria was asleep by the time I got here."

He made an annoyed sound.

"Don't blame her. It was pretty late," I said, worried that I'd gotten Gloria in trouble with Connor.

The housekeeper would hate me now, and we hadn't even met. There was nothing I had resented more in my life as a server than another server ratting me out to management.

"It's Juliet who's the problem," he said. "She was Nina's personal assistant. I don't know what she thinks she's doing, hanging around you. You didn't encourage her, did you?"

"Encourage? I mean, I don't know. I'm really not used to having staff. It would be easier to navigate this stuff if you were here."

"You're going to have to fly on your own for a little bit, Tabby cat. I'm afraid I have to go to Riyadh."

"Where's that?"

"Saudi Arabia."

"Seriously? Connor, no—"

"Baby, don't make it harder, okay? You know I want to be with you. But this is important. I have to finesse things with Hank. I told him we got married, by the way."

"How did he take it?"

"Better than I expected. He's smart enough to realize I have the best claim to the estate, which includes Nina's voting shares. As long as I play ball on the direction of the company, he has no interest in antagonizing me, or in swapping me out for that whackjob sister. Better the devil you know, right?"

"Does he know about the lawsuit?"

"Everybody knows. It's been all over the news. He offered to hook me up with his team of lawyers. He says they're real killers. We need to get aggressive. Fight back. Like, how do we even know this nutjob *Is* Nina's sister? Hank knew Nina for thirty years, and never met her. We have to discredit her claim any way we can."

"Could that really work?"

"It's worth a try. We're not going down without a fight. You keep a low profile, like I said. Don't leave Windswept unless you have to. Got it?"

"Yes."

"Hey, I've been missing you all day like crazy. Do you miss me?"

"Mmm, so much."

As we sweet-talked, one thing led to another, and before I knew it, we were having phone sex. It made me feel close to him across the miles, and by the time we hung up, I wasn't as afraid. I'd forgotten to ask him about changing rooms. But I didn't feel the need to quite so urgently anymore. That portrait was only paint on canvas. Connor loved me. I lived here now, and Nina was gone.

For the rest of that week, I did my best to settle into Windswept on my own. The weather was chilly and bright, and I took long walks on the beach every day. Nobody stopped me. Nobody cared where I went. In my new life, I had no responsibilities, no shifts to miss, no hours that I needed to log. And I was grateful. My life had been a terrible grind, almost unbearable through the first trimester. My energy returned now that the morning sickness was gone, and I walked for miles, feeling at home in my body for the first time in months, mesmerized by the ocean. The waves bubbled and churned on the cold sand, every color of blue and green and gray and silver. Gulls reeled overhead. Geese were beginning to fly south. There were plovers on the beach, and crabs, different kinds of seaweed, shells. The wind smelled fresh and briny. When I came back indoors, my nose would run in the warmth, and I'd make my way to the library, with its elegant walnut paneling and plushly upholstered sofas and chairs. I'd mock-salute the Warhol of Edward Levitt, fall into a chair, press a buzzer, and Gloria would come and bring me tea.

Gloria was in her fifties, with hair of such jet-black that it must be dyed, and brown eyes that always looked tired and sad. The soft, jowly roundness of her face reminded me of Grandma Jean. She moved about quietly in her sensible shoes and starched uniform, always calm, never seeming to mind my questions or requests. She was there with a hot drink when I needed one, but when I said I preferred to cook for myself, she showed me the kitchen, and left me to it. When my boxes arrived from New Hampshire, she laid out my jeans and sweaters in the small corner of Nina's dressing room that had been cleared for my use by Juliet. My old clothes looked incongruous among the furs and ball gowns, but Gloria treated them respectfully, the same way she did me. I sometimes got the sense that she felt sorry for me—the new bride knocking about alone in this giant house, her husband gone off to some exotic land—but always, Gloria accepted me without judgment.

Toward the end of that first week, Dennis drove me into the city. I asked him to drop me off at Bergdorf's, a place that Juliet said Nina had liked to shop. I wasn't planning on buying anything. It was a ruse, a cover, for the visit to the obstetrician whose name Connor had gotten for me.

Dr. Jennifer Klein had a kind face, graying dark hair, a degree from the Yale School of Medicine, and an office on Park Avenue decorated in soothing pastels. Lying on the examination table as she did the ultrasound, I wished so much that Connor was with me that there was a catch in my voice when I spoke.

She patted my arm.

"Cry if you want to. It's emotional, the first time you see the baby," the doctor said.

And I did—just a few tears as I stared at the screen. The doctor spread cold gel on my stomach, moving the wand around to get images of the baby from various angles.

"Do you want to know the sex?" she asked.

I had to choose between Connor missing the big moment or waiting another month to find out.

"Yes."

She manipulated the wand to get a view of the space between the legs.

"Congratulations, it's a girl."

My daughter was perfect. Tiny nose and lips, a delicately round head, little hands balled into fists.

"Amazing," I whispered reverently.

As I watched, she kicked, and for the first time, I actually felt it—like the rustle of butterfly wings inside me. And with that, the baby was a person to me—someone I knew, loved dearly, and had a sacred obligation to protect. I decided on the spot to name her Margaret, which had been my mother's name. My mother was Peggy. My daughter would be Meg, a name I'd adored ever since reading *Little Women* when I was twelve.

Dr. Klein texted me the sonogram video, which I forwarded to Connor, with a text that just said, our daughter. I wanted to save the name and tell him on the phone. I hoped he'd love it as much as I did.

I was in the backseat of the Mercedes on the way back to Windswept when he called.

"Hey, babe," I said, my smile a mile wide.

His voice was cold. "Tabby, that was a mistake, sending me the video. You have to be more careful. How many times do I have to tell you that nobody can know about the baby."

Shocked, I glanced up to make sure Dennis wasn't listening. The glass barrier was up. His reflection in the rearview mirror was neutral, staring at the road.

"But—I only sent it to you. I didn't—"

"You have to assume your phone is not secure. Do you understand? This woman could've hired someone to bug us."

"That's so paranoid. Besides, if you really believe it, why are you talking about this over the phone?"

"Do I think the phones are actually bugged? It's not impossible. People do crazy things for this much money. The knives are out for us, Tabby. You don't understand the world you live in now. Delete the video from your phone, okay? I deleted it from mine. I'll call you in the morning."

"Wait! . . . Hello? Connor?"

The call had dropped. He'd deleted the video of our baby? How could he? What would it even achieve? My pregnancy was beginning to show. I wouldn't be able to hide it for much longer.

As it turned out, I couldn't even hide it for the rest of that day.

That afternoon, I went out for a walk on the beach without checking the weather forecast. Within a few minutes, the skies opened, sending me scurrying back to Windswept, soaking wet. I went up to the master suite to change, and was shocked to walk in on Juliet, standing in my bathroom. She was staring at the prenatal vitamins I'd left sitting out on the vanity so I wouldn't forget to take them.

"What are you doing?" I said.

She whirled, startled. She hadn't heard me come in.

"You're *pregnant*?"

Her tone made it sound like an accusation.

"That's none of your business. Why are you in my bathroom?"

I watched the emotions play across her face—shock and anger, followed by the guilty look of someone who'd been caught out. And then, panic.

"Ma'am, I apologize. I was cleaning out Mrs. Levitt's things, and I realized, I hadn't checked the medicine cabinet. I thought this might be hers—lying around. I—I'm so sorry if offended you. I had no intention of invading your privacy—"

"It's okay. Relax."

"Please don't tell Mr. Ford I was in here."

"He doesn't care."

"He does. You won't tell him? I think he wants to fire me."

"Juliet, no. That's not true. You've been nothing but helpful."

"Seriously. If you tell him, he'll ask me to leave."

"I won't let that happen. I've worked for a living my whole life. Nobody is getting fired on my watch. Rest easy, okay? You're keeping your job."

The gratitude in her eyes moved me. I knew how it felt to think you might get fired. The uncertainty, the feeling of unfairness. Juliet was probably around the same age as me. A month ago, I would have envied her position. I would've thought her job was cool and hoped we could be friends. And now she needed to be afraid of me. That was a strange feeling, and an uncomfortable one.

"Thank you, Mrs. Ford. And if it's not too intrusive of me to say, what wonderful news. You must be very happy."

She smiled brightly, and I wondered if I'd imagined that flash of anger a moment ago.

"It wasn't planned. We would've preferred to wait. But yes, thank you, I am happy."

"And Mr. Ford? Is he happy, too?"

"Thrilled. He always wanted children. Even so, I would appreciate it if you didn't mention this to anyone just yet. It's still early."

"I wouldn't dream of it," she said smoothly. "It's for the proud parents to announce when they're ready. Now, I have some paperwork for the auction to take care of, so I'll get out of your hair."

After she left, I changed into sweatpants and a cozy sweater and sat on the window seat, watching the storm rake the ocean. I felt like we'd connected. But now that the moment had passed, I was gripped with anxiety that she'd found out my secret. Not just any secret. A dangerous one, life or death. Would she keep quiet? I hoped she saw me as an ally, even someone who might become a friend. But her loyalty to Nina might make her resent me. The new wife, the interloper, whose prescription bottle told a tale of infidelity predating Nina's death. Was Juliet trustworthy? I couldn't tell. Connor had gotten one thing right on the phone earlier. I didn't understand the world I lived in now.

24

I'd been at Windswept for an entire week without Connor, but finally, the end of our separation was in sight. He'd be flying home tomorrow, and I was expected to join him in the city that same night for a dinner celebrating the closing of the Saudi deal. The top brass of Levitt Global would be there, along with the Saudi executives.

"Is that a good idea?" I said nervously, when Connor told me this over the phone the night before. "I thought I was supposed to keep a low profile."

"True. But Hank Spears wants to meet you. He's the CEO, and things will go easier if he's in our corner. This is a small dinner in a private room at a restaurant. Nobody from the public will be there. It should be fine, and it's a good opportunity to introduce you."

"But I won't know what to say."

"It's just a meet and greet. You don't have say much. The focus of the dinner is on the Saudis."

"I don't have anything to wear."

"Whatever you wear, you'll look beautiful. Be ready by six tomorrow night, okay? Dennis will drive you."

The next morning, I asked Juliet to come to the master suite and give me pointers on what to wear. We stood in the dressing room, which had been stripped bare except for the tiny corner where my clothes now hung.

"Too bad I already sent off Mrs. Levitt's things," she said. "She had the most glamorous Saint Laurent tuxedo with sequined lapels. It wouldn't've fit you, though. She was very petite."

She looked me up and down skeptically.

"I wouldn't feel right, wearing her clothes."

"I know. I just meant, that suit strikes the right balance for this event. Discreet, but impactful. Show me what you have. Let's see if we can find something similar."

It took literally three minutes to go through my wardrobe. I owned five pairs of jeans in various washes, three sets of black pants and white tops that I wore to work, sweats, leggings, a large pile of T-shirts, a few cute tops, and several dresses from Target and Old Navy that I'd worn on my honeymoon.

"What about this? It looks good on," I said, holding up my favorite of the dresses, a flowy, floral print.

"Honestly? That looks like something a sorority girl would wear on a Tinder date."

"I'm sorry, Juliet. As you see, my wardrobe is basically jeans, and the black pants and white shirts I wore for work."

"Work? What did you do before?"

"I was a waitress."

She gave me a strange look, and my stomach clenched. Unlike with Gloria, I always felt that Juliet was judging me.

"As you can imagine, I'm kind of out of my league here. Could I possibly impose on you to help me find something to wear?"

"Mrs. Levitt had a stylist in the city who chose clothes for her, but I could never get you an appointment on such short notice."

"That seems like a lot of fuss, anyway. You can help me, can't you? For this dinner, I'd just like to wear something simple. Maybe something like what you're wearing."

"This is just a Theory pantsuit. It's the uniform for Mrs. Levitt's assistants. The girl before me wore them, and the girl before her. It's fine, but they'll be expecting something more. As Mr. Ford's wife, you really should wear couture to an event like this. To find something, to have it tailored—we just don't have time."

"Is there a mall nearby?"

"There's a boutique in town that carries high-end things. I'll call Dennis to bring the car. Let's hope they have something."

I ended up with a simple V-necked black dress and a pair of stiletto-heeled black pumps with crystal buckles. The items totaled over a thousand dollars, which Juliet had to charge to the Windswept household account because my credit card was declined. The beauty people who normally did Nina weren't available on short notice, which was fine with me. I was more comfortable doing my own hair and makeup.

At five minutes to six, I was putting on mascara when there was a knock on the master-suite door.

"Come in."

Juliet walked into the dressing room. She looked me over as I stood in front of the full-length mirror.

"What do you think? Am I okay?"

She frowned. "It's a little—"

"A little what?"

"—a little too *basic.* Maybe an updo?"

My blond hair hung past my shoulders, thick and wavy and guileless.

"I'm not good with hair."

"Me, neither. We need to dress you up a little. Hold on, I have an idea."

She punched the combination into the safe, and the door swung open.

"The clothes are gone, but the jewelry is still here."

"Oh, I couldn't," I said.

"Jewelry isn't like clothing. It's much less personal. Here, this will look nice with that dress."

She held up a glittering emerald choker. Standing behind me, she fastened it around my neck. It lay cold and heavy against my throat, but the effect was instantly transformative. I went from being an average girl in a basic black dress to looking like a starlet.

"It's beautiful. Are you sure this is okay?"

"The jewelry belongs to Mr. Ford, and he'd want you to look nice when you meet his colleagues. Dennis is downstairs with the car to take you to the helipad."

"*Helipad?*"

"Yes, how did you think you'd get to the city? The dinner starts in an hour. You'd better go."

"Thank you. You've been such a help."

I hugged her and ran out.

I'd never been in a helicopter before, but Dennis assured me it was a normal way to get into Manhattan from out east. Normal, that is, if you were fabulously rich. He introduced me to the pilot, who strapped me in and gave me headphones to protect my ears from the noise. I raced into the sunset, as lacy waves tumbled on the shore below, and the lights of Manhattan glittered in the distance like Oz, unable to believe that this was my life.

When we landed, a driver sent by Levitt Global waited to take me to the restaurant. The dinner was being held in a private room at Le Bernardin, a famed Manhattan restaurant with three Michelin stars. I'd looked it up online and knew those stars meant the most exquisite food on the planet. I was so excited to eat there that it kept the butterflies in check at meeting Connor's business associates for the first time. The driver came around to open my door, and I stepped from the car carefully, teetering in the high heels. As I maneuvered to the curb, a dark-haired man dressed entirely in black ran up and took my picture. As the flash went off, I cowered, allowing him to get off several more shots.

"What's happening?" I said to the driver.

"Get lost," the driver said, waving the photographer off. He stepped between me and the camera, blocking the photographer's view, and hustled me to the door.

"Sorry about that, ma'am."

"Who *was* that?"

"Paparazzi. They used to swarm Mrs. Levitt like flies."

The dinner was just beginning. I followed a group of beautifully attired guests into a sleek, modern room set aside just for this event. The grandeur of the scene overwhelmed me. The ceiling was made of precious woods, the long table laid with white linen cloths, crystal and fine china, exotic-flower arrangements at intervals along its length. Waiters circulated with trays of champagne and hors d'oeuvres. The crowd was mostly men in dark suits, some in Arab dress, and here and there a few women in elegant outfits and jewels. Connor stood at the far end of the room, talking with a tall silver-haired man and a beautiful woman in a red dress. They turned as I approached. Connor's look of welcome was instantly replaced with one of horror as he caught sight of me. His mouth fell open. And I realized—he was staring at the necklace. I knew then that I'd made a terrible mistake by wearing it.

"This must be the new Mrs. Ford," the silver-haired man said.

"Ah, yes. Yes, my wife, Tabitha. Hank Spears and Lauren Berman from Levitt Global," Connor managed. But he'd gone white.

Hank had mild eyes behind wire-rimmed glasses. He took my hand in both of his.

"Ah, Tabitha. I've heard so much about you. Welcome to the Levitt Global family," he said, with a warm smile.

Lauren nodded coolly and didn't say anything. A couple of the Saudis joined the group, and the conversation went on. They were talking about the deal. I couldn't focus enough to follow the conversation because my whole body surged with anxiety. At a moment when the others seemed distracted, I leaned in and murmured to Connor.

"I missed you so much. Did you miss me?"

"What the hell were you thinking, wearing that necklace?" he whispered, between gritted teeth.

I felt sick, horrified. "Juliet said I should be more dressy."

"Is she behind this? She's gonna hear about it from me."

"She was only trying to help."

He snorted dismissively.

"Please, Connor, don't say anything to her. I'm trying to settle in here, to get along with people."

"We'll deal with this later," he said.

It was time to sit down. A waiter escorted me to an assigned seat. I wasn't seated with Connor. I saw him at the opposite end of the long table, taking his seat at Hank's right hand. I gazed at Connor steadily, willing him to look up and give me a signal. A signal that everything was okay. That I hadn't just blundered into a ruinous faux pas that would bring our world crashing down. That he wasn't regretting that he'd ever reconnected with me. But he didn't so much as glance in my direction.

The few women in attendance had all been seated together at the far end of the table. My calligraphy place card read, "Mrs. Connor Ford." I wondered whether they even knew my first name. I didn't belong here. I didn't understand this world. I didn't know the rules. I couldn't even communicate. On my left, a woman in full black veil sat scrolling through her phone. All I could see of her face was her beautifully made-up eyes. Lauren Berman sat down on my right. She was looking at her phone, too, ignoring me. Waiters were placing elaborate tiered serving trays in front of all of us. Trying to distract myself with the food, I nibbled a crab tartlet. Lauren threw down her phone with a dramatic sigh.

"I can't believe I'm down here in fucking Siberia," she said, her language a contrast with her elegant red dress. She was beautiful, with dramatic eyebrows and full lips. I was a little afraid of her.

"So, you're Connor's new wife," she said, looking me up and down brazenly. "I see you didn't waste any time helping yourself to Nina's jewelry."

I flushed crimson. "Uh—I, but I didn't know that I—"

"You didn't know about the Levitt emeralds? That piece is famous."

I started stuttering. "No, just, well, there was no notice, you know, this dinner, so sudden. Nothing to wear. I borrowed something. I didn't think anyone would mind."

"Oh, trust me, Nina would mind. She'd mind *very much.* You're lucky she's not here, she'd rip that thing off you so fast. Nina had claws."

Shaking her head, she signaled for the waiter.

"Vesper martini, make it strong," Lauren said.

He turned to me. "Ma'am?"

"Just soda water, please."

"I don't trust people who don't drink," she said. "It's like they're trying to gain some advantage over me."

I couldn't tell her the real reason I wasn't drinking. "I just—I'm a little under the weather tonight."

"That was a joke," she said.

But it hadn't sounded like a joke. It had sounded hostile, and I could understand why. I'd stolen Nina Levitt's emerald necklace. More important, I'd stolen her husband. I wondered how many people in this room tonight were angry at me for that.

"You were a friend of hers, I take it?" I said.

"A friend of *Nina's*? Hah, no. I'm the head of the PR department. I'm here tonight to figure out how to sell this stinker of a deal to the shareholders."

The waiter returned with our drinks. I sipped my club soda. Lauren took a long pull of her martini. A couple of women sat down across from us on the other side of the table. They said perfunctory hellos to Lauren, who didn't bother introducing me. I noticed them shooting glances in my direction, whispering behind their hands. Were they talking about the emerald necklace, too? A waiter came around, filling glasses with white wine. I put my hand over my wineglass. The meal service began, and I focused on the food, taking a bite of buttery langoustine. As delicious as it was, I no longer had an appetite.

"The Real Housewives are trash-talking you, I see," Lauren said, leaning close enough that I caught a whiff of gin.

"I don't know why they'd waste their time on me."

She'd finished her drink and proceeded to drain the glass of wine.

"Oh, you're a very interesting topic. Nobody can understand how you pulled it off. Connor's a free man, in line to inherit Nina's fortune, and he turns around and gets married to some waitress he meets at a dive up in the boondocks. Some might wonder what you have on him."

"Did you ever think that maybe he fell in love?" I said, starting to get annoyed.

"Please, Connor Ford is not capable of love."

That upset me. Who did she think she was, talking about my husband like that?

"What the hell do *you* know?"

"Oh, I know plenty," she said, setting the glass down unsteadily, her eyes lit with fierce urgency. "Connor used to work for me. And when he did, we were *very* close, until someone better came along.

Hindsight is twenty-twenty. By the time I realized what a player he was, he was already Mr. Nina Levitt. He forgot me so fast. Anyway, karma, right? Nina got hers. Look at Connor now, so cozy with Hank, in the middle of every deal. They used to hate each other. Then Connor signed off on getting in deeper on this Saudi thing when Nina was against it. She would've found a way to tank this deal if she were alive. But what do you know?" She raised an eyebrow drunkenly. "She's dead, conveniently for some people."

Lauren was obviously drunk, plus, she had an agenda. Yet, Connor had as good as admitted to me that he'd married Nina for her money. It was plausible that he'd been with Lauren at some point for career advancement, too. Being with me had changed him. He'd told me that repeatedly. I'd ignore Lauren, except for the fact that, in her drunken ranting state, she'd made the one accusation that I most feared. And loudly enough for others to overhear.

"I'm just trying to understand, since you're slurring your words so badly," I said, in a low tone. "Did you mean to insinuate that Nina was murdered? If you did, I need to let my husband know that you're over here slandering him."

Her eyes widened in alarm, and she laughed.

"You go, girl. No, the party line is absolutely that Nina killed herself. And why shouldn't she? She was a nasty old bitch who everybody hated, including yours truly. Don't pay me any mind. I'm nobody. Just a flack who's had a few too many. Speaking of."

The waiter was going around the table with bottles of wine. Lauren pushed her glass forward to be refilled.

"The white burgundy is excellent. Six hundred a bottle on the menu, you really should try it."

"No, thank you," I said, shaking my head at the waiter.

She looked at my empty glass, then at my face, then at my midsection, which was looking rather pronounced in the fitted black dress.

"God, I'm such a dolt. So that's why he married you. Holy shit."

I stood up. "I don't know what you're talking about. If you'll excuse me."

I teetered away on the stiletto heels, going to hide out in a stall in the ladies' room. I stayed there for long enough that Connor texted to say he'd noticed I was gone and was I okay.

In the bathroom, not feeling great, I wrote.

My poor girl. Sorry I got mad. Everything feels shaky. Do you need to leave? Should I come get you and bring you home to bed?

Feeling a little better, be out soon.

If Connor was willing to walk out of his important business dinner to take care of me, then things must be okay. At the very least, I hadn't ruined our marriage. And nothing else mattered. Even if everything Lauren had said was true, I wouldn't care. Connor had made mistakes in the past. He was honest about them. He'd told me he'd married Nina for the wrong reasons. Not to use her, but because he'd been dazzled by her wealth and fame. Who wouldn't be? I was dazzled by his now. Did that make me a user? I didn't think so. We've all done things we're not proud of. I was no different. I had an arrest record that Connor didn't know about. I kept struggling for a good moment to tell him that, along with the fact that I'd been at Windswept the night Nina died. And so had Derek. But I didn't murder Nina. Connor didn't either. The miracle was, he and I were together again. We were having a baby. He was a changed man because of it. I believed that. I believed in him. I couldn't let some drunken ex-girlfriend with an ax to grind shake my faith in the man I loved. I shouldn't even let her ruin our evening.

We helicoptered home together, our hands entwined, our mouths locked together as we rushed through the air. At Windswept, Dennis took Connor's luggage from the trunk, but Connor waved him off.

"Leave it. I'll get it later," he said, pulling me up the stairs in a rush.

"Yes, sir."

I blushed, self-conscious at the thought that Dennis knew what we were going to do. But as soon as Connor slammed the bedroom door, there was only him and me.

"I missed you so much, Tabby," he murmured. "I hate being away from you."

The sex was different now that I was pregnant. Gentler, more emotional. Afterward, he stroked my abdomen, cooing to the baby, and I wondered how I'd ever doubted us.

I went to the bathroom. When I came back, he was gawking at his phone, his face slack with dismay.

"What is it? Is something wrong?"

I hurried to his side, leaning over him to see the screen. My own image stared back at me, stepping from the car in front of the restaurant. Eyes wide, I looked like a deer caught in the headlights. But it wasn't my face that Connor was staring at. The Levitt emeralds glittered at my throat, as lavish as the crown jewels.

"You let yourself be photographed in that necklace?" Connor said, his voice flat with shock.

"Some guy jumped out at me with a camera. I didn't ask him to."

"You should've told me."

"I don't understand. Did he send you the picture? Why is it on your phone?"

"He's a photographer for ChitChat. The online gossip rag? I have a Google alert on my name, and it popped up. There's a whole story with it. Listen to this—'A mere three months after Nina Levitt's suspicious death'—"

" 'Suspicious'? How can they call it that, when the cops—"

"They say whatever they want. 'Nina Levitt's *suspicious* death, Connor Ford has a hot new wife. Tabitha Ford didn't waste any time in helping herself to the famous Levitt emeralds.' "

" 'Helping herself'? It wasn't even my idea. They don't know the first thing about me. How can they write that?"

"Tabby, they don't care if it's true or not. They'll say anything for eyeballs. Jesus, listen to this, they're talking about the lawsuit. 'The late Mrs. Levitt's sister has raised doubts about the cause of her death.' Yeah, because she's trying to steal the money. Nina hated her guts. She wouldn't want that witch to see a penny. *Fuck.* This is bad."

When I rubbed his shoulder to try to comfort him, he glared at me and flinched away.

"How could you be so reckless?"

"Wait. You're blaming *me*?"

"I told you to keep a low profile."

"This isn't my fault. You made me go to that dinner. I had no idea what to wear. It was Juliet who gave me the necklace."

"You can't trust her."

"Why not? These are the people you left me with. Why wouldn't I listen to them?"

"You don't know where people's loyalties lie. This whole place is a vipers' nest."

"It's understandable that the staff cared about Nina and might take a while to accept me. But if we can't trust them, that's a problem, Connor."

"What do you want me to do? Start firing people? That's not smart."

"I didn't say that."

"They'll sell stories to the press. Keep your friends close, and your enemies closer."

"I understand. I don't want anyone getting fired. But what about Lauren?"

"What does *she* have to do with anything?" he asked, a sick look on his face.

"I sat with her at the dinner. She'd been drinking, and she had a lot to say about you, none of it very nice. She said you were a gold-digger, that you use women. You used her. She basically insinuated that you killed Nina."

"She's full of shit. Don't tell me you believed her."

"This is someone you were involved with?"

"We had a fling, before I met Nina. It was nothing. Lauren and Hank were in the middle of a divorce—"

"Lauren was married to Hank?"

"Yes. But he left her for Nina."

"Wait, Hank and Nina were together?"

"For about five minutes once, but long enough to cause Lauren's divorce. She rebounded with me. I thought it was just a fling, that it didn't mean much to Lauren. But when I got involved with Nina, she went ballistic. She hated me. She hated Nina more. If someone wants to suggest that Nina was murdered, they ought to be looking at Lauren, not me."

"You think Lauren killed Nina?"

"No, I think Nina killed herself. I'm just saying, if push comes to shove, Lauren would make an excellent suspect."

"If push comes to shove. You're saying we should frame her?" I asked in astonishment, a sick feeling in my stomach.

"Jesus, no. I wouldn't do that. But you can't take anything she says at face value. She's out to get me."

"Connor, it's disturbing to me that you have all these enemies. Stalked by the press, surrounded by people who want to hurt us. What kind of life is this?"

"I tried to warn you. That very first night. I told you how terrible it was in Nina's orbit."

"That was Nina. She's gone now. We can't be like her. It's no way to live, and not what I want for our baby."

"Well, we don't always get to choose. Maybe I shouldn't've married you and brought down this scrutiny on us. But with the baby coming, I wanted to be with you so much, I couldn't wait. We're living the consequences."

"You regret marrying me?" I asked, my eyes flooding with tears.

"Never. I love you, Tabby cat, and I don't regret it at all. I *am* sorry you have to suffer through this ugliness, and I'll do anything I can to make it better. We have to be prepared. To protect you as much as possible. C'mere."

He kissed my eyelids and wiped away my tears, then gathered me against his chest. I listened to his heartbeat as he stroked my hair. Being held like this should make me feel protected, like everything would be okay. But it didn't. We hadn't resolved anything.

"Connor, all I want is you. I don't need this house, the money. Maybe we should just give it to that Baxter woman, and find a way to disappear. Move somewhere far away. Lead a normal life. Otherwise, I'm afraid of what will happen."

"Shush, baby. It'll be okay. I promise."

He took my face in his hands, kissing me on the lips. Gently at first, then harder. As the kiss went deeper, he caressed me, pulling me on top of him, and my breathing sped up. But I couldn't get lost in the sex this time. I was too bothered by the things he hadn't said. He didn't want a normal life. He had no interest in renouncing Nina's money. Her fortune was his, and he'd do everything in his power to keep it, no matter what the cost. If I wanted to be with him, I needed to quiet my doubts and accept that.

25

Connor immediately set about protecting me from the paparazzi. One morning the following week, as he was about to leave for the city, he asked me to join him in the library.

"What's this about?" I asked, as we made our way down the sweeping staircase.

I was dressed in dark leggings and a knit hat for my morning walk on the beach. Connor wore a beautifully tailored dark suit with a gold tie that brought out the color of his eyes. He was so handsome that he gave me butterflies, and I still couldn't get over that he belonged to me.

"This is about your safety, my love. The paparazzi harassed Nina constantly, and I'm not going to let that happen to you. I called in an expert to handle the situation. He's here to brief us."

"A publicist?"

"A security consultant."

We hurried through the east wing parlors, our footsteps echoing on the parquet floors. Windswept was like a museum, its high-ceilinged rooms full of exquisite furniture and artwork. After two weeks here,

I was still overawed by the place, to the point that I was afraid to touch things for fear of damaging some priceless object.

As Connor pushed open the library door, the man who'd been sitting on the sofa sprang to his feet. He was tall and brawny, with a smashed nose and colorless eyes. It was the guy who'd caught me trying to sneak into Windswept the night Nina died, the one who'd fought with Derek and called the police on us. I watched his eyes flicker as he tried to place me, feeling like someone had walked across my grave.

The man turned to Connor.

"Steve, great to see you. Thanks so much for coming by," Connor said, pumping his hand. "Darling, this is Steve Kovacs. He's a top-notch security consultant. Steve, my wife, Tabitha."

"Mrs. Ford, pleasure," Kovacs said.

"H-hello," I said, my throat dry.

My hand sweated as we shook. His powerful grip brought back the feeling of his hand on my arm as he walked me to the police cruiser that night. How was it possible that he didn't recognize me? Was I saved by my ponytail, my long blond hair hidden under a cap? That reprieve couldn't last. I should say something before Kovacs did. People survived in this dog-eat-dog world by getting out ahead of the story and spinning it to their advantage. But there was no good spin here. I'd been at Windswept the night Nina died, accompanied by my drug-dealer ex who was now in prison for assaulting this security guard. How do you make that sound better? I could tell the truth, give the innocent explanation, but who would believe it?

"Please, have a seat," Connor said.

Kovacs and Connor sat down on the couch side by side. I sank into an overstuffed chair, limp with the fear that he'd recognize me any minute now. But his face was perfectly blank.

"I hear you've got a nasty paparazzi problem," he said.

"Yeah, some asshole from ChitChat snuck up on her at Le Bernardin last week when we were there for a Levitt Global dinner. I don't know whether it was dumb luck, or if somebody tipped him off. But now they're interested in her, and I'm worried she'll be targeted wherever she goes. With this lawsuit nonsense, it's a sensitive time. We don't need the scrutiny."

"Absolutely. I understand."

"What can we do to protect her, so she's not hounded? And protect me, too, of course."

"Sure. Well, first, thank you for the opportunity to discuss your security profile. I always believed Mrs. Levitt's risk management was not as robust as it should be given her high net worth and public presence. I think it's wise for you to reassess. My advice is to bring your considerable resources to bear on the problem. In other words, you get what you pay for. Let's be real. People are out to get you. The press, the woman who brought the lawsuit, her investigators, who knows what other bad actors are out there every day, thinking about you, and how they're gonna bring you down. Let me think about how to stop them. How to frustrate their access to you, and how to set up a muscular program of counterintelligence."

"Go on."

"At a minimum, you need daily personal security, a complete overhaul of on-site security here at Windswept, and an investigative capability aimed at neutralizing threats *before* they arise."

Kovacs proceeded to outline a series of measures, including the installation of multiple security cameras on Windswept's grounds, a twenty-four-seven security team including live-in bodyguards, guards to accompany us whenever we left the house, and investigators who could dig up dirt on Connor's adversaries. When Kovacs said it would cost thousands of dollars a week on an ongoing basis, Connor didn't bat an eye. He agreed to everything.

If Kovacs became a regular presence in my life, I'd live in constant fear of the moment he remembered me. I protested based on the expense and the intrusion, but Connor wouldn't hear it.

"Let me handle this, okay, babe? You're new to this lifestyle. You're just not in a position to make an assessment of our security needs the way I am."

They agreed that Kovacs would implement a large-scale security program at Windswept as quickly as possible. In the meantime, it would be best if I didn't leave the grounds, not even to walk on the beach.

"Is that really necessary?"

"It's a public beach. Anybody could be out there, and I can't protect you until we're on site," Kovacs said.

"Please, Tabby. For my peace of mind," Connor said.

"If you really think so."

"I do. And now I've got to get into the city. Steve, I'd appreciate it if you could forward the contract and put your team in place as soon as possible."

"Absolutely, sir."

They left, and I sat on the window seat with my chin in my hand, looking out at the bright, blustery day. Down on the beach, whitecaps crested jauntily as gulls swooped across the sky, but I was a prisoner here because some stranger had taken my picture. Surely, an overreaction. Right? If Nina had committed suicide, Connor should have nothing to worry about. There wouldn't be evidence proving him guilty if he wasn't, so there shouldn't be a way to pin her death on him. Unless there was evidence. Unless he was behind it.

If I let myself doubt him even for a minute, I'd go down a rabbit hole and never get out. Connor stood to gain hundreds of millions of dollars from Nina's death. It would be so easy to believe he was guilty, but then I'd have no one, and nothing. I had to have faith. Yes, there was a lot of money at stake, but that didn't make him guilty. You could say I had that same motive, and I was innocent.

You could say I had the same motive. That train of thought continued, bringing me to an uncomfortable truth. I was as good a suspect for Nina's murder as Connor was. Better, actually. Connor had access to Nina's money while she was alive. I didn't. I was struggling to make ends meet, with a baby on the way. The only way I could get my hands on Nina's money would be through her husband, and for that, she had to die. Not only did I have the most compelling motive, I had the opportunity to kill her. I was at Windswept the night she died. Kovacs knew that. He just hadn't recognized me yet. All it would take was that lightbulb going off in his head, and I could find myself accused of Nina's murder.

I ought to tell Connor the truth, tonight. The whole truth. Or else Kovacs could end up telling him first.

As if conjured by my thoughts, Kovacs strolled out onto the terrace and down the steps to the beach. He was talking on his phone, heading west, away from Windswept. He walked down the beach until he became a tiny dot and disappeared. I picked up the binoculars that sat on the windowsill to see him better. Almost immediately, he turned around and headed back, taking up position on the stretch of beach in front of Windswept. Putting up the collar of his jacket against the wind, he checked his watch as if he was waiting for something.

A few minutes later, Juliet emerged from the house and walked down to meet him. It didn't appear to be a chance encounter. There was no look of surprise, not even any greeting. They spoke several minutes, intently. At one point, Kovacs turned and gestured toward the house. Juliet looked up and nodded. The feeling that they were talking about me was so strong that the back of my neck prickled. After a few more minutes, Juliet went back into the house, and Kovacs strode off toward the brick path that led past the garage and up to the front gate. I crossed my fingers that walking on the path where Derek had attacked him wouldn't jog his memory. To me, it evoked memories uncomfortable enough that I'd avoided it since my return, just as I'd avoided visiting the swimming pool where Nina had drowned. To me, they were haunted places.

I heard a noise behind me and turned with a start. But it was just Gloria, coming to dust the room.

"Good morning, Mrs. Ford," she said, nodding unsmilingly, her black hair and dark eyes making her seem even more somber.

"Good morning, Gloria."

"Okay if I tidy up in here now?"

"Sure thing. Go right ahead."

She made her way around the room on soft-soled shoes, flicking a feather duster, straightening the knickknacks. Juliet had referred to Gloria as a fixture at Windswept. The term was apt—she moved so soundlessly that, at times, she seemed to blend in with the furniture. More than once, I'd turned a corner in the immense house and been startled to stumble across Gloria going about her work. I wondered if Nina had insisted on that level of discretion, if she'd been the type who hated to see or hear her staff. Personally, I found Gloria's silence disconcerting. She could be watching me, and I would never know.

"How long have you worked at Windswept, Gloria?"

"A long time."

"Did Mrs. Levitt hire you?"

She stopped dusting for a moment, averting her eyes, as if deciding whether to reply.

"No. He did. He brought me here."

She gestured at the Warhol of Edward Levitt hanging over the fireplace. A candy-hued silk-screen of a photograph, it was realistic in a way that the ghoulish Lucian Freud of Nina was not. It showed Edward in minute detail, with a pockmarked face and bright blue eyes, wearing a smoking jacket and holding a cigar, a cruel smile playing about his lips. He was probably in his forties when it was done, and he looked commanding and dangerous, like someone who ruled his corner of the world. Like a pirate.

"Everything I've read makes him out to be a tyrant. What was he like to work for?" I asked.

She continued dusting. I thought she wasn't going to answer, but eventually she started talking, in a soft, faraway voice.

"That's true. He did what he wanted. He didn't like to hear the word 'no.'"

"You mean, in business?"

"Everything. But business, sure. Like, years ago, Mr. Levitt came to my town to open a mine. There were protests, but the police arrested everyone. My brother went to jail. He got beat really badly, and he died."

"My God, that's awful. I'm so sorry. Your brother died in the protest, yet you still came to work for the Levitts?"

"A lot of people agreed with the police, because the mine brought jobs. My other brothers went to work there. And when Mr. Levitt came back to the U.S., my family sent me with him. It was a chance to send money home. The Levitts paid me good money. I sent my nieces and nephews to school. I bought my mother a house. Maybe I wanted to leave sometimes, but I had reasons to stay."

"I feel like that myself sometimes, too."

"You? You can leave whenever you want to."

"You're right. I don't mean to equate our situations. I'm sure what you went through was very difficult. How old were you when you came here?"

"Seventeen. The first Mrs. Levitt was here then. She was a nice lady. Good to me. I was sad when she left."

"You mean, when Edward divorced her for Nina?"

"Yes."

"How long did you work for Nina?"

"Long time. Thirty years. Until she died."

"That must've been hard, too."

"People say Mrs. Levitt was difficult. Not to me, she wasn't. We got along. We understood each other. It might sound funny, but we went through a lot of the same things."

I didn't really understand what she meant by that.

"The papers said you were the one who found her body."

"Oh, I don't talk about that," she said, turning her back abruptly. She took up the feather duster again, moving to the other side of the room.

"I'm sorry. I should've realized it would be a sensitive topic."

"The police told me, don't talk about it, in case I have to testify."

"Testify? Isn't the case closed?" I asked, alarmed.

She shrugged. "That, I don't know. They don't tell me much. Just not to talk about it."

"Got it."

"So, you say you want to leave. Why don't you, then?"

"Leave Windswept? I didn't really mean that. It's just that I feel alone here sometimes. I imagine you felt the same way when you first came. I was a waitress before, and I'm really not prepared for this life. Connor and I got married fast. I didn't exactly know what I was getting myself into."

"Because of the baby?"

"What?"

She patted her stomach. "You got married because of the baby."

"Did Juliet tell you that?" I said, astonished.

She'd promised not to, but then she'd gone and blabbed to Gloria?

"Oh, no. No, she didn't say anything."

"Then how did you know?"

"I can see it, in your face, your body."

Was that true, or was Gloria covering for Juliet's indiscretion? The pregnancy didn't show much yet, especially to someone who hadn't known me before. That raised the troubling prospect that two members of the staff were gossiping about my pregnancy behind my back, and lying about it. Plus, if Juliet had told Gloria, what were the chances she'd also tell Kovacs? Worse, that she already had, during their tête-à-tête on the beach just now?

"Please don't tell anybody, okay, Gloria? Not until I'm farther along."

"I won't. I don't talk to anyone outside this house," Gloria said.

"Don't tell anyone in this house, either."

"But you just said Juliet already knows."

"I didn't tell her. She found out because—well, it doesn't matter. The point is, I swore her to secrecy."

Gloria raised her eyebrows skeptically.

"Why are you giving me that look? Did she keep my secret, or not?"

Gloria held her hands up, shaking her head. "She didn't tell me. I don't who else she talks to."

"Well, can I trust her, or not?"

"*You* have to decide who to trust."

"I'm asking your opinion."

"You want my opinion? Fine. You say you want to leave. So, leave. And soon, before the baby comes. Nothing good happens at Windswept, and it's no place for a baby. But that's just my two cents, and I'm only the housekeeper. Now, if you'll excuse me, ma'am, I have things to do in the kitchen."

26

I knew I had to tell Connor that I'd been at Windswept the night Nina died before Kovacs remembered, and gave me up. I spent the day agonizing over how best to break the news. What tone to strike, how much to reveal, to make him the least upset. Should I cook dinner first? Get him into bed and tell him afterward, when we were relaxed in each other's arms? Or just sit him down the minute he walked in the door and treat this like the crisis it was?

In the end, my stewing was for nothing. Connor called me from the airport. He was on his way to Dubai on business and wouldn't be home for days.

"Can I come? I hate being alone here."

"We can't be seen together publicly right now. That ChitChat piece is all over the internet."

"The one about me and the necklace?"

"Not just that. They did a piece on that Baxter woman's lawsuit, repeating her lies like they're gospel truth. Lauren says we have to fight fire with fire and dirty up the Baxter woman in the press ASAP.

Make *her* the villain. Once the Twitter mob picks a side, there's no turning back. They'll come for us with pitchforks."

"What's Lauren got to do with this?"

"She's advising me."

"Connor, you can't trust her. I told you what she said about you."

"She apologized. Look, Lauren shoots her mouth off when she's had a few. She doesn't mean anything by it. We'll come up with a strategy by the time we land."

"Wait, Lauren's going to Dubai with you?" I said.

"She's staffed on the deal. But since we're taking the company plane, we'll have some privacy to work out a strategy for the PR problem."

"Oh, no. That makes me really nervous."

"What?"

"You, alone with Lauren on a long flight. You used to be *with* her. And now she thinks you killed Nina. What kind of twisted thing do you have going on with her?"

"You're overreacting. Lauren and I were over long ago. And she'd had too much to drink that night when she said those things. Besides, we won't be alone. Hank's here, and the entire team. Don't get jealous, okay? I hate that. It reminds me of Nina."

I felt like I'd been punched in the gut. "You're comparing me to her because I don't trust Lauren? I don't even believe you anymore that Nina was paranoid. She wasn't paranoid. You were cheating on her. You can't deny it. I was there."

"Look, I don't want to fight right before I get on a plane. I'm sorry for comparing you to Nina. You're nothing like her. That marriage was wrong from the beginning. I'm a different person with you. And I have no interest in anybody else, so there's no need for you to worry about anything. I love you more than I've ever loved anybody."

Connor Ford is not capable of love, Lauren had said at the dinner. Did she know something I didn't?

"They're telling us to board. Tabby, you have to have faith."

"Okay."

I'll try, I thought. But it was getting harder.

"Now, listen. Steve Kovacs is coming tomorrow afternoon to start implementing the security plan. Until then, don't go out. Don't accept calls from numbers you don't recognize. Don't do anything that could attract more press scrutiny. Understood?"

"I—"

"Just say yes. Otherwise, I'll be worrying about you the whole time I'm gone."

"Yes."

"Gotta go. I'll call you when I land. I love you."

I didn't say it back. Not because I didn't love him. If anything, I loved him too much—painfully and overwhelmingly and with the dawning fear that our love would not bring me happiness.

I searched my name online to see what Connor had been upset about. The photo of me in the emerald necklace had been picked up on scores of news and gossip sites. I read the article about Kara Baxter's lawsuit. She'd obviously fed information to the reporter, who reprinted her claims verbatim. "I want justice for my beloved sister," said the woman who hadn't spoken to Nina in decades. "The police need to reopen this investigation because I know in my heart she would never take her own life."

Normally I avoided looking at Nina's portrait, but now I went to stand before it, trying to find the real woman in the ghostly form splayed across the canvas. I wanted answers. I wished I could make her talk to me. Tell me what happened.

"Did you kill yourself? Did you try to kill me?" I said.

My words echoed in the cold bedroom. I'd accepted that Nina

was a head case, like Connor always said. I had good reason to believe him. Some goon in a Suburban tried to run me down and kill me. Nina was behind that. She had to be. I couldn't prove it, but I'd seen the Suburban here, on Windswept grounds, the night she died. I even took a photo of its license plate, then wasted two hundred bucks so some PI back home could tell me the car was registered to a shell company. Protocol Shipping Solutions, an entity with no known ties to Nina Levitt. But it had to be her, right? *Right?* And yet. When Gloria told me what a monster Edward Levitt was, for the first time I felt sorry for Nina, and wondered if I had the full picture. Who was she, really? If only I knew that, I could understand what had happened to her.

"Who *are* you?" I demanded, my fists clenching in frustration.

But daubs of paint on canvas couldn't answer questions. And the woman herself was cold in the ground.

I was lying in the dark when I heard a scratching sound. A strange chill pervaded the room, a sort of mist, that smelled of chlorine. The scratching sound seemed to be coming from a shutter blowing in the wind. Funny, I didn't recall that window being open, or even having shutters before. I got up to close it, and looked down to the beach, which was much closer than I'd remembered, as if the bedroom had fallen to the ground. The mist cleared suddenly, and I gasped as I saw Nina standing there looking back at me. Not Nina herself, but the painting come to life—naked, with mottled skin, spindly limbs, and vacant eyes. The chlorine smell was overpowering now, and it was coming from her. As I watched, a big black SUV barreled down the beach heading for her. I knew it was the car that had tried to kill me, and I screamed to warn her, but my voice wouldn't come. The Suburban hit her at full speed, sending her fragile body arcing high into the air. She landed in the swimming pool with a loud splash, a mangled corpse, as blood and red hair fanned out against the blue water.

I woke up in a cold sweat. The crack where the drapes came together glowed pink. I threw them open, letting in the morning light to banish the nightmare. But the vision of Nina broken and floating in the swimming pool wouldn't go away. I felt like it was there for a reason, urging me to take action. In my heart, I no longer trusted the official version of Nina's death. I needed the truth. Not knowing could be dangerous. I'd never searched the grounds for that Suburban. I'd never visited the swimming pool where Nina drowned. Okay, I was no detective, and maybe I wouldn't be able to solve the mystery on my own. But the time had come to stop being passive. I inhabited this woman's life like a borrowed coat. If I didn't find out what happened to her, I could end up suffering the same fate.

I pulled on sweatpants and a down jacket and made my way through the silent house to the back terrace. The sky was brightening, and the air was calm and frigid, with a bracing smell of seaweed. I inhaled deeply as I walked up the footpath past the spot where Derek and Kovacs had struggled the night Nina died. The memory was upsetting enough that I'd avoided this area ever since. That could've come with a cost. For all I knew, the Suburban was parked in the motor court right now. It might belong to someone I saw every day. Better to know.

I followed the path over the frost-covered lawn to the motor court on the west side of the property. The night of the party, rows of cars belonging to Nina's guests had been parked there. But as I crested the rise, I saw it was empty now. A brick garage with six bays ran along the edge of the motor court. There was an apartment above it, where Dennis lived. The shades were drawn—hopefully he was asleep. I walked up to a garage bay and tugged the metal door handle, but it wouldn't budge. I tried a couple of the others with no success. Around to the side was a pedestrian door. Gloria had given me a set of keys when I first arrived. Most of them I'd never used, but now I tried them until I found the one that worked. The door squeaked so badly that I cringed. Immediately to my left, stairs led up to Dennis's apartment. If he came down to investigate, I'd brazen it out. I was Mrs. Ford, after all. I had the right to be here. I even had a key.

The separate garage bays were connected internally, making one long, open space that smelled pleasantly of concrete and motor oil. I walked the length of it, surveying the cars. Connor's beautiful Lamborghini sat idle and neglected. That car reminded him of Nina, which was why he didn't drive it. There was an antique Porsche roadster, a Jaguar, a rugged, military-looking Mercedes SUV, and the Mercedes sedan that I'd ridden in on numerous occasions. In the farthest bay, a large, square vehicle was hidden under a silver car cover. I walked up to it with a sick feeling. The cover turned out to be held on with cables fastened with a padlock. The only way to remove it would be to cut it off, and then I'd be left with some explaining to do. The shape of that Suburban lived in my nightmares. I knew it was the same car, but now I wouldn't be able to prove it. When Connor returned from Dubai, I could demand that the cover be removed, and an inquisition undertaken to find out who'd driven it. But was that smart?

I should find out what I could by investigating on my own. I left the garage, crossed back over the terrace, and went around to the east, where a lavish pool and tennis complex hid behind a tall fence. The gate was locked, but I had the key. Inside, the complex had the forlorn air of a summer retreat after the cold weather set in. The lawn, though perfectly trimmed, was brown in places and speckled with fallen leaves. The Olympic-size pool had been drained and closed. Its sturdy vinyl cover was held in place with metal cables and dotted with pools of stagnant water. I walked the pool's perimeter, trying to understand what had happened here that night. A woman lost her life. Not just any woman. Connor's wife. She'd been diagnosed with a terminal illness, thrown a party, and come here at its end, determined to end her suffering. Did that make sense? Not to me. If I'd been in mental anguish, I could never have held up my head and entertained my guests, like I'd read she did that night. Then again, I hadn't known her. A lifetime spent as Edward Levitt's wife had probably taught Nina to smile for the cameras even when she was bleeding inside.

Camera. Shit.

Lost in my reverie, I'd failed to register the sound as I walked around the pool. A camera shutter was clicking somewhere nearby, when it shouldn't be. I looked about wildly to find the source of the noise. He was up in a tree, sitting on a branch that ran along the fence, dressed all in black. The long lens of his camera had recorded me as I visited the place where my predecessor died.

27

The photos were a viral sensation, beamed around the world at warp speed with the caption "Tabitha Ford revisits the scene of the crime," translated into many languages. Within a matter of hours of my visit to the swimming pool, Connor had seen them in Dubai. He texted me a photo with the message What did you do? I tried to call him, but he wouldn't speak to me.

Around dinnertime, I was in my room. I hadn't eaten anything all day. I sat on the edge of the bed, staring at Nina's portrait. For the first time in my life, the thought of suicide crossed my mind. I could understand how, when faced with an unsolvable problem, it might seem like a solution. But it wasn't available to me as an option. I had a baby to think of.

Juliet knocked on the door.

"Come in."

"Ma'am, the police are downstairs. They have a search warrant."

"Why?"

"They say it pertains to Mrs. Levitt's death."

"But that was resolved months ago. They ruled it a suicide."

She looked as upset as I'd ever seen her look. "I thought so, too."

"Didn't they search the area back then?"

"I have no idea, ma'am."

"What should I do?" I said, breathing hard, wringing my hands together. "What do I tell them? Should we let them in? What does Connor say?"

"I haven't spoken to him. Maybe you should call?"

I plucked my phone from the bedside table and tapped his number, pacing the floor nervously. He hadn't returned three texts and two messages. I had no reason to believe he'd answer this time. No answer. The call rolled over.

"It went to voicemail. Juliet, help me, what do I do?" I said, hanging up.

"I'm not the expert, ma'am. Steve Kovacs is downstairs with a technician, installing the security cameras. Should we ask his advice?"

"Good idea."

"Hold on, I'll have him come upstairs. You might want to—"

She waved her hand around her head, which had the general effect of sending me to the mirror. She was right. My face was puffy and streaky, my hair a wild mess. I looked like a woman in trouble, like someone who felt the walls closing in. Even I knew that was a bad look if the police asked to speak with me. I pulled on a fresh shirt, splashed water on my face, brushed my hair, put on lipstick and blush. By the time Kovacs arrived, I appeared calmer and more in control, even if I didn't feel that way.

"Mr. Kovacs, I'm glad you're here," I said.

He shook his head, his face grim. "I only wish I'd come sooner. If we had the cameras installed this morning, I would've caught that asshole before he got close to you. Excuse my French, I'm just pissed off."

"I understand. So am I."

"The nerve of these leeches, invading your privacy. On your property no less."

He was right. I'd been blaming myself all day long for letting that man take my photo. Worse, Connor blamed me for it. But was it my fault that someone had spied on me? That a stranger trespassed on Windswept property and climbed a tree to be able to photograph me while I walked inside a fenced compound? I hadn't taken greater steps to protect myself because I wasn't used to living this way—stalked, harassed, lied about in the press. I was out of my league here.

"The immediate concern now is the police. Juliet told you they have a search warrant?"

"Yes, ma'am, and I took the liberty of speaking with them. The warrant pertains only to the pool complex. They won't be coming in the rest of the house, at least not under this warrant."

"Was the pool complex searched before?"

"It was, at the time the bod—at the time Mrs. Levitt was found."

"So, why come back?"

"I asked. They say they're not at liberty to discuss the investigation. They want to speak to you, though."

"*Me?* Why? I never met Nina. I don't know anything about this."

Something flickered in his eyes. Was he remembering me with Derek at Windswept that night? I held my breath, waiting for him to accuse me.

"I expect they just want to talk to someone in authority. I can speak to them for you if you like," he said.

I breathed out. Since seeing the photo caption accusing me of returning to the scene of the crime, I was no longer confident that I could explain away my presence here the night she died. It would be best if it never came out.

"Yes, thank you. If you could just say . . . I don't know. What *should* you say?"

"There are two choices. We could call a lawyer in to review the warrant. But the detectives who are working this case are professionals. I doubt a lawyer would find it worth challenging in court. The other option is for me to let them into the pool complex, so we appear cooperative and like we have nothing to hide. I stay with them during the search just to make sure they don't go beyond the scope of the warrant."

"That sounds like the right approach. But I think you should call my husband and get his approval. I'm worried that he'll be upset by this."

"Probably. I'm sure he'd prefer the investigation to remain closed."

I searched his face, wondering what that meant. But I was afraid to ask.

"You'll call him?" I said.

"Will do. I'll report back, ma'am," he said.

"Thank you."

"Mrs. Ford, I hope I'm not speaking out of turn," Juliet said when he'd left.

"What is it?"

"I know the detectives. They interviewed me after Mrs. Levitt died. I'm just saying, they're pretty low-key, reasonable people. Are you sure you want to send Steve to deal with them, rather than speaking to them yourself?"

I'd forgotten that Juliet was the one who'd told the police about Nina's cancer diagnosis. But she didn't have skin in the game when she talked to them. My own experience of speaking with the police was a traumatic one. When they opened the secret compartment in Derek's truck and pulled out bags full of pills, I was shocked. I'd never been in trouble in my life. I wanted to cooperate, to prove that I was an honest, law-abiding citizen. I remembered how they separated us by the side of the road, then put us in different cruisers and took us to separate rooms back at the station. They just had a few questions, they said, then set about pressuring me to give information on Derek. Maybe I would have, but I had none. I was innocent, and I said so. They refused to believe me. At the end of the interview, they put me in handcuffs and took me to the holding cell. What little information I gave was used against me. Later, my lawyer said I'd been a fool. *The next time you find yourself in a tight spot,* he said, *don't trust the cops. Keep your mouth shut and call your attorney.*

"Do you have reason to think Mr. Kovacs won't represent our interests properly?" I asked.

"I never said that."

"Then why would I talk to them? I know nothing about Nina's death."

"Okay. That's your call, ma'am."

"I mean, what could I possibly say?"

"Of course."

"Seriously, Juliet. I don't get why you're telling me to talk to them."

"You're right. That doesn't make sense. I'll let you rest," she said, and walked from the room.

My phone rang. Grabbing it from the bedside table, I saw Connor's number flashing on the screen. He'd blamed me for the paparazzi. Was he going to blame me for the search warrant, too? I hit Decline and tossed the phone on the bed. Let him wait for me to call back, like I waited for him. After a pause, the ringing started again. I ignored it.

A couple of minutes later, the phone dinged with a text.

Tabitha, it read—a name he never called me—I just heard the police are there with a search warrant. Pack a bag right now. Dennis will take you to the airport. There's a plane waiting to bring you to Dubai. I want Juliet to go with you. We can't risk having you interviewed or letting the media anywhere near you. Connor.

The undercurrent of blame in his text made my blood boil. He'd left me at the mercy of the paparazzi and the police, then acted like it was my fault when things went south. Now he was ordering me to flee the country, with Juliet as my babysitter, so I didn't screw things up worse. I should just say no. Better yet, I should go talk to the police right now and tell them I honestly didn't know whether Nina killed herself, or if Connor had anything to do with it. That would show him.

I might be furious. But acting out of spite like that would be a huge mistake. I was out of my league here. I'd say the wrong thing. The cops would trick me again. The press was already accusing me of Nina's murder. Next thing I knew, I'd be in jail. Or Connor would. And as much I hated him right now, I loved him. And didn't believe he'd commit murder.

The time had come to ask him. I needed to ask him to his face.

I found my passport and started packing.

28

Stepping onto the plane was like entering a different world—a world in which nothing could touch me. The police investigation, Nina's death, the bad press, even my husband's guilt or innocence—all the bogeymen faded away. I was a one-percenter flying first class on an exotic journey. The flight attendants lavished attention on me, bringing pillows and chocolates and drinks. My seat compartment was the size of a small bedroom, with its own fully stocked mini-bar that popped up from a lacquered console, and a giant television that showed a map of the route. I loved reading the names of the places we'd be flying over. Paris and Madrid, Athens and Tangiers. The world had been closed to me before, but with Connor, any destination was possible.

I'd arranged to meet Juliet in the bar for a drink as soon as the seat-belt sign went off. My OB had said that one alcoholic beverage per week was permitted in the second trimester. Though I still wasn't sure I wanted a drink, Juliet insisted the bar was not to be missed, and she was right. I walked in with eyes like saucers. White leather banquettes lined the sides of the cabin, which was glamorously lit with blue neon and full of beautiful, well-dressed people. A uniformed bartender stood behind a marble-topped, circular bar. There were trays of appetizers for the taking—mini quiches, caviar on crackers, cocktail shrimp. A calligraphy menu of artisanal cocktails. Fine wines and champagnes and brandies. As I took it all in, Juliet walked up behind me.

"Can you believe this?" she said, a wide grin on her face.

The tension I'd felt building between us at Windswept evaporated in the rarefied air. She ordered Veuve Clicquot Brut Rosé, and when I saw the bartender pour it, I realized it was a pink champagne. I smiled and said I'd have one, too. We sat on a banquette and clinked glasses. The champagne bubbles tickled my nose, and my first taste of alcohol after so many months loosened my tongue. I'd been so lonely. I found myself telling Juliet about my life. My rootless childhood, my mother's death, the grandparents who saved me. Somehow, I got on to talking about Connor. How glorious he'd been that summer at the lake. How I'd never stopped loving him. What a miracle it was when he walked into the restaurant after all those years. I was lost in time, visualizing him in my mind's eye, when I noticed Juliet's horrified expression.

I'd been indiscreet.

"But nothing happened then, of course. We only reconnected later, after Nina died," I added, in a hurry.

"You have to be more careful," she whispered, glancing around meaningfully. "We don't know who these people are. They could be reporters."

"I'm sorry."

She got up for another drink, and this time, I noticed, it was straight scotch. That careless confession put a damper on our rapport. It was her job to keep me in line, but how could she, when

I was so careless? Maybe this mess was my fault after all. Maybe I didn't belong here, on this flight, in this life. Conversation grew stilted, so I finished my champagne and excused myself, returning to my seat.

In the morning, when we reunited on the Jetway, she was back to her pleasant, efficient self, seeing to the luggage, finding our driver. The hotel was famous, an architectural marvel designed to look like a ship in full sail, perched on the edge of the Arabian Sea. The lobby was a kaleidoscope of color, gold leaf and leopard print, exotic flowers, exotic people. Juliet went to check into her room. I was assigned a personal butler to take me to the suite that Connor already occupied. We got off the elevator, and my jaw dropped. The upper floors were designed around a soaring atrium like nothing I'd ever seen—honeycombed white balconies rising to an elaborate blue-and-gold ceiling. I had to stop and take pictures. The suite was two stories with a curving staircase and floor-to-ceiling windows that looked out on the sea. The view went on forever, with sailboats and yachts and tanker ships passing in the distance. There were fresh flowers everywhere, and an elaborate fruit basket set on the gilded bar. The butler gave me his card and said he could arrange shopping or spa appointments if I liked, and that in the meantime he'd send the maid to unpack my things. I almost told him not to, that she'd be disappointed.

The butler left, and I was alone. The windows were thick, the room silent except for the subtle purr of air-conditioning. It was cold in the room, and my legs were shaking. I hadn't slept much on the plane. I hadn't slept well for the weeks I'd been at Windswept, really. I sat down on the velvet sofa to regroup, and suddenly found myself sobbing. This life was magnificent. But it felt dangerous. And it wasn't mine.

Someone knocked on the door, and I dried my eyes. It was the maid, come to unpack my suitcases. Juliet called to say that Connor was in meetings for the rest of the day. We could go to the pool. There was a section reserved for guests, where we could be comfortable that the press wouldn't find us. Trying on my old bikini, I saw that my stomach had popped. I couldn't go out in public wearing this without flaunting a bump for the world to see.

Turns out I forgot my bathing suit, so I'll take a rain check, I texted Juliet.

She told me to go to the boutique in the lobby and charge whatever I needed to the room. I emerged with a black one-piece, a flowing white chiffon cover-up, a wide-brimmed straw hat with beaded trim around the crown, and crystal-embellished sandals. The total was twelve hundred dollars, and all I had to do was sign my name. I spent the afternoon drinking exotic fruit juices at an infinity-edge pool, surrounded by swaying palms, looking out at an aqua sea, trying to appreciate the luxury of this life. But that was hard to do when it might be taken away at any moment. I couldn't help thinking—if Connor divorced me. If he got arrested. If *I* got arrested. They'd never let me in the door of a place like this again.

He finally texted around six that evening.

I'm in the room. Where are you?

By the pool with Juliet.

I'll come down, he wrote.

No, we need to talk. I'll come up.

I turned to Juliet and told her I had to go.

"Was that— Did Mr. Ford just text you?" she asked. Her own phone was in her hands.

"Yes. I'm going to meet him in the room."

"Oh."

"Thanks for keeping me company. Enjoy the rest of your evening."

She nodded. I had the sense she was upset about something. But with her hand over her eyes, shielding against the sun, I couldn't read her expression.

Connor opened the door and tried to pull me into his arms. I resisted.

"Wait, I thought you were mad at me," I said.

His hazel eyes were troubled.

"I'm sorry if I was harsh on the phone, but I was losing my mind. Steve had just told me the cops were at the door. It was like my nightmare coming true. The lawsuit set the tabloids after us, then the tabloids brought down the police. It's a death spiral."

"Why are you so worried if there's no truth to it?"

He took a step back, his face stricken. "Why are you asking me that? You think I killed her, don't you?"

"I don't want to believe that. But there are some facts that I can't square. Like, you wanted to leave Nina and be with me. But you didn't want to give up the lifestyle. That's only human nature. I understand why, now more than ever."

I gestured at the wall of glass, the endless view of swimming pool and sea.

"But you have to admit, it was awfully convenient that Nina died when she did," I said.

"It was convenient for both of us. Why shouldn't I suspect you, then?"

"Go ahead, ask me. I'll swear on our baby's life. I didn't kill her."

"Neither did I."

"What's under the car cover in the garage at Windswept?"

"What are you talking about?"

"There's a large vehicle hidden under a locked car cover. I think it's the Suburban that tried to run me off the road."

For a split second, something flickered behind his eyes, but then it was gone.

"I have no idea," he said. "I haven't been in that garage in months."

"If it's there, then it was probably Nina who had me followed, who tried to have me killed. Right?"

He shrugged. "Sure, but this is all speculation."

"And if she was doing that, then she knew about us. And she would have confronted you. She would've divorced you and left you with nothing."

"We're back to me being a murderer again."

He held my gaze, a mournful expression in his eyes.

"I don't know how to convince you, Tabby, except to put my heart and soul into promising you that I didn't do it. Yes, I wanted to be with you, more than anything. Even with that motive, I'm not capable of ending someone's life. I couldn't even bring myself to tell her I was leaving. You could say I'm a coward. But I'm not a killer. I need to know you believe that, in your heart."

He rested his hand on my chest.

"I have the feeling there are some rough days ahead. I need to know we're in this together."

I nodded, my eyes filling with tears. I wanted so badly to believe him.

"I can't stand it when we argue. I hate it even more when you doubt me. All I want is for things to feel right between us again."

"That's what I want, too," I said.

He kissed me, then led me up the curving staircase. The dressing room off the bedroom was paneled in fine-grained wood, with benches for the suitcases, built-in closets, and a wall of mirrors. He turned me around to face my image and stood behind me, running his hands slowly over my body as our eyes met in the glass. Kissing my neck, he slipped the cover-up from my shoulders. It pooled at my feet. I kicked it away. The bathing suit was from a French brand, a black one-piece with a plunging halter neckline, sexy and obscenely expensive. He untied the neck, taking my breasts in his hands. They were fuller than they'd ever been.

"So perfect and ripe," he said, then worked the bathing suit down over my hips.

I stood naked, flesh goose-pimpled, nipples hard in the chill of the air-conditioning, looking at us in the mirror. It was a miracle that I was with him. I watched him strip off his clothes. My eyes lingered on his perfect body, and I wavered for a moment. He'd been unfaithful to Nina. Could I trust him to be faithful to me? Then he embraced me from behind and I thought, *Worry about that later. This life might not last. Enjoy it.*

He led me to the bed, lowering me down onto it with such gentleness, opening my legs with his hands. He got down on his knees.

I noticed the mirror over the bed, and my body tensed.

"Relax, baby. It's okay. Let me take care of you."

Looking at us in the overhead mirror, on this lavish bed in this amazing suite, I didn't feel like myself. This life was too unreal, like some perfect dream. I couldn't believe Connor was here with me—the man I'd wanted so badly for so long, now with more money than God. If something's too good to be true, then is it true? Or is it just lies? I had to close my eyes and force the dark thoughts from my mind to enjoy the sex.

When we were done, he held me, and I sighed like the weight of the world was on me.

"What is it?" he said.

"I wish time would just *stop*. I wish we could stay here forever."

"I've been thinking about that, too," he said. "Especially if things go south back home. If we wanted to, it's possible we could make that happen. Levitt Global has an office here. I could transfer. We could get a penthouse in a high-rise, with a fabulous view. The UAE doesn't have an extradition treaty with the U.S. I checked. What do you say we never go back?"

I forced a laugh, but I was chilled to the bone.

"That's a joke, right?"

He'd looked in my eyes and sworn he wasn't guilty, and I'd believed him. Basically. But why would an innocent person research an extradition treaty?

"Yes, it's a joke," he said.

Connor smiled at me, but the smile didn't reach his eyes. I was in over my head. No question about that. For the first time it occurred to me that he was, too.

29

That night, we went to dinner at the hotel restaurant. The maître d' fawned over Connor and called me Madame Ford. The wall of the restaurant was a floor-to-ceiling aquarium. Schools of brightly colored fish darted around playfully right beside our table as we ate. We'd gotten to the dessert course, and I was eating my first-ever soufflé—hazelnut, light as air—when Steve Kovacs called.

As Connor listened, I saw his expression change. By the time he hung up, he was ashen.

"What is it?" I asked, holding my breath.

He glanced around before answering, making sure nobody was close enough to overhear.

"Nina's doctor was arrested."

I stifled a gasp. "For her murder?"

"Hah, I wish. For drugs. He got swept up in some sting operation, accused of trading opioid prescriptions for sex and cash. And to quote Kovacs, he's singing for his supper."

"What's that got to do with us?"

"Without him, there's no basis for saying it was suicide. The whole inquest was built around his testimony. He said he diagnosed her with terminal cancer a week before she died, that she was despondent. That he gave her a prescription for painkillers. That's how they explained the drugs they found in her system."

The silence stretched out as we looked at each other.

"But that wasn't true?" I said finally.

"I don't know."

"You don't know?"

"I told you, I wasn't involved with Nina's death. I don't know whether he was telling the truth or not."

"*You* weren't involved. Was someone else?"

He looked away. "How would I know what anybody else did? She had a lot of enemies."

"Why won't you look me in the eye?"

He met my gaze.

"Because the fish are distracting," he said, and signaled for the check.

The Levitt Global team had been invited to go on a yacht belonging to the chief executive of their Saudi counterpart. It seemed to me to be an awkward moment to party on a boat with Connor's business associates. But he couldn't say no without giving offense, and he refused to leave me behind at the hotel.

"Besides," Connor said, "it's not the worst thing if we're out of reach in the middle of the ocean for a few days."

That afternoon, we boarded a helicopter, flying for an hour high above sparkling waters before touching down on the deck of an enormous yacht. Connor gave me a peck on the cheek and went off to find the conference room where they'd be meeting to finalize the agreement. Juliet and I were escorted to a lounge to wait for our rooms to be ready.

The lounge was decorated in pristine white, its walls made entirely of glass, retracted and open to the air. Music played softly and a delicious breeze blew in from the deck. A uniformed steward brought us figs, watermelon juice, and a tray of cold towels. I buried my face in the ice-cold towel, drinking in its lemony scent and sighing with pleasure.

"I guess I knew people lived like this. But to see it for real. Just, wow," I said.

Juliet had gotten up. She was standing at the open wall, staring out at the deck with a hard expression.

"What's wrong?" I asked.

"Lauren Berman is here. I see her by the pool."

"Oh." I paused. "I knew she was on this trip. She's part of the deal team."

Juliet looked at me like I was crazy. "And you're okay with that?"

I swallowed hard. "Why shouldn't I be?"

"Lauren's a snake. Don't ever turn your back on her."

I was surprised by the venom in Juliet's voice.

I put it down to, they must have a history.

The steward came back and escorted us to our cabins. My room had picture windows, its own balcony, an en suite bath, and décor straight out of a magazine. It also had twenty-four-hour room service and spa treatments on call. I booked a massage and facial, and ten minutes later a matronly woman who spoke heavily accented English showed up with a massage table. For the next two hours, she rubbed my back and legs with essential oils and applied various potions to my face. At the end of the treatments, I was refreshed and glowing, smelling of lavender. I asked her for the bill.

"No bill. Compliments of host."

I realized I had no idea who the host was.

"Please thank him for me. And this is for you."

I handed her a hundred bucks from my handbag. She looked shocked, but the waitress in me always tipped, whether it was expected or not, and the amount I tipped had gone up commensurate with my newfound wealth. It just seemed like I had so much, it would be wrong not to share.

Hungry now, I got dressed and made my way to the lounge, hoping to find Connor so we could eat dinner together. I paused on the deck to admire the setting sun, its blazing circle just touching the water, spreading vivid pinks and oranges in all directions. In my old life, at this hour, I'd've been in the middle of dinner service at the Grill, sweating, carrying heavy trays, my clothes reeking of that night's special. Instead, I was on a fabulous yacht in the middle of the ocean. But was it worth the pit of dread in my stomach, the certainty that everything was about to come crashing down?

In the lounge, there were no men in sight, only a gaggle of tall, gorgeous young women in tiny bikinis, speaking a language I didn't recognize. They lounged at the bar, giggling, and shot me hostile looks when I came in. The proportions of their bodies were so extreme that they looked more like gazelles than humans. I felt like I'd landed on a distant planet.

"*Russians,*" a voice behind me said.

I turned to find Lauren Berman, dressed for dinner in flowy white pants and a beaded halter top, a martini glass in her hand. I realized that I looked wrong, wearing the black dress I'd bought for that other dinner, which was too hot for this climate.

"They're Russian? I figured they were the Saudi wives, talking Arabic."

"God, you really are from the farm. They're prostitutes."

Lauren had been drinking again and spoke much too loudly. One of the young women turned and actually hissed at her.

"I think they understand English," I said.

"Hey, if the shoe fits."

I believed her about the Russian women, and it bothered me. But who was I to judge? This was a world I didn't understand. Maybe inviting prostitutes on your yacht was normal.

"Pax, by the way."

She held out her hand to me. I stared at it, not sure what to do.

"Look, I was drunk, okay? Yes, I had a thing with Connor, but it was two wives ago. Even if I were still interested, which I'm not, he's obviously mad about you, and not in the market."

"You're not interested?"

"No. If nothing else, he's a risky proposition right now."

She saw the expression on my face and guffawed.

"You are too much. Just kidding, okay? Hank and I are reconciling."

"Really?"

"Yes. Really. Now, chillax. We can do dinner on the deck or in the dining room. I just have to tell the purser."

"I'm waiting for Connor."

"Of course, so am I," she said, adding, "*And* the rest of the team. But we can sit and chat until they arrive."

A crew member escorted us to a table in a secluded part of the deck. It had been set with flowers, crystal, fine china, and silver. Twinkling white lights strung from the bow combined with soft music to create a lovely ambience. A warm breeze blew. With no lights visible as far as the eye could see, we might have been a thousand miles from land. As a waiter in a white jacket took drink orders, Juliet joined us. She wore her long, dark hair down, and a pretty floral dress. It brought up a memory that I couldn't quite put my finger on. The tension between her and Lauren was palpable. I looked back and forth between them, trying to discern what it was about. There was an undercurrent of something, but it was beyond my ability to understand.

"Have you seen the latest ChitChat garbage?" Lauren said.

"Do we have to talk about that?" I said.

"It's smart to know what's being said about you."

"About *me*?"

"Yes, girlfriend. They're digging into your background. I saw photos of the restaurant where you worked, and your apartment complex. My, but you've come up in the world. And so quickly. They made a point of noting that."

"Is that it? That's all they said?"

She looked at me cannily. "Why? Is there more?"

"What you've described doesn't bother me at all. Being middle class is nothing to be ashamed of."

Lauren raised a luxuriant eyebrow. "*Middle* class?"

"God, would you leave her alone?" Juliet said, glaring at Lauren.

"Hey, you know what I wonder, Juliet? What do you have against me? One of these days I might take it upon myself to find out."

The rest of the party arrived, putting an end to the squabbling. Hank, Connor, and the other Levitt Global execs were accompanied by several Saudis and the Russian women we'd seen in the lounge earlier. Hank kissed Lauren on the lips and took a seat beside her, his hand on her bare back. Maybe she was telling the truth about their reconciliation. Connor sat across from me, between Hank and one of the Saudi men. Now and then during the dinner he would catch my eye and smile. I relaxed a little. The food was Middle Eastern and delicious. Grape leaves, hummus, broiled lamb, rice pilaf, yogurt and honey for dessert. The wine was French and expensive. Everybody drank copious amounts of it, except me and the Saudis, who abstained from alcohol. We retired to the lounge for a nightcap. The steward served a flight of rare artisanal scotches, flown in from an award-winning distillery in Scotland. Everybody drank, and laughed loudly, though with an edge of hysteria like they were partying through the sack of Rome.

I was returning from the bathroom, lingering to appreciate the moonlight on the water, when Juliet stumbled out of the lounge onto the deck, about twenty feet ahead of me. She glanced over her shoulder, and I drew back into the shadows. Connor came flying out of the lounge after her.

"What the hell was that? Don't you walk away from me," he said.

"Fuck off."

She started up the stairs to the flybridge.

"Don't be like that. Come on."

He followed her up the stairs. I emerged from the shadows, heart pounding, and stood at the bottom of the staircase, looking after them in shock. I couldn't hear them anymore, over the sound of the breeze and the waves lapping at the boat. I had to get closer. I climbed slowly, one step at a time, until I was a couple of steps below the top. One more rung, and they'd see my head. But it wasn't enough. I could make out the tone of their conversation—angry and filled with recriminations—but not the words. Then I heard a sound. Was that—? Juliet. Sobbing. Connor was silent, and a terrible thought crossed my mind.

He's holding her.

I backed down the stairs like I'd been burned and made my way to our cabin, where I threw myself onto the bed. What had I just witnessed?

Connor and Juliet knew each other better than I'd ever imagined. That much was clear. But—in what way? Were they lovers? Co-conspirators? Something else? And which answer would hurt worst? I'd been grappling with the idea that Connor had slept with Lauren. Yes, it was years ago, and things between them were over. Yet, it still upset me very much. And now Juliet? If there was something romantic between them, even if it was in the past, I was not okay with that. Already, I felt like the earth had shifted beneath my feet. Juliet lived in our house. She'd snooped in my room and found out about my pregnancy. When she'd seemed angry about it, I'd put that down to her loyalty to Nina. Was there a different reason? She was the one who'd suggested I wear the Levitt emeralds, setting off the tabloid scrutiny that had caused so much trouble. She pretended she was trying to help, but in retrospect, it seemed obvious she wanted to hurt me. The Juliet I knew was pleasant, somewhat distant, formal, a bit dull. I couldn't reconcile that persona with the woman I'd just seen tell Connor to fuck off, arguing with him, sobbing on the flybridge. The face she showed me was a false one. That must mean that she was hiding something. That they both were.

Connor didn't come back to the room for another hour. I pretended to be asleep. I heard him stumbling around, swearing as he bumped into things. When he got into bed, I could smell the liquor on him. He was asleep as soon as his head hit the pillow, snoring loudly, keeping me awake. I lay beside him, wondering who I'd married.

The next day, the yacht set sail. People kept to their cabins. Everyone but me was hungover. I spent most of the day sitting by the pool, under an umbrella, taking in the exotic sights and sounds and smells. We were somewhere in the Arab world; exactly where, I never learned. By sunset, we'd docked in an industrial-looking port city in an unnamed country. I saw the towers of the mosques silhouetted against the sky and heard the call to prayer blaring from loudspeakers. The wind blew from the direction of the city, carrying the scent of smoke and oil. There was another fancy dinner that night, but I begged off, claiming illness, and had a tray in my cabin. By the time Connor came to bed, I was asleep. We sailed overnight, reaching Dubai early in the morning, and transferred to the airport.

Hank and Lauren were staying on in the UAE for another few

days with the rest of the team. Connor, Juliet, and I would fly home. Her ticket was business class, and ours was first. I was relieved that we wouldn't have to sit with her, not even in the lounge, which was segregated by cabin class.

My mental state fluctuated between denial and panic. At moments, it seemed not only like nothing was wrong, but like I was living a dream life. Connor and I waited in the first-class lounge, side by side in luxurious leather chairs, surrounded by well-heeled business travelers filling up on free food and booze. When I got bored, I took a stroll to the duty-free to stretch my legs and bought anything I liked. Makeup and magazines and a cashmere wrap in case I was cold on the plane. But Connor was distant, absorbed in his phone. He said he had a headache. He claimed to have documents to review for the Saudi deal. He barely spoke to me, though that came as a relief. If we'd started talking, I doubt I could've held my tongue about what I'd seen. But neither did I want a confrontation in public that might end up in the tabloids. On the flight home, he was seated in the row behind me, so I couldn't even see him. I lay wide awake on my lie-flat seat, worrying about the days ahead. The baby was unusually active, and I put my hand on my abdomen, trying to feel her, wondering what her future held.

At the baggage claim, Juliet smiled and nodded as she collected our luggage tags. She'd wait for the bags, then follow us to Windswept in an Uber. She seemed so calm, so normal, so much her pleasant, efficient self, just doing her job, that I started to question what I'd overheard on the boat. It was so far away—another climate, almost another planet. Maybe I'd misunderstood. Maybe it was nothing.

That would be so much easier.

As Connor and I exited through Customs, I saw that it was evening here. We'd been on the plane forever, and I'd lost all track of time. The smell of car exhaust and cigarette smoke hung on the chill air. The pavement was slick with rain as Ubers and limos jostled one another for space at the curb. Connor took my arm protectively.

"I see Dennis. This way," he said.

Dennis waited by the Mercedes. As we approached, he nodded crisply and opened the rear door. Connor stepped aside to let me get in first. Out of the corner of my eye, I saw two figures approach the Mercedes, a man and a woman. The woman was pulling something from her pocket. The long flight, the jet lag, the lack of sleep—it took me a moment to understand that it was a badge, and that they were coming for me. They'd been waiting.

"Mrs. Ford?" the man said.

He stepped up and grabbed me by the arm.

"Tabitha Ford, I'm Detective Ryan Hagerty. I have a warrant for your arrest. Come with us, please," he said.

"What the hell are you doing?" Connor demanded. "Get your hands off my wife."

The female detective held up a piece of paper.

"Sir, Detective Denise Pardo. This is a copy of the warrant. You can have your lawyer review it if you like. You'll find it's in order."

"You're under arrest for the murder of Nina Levitt," Hagerty said. "You have the right to remain silent. Anything you say . . ."

My knees buckled, and the world went dark.

30

I woke up on a cot in the secure medical facility at JFK Airport with an IV stuck in my arm. Detective Pardo sat on a chair next to my bed, scrolling through her phone. After a moment, she looked up and noticed that I was conscious.

"She's awake," she called.

The medical personnel were busy with other patients and ignored her.

Pardo explained that I'd fainted and had been taken to the "van," which was actually a trailer in the middle of a parking lot somewhere, fitted out with medical equipment and staffed by a doctor, a couple of nurses, and numerous law-enforcement officers. It was there to treat drug mules who'd been arrested smuggling heroin-filled condoms in their stomachs. I felt like Cinderella at midnight. The day before, I'd been on a yacht. Now I was here, surrounded by men and women of every age and color who looked beaten down and exhausted. Some looked angry. One woman sobbed pitifully, repeating over and over that she was innocent and didn't belong here. *You and me both, sister.* I knew how this went. I could protest my innocence, but no one would care.

Eventually, a nurse came by and checked my blood pressure. She removed the IV, then had me sit up in a chair and drink some orange juice from a can. The juice tasted sour and metallic. But it had enough sugar in it that the baby suddenly kicked me hard, making me gasp. I put my hand on my abdomen. The nurse asked how far along I was. Feeling Detective Pardo's eyes on me, I just shrugged and didn't reply.

It was after midnight by the time the doctor signed my discharge papers. Detective Pardo handcuffed me and walked me down the steps of the van to the parking lot, where an unmarked police car sat spewing exhaust into the cold night. It was raining steadily, and the handcuffs were cutting off my circulation. Hagerty got out and opened the rear door, and only then did it hit me that I wasn't going home tonight. I was going to jail.

"Where's my husband? I want to see him."

"We told him there was no point in waiting around for you tonight," Pardo said.

Anger seared me. How dare she send Connor away? In that moment, I hated her so much I could have hurt her. Her sharp, nasty features, her smug, clipped way of speaking. Hagerty was just the opposite. He had a soft face, blondish hair. He reminded me of a golden retriever.

"Let's get you out of the rain," he said, sympathy in his eyes.

Hagerty put his hand up to protect my head as I slid into the hard, cold backseat. It occurred to me that they were playing good cop/bad cop, and they were just right for those roles. The mind games were having their intended effect. I hated Pardo's guts, and felt a powerful rush of emotion toward Hagerty, like he was my best friend, and I should tell him my secrets. I had to be stronger than this, to remember what my lawyer up in New Hampshire taught me about when to talk to the cops. The right answer was *never.*

We merged onto the highway, heading out toward Long Island. The rain was heavy for a bit, and nobody spoke. But once it let up, Hagerty started working on me, trying to get me to talk.

"So, Tabitha, that must've been a shock, us meeting you at the airport, huh?"

I didn't reply.

"I'm sorry if we frightened you. And I'm really sorry you fainted. I understand you might be expecting?"

He tried to catch my eye in the rearview mirror. I stared out the window.

"Look, though, I just want to explain where we were coming from. We have some pretty heavy evidence against you. We were just working through it, deciding whether to seek a warrant, when we learned you left the country. I'm wondering if it was your idea to skip town? Or was it Connor's?"

I saw what he was doing. Either way I answered would implicate someone. I could try to exonerate myself by giving up Connor. Or I could protect my husband at my own expense. The entrapment was so obvious that I felt a surge of rage. I was determined not to repeat the experience I'd had with the police last time. I'd played into their hands, and taken a plea for something I knew I didn't do. I wouldn't be such a patsy this time. I had to use my wits and fight back. But carefully, so I didn't give them anything they could use against me in court.

"What evidence?" I asked.

"Beg your pardon?"

"What exactly is the evidence you claim to have against me?"

"I think you know."

"If you tell me what your evidence is, I'll talk to you. If you don't, I'll ask for a lawyer."

Hagerty and Pardo exchanged glances.

"Where were you the night Nina Levitt was killed?" Pardo said.

Pardo's question told me two things. One, they knew I'd been at Windswept that night. And two, they now believed that Nina had been murdered.

"I'm assuming you don't have any actual evidence against me, or you'd tell me?" I said.

They looked at each other again.

"That's an incorrect assumption," Pardo said. "We couldn't get a warrant without evidence. So, you know, you really should cooperate."

"I don't believe you. I think you arrested me because of something you read on ChitChat, and you're hoping I'll confess to killing Nina, when I didn't," I said.

I sounded more defiant than I felt. Her point about needing evidence to get a warrant seemed plausible to me. They must have told the judge *something.* What was it? Presumably that I'd been at Windswept that night. That didn't prove my guilt, but it didn't look good, either. It felt hot in the car suddenly, and sweat broke out on my forehead. I had no way to lower the window, but I didn't want to ask them to do it because then they'd know they were getting to me. If I felt trapped, it's because I was trapped. My fate was in their hands, and they already believed I was guilty. Nothing I could say would change their minds, so best to stay silent. I pressed my lips together into a hard line.

"I heard you say you want to see your husband," Hagerty said. "That won't be possible tonight just because of the hour. But, you know, I wanted to raise the idea that seeing him might not be good for you right now. I'm not sure Connor has your best interests at heart."

He caught my attention with that last remark. I turned back from the window and met his eyes in the mirror.

"He's planning to get you a lawyer," Hagerty said. "Ask yourself, Tabitha—who will that lawyer work for? You? Or Connor?"

That got under my skin. Hagerty was suggesting that Connor might set me up. I couldn't believe he would do that. Yet, if I was honest with myself, I couldn't rule out the possibility that he was involved somehow in Nina's death. The police no longer believed that she committed suicide. My arrest proved that. *My* arrest. Why *me,* when I was innocent? When Connor might not be? Maybe Hagerty had a point.

"You asked what our evidence is," Pardo said. "We think you two were in on this together. Admit what you did, testify against Connor, and we might cut you a break. That's your best bet."

They wanted me to testify against him. But, just like with Derek, I had nothing to offer. I didn't know how Nina died, because I wasn't involved in killing her. If Connor was, I knew nothing about it. I might have my suspicions. But that's all they were—suspicions. What if he was innocent, too? I still loved him. I was carrying his child. I couldn't let myself be maneuvered into implicating him in a murder that he might not have committed.

"I had nothing to do with Nina Levitt's death," I said. "I don't know anything about it. You're asking me to lie, to invent evidence that doesn't exist."

In the rearview mirror, Hagerty looked alarmed. Pardo shot me an annoyed glance.

"She's playing games," Pardo said.

"You're the ones playing games—with people's lives," I said. "I told you I'm innocent. Instead of taking my word for it, you're trying to get me to set up my husband. You're asking me to lie."

"That right there is going to wreck your chance at a plea deal," Pardo said.

"I don't want a plea deal from you, and I don't need one. I'm innocent. You're only doing this because of a tabloid story. And that story is a lie. Your case is based on nothing. It's made up out of thin air. I see no point in talking to you when your minds are closed against me. That's all I have to say. Now, I choose to remain silent. I want a lawyer."

31

I spent a few sleepless hours in a freezing holding cell before being transported to court, where I was placed in another freezing holding cell to wait for a lawyer. I hadn't showered since Dubai, and I'd had nothing to eat. I had to wait to use the bathroom until a female officer was available. I was desperate to talk to Connor, but they wouldn't let me make a phone call. I couldn't wait to get to court, so I could talk to him. I didn't understand what was happening, and why they'd arrested *me* for Nina's murder. But Connor would know. He'd have a lawyer with him. They'd have information, a plan, a change of clothes. They'd get me out of this nightmarish place.

Hours passed. Nobody would tell me what the schedule was. The uncertainty sent me into a kind of grim coma. I was practically catatonic, so exhausted that I tried to sleep on the hard, grimy metal bench. At least, as the only female prisoner going to court that day, I had a small cell to myself. The female guard came back with a plastic cup of water and a ham sandwich. She told me to hurry up and eat because my lawyer was waiting for me in the courtroom.

"Don't I get to talk to him before we go to court?"

The guard shrugged.

Ten minutes later, I was brought in an elevator to a crowded courtroom, where I was seated in the jury box with two male prisoners. One was muscular and heavily tattooed. The other was slight, much older, and might've looked distinguished had he not been unshaven and wearing prison blues. They both nodded politely to me.

The judge, an African-American woman who wore pearls over her black robe, was already on the bench, hearing another case. The courtroom was full, but I didn't see the one face I was searching for. Connor must be here somewhere. Maybe he was in the hallway, talking to my lawyer.

A woman approached the jury box and leaned down to whisper. She had a round face and dimples and looked younger than I did.

"Hey, Tabitha, I'm Courtney McCarthy. I'm a lawyer for Levitt Global. Your husband asked me to represent you today at your bail hearing."

"Oh, thank God. Where is he?"

I craned my neck to see past her, scanning the benches for Connor.

"He asked me to send his apologies. He couldn't make it to this hearing."

Anxiety beat in my chest. First like a flutter, then, as I absorbed her words, like the roar of a giant wave.

"*What?* No! No, that's not possible. I'm in jail. How could he just leave me here?"

She glanced up at the bench nervously, motioning with her hand for me to keep my voice down.

"I'm sorry. He didn't share his reason with me. There is kind of a media circus outside the courthouse right now. Maybe he thought it wouldn't be helpful for him to contribute to that?"

"I'm arrested for murder, and he doesn't show up to court because he's afraid of getting his picture taken?"

What could that mean? Was he abandoning me? Did he believe I was guilty? I felt like I'd been punched in the stomach. I doubled over, holding my stomach, tears prickling behind my eyes.

"You go call him. Call him right now. Tell him I need him here."

"Uh, I'm worried they'll call the case when I'm out, and I'll get in trouble with the judge."

"What are you, five years old? Do it."

She flushed. "Fine, if you insist."

She left the courtroom, returning mere moments later.

"I'm sorry, I couldn't get through," she whispered.

"Did you really try?"

"Yes, I tried. And look, I know it's disappointing, but he's very busy."

"He's my fucking husband, and I'm arrested for murder. What reason could he possibly have for not showing up?"

"I'd be speculating to answer that. I honestly don't know the reason. Looking on the bright side, *I'm* here, so you're represented. Though I ought to advise you, I'm really a corporate attorney. My only criminal background is one course in law school, and I'm wondering if it wouldn't be smarter to—"

The judge pounded her gavel, glaring at my lawyer. "Silence. We're conducting a hearing here, Counselor."

Courtney blushed crimson. "I apologize, Your Honor, but I needed to speak to my client, so—"

"If you wanted to talk to your client, you should've asked the marshal to let you back to the holding cell. You don't take up my time in my courtroom. Do you understand?"

"Yes, ma'am."

"Do it again, and I'll sanction you. Now, sit down."

My lawyer slunk away and took a seat in the back. I couldn't help remembering Hagerty's words in the car last night. *Ask yourself, Tabitha—who will that lawyer work for? You? Or Connor?* I had to face the facts. Connor was not here for me, and that was a bad sign. The lawyer he'd sent seemed barely qualified, and that was an even worse sign. I wouldn't have the advice I needed to defend myself against the charges. For some reason, Connor didn't want me to defend myself. Could he be washing his hands of me, because he believed I was guilty? Or—worse, to the point of being unthinkable—could he be guilty himself, and looking for me to take the blame in his place?

"That one's out of her league," the tattooed guy said under his breath. "You say they got you up on a murder charge?"

"That's what they said when they arrested me last night. I can't believe it. I'm completely innocent."

He shook his head. "That's some heavy shit, sister. And that lawyer you got is green as grass. Is she the best your husband could do?"

"I don't know. He's not here. I can't believe he's not here to support me."

"That shit happens all the time. I'm lucky my girlfriend stuck by me. Plenty of guys get dumped the second they get locked up."

He blew a kiss to a young woman sitting in the stands, who took the hand of the toddler sitting in her lap and waved it at my seatmate. I'd done just what he was talking about—dumped Derek when he was in jail. He deserved it. For lying to me, getting me arrested, being an abusive jerk. But in my weakened state, I started thinking this was karma, and my eyes misted over. I would never have a decent life. Connor wasn't here for me. He'd abandoned me in my moment of need, possibly for nefarious reasons. Our marriage was over. My baby would be born in prison. Hysteria was building inside me. I felt like screaming or beating my head against the wall.

The older prisoner was staring at me. I raised my manacled hands to wipe away a tear.

"What are you looking at?" I said defiantly.

"I'm feeling sorry for you, young lady. You need to get yourself a better lawyer right away. This is a very serious predicament you're in. It would be a huge mistake to rely on someone inexperienced in criminal law."

"You're right. But what can I do?"

"The public defender ain't half bad," the tattooed prisoner interjected.

The older man looked me up and down. My jewelry had been taken and catalogued when they booked me. But I still wore my street clothes from the plane, complete with the cashmere shawl from the duty free.

"I doubt she qualifies for free legal assistance," the older man said.

"Not if they count my husband's money, I don't."

"Then you can pay?"

"*He* can. But the fact that he sent this Levitt Global lawyer makes me wonder if he plans to."

"Levitt Global. I'm familiar with that company. Who's your husband?"

"His name is Connor Ford. He's—"

The judge rapped her gavel again.

"Marshals, separate those prisoners immediately."

Two guards marched up to the jury box. One of them grabbed my arm and hustled me into the back row. The other prodded the tattooed prisoner to move over several seats, then took the older man out of the box and brought him to the defense table up front. I'd already felt alone, but now my spirits plummeted. My jailhouse companions at least seemed to know what they were doing, and cared to help me, in contrast to the lawyer Connor had sent.

Slumped in my chair, with no windows in the courtroom, I lost track of time. Cases were heard, but I was lost in my misery, and barely paid attention. Eventually, the judge called a lunch break, though to me it already felt like ten o'clock at night. The older prisoner, escorted by two guards, passed by on his way to detention, and winked. Our conversation of an hour ago felt like it had happened in another century.

I was brought back to my solitary holding cell and given a second ham sandwich. I knew I needed to eat, but I took a bite and gagged. The thought of food was repugnant to me. I saw no way out of my predicament. I put the sandwich down, hung my head, and cried.

32

The clanging of the cell door opening awakened me from a fitful sleep. I sat up, my back and neck stiff from lying on the hard bench.

"Lawyer meeting," the guard said.

She escorted me back up to the courtroom, and then to a holding cell behind it that I hadn't seen before. I waited there for about ten minutes, until the guard admitted the Levitt Global lawyer, Courtney whatever-her-name-was, along with a second woman, whom I recognized from the courtroom as the older prisoner's lawyer.

"Hey, Tabitha," Courtney said. "Look, I know your husband asked me to represent you. And I'm happy to do that. But I was just speaking with Ms. Cohen here, who represents Howard Bishop. I don't know if you know who he is, but he has a major hedge fund. *Had,* I should say. He's in for embezzlement, and—"

"He was the gentleman you spoke to in the courtroom earlier. He told me you were in need of further advice," the other lawyer said.

"Okay, yes. Definitely."

"The point is, I don't have much criminal experience—"

"I can tell," I said, and pointed to the other lawyer. "If you're saying she could represent me instead, then I want her. You can go."

"Okay. Wow, great. Thank you. And you'll tell Mr. Ford that I offered to stay, right? I mean, I *can* stay, to observe. In fact, he might prefer that I do that. He did ask for a full report."

"No. This is my new lawyer. I want to meet with her privately. Please leave."

"Oh, right, sure."

My new lawyer pressed a buzzer. A few moments later, the door to the courtroom opened, and Courtney McCarthy disappeared through it.

"Thank God she's gone," I said.

The new lawyer laughed and pulled a chair up to the bars of my cell. When she sat down, we were at eye level with each other. She was in her fifties, with short dark hair and glasses, wearing a navy-blue business suit. She stuck her hand through the bars, and we shook.

"Suzanne Cohen. It's a pleasure to meet you, Mrs. Ford, though I'm sorry it's under such difficult circumstances. Call me Suzanne. May I call you Tabitha?"

"Certainly."

"The judge is hearing a civil case now. We have about an hour till they call us to court, and there's a lot to cover."

In my agitation, I jumped to my feet and paced the tiny cell.

"Okay, but first, before I can focus on anything, where is my husband? I just can't believe he would abandon me. It's his money that would have to pay your fee. Maybe I shouldn't tell you that. Please, don't *you* abandon me. But—*has he*? Why would he do that? I'm scared."

"Tabitha, please, sit down. Come on, here. Have a seat. Give me your hand."

I sat down on the hard bench and clutched her hand through the bars. It was cool and dry and felt like a lifeline.

"Ever do yoga?" she asked.

"Sometimes."

"Deepen your breath, in and out. I need you to be calm enough to work with me on your defense."

I sat for a moment, looking into her eyes, breathing in and out deeply. I felt my concentration come back.

"Better," I said with a nod, and dropped her hand.

"Good. We're under time pressure, so let's not worry about the fee right now. As to where your husband is, that's an important question. Do you know whether he's distancing himself from you, and why that might be?"

"I don't know it for a fact, but he's not here, so—" I shrugged hopelessly.

"That may be for some reason that has nothing to do with your case. But if it does have to do with your case, it would be important to know, and we're going to cover that. Rest assured that anything you say to me in the course of this representation is confidential. Do you understand?"

"Yes."

"First, I want to make sure you understand the charges against you. DA Neely gave me a copy of the criminal complaint. Let's review the evidence they have against you, before I ask you for your side of the story, okay? It's important for you to know where you stand before saying anything."

She took a paper from her briefcase and held it so I could see. The first shock was the title. "People of the State of New York v. Tabitha Ford." Me, charged with a crime in New York State. But it was the next part that knocked me over. The charge. Murder in the second degree.

Murder.

I had to reach for the bars and steady myself.

"Are you all right?" Suzanne asked.

"I'm sorry. I'm five months pregnant, and I get faint sometimes."

"Oh. Congratulations."

"Thank you. It's hard to be happy about it under present circumstances."

"I understand. It's good you told me about the pregnancy, though. I can use it to our advantage in the bail hearing. It may not get you out, but I can ask for Bedford Hills over Rikers. It's a much better facility, meant for female prisoners, with better medical care."

"You mean I might not get bail?"

I started to cry. She handed me a Kleenex.

"Tabitha, I know this is hard. But you have to focus and face facts. I need your help to defend you."

I nodded, pressing the Kleenex to my eyes.

"Are you sure it's okay to say I'm pregnant? Won't they use it against me?"

"Five months pregnant, you said?"

"Yes."

"In other words, your relationship with your husband began prior to Nina Levitt's death?"

"Yes."

"Well, yes, that *could* be used against you. Let's hold off on telling them for now, until we figure out our approach to the case and to bail. Getting back to the complaint, as you know, Nina Levitt's death was originally ruled a suicide. It's unusual for the ME to reopen a case after ruling on it, but the police presented new evidence to the ME."

"What evidence?"

I leaned forward, wringing my hands. As shaken as I'd been by the events of the last twelve hours, I'd still held out a faint hope that Nina had actually killed herself. The alternative was terrible to contemplate—that Connor was a murderer.

"Barry Ogilvy—the doctor who testified that Mrs. Levitt had terminal cancer—was arrested for trading opioid prescriptions for sex and cash. He's in jail now, and he's cooperating with the police in exchange for a reduced sentence. He now claims he was bribed into making that statement about Nina Levitt, and that in fact she was never his patient."

"Who bribed him? Do they say? Was it Connor?"

"They don't name names in the complaint, which at least tells us it wasn't you. If they had Ogilvy saying you were the one who bribed him, they'd say so. That would be very damning evidence."

"It wasn't me. I can promise you that. Whoever bribed him was behind Nina's murder, right? And I'm innocent of that."

"Okay, let's put your guilt or innocence to one side. We're going to plead you not guilty at this appearance. It's about gauging the strength of their case."

"But can you ask if it was Connor? I need to know if he's involved."

"They're not going to tell me that. If they had enough to arrest your husband, they'd do it. He's not named in the complaint. My guess is, their investigation against him is ongoing. I think they're trying to shake you down and get you talking against him. Based on this complaint, they don't have a viable murder case against you—"

"Thank God," I said, collapsing back against the wall. "Then you can get me out, right?"

"No. Tabitha. Please, let me say my piece without interruption, okay? This is not a good situation for you. They may not have a murder case, but they *do* have a viable murder conspiracy case, and the punishment is the same."

I snapped forward. "What? How is that possible?"

"The complaint puts you at Windswept on the night of the murder, accompanied by your ex-husband, Derek Cassidy, who was arrested that night for assaulting a security guard. It also states that you each have a prior conviction for distribution of oxycodone. Oxycodone was found in the tox screen performed during Nina Levitt's autopsy, in an amount about ten times the recommended dosage. It was enough to kill her even if she hadn't drowned."

My words came out in a rush.

"Okay, look. I was there, but I can explain everything. I'd just found out I was pregnant. I was trying to tell Connor, but he wouldn't take my calls. I knew he was at Windswept, and I went there to find him. Derek followed me. He'd done it before. He was stalking me. I can prove that. I called the police on him. There's got to be a report. I didn't even know he was behind me until he started fighting with Steve Kovacs—"

"Kovacs?"

"The security guard. He works for Connor. And that drug arrest—it was Derek's. I was just in the car. I didn't even know the drugs were there. I took the plea because my lawyer said it was the best I could do. A misdemeanor, no jail time. Otherwise they'd charge me with a felony, and I might lose. You understand, right? You believe me?"

"On the drug charge, the fact that you took the plea—I'm afraid that leaves us limited room to maneuver."

"Okay, I get that. Taking the plea was a terrible mistake. It's been following me around forever. But that's the truth. And you have to believe me, I was there to talk to Connor that night, not to hurt Nina. I never even met her. Seeing her across the terrace was the closest I ever got. Please, Suzanne. Tell me you believe me."

She reached through the bars and patted my hand.

"Tabitha, please, try to calm down. We need our wits about us. My job is not to believe or disbelieve, but to help you do what's best for yourself and your case. I have to be honest. This looks very bad for you. If by any chance you're not being truthful—and especially, if Dr. Ogilvy could say you were the individual who bribed him—"

"No. Absolutely not. Unless he's been double-bribed to say that."

"Okay, then. I'll take your word on that. And on the drug charge.

I believe you didn't know about your ex-husband's drugs, and yet, that doesn't really matter. You took the plea. They plan to use it to argue Nina OD'd on the same substance at issue in your prior conviction. I can ask to have your prior kept out, and it's possible I would win. Prior convictions are almost never admissible. This one is six years old, and a misdemeanor. On the other hand, this is not your usual instance of the DA trying to admit a prior just to dirty you up. It's not 'Tabitha Ford is a proven criminal.' It's 'Tabitha Ford had access to the type of drugs used in this murder.' This prior has a special relevance, even more so because your ex-husband was there that night. I understand he's currently incarcerated?"

"Yes."

"Is there anything you'd like to tell me about him?"

"Like what?"

"Do you have an ongoing relationship? Was he somehow involved in this crime in a way you're not disclosing? I can't defend you if I don't know the facts."

"Maybe I didn't explain clearly. Derek ruined my life. He was dealing drugs without telling me, and he got me arrested. I divorced him. The only reason he was at Windswept that night is because he was stalking me. I want nothing to do with him, for the rest of my life."

"Got it. That simplifies things. But your association with him is still damaging to your case. The prosecution will try to introduce evidence of his prior drug conviction and his presence at the house that night."

"But why would I want Derek there? I hate Derek."

"They might try to argue that he supplied the drugs you used to kill Nina—"

"I didn't kill her."

"I'm not saying you did, but they are saying that, Tabitha. That's what you need to understand. And your prior drug conviction works against you. You can't just assume that, because you're innocent, the charges won't stick. When things look bad, that can sway a jury's opinion, even if it's unfair."

"That's what my lawyer said the last time. That's why I pleaded guilty to something I didn't do, and I'm not going down that path again."

"I would never ask you to do that. Look, I'm going to make a suggestion. The DA, Brad Neely, expressed interest in having you proffer."

"What's that?"

"It means he wants to sit down and interview you—with me present, of course. They think Nina Levitt was murdered. You and your husband are the obvious suspects. My read is, they don't have enough to arrest your husband, so they picked you up first, hoping they could flip you on him."

"I won't lie about Connor to please them."

"Nobody's asking you to lie."

"Yes, they are, because I don't know anything. I told the cops that last night. If Connor killed Nina, he didn't tell me about it."

"What if we agree to an initial listening session? We postpone the bail hearing and sit down with the prosecution just to see what we can find out about their case against you."

"Can we do that?"

"We can try. We let them make a pitch for you to cooperate, and I use that opportunity to ask questions. Before you say anything substantive, we break for a consultation. Then you and I can decide if it's going to be fruitful or not. If not, we haven't lost anything. But if their case against you looks strong, giving evidence against Connor may be your only option. I know that's tough to hear. But you need to think of your child."

Think of my child. That's what I'd been doing when I plunged headfirst into a marriage with a man I really didn't know. And look where it had gotten me.

33

Later that afternoon, Detectives Hagerty and Pardo escorted me to a conference room on an upper floor of the courthouse, where my lawyer and the DA were waiting. The DA, Brad Neely, was a fortyish guy in a dark suit with heavy five-o'clock shadow. Gulping from a coffee cup as I entered, he stood up and shook my manacled hand.

"Mrs. Ford, thank you for agreeing to meet with us," he said, ducking his head in greeting. "Please, make yourself comfortable. Detective, could you please remove her handcuffs? Thank you."

I sat across from him, with my lawyer beside me.

"Can I offer either of you ladies a cup of coffee?" Neely said.

I'd been expecting coldness and hostility. His courteous attitude had the effect of lowering my guard. That could be a ploy, just like the good cop/bad cop routine the detectives had pulled in the car last night. In my exhausted state, I wasn't confident that I could avoid getting played. I'd sworn off caffeine because of the baby, but my screwing up here today would hurt her more than a cup of coffee ever could.

"Yes, thank you. With milk, please."

Neely called somebody to bring the coffee. In the meantime, he reviewed the agreement where they promised not to use anything I said today against me in court. The only exception was if I took the stand at trial. If I had to take the stand at my murder trial, this interview would be the least of my worries.

"That's fine with me. I'll sign the paper," I said.

He handed me a pen. The coffee came. It was hot and strong, and in combination with the utter terror coursing through my veins, had the effect of focusing my mind. I listened intently as Neely spoke.

"Your lawyer, Ms. Cohen, tells me that you're on the fence about cooperating against your husband. I get it. It's a tough decision. I'm married myself," he said, flashing the gold band on his ring finger. "For now, all we're seeking is information. You might not ever have to testify against Mr. Ford in court, because of the marital privilege."

"*Or,* you might," Suzanne said. "Sometimes, the marital privilege doesn't apply. The judge decides. Let's just be clear, Brad. You can't promise her she won't have to testify against him."

"That's true. But *for now,* all we want is information, and anything you tell us is confidential. Your husband won't find out we had this conversation unless you tell him yourself. And, by the way, if you're afraid of him—"

"Afraid of Connor, you mean? Not my ex-husband?"

"Your ex-husband? You're referring to—" He consulted a notepad that lay on the table in front of him. "—Derek Cassidy?"

I nodded. "I *am* afraid of Derek."

"My notes indicate that Mr. Cassidy is currently incarcerated on an assault charge stemming from an incident that took place at Windswept the night Nina Levitt died. He was there."

"Yes, but I don't know anything about Derek's case. How long he's in for. When he might get out. If I'm going to talk to you, I'll have to speak against Derek. *That* scares me. *He* scares me. Connor doesn't."

"Okay, why is that? Are you saying Derek—no, wait a minute, I don't want to get ahead of ourselves. Let me just assure you that if you have a specific security concern, we have the resources to protect you, okay?"

"Okay."

"Now. Ms. Cohen has asked me to give an overview of the evidence against you to help you decide whether to proceed with your cooperation. That isn't something I would normally do. But I'm willing to do it in this case, for a couple of reasons. One, this is blowing up in the press even as we speak."

"You know that's all orchestrated by Kara Baxter, right?"

"Who?"

"Kara Baxter. She *says* she's Nina Levitt's sister. We don't even know if that's true, but she's after the money. She sued Connor for the estate, and the only way she can win is by proving he killed Nina. She got the tabloids to say he did by granting exclusive interviews. Now that they printed it, you guys are falling in line, trying to lock him up."

"Who told you that?"

"Connor did."

"I don't know whether he's trying to snow you, or if he genuinely believes that. But I assure you, Ms. Baxter's lawsuit has nothing to do with our case. The information that led us to reopen the case came from Barry Ogilvy, the doctor who testified at the inquest. He got caught in a federal sting operation, trading opiates for sex. That obviously undermined his testimony. So, we brought him in, and he had quite a story to tell. A young woman visited his office and bribed him to say those things about Nina Levitt."

"A—a young woman?" I said, shocked.

I sat back in the chair, feeling faintly sick. Neely's eyes were locked on my face.

"Yes. Was that young woman *you,* by any chance, Tabitha?" he asked.

"Did he *say* it was me?"

"Answer the question, please."

"Hold on one minute," Suzanne said.

"No! Absolutely not, it wasn't me. Did you ask the doctor who she was?"

"We did. He gave us her name, and we couldn't associate it with a legitimate identity. In other words, the name was fake. She used an alias."

"Show him my picture, then. It wasn't me, I swear. Did he say what she looked like?"

"He said she had dark hair, and I note your hair is blond."

"Dark hair. Okay, then. That could be a couple of people I can think of. But it's not me. You believe me, right?"

"A woman smart enough to use an alias would probably think to wear a wig."

I threw up my hands. "I don't know what to say. Put me in a lineup, then. It wasn't me."

Suzanne put her hand on my shoulder and leaned forward.

"Tabitha, stop talking. For the record, Brad, we don't agree to a lineup."

"You don't have to agree," he said. "She doesn't have a Fifth Amendment right to refuse a lineup. I think it's a brilliant idea."

"I need to speak to my client alone, please," Suzanne said.

"Fine. We'll be outside. Knock when you're done."

The DA and the detectives left the room, closing the door behind them. When we were alone, Suzanne turned on me with a troubled expression.

"Tabitha, what are you doing? We agreed that we're here to get information, not give it. You can't just go running off at the mouth like that—"

"Suzanne, you don't understand. What Neely just said is huge. The woman who bribed the doctor? That wasn't me, I swear to you. Who was it?"

"I don't know. Who do *you* think it was?"

"I don't know either, but whoever it was killed Nina. Maybe working with Connor, maybe not. There were two dark-haired women in Nina's life. Lauren Berman, the head of PR at Levitt Global. She had a motive. Her husband left her for Nina, then she had an affair with Connor, and he left her for Nina, too. There's Juliet Davis, Nina's personal assistant. Whether she had a motive, I don't know. But she was around constantly, in the middle of everything. Actually, there's a third dark-haired woman. Nina's yoga teacher, Dawn something. I only met her once in passing, but people say she's a real whackjob. We have to tell the DA."

"I explained the rules earlier. This session is for us to get information. We're not telling the DA anything yet. You understand? We don't just blurt things here. That's not smart. You've been arrested on a murder charge. You. Not Lauren, not Juliet, not— Who was the third one?"

"*Dawn.* The yoga teacher."

"Whatever. You're in a very difficult position, and we need to proceed with caution. After the interview, I'll follow up. I'll research these women. Figure out if that's information we want to trade. But only if we get something in return. You need to keep quiet and let me do the talking. Do you understand?"

"Yes. I'm sorry, you're right."

"Promise you won't say anything more without clearing it with me first. Otherwise, I'll end this session right now. I can't sit here and let you dig yourself into a hole."

"I promise. Forgive me, Suzanne. I appreciate your advice, and I'll follow it."

"All right. Ready? Deep breath."

I nodded. She called the DA and the cops back to the table.

"Tabitha has information to give," Suzanne said. "But cooperating against her husband is a big step, and she's not there yet. She's not the woman who bribed the doctor. You won't be able to prove that at trial. What else have you got?"

"We've got lots of witnesses who put her at the scene on the night of the crime, starting with an Uber driver who remembers her because she gave a cash tip."

"No good deed," Suzanne said, shaking her head.

"Not just him. A Southampton police officer named Beth Rossi who remembers Tabitha, and who arrested her drug-dealing ex-husband, Derek Cassidy, that same night for assault. Plus, the guy who was assaulted, Steve Kovacs, who worked for Nina Levitt—he could be a witness, too."

I opened my mouth to ask whether Kovacs was actually talking, or if he was just a hypothetical witness, but Suzanne put a restraining hand on my arm.

"Brad," she said, "let's say Tabitha admits to being at Windswept that night. But she has an innocent explanation for the visit, and her ex was only there because he stalked her to the scene. I'm not sure what that gets you."

"Innocent explanation? Are you kidding me? She and Cassidy, who both have a record for oxy distribution, were at the scene that night that Nina Levitt died. Not just momentarily. For a long time. Cassidy was arrested lurking in the area around midnight, after assaulting the guard an hour earlier. Midnight is smack in the time-of-death range the coroner gives for Nina. As for Tabitha's presence, the evidence is damning. She wasn't there like some guest at the party. She was trespassing, stalking Nina. Denise, show them."

Neely nodded at Detective Pardo, who reached into a manila folder, pulled out three eight-by-ten photographs, and laid them down, one by one, facing me. Suzanne cast a dire look in my direction. They were color pictures of *me,* taken at Nina's Fourth of July party, so vivid that I could feel the soupy heat under the tent and hear the band playing. In the first one, I stood against a wall stuffing my face, my eyes darting sideways furtively, like I was up to no good. In the second, I was even more shamefaced, looking over my shoulder as if I knew the law was on my heels. The third was the worst of all—a wide-angle shot that captured me in the same frame as Connor and Nina. The two of them were side by side, his hand on her arm, a unit, a married couple. I stood alone, glaring at them with undisguised hostility.

I looked like I was thinking about killing her.

Neely tapped that one with his finger.

"This will be Exhibit A at your trial. They say a picture's worth a thousand words. This one's worth twenty-five to life," he said.

Sick, cold fear spread through my body from the pit of my stomach down to my fingers and toes. I tore my eyes from the photos and stared at him. My heart beat so loudly, I could hear it in my ears.

"Who took these?" I demanded, my voice quiet and deadly calm.

"I won't answer that."

Who was it? Lauren? Juliet? Kovacs? Why would they take my picture months before they knew me, before Connor and I were even married? How would they know to do that? There was only one way. Connor told them to.

In that moment, I began to accept that I was probably being framed for murder by the man I loved.

"Whoever took these pictures is your killer, not me. I'm just the patsy."

"Oh, your story is that you're being framed?" Neely said. "That's a Hail Mary if ever I've heard one. The jury won't buy it. I have phone records showing that you called Connor's phone just minutes after this photo was taken, and he didn't answer. We can prove at least ten unanswered calls from your phone to his in the days leading up to the murder. So, here's my current theory. You were a financially strapped waitress who had the good fortune to have a fling with a wealthy, married man. To him it was nothing. You saw it as the opportunity of a lifetime. You pursued him. But he wasn't interested. So, you took matters into your own hands, and solicited your violent ex to assist you in murdering his wife. Then you married him, a mere three months after she passed away. You now live a life of untold luxury. If that's not the truth, Tabitha, then you'd better tell me what is."

34

It was after eight o'clock and pouring rain when the unmarked car pulled up to the Windswept gates. I'd been released to the custody of Detective Hagerty, who was escorting me to Windswept to set up the electronic monitoring that was a condition of my bail. This would also be the start of my undercover cooperation with the DA's office. I was so nervous about that part that I had to clench my hands in my lap to stop them from shaking.

The gates parted, and Steve Kovacs emerged from the gatehouse, wearing a navy windbreaker with the hood up. I searched Hagerty's face for any indication that he knew Kovacs, but he didn't blink. Was that a no? Somebody had fed the DA those photographs of me. That person was a prime suspect in Nina's murder, and a danger to me. If it was Kovacs, I wanted to know.

"Who's that?" Hagerty asked.

So, they didn't know each other. Did that mean I could rule Kovacs out?

"Steve Kovacs, the security consultant."

Kovacs rapped a knuckle on the driver's-side window. Hagerty dug his badge from his pants pocket, flashing it as the window went down.

"Detective Ryan Hagerty, escorting Mrs. Ford pursuant to court order to install her electronic monitoring device."

"I'm sorry, come again?"

"She's charged with a crime. Her bail was home confinement with an ankle bracelet."

"Is that right?"

Kovacs shot me a hard, measuring glare. He must've heard by now that I'd been arrested for Nina's murder. It was all over the news. They'd had to smuggle me out through the courthouse basement to avoid the mob.

"Detective," Kovacs said, "I'm in charge of security at Windswept, so if you're planning to install any equipment, I need to be involved with that. Can I see the warrant?"

Hagerty pulled a piece of paper from his jacket pocket.

"This is a court order directing persons in the home to allow installation of electronic monitoring devices. Obstruction of this order will subject you to contempt proceedings."

"I'm not trying to obstruct. I just need to know what you're doing."

"Sorry, that's not in the program. The installation and functioning of our equipment is confidential. Otherwise it would be too easy to subvert."

"Nobody's trying to subvert. My concern is interference with the other monitoring equipment on the property."

"Tell me what you've got and where it is. I'll make sure I don't interfere."

"I can't do that."

Hagerty shrugged. "Then I can't help you, my friend. I have a court order to install my system, and I'm going to do that without anybody looking over my shoulder. You got a problem, talk to the judge."

Kovacs grumbled, but signaled us to pass. We proceeded up the driveway to the porte cochere.

"Why did he give you a hard time? Is he on to us?" I asked Hagerty.

"I doubt it. He probably just doesn't like having his authority challenged."

I'd never been able to get a read on Kovacs. To this day, he'd never given any indication of recognizing me from the Fourth of July party. Yet, I had to believe he did. Maybe he was involved in setting me up by taking those pictures at the party. The one thing I could be sure of was that he was not on my side. I shouldn't trust him. I shouldn't trust anybody at Windswept.

"You *doubt* it?" I said. "Somebody at Windswept gave you those photos of me, and that person killed Nina Levitt. How can you not tell me? Was it Kovacs, or wasn't it? I don't feel safe here not knowing that."

"All right, look. The photos were sent to us anonymously. There's no reason to think it was him."

"No reason to think it wasn't. It could be anyone at Windswept. How can I protect myself if I don't know?"

"You're the one claiming somebody else killed her. It's up to you to prove that. Our best evidence says it was you."

"I told you, I'm innocent. Are you gonna let them kill me, too?" I said.

"Tabitha, we'll do our best to keep you safe. But wearing a wire, cooperating—that involves risk. My advice is, assume people around you are hostile and don't take any unnecessary chances."

At the moment the DA had suggested I wear the wire, I had felt so betrayed, so angry, that I jumped at the chance. Whoever thought

I would be their patsy had another thing coming. But here, now, in the rain, with Windswept towering over me like a haunted castle, that nourishing anger was gone, replaced by uncertainty and fear.

"What happens if I get caught?"

"The ankle bracelet is equipped with a panic button. I'll show you how to use it before I leave."

"Panic button? Why can't I just call you?"

"If you've been outed as a snitch and you're in imminent danger, you probably won't have time to make a phone call."

"You're scaring me, Detective."

"Hey, if you're uncomfortable, I understand. I'll take you back to jail, and we can forget about the cooperation. Who knows, maybe you can beat the murder rap. But if not, you're looking at life in prison."

We'd pulled up to the door.

"What do you want to do?" Hagerty said.

I couldn't breathe. Life in prison? Was this real? If I could've snapped my fingers and been back at the Baldwin Grill, setting up the dinner shift, I would have, in a heartbeat. If I could make it so I'd never met Connor—not now, not before—I would.

"You're threatening me with *life in prison*?"

"It's not a threat. It's reality. I'm not the person who put you in this situation."

He meant I'd put myself there, but he was wrong. Somebody else had, by manipulating the evidence to make it look like I murdered Nina Levitt. That person was willing to put me away for life, then go home and eat a nice dinner. I had to pull myself together. I had to get mad again. Not just mad—filled with a cold rage that made me smarter, bolder, more strategic. I should do it for my daughter. No way was she growing up without me. Never. I had to beat this rap, no matter what it took.

"I'll do it."

"All right, let's go."

I got out of the car. Hagerty took a briefcase from the trunk and came to stand behind me.

"Kovacs might've warned anyone inside that we're coming, so just in case, don't ring. Use your key. Let's enter quietly and see what we see."

I let us in. The cavernous foyer was silent and dark. I didn't know where the light switch was. I had to hunt for it along the walls before I managed to turn on the lights.

"Can you call the staff? I'd like to know who's home before I set up the monitoring system. I don't need an audience."

"Hello? Hello? It's Tabitha. Anyone home?"

My words echoed off the walls. I turned to Hagerty and shrugged.

"Who would normally be here?" he asked.

"Gloria and Juliet at least. Maybe Connor."

"Where would they be?"

"The housekeeper is probably in the kitchen, which is that way." I gestured. "When they're done working for the night, Gloria and Juliet have rooms on the third floor. Connor could be upstairs in our bedroom, or in the library, that way, in the opposite wing from the kitchen."

"Wait here," Hagerty said, then lowered his voice. "I don't want you encountering anyone until the monitor is activated and you're wired. That first conversation could be critical."

He walked off toward the kitchen, leaving me alone in the hall.

My clothes were wet from the rain and stale from two days of travel. Rather than sit in the beautifully upholstered chairs that flanked the grand fireplace, I stood there, huddled into myself, rubbing my arms for warmth. The bleakness of this place descended on me. I'd never felt at home here. I'd always been an outsider—alone, afraid. Now I was actually a spy, returned to trick the occupants into confessing their crimes. *The occupants.* My husband and his accomplices. I told myself that he deserved it. That he'd murdered his first wife for the money and was now framing me for that crime. *Me,* his wife, the mother of his child. I couldn't believe it. I didn't believe it. I was in denial. I'd loved him. I still did. To think he could do such a thing—it tore me apart.

Hagerty strode back into the hall.

"I found the housekeeper," he said. "She claims to be alone in the house. Your husband and the assistant are both out. I told her to stay in the kitchen until further notice. That gives us the opportunity to install the system without prying eyes. Let's get a move on, before anyone else shows up and starts asking questions."

For the next hour, I followed Hagerty around Windswept as he set up the monitoring system that he'd brought with him in his briefcase. He fitted me with a padded monitor that clamped around my ankle and tightened with screws. It was an unwieldy black plastic thing that looked sort of like a giant Apple watch. No matter how he adjusted it, it wouldn't get comfortable. Finally, he gave up and told me I needed to live with it.

"It's not a bedroom slipper," he said.

Once activated, the ankle bracelet would send a continuous signal to a receiver installed in Windswept's landline telephone system. He installed receivers on several phones throughout the house, to ensure that I would always be in range.

"Never used one of these in a place this size. Hope it works," he said.

The receivers would give the police department a twenty-four-seven readout of my location. If I left the premises, they'd know. If I cut the bracelet off, they'd know. And unlike your average ankle bracelet, mine had a bonus feature—a recording device. The bracelet was bugged. It would record anything said within range of it.

"*Record,*" Hagerty said. "Not transmit. We don't have a van stationed outside listening to every word you say as you say it. That's

FBI stuff. We don't have the resources. Anytime, day or night, you can get a confession out of your husband or anybody else who might be in on the crime, as long as they're speaking within range of the device, it will be captured and stored. In forty-eight hours, you'll go to your attorney's office, and I'll meet you there to retrieve and download whatever you got."

Hagerty claimed the bug was hidden in the ankle monitor for my protection. A wire worn taped to the body was easily discoverable, he said, and could result in me being outed, retaliated against, even killed. The ankle monitor was a condition of my bail, ordered by the judge. Everyone expected me to be wearing it. Nobody would bat an eye. They'd never suspect. But, unlike a wire, the ankle bracelet and its recording device couldn't be turned off by me. The DA and the cops would hear everything I said for the next forty-eight hours, and there wasn't a thing I could do to stop them.

Before he left, he showed me that one of the screws on the bracelet was actually a panic button. The screw was flush with the plastic of the device in order to avoid triggering it unintentionally. But if you pressed it hard with something pointy, it would send an emergency signal to the police.

"Only use it if you really need to. If we get that signal, we rush over here and break the door down. At that point, your cover's blown, and your cooperation is done. You won't be any good to us, which means you won't be any help to yourself. Got it?"

"I understand."

"Your monitor is live now. You're alone in the house at present except for the housekeeper. That gives you a window of opportunity. Use it. Poke around, see if you can find evidence to help the DA's case. Get your husband talking, or anyone else who might know something. You need to produce if you expect to gain."

I nodded. The fear must've been plain on my face, because Hagerty broke into a pep talk.

"Buck up. Keep your head down, watch your back. If things go south, trigger the emergency alert. We'll come and get you out. All right?"

I nodded.

He swatted me on the arm in what I guessed was supposed to be a gesture of encouragement. Then he was gone.

35

I was supposed to be looking for evidence. Steeling myself to betray the man I'd loved into confessing a terrible crime. But all I could think of was taking a hot shower, crawling under the covers, and crying myself to sleep.

The master bedroom was cold and dark. I turned on every single light before going to stare at Nina's portrait. It looked like a death mask, reminding me of how much was at stake. In the bathroom, I ran the hot water until steam poured from the shower stall. My clothes stank of the jail cell. I wished I could burn them, but I couldn't even get them off my body. I yanked my jeans down until they got stuck on the ankle bracelet. How could I shower with this monstrosity attached to me? Was it waterproof? Or would it electrocute me the second the water hit it? Screw Ryan Hagerty for not cluing me in. I turned the shower off, pulled my pants up, and went in search of a plastic bag to cover it.

Gloria sat at the kitchen table with a bottle of Dewar's in front of her. She jumped up when she saw me.

"Sit. It's okay. I could use a drink myself."

I took a glass from the cabinet and grabbed the bottle. She glanced at my stomach, then raised an eyebrow at me.

"Seriously?" I said, my voice thick with tears as I sank into a chair across from her. "I'm five months pregnant, okay, and I just spent the night in jail for a murder that I didn't do. Don't judge me."

"I don't judge anybody."

"You probably think I did kill Nina, so I could live in her house and have her money."

"I don't think that."

"I don't care about any of that. I wish I'd never seen this place. I wish I'd never met Connor Ford."

I took a gulp of scotch. It burned going down, setting off a pain in my chest that told me this was wrong. My life might falling apart, it might even be over. But my baby's was just beginning. I got up and dumped out the scotch in the sink. I couldn't run. I couldn't hide. Getting drunk wouldn't help. I caught sight of my reflection in the window. My face was as gaunt and ghostly as Nina's in the painting. I was going to suffer her fate, I could feel it coming. Maybe I deserved it. Hot tears rolled down my cheeks. I bent over the sink, sobbing.

"I tried to tell you," Gloria muttered, behind me. "She's her father's daughter, all right."

I turned on her, struggling to get words out, my body heaving with sobs. "Her father's daughter? Who are you talking about?"

Her big, dark eyes took my measure.

"Gloria, if you know something, please, I'm begging you. Tell me before it's too late."

"The police really think you did it? Because that's not right," she asked.

I was sobbing so hard, I couldn't get any words out, so I just nodded.

"Don't go anywhere. I'll be back in a minute," she said.

She left the room. Collapsing into a chair, I cried until I felt hollowed out and drained. I was still trying to catch my breath when Gloria returned. She glanced over her shoulder, put a finger to her lips, then came up beside me.

"Go upstairs now," she whispered. "I left something for you, under the pillows on your bed. Nobody can know about it, and they can't know it came from me. But it's gonna help you. You shouldn't pay for something you didn't do. That's wrong."

"What is the thing that you left for me?"

"Lock the bedroom door, and you'll see. Make sure you hide it good when you're done, because if they find it, they'll destroy it."

I sat there with my mouth gaping. She shook me by the arm.

"What are you waiting for? Go, before they come home."

I got up and ran back to the master, locking the door behind me like Gloria had said. Under the pile of pillows, I felt something hard, and pulled out a package wrapped up in a towel. Unwrapping the towel, I found a book bound in rose-pink leather, with the initials "N.L." embossed in gold on the cover, closed with a brass clasp.

Nina's diary.

There was something stuck inside. I saw the edges protruding. The clasp opened easily when I pressed it. A manila envelope had been folded in half and tucked inside the front cover. It was marked CONFIDENTIAL on the front. I'd get to that in a minute. My eyes were drawn to the first page, where a scrawling, left-tilted hand had noted the date. *July 4.*

Nina wrote this on the day she died.

I'm writing this to raise an alarm in the event of my untimely death. This is hard to admit, even to myself, let alone to the world. My husband is planning to kill me. For obvious reasons. He's in love with someone else. And he wants my money.

Was she talking about *me*?

Fighting tears, holding my breath, I read obsessively to the bitter end, my eyes racing over the pages. The good news was, I wasn't the woman whom Nina had accused of conspiring to murder her. And the bad news was, I wasn't the one. It was somebody else. Somebody much too close for comfort.

36

NINA'S DIARY

July 4

I never suspected her, not for a single second.

How could I be so blind??

I don't know how I can ever trust again after this.

I'm so angry!!!!

Deep breath.

Okay, I didn't know about *her,* but I've known Connor was cheating on me for a while now, since at least Memorial Day weekend. Edward's behavior left me feeling so insecure that I would've worried about cheating in any relationship. With Connor, it was even worse, because of who he was. A party boy. A player. Somebody who likes the finer things but doesn't want to work for them. I knew those things about him. I saw the danger and married him anyway. Because he made me happy. Because I loved him. But I wasn't stupid. I made him sign a prenup that gave him *nothing* if he left me or cheated on me. And I hired an investigator, a former cop named Teddy Bruno, who was recommended by Steve Kovacs.

Steve. I trust him. *I think.* I'm certainly relying on him to keep me safe tonight, so I'd better be right. But if something goes wrong, well—the authorities should look at him, too. I'm writing all this down. The good, the bad, and the ugly. The ones who lied, the ones who hurt me, the ones who might even be willing to kill me. If the worst happens, they won't get away with it.

Anyway, I hired Bruno right from the start because Hank, who wanted to stop me from marrying Connor, gave me this file on Connor's ex-girlfriend. Her name was Lissa Davila, and she'd gone missing about two years before Connor and I met. Hank claimed Connor was a suspect in her disappearance. I didn't buy it. Maybe I didn't want to. But there was also the fact that I didn't really trust Hank. He was the king of the hatchet job, the smear campaign. I thought he was making it all up. So, I hired Bruno to get to the bottom of the allegations. When Bruno came back and said there was nothing to it, that Connor wasn't involved, I was so relieved that I put him on permanent retainer.

Big mistake.

Bruno was either incompetent, or complicit. Either way, he was wrong. Connor knew everything about Lissa's disappearance. Including where she is now. *Who* she is now.

I started suspecting something was amiss this past Memorial Day weekend, when Connor went up to New Hampshire without me. He told me a parcel of land had come on the market, at the lake where he'd spent his summers as a kid, and that it was a prime candidate for development. I immediately smelled a rat. Things had been rocky between us. The timing seemed bizarre—a business meeting over a holiday weekend? And Connor is in the middle of some of the biggest real-estate deals in the world right now. Why would he waste time on some country club in New Hampshire? So, as a test, I said fine, Hank has a place up there, let me ask him if you can stay. When he gave me a hard time about staying at Hank's place, I knew something was off. Either he had some rendezvous planned, or he was worried that I'd spy on him there. Which—yes, I would have, except Bruno turned out not to be available.

I had no eyes on Connor that weekend. He went up there, and *something* happened. I didn't know exactly what. But he came back different. Dreamy. Distracted. Like he'd been with someone and was still with her in his mind. I could feel her, clinging to him, haunting us both, like maybe he was in love. And it hurt. A lot.

I wanted to know what I was dealing with. So, after that weekend, I set Bruno to looking at the obvious suspects. Lauren. Dawn. A few other women at Levitt Global whom Connor had contact with. Bruno came back empty-handed, and I knew that was wrong. There were more rocks to be turned over. But it wasn't just the lack of result that bothered me. Bruno told me I was being paranoid, that I had no evidence to justify continuing to monitor my husband. Like he knew Connor better than I did. Right. He'd obviously lost confidence in the mission, so I fired him.

And that's when the truth came out. It took the new investigator to show me what was right in front of my eyes all along.

This time, I didn't ask Kovacs for a recommendation. I didn't ask anybody around me, because by that point, I knew better than to trust them. Instead, I asked a woman I know from a museum board, a lawyer, who's very smart. She recommended a guy named Kendrick Charles, another retired cop, but this one was actually good at his job. I gave him all the material I had on Connor, including Hank's original "Lissa" file, and everything Bruno gave me, and I asked him to start from scratch. He went and he worked and he didn't come back until he had answers—including a photograph of Lissa.

Julissa is her full name. Julissa Maria Davila.

The photograph showed Julissa sitting in Connor's lap, looking into his eyes, her face bright with young love. It was so surreal that I wouldn't've believed it if I wasn't holding the proof in my own two hands. Because Julissa Davila was *Juliet Davis.*

I looked at that photo, and the bottom fell out of my world. The two of them have been lying to me for years. An elaborate con. Juliet came to work for me right after Edward died, nearly three years ago now. I was a fool for not vetting her more intensively, but I'd lost my assistant at the very moment I took on new responsibilities at Levitt Global, and I was desperate. Juliet seemed perfect for the position. So unremarkable, so bland and efficient and unthreatening, exactly what I looked for in an assistant. Her references checked out, though now I realized she must have faked them somehow. I hired her, and once she was in, she turned around and reached back for Connor.

He was a plant, from the beginning.

They were in on it together.

They're after my money.

My marriage is a lie.

I'm getting rid of them tonight. Both of them. As soon as the party is done, I'll have Steve Kovacs bring them here, to my office. And I'll tell them this charade is over for good.

37

After the party

This turned out wrong.

I told Kovacs, bring them to my office after the party, but—I can't remember, something about an arrest. My head is foggy, but I need to get this down. I was sitting here just a little while ago at this desk when there was a knock at the door. It was Connor, with Juliet right behind him. You wanted to talk to us, Connor said. Yes, that's right.

But why was I alone with them? That wasn't how it was supposed to be.

Kovacs left me alone, and I was afraid. I picked up the letter opener from the desk to defend myself. She laughed. That's when I knew this was bad bad bad.

Everything echoes.

Nina, what is it? You don't look well, he said.

You did something to me. What did you do?

He looked at her. What is she talking about? What did you do? Did you do something?

She denied it. Juliet denied it.

He doesn't believe her, I can tell.

How could she—what was it? How did she manage—? She makes my drinks. But tonight, no. I thought I was careful. But something's wrong. It's hard to keep my eyes open and my hand doesn't want to write. Julissa did something. Julissa is her real name. It's all in the report. Read the report.

I said, I know who you are. You're not Juliet. You're *Julissa.* Call 911.

You call, she said.

Where's my phone? You're my assistant. Find my phone.

Find it yourself.

You're together; you're both lying. It's all a fraud. She came here under false pretenses then she brought you so I would fall for you. Lies lies lies. Get out of my house.

Your house? This house is mine by right. *It's mine.*

And I understood.

The baby crying. Was that you, I asked. Were you the baby? Funny, I was just talking about you earlier tonight. Edward said you weren't real. I thought you were a ghost.

You knew, she said.

No, never. I didn't know. *I did not know!*

You sent me away.

Not me. It wasn't me. It was him.

You ruined my life.

Connor said he was going to call a doctor, and Juliet said, don't you do that. You reap what you sow. She should pay the price.

I blacked out. Then I woke up again with my face on the desk and took out the book to write. The report is here. Read the report.

JULIET!

They left. They're gone now. Where's my phone? Did she take it? I need a doctor. Call 911.

Gloria. Somebody. Help me.

38

TABITHA

I sat on the bed, shaking from head to toe. If the things written in this diary were true, then Nina had been murdered. By Connor and Juliet. Who were lovers. And had been together for years.

For the first time, I understood what it felt like to want to kill someone. The betrayal burned like acid. If I had a gun in my hand, and Connor or Juliet walked in that door right now, I would use it. I'd loved him so much. I'd believed in his love for me. How was it possible that—

But, wait. What if this wasn't true? What if Nina was wrong? What if she was making it up? Stop and think. Assess the evidence. How did I even know this was her journal? There was something off about it. A normal diary would have entries for multiple dates. The entirety of this journal was written on July fourth, the day of Nina's death. Correction, of her *suicide.* Before she killed herself, Nina Levitt sat down and wrote out an accusation to hurt the husband she left behind, who, she believed, had been unfaithful to her. She left the journal where it was sure to be found, in order to get him in trouble with the law. That was straight-up revenge. Made up. A lie.

But this Juliet thing . . . *crazy.* It couldn't be real. I didn't want it to be real.

Though—why would Nina say those things about Juliet, if they weren't true? The outrage, the sense of betrayal, that came through on the page was as white-hot as her fury at Connor. I believed the emotion. But the accusations seemed too far-fetched to be true.

Read the report, she'd said.

I cast the diary aside and opened the manila envelope. The word "Confidential" was typed on the front, but no sender or addressee was shown. I pulled out a sheaf of papers with a photo paper-clipped to the top.

No.

I rubbed my eyes and looked again. It was still there. The awful truth.

Connor, with Juliet sitting in his lap. They were both much younger in the photo. Connor looked softer around the eyes, with longer hair—much as I remembered him from that summer when we fell in love. And Juliet? She looked so *familiar.* She wasn't wearing glasses. Her hair flowed over her shoulders. Suddenly, I remembered. I'd seen her before I ever came to Windswept. She was the woman who'd had dinner with Connor at the Baldwin Grill the night he walked back into my life. They'd spent maybe an hour together, and then she disappeared. What could that mean? Juliet was in New Hampshire with Connor the weekend he and I got back together. The weekend my baby was conceived.

Why was she there?

I put myself back at the ski house that night, and I remembered. The noise outside that Connor went to investigate. Was that Juliet? What about the blackmail photo? Was that her, too? And the

Suburban—following me, trying to run me down—was that her? I caught my breath. It had to be. It had to be Juliet behind the wheel of the Suburban. She'd tried to kill me.

Jesus. Now I believe that Nina was telling the truth. Connor claimed he'd come back to the lake looking for me. It hadn't made any sense at the time. It did now. They were looking for someone to take the fall for a murder that hadn't been committed yet.

Our whole relationship was a lie. That's exactly what Nina had said. She and I weren't that different after all. We both fell for the same beautiful, charming con man.

I hated him. I wanted to rip him apart.

I still loved him. I wanted him to tell me I was wrong about this.

I sank back against the pillows and covered my eyes, with no idea what to do. Was there some way out of this awful scenario? Something that didn't fit, that suggested my interpretation was wrong? I thought, and I thought, until I found it. It was this: If they'd been planning all along to set me up for Nina's murder, why did Juliet run me off the road before Nina actually died? That made no sense. She'd need me alive later in order to take the fall for Nina's murder.

Unless. Maybe they weren't in on it together. Maybe this was all Juliet. Oh, God, how I wanted to believe that.

I looked at the photo of the two of them again. Connor was looking at the camera. Juliet was looking at Connor, and she was dazzled. Completely gone. Madly in love. You could see it on her face. But him? He was just enjoying the attention.

Maybe he never really loved her.

The report. I skimmed the pages, looking for something, anything, to back up that faint hope. And there it was in black and white. The account given by Juliet's college roommate of their relationship. The relationship was unhealthy, obsessive, one-sided. "When Connor left school to try to make it in the music industry," the roommate had said, according to the interview transcript included with the report, "he told Lissa he needed space, that they should just be friends. She flipped out and attempted suicide. She had to be hospitalized. She was really messed up over him."

There you go. She loved him. He never loved her back.

Right. Keep telling yourself that, Tabitha.

I didn't know what to believe, so I kept reading. According to the report, Julissa had disappeared from New York about three years before she turned up as Nina's assistant using the name Juliet Davis.

Okay, question. Why not just use her own name? Was there something about her name that would have stopped Nina from hiring her?

I continued reading. There was evidence that Juliet had been in touch with Connor right before she disappeared. The report included a xerox of a grainy surveillance photo showing the two of them together outside her apartment mere days before she disappeared. They were facing away from the camera.

I studied that photo. It was him. I knew him by heart, even the back of his head, the slant of his shoulders. And there was more. The private detective had gone back through Connor's Levitt Global personnel file. When Connor applied to the Levitt Global PR department, he was asked how he learned of the job opening. He wrote, "Referred by: Juliet Davis, personal assistant to Nina Levitt."

Julissa went to work for Nina, then brought Connor into the company. I wondered if she'd introduced the two of them, or had it happened some other way.

And then, this. Buried on page three of the report, a fact that might have seemed minor to someone else leaped out at me. Juliet's employer before Levitt Global was Protocol Shipping Solutions, the company that owned the Suburban she'd used to run me off the road. Proof positive that it was her.

Juliet and Connor had murdered Nina. Juliet tried to kill me and failed. And now they were setting me up to take the fall for Nina's murder. Not just trying to set me up. Succeeding in setting me up, since I'd been arrested and charged with the crime.

I had to give this diary to the police. Immediately.

I pulled out my phone. Detective Hagerty had warned me to take precautions against anybody finding out that I was working with them. *The line "snitches get stitches" exists for a reason,* he'd said. *The threat of retaliation is real.* I'd listed him not as Hagerty, but as "Hayley from the restaurant," in case someone at Windswept searched through my contacts. I found his number, but then hesitated, my thumb over the screen. Handing over Nina's diary would be an irrevocable step. The journal implicated both Connor and Juliet. They could go to prison. They would. Not just her. Him, too. Deep down, I didn't want it to be true. I didn't want to lose him. Was I ready to give up hope of his innocence? Did I honestly believe he'd been lying to me all along—not just about Nina, but about his feelings for me? At least, before taking this very final action, I could talk to Gloria. There were so many unanswered questions. Where and when did she find the diary? Why did she keep it hidden, instead of giving it to the police? And why did she turn it over to me? Gloria must have read the journal and known about Nina's accusations, or else she would have had no reason to give it to me when I'd begged her to tell me what really happened. Did she believe that what Nina had written was true? Did she have evidence that could prove that? There had to be more that Gloria could tell me. At the very least, I should ask her, before turning in my own husband for murder—even if he'd done that to me.

I unlocked the master-bedroom door and stuck my head out, straining to hear if Connor or Juliet had returned. But Windswept was so big that there was no way to tell just by listening. The sound of footsteps, or even voices, would be lost amid the creaks and sighs of an old house and the distant crash of surf on sand. Playing it safe, I wrapped the diary in the towel and shoved it back under the pillow. I put the photo in my pocket and went in search of Gloria.

She was no longer in the kitchen. I wandered the darkened first floor, afraid to turn on lights for fear of attracting attention. The echoing parlors, the glittering, high-ceilinged dining room, the ornate library were all empty and silent except for my own footsteps. Gloria must've gone back to her room. I knew she lived in the staff quarters on the third floor, but so did Juliet. I'd never been up there. As I climbed the two sets of steep stairs, I worked on my cover story, just in case I ran into Juliet.

There was a door at the top of the stairs to the third floor, but it was unlocked. I pushed it open and stepped into a space that felt like a different planet from the rest of the house. The first two floors of Windswept boasted ceilings of twelve or thirteen feet, even higher in the ballroom, with elaborate moldings, murals, sconces, chandeliers, exquisite carpeting, expensive wallpaper, paintings, and objets d'art. This floor was cheap and dingy, with grimy, old carpet, faded paint, and ceilings so low that I felt claustrophobic. How the other half lives—and for most of my life, I'd been in that half.

Four doors opened off the narrow, windowless hall. The only way to find Gloria's room would be trial and error. The first door on the right was not only unlocked, it was ajar. I pushed lightly, and the door opened inward. Lit only by the moonlight that filtered through the single, dormered window, the room was clearly lived-in, though unoccupied at the moment. It was tucked under the eaves of Windswept's great roof, and the sharply slanted ceiling made it impossible to stand along one side. I flicked on the flashlight from my phone. The cramped space was cluttered with furniture and personal effects, as if it had been lived in for years. There was a narrow bed, a dresser, a wardrobe, and a rickety chair covered with clothing. I recognized a black uniform on top of the pile. I was in the right place, but Gloria was not here.

I was just turning to leave when a framed photograph on the

dresser-top caught my eye. I stepped over to the dresser, its battered surface strewn with her things. There was a bottle of Tylenol, several pairs of earrings, a couple of lipsticks, a hairbrush with black hairs clinging to it. And a photo—of Gloria and Juliet, standing in front of a massive Christmas tree in Windswept's entry foyer. Their arms were around each other's waists. Juliet looked happier than I'd ever seen her before. Gloria appeared uncomfortable. Yet, there was something about the photo, something I couldn't put my finger on, that troubled me.

Were the two of them closer than I knew? Then, why would Gloria give me Nina's diary, which implicated Juliet so unequivocally? Still, I needed to be careful. I didn't understand this place well enough to know where people's true loyalties might lie.

As I backed out of Gloria's room, leaving the door the same amount ajar that I'd found it, my gaze fell on the room next door. Juliet kept a room here, on this floor. She had a place of her own in the city but stayed over frequently when Nina was alive because her job required it. She'd continued the practice since I'd been here, living at Windswept full-time, though now I had to wonder why. She claimed it was necessary in order to inventory Nina's things for auction, but was there some darker purpose? Keeping an eye on me? On the investigation? Here was a chance to sneak into her room when she was out, to see if I could find evidence that would be of interest to the DA.

I knocked first, just to be sure she hadn't come back without my knowledge. There was no answer, and the door was locked. I went through my key ring, found a key that fit, and let myself in. This room was the same size as the one next door but felt larger and airier because it lacked the slanted ceiling. It was also sparsely furnished and meticulously kept—bed made, clothes put away, nothing left on the surface of the dresser or the desk. Checking the closet, I found four black pantsuits on hangers, spaced at perfect intervals. I was in the right place. This was Juliet's room, and she was a neat freak.

I heard a creak in the hallway and froze, listening. After a moment or two, when there was nothing more, I crossed to the small desk and sat down in the chair. My blood pressure had shot up. I felt a pulse beating in my temples as I examined the desk. The two file-cabinet-style drawers to the right of the footwell were locked. I tried a few keys from my key ring, but nothing fit. The middle drawer pulled open easily. It contained a tray filled with paper clips and rubber bands. I lifted the tray out and underneath found a small key, which opened the file drawers. The top drawer held little of interest—Kleenex, pads of paper, more office supplies, a pack of gum. But the bottom one was filled with files in hanging folders. The labels made me catch my breath. "Genealogy." "Birth and Custody Records." Those should help prove Juliet's false identity. There was no time to waste. I could be interrupted at any moment. I pulled out the "Birth and Custody" file and opened it on the desk.

The birth certificate was right on top and gave her name as Julissa Maria Davila, her father as unknown, and her mother as—

Her mother as Gloria Maria Davila Maldonado.

Gloria? My Gloria? The woman who'd just given me a diary saying that Juliet was using a fake name, and that Nina believed she planned to kill her? That same Gloria was Juliet's mother? It made no sense, and yet it struck me with the force of truth and I realized now what had troubled me about the photograph of the two of them together in front of the Christmas tree. There was a family resemblance between the two women.

Whatever this meant, I knew it was of critical importance, so I pulled out my phone, photographed the birth certificate, and texted it to Hagerty. Next, I examined the photo of the newborn baby in its mother's arms. This had to be Juliet—Julissa—and her mother, simply by virtue of being in that same file folder. There was no way to tell if the red-faced little baby was Juliet. But was the mother Gloria? I looked more closely at the girl in the photo—for she was a girl. Thin, dark-haired, pretty, and very, very young. A teenager, with an air of sadness despite the baby in her arms. She'd changed so much, but the shape of the eyes and nose gave her away. It was Gloria.

As I looked closer, I noticed something else, so shocking that I gasped out loud. The narrow room, with its slanted ceiling. I'd been in there minutes ago. This photo of baby Julissa had been taken in the room next door. Gloria had given birth while she worked here at Windswept. I remembered something that Nina had written in her diary—something about a baby crying?

Father unknown.

Hands shaking, I photographed the photo itself, then the other documents in the file—adoption papers, a motion for termination of parental rights, a motion for unsealing of adoption records, and more. When I'd finished with that folder, I replaced it and moved on to the next one. I started with the first of five separate folders labeled "Lawsuit." As I laid down a legal document to take its picture, the title of it stopped me cold. "Julissa M. Davila, Plaintiff, v. Edward M. Levitt, Defendant." The date stamp on the front of the document showed that it had been filed in court nearly ten years earlier. As I flipped to the next page, the words leaped out at me—"rape," "acknowledgment of paternity," "abandonment," "child support." Juliet had sued Edward Levitt, alleging that she was Edward's biological daughter, the product of his rape of his employee, Gloria Maldonado.

Juliet had told Nina this house was hers by right. This was what she'd meant.

Gloria had said, *She's her father's daughter.* And this was what *she* had meant—that Juliet—Lissa—was Edward Levitt's offspring.

Just then, I heard footsteps outside the bedroom door. I put the file back, closed the desk drawer, and locked it. As the door to the room began to swing inward, I jumped up and moved away from the desk.

Connor stood in the doorway. His figure in the dim light had an air of menace.

"What are you doing sneaking around up here?" he said, as he advanced toward me.

39

He stopped a few feet away from me. I searched his eyes in the semi-darkness, looking for the Connor I knew, the one who loved me, the father of my child. But his face was a mask of suspicion and anger.

"I—I was looking for Juliet," I said.

"Alone in her room in the dark?"

I felt vulnerable, in this cramped room on this empty floor, cut off from the rest of the house. I needed to put some space between us.

"I was just—I was going to leave her a note, but it can wait. Come downstairs. I need to ask you something important."

I pushed past him, heart hammering, afraid he'd try to grab me. But he simply followed me down the stairs and into our room, shutting the door behind him. In the bright light of the master bedroom, I could see that stress was taking its toll on him. He looked as bad as I did, his skin gray, his eyes red, his tie hanging askew against a crumpled white shirt. I had to fight a rush of sympathy. This Connor didn't deserve my concern. This Connor had let me be charged with murder, and had not even shown up to the courthouse.

"Where were you today?" I said, my voice dripping with disgust.

"Don't lie. It'll just make me hate you more."

There was a tortured look in his hazel eyes. "I'm not lying. *Tabby.* How can you think I faked my feelings for you? It's the most I've ever felt for anyone."

"You faked your feelings for Nina. I know that to be true. So, why not with me, too?"

That brought him up short. "Well, okay—*maybe.* I mean, not exactly, but there's some truth to what you just said. Since we've been together, I've changed. I sincerely have. Still, I deserve your doubts. I see that, because of my past."

He rubbed his eyes, which were red and watery. He was fighting tears.

"Please, hear me out. I'll tell you the whole truth, even if it makes you hate me. But you have to try to see my side, like I'm doing, with you and the drugs. At least keep an open mind. Please?"

"Yes. I'll try. Go ahead."

"This will only make sense if I start at the beginning. *Okay.*"

He took a deep breath. "I met Lissa in college, and we were together briefly. The relationship meant more to her than it did to me. Honestly, I still had you on my mind, and that's not a lie. I wasn't happy with myself. I was confused. My grades suffered. I left school for a while. Lissa and I broke up. She was fragile. Mental health issues. She had a tough upbringing—foster homes until she got adopted when she was ten. She actually attempted suicide after we broke up. I felt guilty, and protective of her. So I kept in touch. Not out of love. It was obligation. And friendship. Maybe it was more to her, though."

He paused for breath. I watched his eyes. I believed he was telling the truth about Juliet, but so what? His sob story didn't change the facts that Nina had been murdered and I was being framed.

"You think your protectiveness of her justifies what you've done?"

"*I* didn't do anything. Just listen, okay? This isn't just background,

"I went to *jail,* with our baby inside me, and you didn't bother showing up. You didn't come to court. You sent a useless lawyer. You didn't even call. For all you knew, I could still be rotting there, and you wouldn't care."

Connor's face went red, but he kept his voice calm as he replied.

"If you want to know the truth, I was trying to cool down before I had to face you. I was so angry."

"*You're* angry at *me*?" I demanded, pacing up and down just out of his reach, so furious that I was panting.

"Calm down. This is bad for the baby."

"Don't tell me to calm down. You know what's bad for the baby? Sleeping on a hard bench in an ice-cold cell. Going to jail for a murder I didn't commit."

"I sent a lawyer."

"Courtney Whatever-the-fuck? Please. She had no clue, and you knew it. You wanted her to fail."

"What are you talking about?"

"I'm talking about the fact that you framed me."

"First of all, I didn't. And second, you put yourself in this position. When were you planning to tell me that you have a rap sheet? That you're a drug dealer? That you sold exactly the same type of pill that Nina died from? Don't you think that was something I had a right to know before deciding to marry you?"

For a moment, I had the strangest sensation of staring down at us from above. If I stepped outside myself, I was the one who looked guilty, not Connor. Maybe his anger was justified. Maybe he hadn't killed Nina and wasn't trying to frame me. But then, how did he explain Juliet? I had proof right there in my jeans pocket not just of her false identity, but of their preexisting relationship. I ran my finger over the smooth surface of the photo of the two of them together. I was tempted to pull it out and throw it in his face. But I had to be more strategic than that. I was supposed to be tricking Connor into implicating himself in Nina's death for the benefit of the police who were recording our conversation. I didn't exactly have a plan for doing that, other than getting him talking about the murder.

"I had nothing to do with Nina's death," I said to Connor. "And you know that."

"I'm not accusing you of killing her," he said. "I don't believe you'd do that. But you have a criminal record for selling drugs. You were here at Windswept the night she died, along with your ex, who attacked Steve Kovacs. What the hell am I supposed to make of that? You know how bad it looks?"

"Yes, bad enough to get me arrested for a murder I didn't commit. I'm surprised you're upset, given how convenient that is for you."

"What are you talking about?"

"Look, I'm sorry I never told you about Derek. I was waiting for the right time. Those were his drugs, not mine. I didn't even know they were there. I only pled guilty because they offered me a misdemeanor with no jail time, and my lawyer said it was the best deal I could get."

"You expect me to believe that?"

"It's the truth. And here's another truth. You're the one with the motive to kill Nina. Not me. What would I gain from her death?"

"What would you gain? *Me.* This house to live in. Clothes and vacations, servants, private jets."

"You had that, and you cared about it more than I ever could. Yet, you were about to lose it. Nina was going to divorce you."

"You don't know that."

"Yes, I do, Connor. I know it for a fact."

"How?"

I sat down on the bed. Nina's journal was hidden under the pillows, inches from my fingers. I was itching to pull it out and toss it at his head. If only the police were listening in, I would have. But the recording device in the ankle bracelet was not a transmitter. They

couldn't hear me in real time. The only way to summon them was to push the panic button. How was I supposed to do that with Connor standing over me?

"Because, I know you were planning to use my record against me. At least, Julissa was."

Connor's jaw dropped. "Ju-Julissa?"

"Why else did you two show up at my restaurant Memorial Day weekend? She knew all about me. She set me up," I said.

I'd been trying hard to keep my voice steady, but it came out small and shaky and filled with sorrow. Hot tears started rolling down my cheeks. We stared at each other, everything between us so broken. He hung his head.

"Nooo," he said. "Tabby, no."

"No, what? Are you saying it's not true? Then explain this."

I reached into my pocket and pulled out the photo. It had gotten crumpled along one edge. I smoothed it against the fabric of my jeans. He stared at the picture in stunned silence.

"This is very much how I remember you. Back then, that summer when we fell in love—I thought. But here you are with her, not long afterward."

"You got that from her room?" he asked.

Let him believe I'd found the photo in Juliet's room. That way, I'd protect Gloria, who had at least tried to help me.

"She's not who she says she is," I said. "She wormed her way into working for Nina under a false name. Then the two of you killed Nina for the money."

"That is completely wrong. Please, tell me you don't believe that. You can't."

He grabbed my hands, but I pulled them away.

"You brought me here to take the fall for Nina's death. You were with Juliet this whole time."

"*No.* I completely deny it."

it's my explanation, and you said you'd keep an open mind. About ten years ago, Lissa got her adoption records unsealed, and she discovered that her birth mother was *Gloria.* Gloria, the housekeeper here."

I knew that was true. Again, it didn't justify his conduct.

"So what?"

"I'm about to tell you what. Lissa was desperate to know her birth mother. She wrote to her begging for a meeting, but Gloria said no, it would be too painful. That's when Lissa found out the truth about her identity. Gloria wrote her a letter explaining that she'd been raped when she was seventeen and forced to give the baby away. Well, it didn't take much digging for Lissa to figure out that Edward Levitt was the perpetrator—and her father."

"I believe that Edward would do something like that. But don't think you can use it to excuse what you and Juliet did."

"*I* didn't do anything. Will you please not say that, at least until you've heard the whole story? Okay?"

"Go on," I said grudgingly.

"At that point, Lissa had nothing. She was twenty years old, a college dropout, with no money, no job, no prospects, fragile mental health. And she'd just discovered she was the daughter of this fabulously wealthy man. So, she sued for paternity. But the case wasn't viable. Because she was over eighteen, Edward no longer had any support obligation, and there was no requirement that he give her a penny. She settled for a hundred thousand bucks, plus a no-show job at some shell company of Edward's."

"Protocol Shipping Solutions?"

"Yes, how did you know?" he said, taken aback.

"Finish your story, then we'll talk."

He nodded. "So, they settled. Lissa was required to sign an NDA and agree never to contact Edward or his family."

"You're trying to tell me that's the reason for the false name, so she didn't violate the settlement?"

"Partly. But the main reason for the false name was because of Gloria. Everything Lissa did—at least at the beginning—was because of Gloria. She'd never given up the idea of knowing her birth mother. But the lawsuit, which was something of a bust financially, had a terrible effect. It set Gloria against her. Apparently, Lissa's lawyer had tried to subpoena Gloria to court, which made Gloria very uncomfortable. And after Edward died, when Lissa reached out again, Gloria basically said get lost and never contact me again. This just made Lissa crazy. To her, it was, like, this huge injustice. She couldn't let it rest. She became fixated. She was obsessively following all things Levitt online, and that's how she discovered that Nina was hiring an assistant. She decided to apply. I know that seems weird. Even twisted. But in her mind, it was a way into that world, so she could get to know her mother. But she had to do it under a different name, or they'd know it was her."

"Okay, fine. Say I accept what you're saying as true. That only tells me about *Juliet's* motive. She's not my concern, you are. Let's talk about you, Connor. Your motive, your lies, your actions."

"Me? I just needed a job. Lissa knew I was looking. She heard of the position in the Levitt Global PR department, and she passed that tip on to me. She offered to put in a good word, but only if I promised to keep her name change between us."

"And you agreed to that? At that point, you knew something really sick was going on."

"Sick? That's an overstatement. You have to understand, Lissa was a friend, with a tragic story, who was trying to help me get a job. I thought what she was doing was weird, yes. But at that point, I'd never met Nina. And whatever Lissa was up to, it didn't involve me. I didn't feel any obligation to out her. Not *then.*"

"Connor, just so you know, I'm not losing sight of the fact that you ended up married to Nina, and Nina ended up dead. This stuff about poor little Lissa is just some smoke screen. You better be honest, because I'll know if you're not."

"Yes. I swear. And here's where the bad stuff starts. This is where I fault myself. This is when I should've known better, should've washed my hands of Lissa, and didn't. As time went on, I realized she had a vendetta against Nina. She blamed her for everything. For forcing Edward to send her away. For making him be ruthless in the lawsuit. Which—I know Nina, and I know Edward by reputation—that just isn't true."

I recalled the words in Nina's journal. *"You sent me away. . . . You ruined my life."* Juliet had blamed Nina. I knew that much was real.

"The point is, I knew she harbored these feelings towards Nina. She started talking about getting back at her. I thought she was blowing smoke. I never took her seriously until—"

He paused, taking a deep breath.

"Until she came up with this crazy plan."

"What plan?"

"To throw me together with Nina and see where it went."

I stared at him, slack-jawed.

"I prayed there was some innocent explanation," I said. "But there isn't. Your marriage was a conspiracy from the beginning. Juliet hadn't succeeded in getting her hands on the Levitt fortune through the lawsuit, so you did it for her."

"*No,* it wasn't like that. She never said, Let's kill Nina and take her money. If she had, I would have done something. She presented it more as, almost, a practical joke. Let's mess with her. To me, it wasn't that. It was just . . . an opportunity. Hell yeah, I'll go to this party. I'll meet this rich, famous, beautiful woman. I'll hang out with her, have sex with her, enjoy what she has to offer. I'm not proud I did that. But it's not the same as conspiring to kill her. *That,* I would never do."

His eyes were pleading. I could feel how much he needed me to believe him. But I couldn't get there. Not yet, not without more of an explanation.

"Nothing changes the fact that you actually went ahead and married her without ever telling her the truth."

"Yes, and that's wrong. But you have to understand, things with Nina went faster than I ever imagined. Within a few months, she wanted to get married. And I wanted to, too. It was an amazing life I could have with her, and I wasn't about to miss out on it because of Lissa's bizarre situation. I know it looks bad. But I didn't see Lissa as my responsibility, and I didn't want to ruin things with Nina by confessing my knowledge of this—*impostor*—in her midst."

I heaved a big sigh, partly convinced by his explanation, yet mad at myself for going along with it. I worried I was missing something. Then I realized that I was. Nina had ended up dead, and Connor with her money.

"None of this explains why Nina's dead, you're rich, and I'm framed for her murder. Go on. Explain all that."

"Around Memorial Day weekend, Lissa told me she wanted to *deal with Nina,* as she put it. And she had this, like, delusion, that I'd help her. We'd kill Nina and split the money. And you know, it's not like she'd never mentioned that concept. But I just put it down to her being crazy. I never thought it was real. And I told her no. I said, I will never agree to that. I want nothing to do with it, and if you're serious, then I'm going to the police. That's when she threatened to out herself in order to ruin me. She was going to tell Nina I'd been in a plot to kill her from the beginning. That was plausible enough that I knew it would ruin my marriage. There was no good explanation for why I'd concealed Lissa's identity for so long. Honestly, I didn't know what to do. That's when I went up to New Hampshire to think things through. And I found you."

"Can I ask you something? Did Juliet follow you there?"

"Yes. It was her, outside the ski house that night. She took that picture of us and that gave her more ammunition to blackmail me with. But, by then, I'd found you again. And I came back here determined to tell Nina I was leaving."

"Yet, you didn't."

"I was looking for a way to tell her without triggering the prenup. I hate myself for dragging my feet over that, because in my moment of hesitation, everything went south. Nina found out about Lissa. She called us to her office after the Fourth of July party, told me she was triggering the prenup, and to get the hell out."

"What was your reaction to that?"

"Honestly? Relief. I wanted to leave, I wanted to be with you."

"Relief? Not rage? Then, why did the night end with Nina floating in the swimming pool, dead?"

"That wasn't me. I had nothing to do with that. If you don't believe me, ask Steve Kovacs. He saw me go."

"Go where?"

"I called an Uber and left. I was on my way to the city when I got the news that Gloria found Nina's body. I turned right around and came back. The next morning, after they took Nina's body away, I confronted Lissa. She admitted everything, said she drugged Nina's drink and pushed her into the pool. She did what I wasn't man enough to do, she said."

"You've known for months that Nina was murdered, that it wasn't suicide, yet you never came forward?"

He sighed. "I wanted to. But when I told Lissa I was going to the police, she laughed. She said she had to do it alone because I was a coward, but she wasn't taking the fall alone. She would tell the cops we did it together, and they'd never believe my denial. But just to make sure, she had an insurance policy. My fingerprints on the glass that she used to drug Nina's drink. *Mine,* not hers. She has it hidden somewhere. That's why I haven't turned her in."

I wanted to believe that Juliet acted alone. I really did. But there was one big, glaring loose end.

"If she really acted alone, why am *I* getting framed for this? Why didn't you stop her? Why not come to court today to proclaim my innocence?"

"Why you is easy. She wants you out of the picture."

"And you're letting her. Connor, she tried to kill me. She was the one in the Suburban, I'm sure of it. She ran me off the road. I could've been killed, the baby, too."

He looked crestfallen.

"I didn't believe that before, but I'm starting to think you might be right. When you first told me about that incident, I was sure it was Nina. That car is a company car. Anybody who worked for her had access to it. Lissa did, too, and the more I think about it, the more sense it makes that it would be her. Especially since, to my knowledge, Nina was not aware of your existence."

"Juliet tried to kill me, and now she's framing me."

"Yes, that's a fair conclusion to draw," he said.

The sadness in his voice made me angry. It was for her as much as for me. He still cared about her—this woman who'd murdered Nina, who'd tried to kill me and his baby.

"You're letting her. You still care about her."

"I understand her. I feel sorry for her. But it's *you* I love. And sweetheart, there is no way I'm letting you take the blame for this. I spent today working out a plan. That's the only reason I wasn't in court. I was moving assets around, looking for an apartment in Dubai—"

"Flee the country? *Never.* That's the same as a confession. And I'm not confessing to something I didn't do."

"It would only be temporary. You would go, and I'd stay behind to clean up this mess. I already met with a lawyer and a private detective. We have a plan to find out where Lissa's got this evidence hidden. Once I have that glass, she has no power over me. I can go to the cops then, without having it come back on me."

"You know what that tells me? After all that's happened, you can't clear my name because you're worried about protecting yourself. I leave the country, and then what? How do I know you don't tell the police that I fled because I'm guilty?"

He grabbed my hands, wild-eyed and agonized. "Please—tell me you don't think that. I would never do that. I love you too much. How can I prove it to you?"

"By coming with me to the police station and telling them the truth. *Now.*"

"I want to. I really do. But it's not that simple. We'd end up taking the fall for Nina's murder. You and I—we need to keep our hands clean. If it gets out there that we were involved, even if it's not true, it would only muddy the water."

"Muddy the water?"

I looked at him warily, a terrible understanding dawning.

"Oh, my God. This is *still* about the money, isn't it?"

"We can't forget about the lawsuit. Tabby, if it looks like you or I were involved in Nina's murder, the courts will rule against me, and Kara Baxter will inherit Nina's money. This is about our future—our future as a *family.* I'm not just looking to survive. I want us to be happy."

"You want us to be rich. It's not the same thing."

"You'll never win by betting on Connor's ethics. You haven't figured that out by now?"

Our heads turned in unison. Juliet stood in the doorway, a gun in her hand.

40

Staring at Juliet down the barrel of a gun, I saw a woman transformed. With her hair down and her glasses gone, in jeans and boots, she looked tough and beautiful, a far cry from the demure wallflower she'd pretended to be. But this wasn't just a costume change. She carried herself like someone else entirely. As I watched a sneer play about her lips, I had a vision of the Warhol hanging downstairs in the library, and realized who. That piratical smile. Those cold blue eyes. She was so like her father. Edward Levitt come back to life—younger, prettier, female, but just as dangerous.

"What do you think you're doing? Stop that," Connor said, jumping to his feet.

"Sit down and shut up."

He advanced on her, hand outstretched. "Come on, Lissa. Enough. Give me the gun."

"God, I'm sick of you."

Before I knew what was happening, Juliet pointed the gun and pulled the trigger. A loud crack sounded, and I screamed. Connor threw himself between the two of us as glass fell to the floor in sheets, tinkling across the parquet floors. She'd shot out one of the tall windows. He extended his arms, protecting me with his body. Was he willing to take a bullet for me, or merely confident that his girlfriend would never shoot him?

"Are you crazy?" he said.

The drapes billowed inward. A damp chill invaded the room, and I shivered.

"Yes, I am, better not fuck with me. Give me your phones. Both of you, hand them over."

"This is ridiculous," Connor said.

"Now. Put them on the floor," she said, and leveled the gun right at my head.

"Connor, just do it," I said, my voice shaking.

I took my phone from the bedside table and dropped it on the floor at her feet. Connor followed suit. Juliet kept her gaze and her gun steady as she knelt down and grabbed the phones with her free hand. She walked over to the missing window, broken glass crunching under her feet, and tossed the phones out into the void.

"I'll do whatever you want," Connor said, as she walked back toward us, still brandishing the weapon. "But Tabitha has nothing to do with this. Let her go."

"Are you nuts? She'll go straight to the police. She's a snitch, Connor. They flipped her. Steve told me a detective was here for an hour, wiring the place for sound. We've got to get out of here, and take her with us, as our insurance policy."

"I'm not going anywhere. Neither are you. Let's calm down and figure this out."

Listening to their words, you'd think they were on the same team. But their body language didn't bear that out. Juliet looked incensed, and Connor was so tense that he practically vibrated.

"Did you hear what I said?" Juliet demanded. "The cops could be listening right now. Ask her if it's true. Ask her."

"Fine. Tabby, did you let the police bug Windswept?"

I was too busy looking back and forth between the two of them, trying to read their expressions, to answer him.

"*Tabby?*"

He was worried she might shoot me. I could hear it in his voice.

"No. The detective was here to give me an ankle monitor for my bail. That's all."

"Satisfied?" Connor said.

"She's lying. There's only one solution, and it goes like this. Tabitha killed Nina. The cops caught her red-handed. The walls are closing in. She's distraught at the prospect of life in prison. She decides to end things and—"

"*No,*" Connor said, taking a step toward her menacingly. "That is *not* happening. You let her go, now."

"What's the attraction here? I honestly don't get it. She's all right, but I'm better. We could have had it all. You were in line to be a very rich man. And you go and bring a wild card into the mix and screw up everything I worked for, everything I planned."

Connor lunged for Juliet, but she was too quick. She stepped back and fired, this time at the ground near his feet. Connor yelped and collapsed onto the bed, grabbing his left wing-tip in his hand. Crimson blood leaked between his fingers.

"Jesus Christ, you shot my foot! You lunatic."

"You need to understand that this is not a joke, and I am not playing. Next time you try anything, I'm shooting *her.*"

Connor tugged frantically at the laces of his shoe. The smell of burnt shoe leather and fresh blood made me gag.

"*You,*" Juliet said, turning the gun on me. "Where is the bug? Tell me now. You know I'm not afraid to use this."

"There is no bug, I swear. Just an ankle bracelet."

"Then, why was that cop here for so long?"

"He had to set up my ankle monitor. I don't think he knew what he was doing, and he couldn't get the signal to work. Do you want to look at the bracelet? It just looks—I mean, I don't know how one is supposed to look—but it looks normal to me."

She nodded, gesturing with the gun. Next to me, Connor had gotten his shoe off. He groaned in pain. The tip of his third toe was missing, and blood spurted over his hands. *We could die here,* I thought, as a wave of nausea swept over me. I slapped my hand over my mouth, fighting the vomit.

"What are you waiting for?" Juliet said to me.

"He—he's hurt. He needs a doctor."

"It's his toe, for Chrissake. He'll live. Show me the bracelet, or no doctor is gonna save you."

I struggled to roll the tight jeans over the bulky black plastic device with shaking fingers. When I finally managed to work it free, I twisted my ankle to see the screws. The panic-button screw looked just like the others, small and deeply recessed into the thick plastic rectangle. Why the hell did they have to make it that way? There was no way to activate it without Juliet knowing I was up to something.

Connor grabbed a pillow from the bed, muttering as he stripped off its case to make a tourniquet for his foot. In the process, he jostled the pile of pillows, revealing a corner of the pink leather diary, which must have slipped from the towel it was wrapped in. Juliet, leaning down to inspect my ankle monitor, didn't notice. The next moment, we were all distracted by the door flying open, and Steve Kovacs sprinted in. For a split second, my entire being sang with relief that this ordeal was coming to an end. Then Kovacs raced to Juliet's side.

"Are you okay? I heard shots fired. Jesus, what's with his foot?"

I saw that Kovacs was in this with her, and my insides went liquid with fear. Juliet with a gun was bad enough. Add Kovacs, and we were doomed.

"I was trying to get her to tell me where the bug is."

"So you shot Connor?"

"She's fucking crazy, Steve. You need to call the police," Connor said.

"Yeah, right. I'm not calling the cops. Let me see."

He grimaced when he saw Connor's wound.

"Jesus Christ. Why'd you shoot him, Lissa?"

"Because he was rushing me to get the gun. He's with her, and she's a snitch and a liar. She claims the guy was just here to install that thing."

Juliet waved her gun at my ankle.

"Maybe he was. I never said I knew for sure there was a bug. What the hell did you do?" Kovacs said.

"I'm trying to protect us. We need to take precautions."

"Use your brain. Now he's shot, he's pissed off. God knows who else heard the gunshot. Any minute, Dennis or Gloria are gonna come around here and—"

"I can handle them."

"They could call the police. Maybe they already did. You forced our hand. Now what do we do?"

"We should get out of here. Now. That's what I've been saying."

"Yeah, and go where?"

"Somewhere we can regroup. We take them with us."

"What, like hostages? That's very ambitious, Lissa. You think very highly of yourself."

"Are you scared? I thought you were some kind of operational genius."

"I am, and I'm telling you, that's not gonna work. We'd need a remote location that isn't tied to either of us, where we could stay for long enough, undetected, to convince Mr. Ford here to get with the program, or failing that, make plans to flee the country. You have a place like that?"

"As a matter of fact, I do."

He paused, frowning. "Oh," he said. "Right."

"What about that?"

"It could work. Cover them, will you."

I didn't know what Kovacs's background was, whether it was military, or law enforcement, or organized crime. But he knew what he was doing, and he was careful. As Juliet held a gun on us, Kovacs had us turn around and lie facedown on the bed. He left the room briefly, presumably to get some restraints, then returned and bound our hands with heavy plastic zip-ties. He then ordered me to sit up, as he carefully unscrewed my ankle monitor. Hagerty had warned me that cutting through the band would alert the police that I was attempting to escape. Kovacs obviously understood that and wasn't taking any chances. He left the monitor intact, on the bed, right where they'd expect me to be. My only hope was that, somehow, the process of unscrewing the "panic button" screw had set the thing off. If not, they wouldn't know I was gone until I failed to show up to my lawyer's office two days from now, as we'd agreed. By the time Hagerty and Pardo figured out I was missing, God knows where I'd be. Hell, I'd probably be dead. So would Connor. And our baby.

I couldn't let that happen.

Kovacs and Juliet walked behind us as we crossed the second-floor gallery and descended the staircase, Connor limping painfully and holding the banister for support. When he slowed down, one or the other of them would nudge him forward with the barrel of a gun. Kovacs warned us in a low, gravelly voice that if we made noise, he'd shoot here and now.

Kovacs had planned ahead. Outside, the Suburban sat in the porte cochere with the engine idling, spewing exhaust into the damp air. It was a cold night, and I shivered without my coat. Connor was barefoot, in shirtsleeves, his breath coming out in clouds, his face pale but determined in the moonlight. Given the way things had played out, I knew for certain now that Connor wasn't in on this with them. It came as an enormous relief. Not just because there would be two of us against two of them if a moment came where we could plausibly escape, but because the man I loved had not been lying to me. As we approached the car, Connor caught my eye. We looked at each other, and for a split second, everything hung in the air between us—the love, the pain, the past, the future. He was gearing up to try to get us out of this. I could feel it. Kovacs and Juliet were right behind us, both holding loaded guns, but Connor was going to try something. Something reckless, to save us, and the baby. It made me love him desperately. Not just love him. Fear for him. I tried to warn him off with a subtle shake of my head, but he nodded back confidently, like a wordless pep talk. He was telling me to get ready.

"Where are we going?" Connor said.

Kovacs shoved Connor toward the car. "Shut up and get in."

Connor planted his feet and swung around, butting Kovacs in the chest with his head, knocking the gun from his hand.

"Tabby. *Run!*"

Juliet aimed at me just as Connor stepped between us. The gun blasted. I took off, screaming at the top of my lungs, but I wasn't fast enough. Someone was on my heels, their shoes pounding and crunching against the drive. They rammed me from behind and I went sprawling. My hands tied behind me, I had no way to break the fall. I closed my eyes as the ground came rushing up. Gravel seared and scratched at me. All the breath left my body. I gasped for air, tasting blood and dirt, grunting with pain. Kovacs was on top of me. I twisted, struggling under his weight, turning my head frantically to see what had happened to my husband.

"Connor! *Connor!*"

"Shut up."

Kovacs tried to put his hand over my mouth. I bit down hard, and he yelped.

"Get, off me, I'm pregnant, you asshole—"

His fist came sailing toward my face.

I woke up with a headache so intense that I couldn't see straight. My mouth and cheeks burned where they'd been scraped up by gravel. I was in the backseat of the Suburban, feeling cold and shaky. The car was moving at highway speed, and there was a smell. Metallic, meaty. *Blood.*

I turned my head fast, and the motion made me nauseous. I had to close my eyes.

I opened them and stifled a scream.

Connor was beside me, belted into the seat, crumpled forward, lifeless. It was dark outside, but in the light from passing cars, I could see that his skin was deathly white, and his shirt dark with blood. Blood coated the backseat. I nudged him with my foot. He didn't stir. I watched his chest. Did I see it rise and fall? *Please, God, let him be alive.* Was he breathing, or was that the motion of the car? Even if he was breathing, with blood loss like this, how long until he wasn't?

"Connor?" I whispered. "Connor, talk to me."

His eyelids flickered. He'd heard me. He was alive.

"Baby, please. We're gonna make it, but you have to hold on. I love you so much. I'm so sorry I doubted you. Can you forgive me? Please forgive me."

Kovacs was driving. Juliet sat beside him in the passenger seat. At least now I knew who the enemy was. The two of them had framed me for Nina's murder. Kovacs knew that I was the same woman he'd seen at Windswept that night. The reason he hadn't given me up was that he'd had another use in mind for me.

If I wanted to keep my husband alive, I'd have to convince him to find a doctor.

I cleared my throat.

"Steve? Connor's lost a lot of blood," I said.

Neither of them turned around.

"He needs medical attention."

Nothing.

"*Do* something. If you don't help him, he'll die."

Kovacs turned.

"Be quiet," he said. "We understand the situation, and we'll deal with it when we can."

"Deal with it now. Please, I'm begging you. He doesn't have much time."

"What are you, a doctor now? Shut up, or else I'll dump him on the side of the road."

After that, I was afraid to talk for fear of antagonizing him. I stared out the window, tears rolling silently down my cheeks. We were passing Springfield, heading north on 91. I'd keep my eyes open, take any chance to escape and get help.

But there was no chance. Time passed. We didn't stop. When we passed a sign for a hospital, I could no longer remain silent.

"Hey, there's a sign for a hospital. You have to stop, or he'll die. Juliet, I know you care! You wanted to kill me, not him. Look at him. He's bleeding out."

Juliet turned around, looked at Connor, and blanched.

"She's right. Steve, we have to do something. We can't let him die."

"I knew it. This is all about him for you."

"What do you care? It's about the money, too. If he dies, we're screwed. We get nothing."

"Should've thought of that before, princess. You couldn't just stick to the plan?"

"I didn't mean for it to happen this way," she said, and I heard the agony in her voice. "I never meant to hurt him. But you told me she had the place bugged."

"I never said that. I said maybe. And so what if the house was bugged? That's no cause for panic. The plan could've still worked. We'd just do it outside, somewhere nobody would hear. A gunshot, or she walks into the ocean. Looks like suicide. She takes the blame for Nina, Connor gets the money, three-way split."

Jesus. When Juliet suggested back at Windswept that nobody would be surprised if I killed myself, that wasn't some off-the-cuff remark. They had a plan. A conspiracy to kill me and blame me for Nina's murder. If this hadn't happened, she and Kovacs would have faked my suicide.

They still might.

"Fine, you're right, okay?" Juliet said. "I don't care who takes the blame. We need to help Connor. Just drive up to the hospital entrance and push him out."

"You really want to get caught, don't you? At a hospital entrance, there are always security cameras. This car can be traced back to us. Both of us—not just you. And then he wakes up in the hospital and starts talking. No way."

"I don't care. I'll take the blame," she said.

"Forgive me if I don't have a lot of faith in you at this point. Enough, now. Let's get where we're going, and we'll figure it out."

Juliet fell silent. By now, that hospital was long gone, anyway. I shook with fear—for myself, for Connor, for our baby, who wasn't moving. It was the dead of night, and the roads were empty. In the flash of headlights on highway signs, the place names grew ever more familiar. We were in Vermont, then New Hampshire, getting on 89, getting off at an exit I knew all too well. We passed the lake, the old country club, the defunct golf course, the ski resort. Everything was shut down tight. No lights in the houses, no cars on the road. The Suburban turned onto the road that wound up Baldwin Mountain.

I knew where we were going. To the place it all began. I looked at Connor, slack and lifeless, and remembered him as he'd been that night, gorgeous and mysterious, his hands sure on the wheel of the Lamborghini. We arrived at the iron gate, and it slid open at our approach, as I remembered. The ski house itself was just as impressive as it had been then, surrounded by dark pines that swayed in the cold wind.

Kovacs pulled me from the backseat and shoved me toward the house. I stumbled, and he grabbed my arm to steady me, holding it in a viselike grip. My legs were like rubber. My hands and arms had gone completely numb from the zip-tie, which had cut off my circulation. I had to be strong and look for any opportunity to get us—all three of us—out of here.

Juliet leaned into the backseat.

"Oh, my God," she said, a catch in her voice.

"He's dead?" Kovacs asked.

Kovacs had to grab my elbow to stop me from collapsing to the ground.

"Check for a pulse," he said.

Juliet put her fingers to Connor's throat, then looked back in horror.

"I don't feel it. Wait, no, there it is. Oh, thank God, he's still alive, but it's faint. He needs a doctor immediately."

"Please, Steve," I said, my voice hoarse with fear. "I'm begging you, help him. Connor and I, we'll tell the police whatever you want. We'll pay you off. As much money as you want. It can still work out how you planned. But he has to live."

"Who's gonna treat a gunshot wound and not call the cops?"

"You can't let him die," Juliet said in a frantic tone.

"I'm not the one who shot him, Lissa. You figure it out. Got any bright ideas?"

"Like she said. Take him to the ER."

"And explain the gunshot in his gut how, exactly?"

"I'm from around here," I said. "I know people at the local hospital. Let's bring him there. I can ask them to keep it quiet."

Kovacs gave a short, barking laugh. "Bring him to your friends? You think I'm stupid? *No.*"

"Then, what? Do you *want* him to die?" Juliet said.

"Of course not. If he dies, we're screwed. Two dead bodies on our hands and no cash."

Two dead bodies—Connor, and me.

41

Kovacs unlocked the front door and shoved me through it. The cold, musty smell of the ski house brought back the nights I'd spent lying in Connor's arms, talking, making love. I was not going to die here, in the place our baby had been conceived. Neither was she, and neither was her father.

He led me through the great room to the hall on the other side. There were three bedrooms off this hallway, I recalled. The first door led to the room where Connor and I had slept. Kovacs pushed me inside and examined the door handle. It had no lock. I could've told him that—there were no locks on any of these bedroom doors. He checked the en suite bathroom, which did lock, but from the inside, with one of those flimsy push-button things. Even with my hands zip-tied behind my back, I'd be able to undo it. Kovacs realized that, because he brought me out to the bedroom and started looking all around, presumably for something to tie me to. I remained docile and compliant, my eyes cast down, so he wouldn't think that I was plotting my escape.

He pushed me down face-first onto the bed, and I heard him

stripping off his belt. Was he going to rape me? Beat me? Adrenaline surged, my body tensing for a fight. Instead, he threaded his belt through my zip-tied hands and yanked me to my feet, dragging me toward the gas fireplace. He pushed me to a sitting position on the hearth, running the belt through the handles of its wrought-iron doors and buckling it so I was lashed to them by my zip-tied hands. The motion forced my arms up behind my back. I cried out in pain.

"Please, that hurts so bad. Can't you tie me in front?"

He stormed out and slammed the door.

I was alone. I caught my breath and took stock of my situation. I had nausea and double vision—probably a concussion from being punched in the head. I was on the edge of hysteria with worry about Connor. I was terrified to try to escape. But I had no idea whether they'd follow through and get medical attention for Connor. If they didn't, he would bleed to death for sure. And then they'd come right back here and get rid of the witness—murder not just me, but my baby. I had to get free of the restraints and get out of here. It wouldn't be easy, and I couldn't be sure that I had the strength or the cunning. But there was no other choice. And there wasn't much time.

Although my hands were tied in back, Kovacs had left the tension on the belt relatively loose. I was able to stand to a crouching position, with enough leeway to move side to side about a foot in either direction. I turned sideways to examine the fireplace. The surround was made from rough-hewn stone, with a sharp edge. It took some maneuvering, but I was able to get myself into position to rub the zip-tie on its corner. That hurt like hell on my swollen wrists, but I kept going—for three minutes, five? Sweat broke out on my forehead and ran down the side of my face. Nothing was happening. It wasn't working. I was using up my strength and getting nowhere.

I needed a different plan. These ties could be broken if you applied enough force. I'd need to slam the tie hard against the stone, but I'd be doing it blind, with my hands behind my back.

On the first attempt, I missed and slammed my hand into rock by mistake. The pain made me dizzy. I waited for my vision to clear, then looked over my shoulder, trying to memorize the distance to get the trajectory just right. I swung. *Success.* The zip-tie popped open and fell to the floor.

There were deep gouges on my wrists and cuts on my hands, but first aid would have to wait. I put my ear to the closed door and listened. The house was quiet, but that didn't mean it was empty. They'd probably both left with Connor, but it was possible that one of them had stayed behind to guard me. I moved silently into the hall, where I stopped and listened again, struggling to focus my attention given the pain and fog in my head. I didn't hear anybody. I had the advantage of knowing my surroundings. This house and Baldwin Mountain were both imprinted on my memory. I bypassed the great room and hurried to the kitchen, where I grabbed a carving knife from the block before slipping into the laundry room. From here, I could access the garage. I couldn't open the garage-bay doors without attracting attention, but I recalled that the garage had a pedestrian door. I wasn't exactly sure where it led, but it had to come out behind the house somewhere. From there it would be a short dash to the woods.

The garage had three bays, all empty. Shelves and hooks along that wall held some basic equipment—rakes, shovels, a coiled hose—but nothing I could use to defend myself, and no jacket to keep me warm. I hadn't changed clothes or shoes since Dubai, and I wore a pair of cute, flimsy flats that were no match for the rugged New Hampshire terrain. I grabbed a couple of trash bags and a roll of duct tape and headed for the rear door. Just as I grasped the handle, the whir of a motor kicked in, and the middle bay door began to rise.

Shit. They were coming back. So soon? What did that mean for Connor? I wanted to run toward the incoming car and find out how he was. But I might be met with a bullet.

Heart racing, I stepped outside, pulled the door closed behind me. It was very early morning, just beginning to get light outside. The ground was wet and uneven, with patches of white from an early snowfall standing out here and there against dead brown grass. My feet got instantly soaked as I sprinted across the lawn and dived into the woods.

There was no trail here, just closely packed evergreens with dense brush in between, and it was almost too dark to see. Branches sprang back as I moved, clawing at my face. I stopped for long enough to slip the roll of tape over my wrist and tuck the trash bags into my waistband. At least now I could use my free hand to keep branches out of my face, clutching the kitchen knife in the other to defend myself. The ground sloped downward treacherously as I forged ahead. My breath rasped in my ears. My feet were going numb from the cold, and I had a terrible stitch in my side. But they could be right behind me, and I couldn't afford to stop again. There was a trail here somewhere—if only I could find it. I'd hiked this mountain in years past, though the last time was probably a decade ago. Unless its path had changed somehow in the years since, it would take me to a trailhead on the main road below. I could flag down a passing car for help.

As I pressed on, the ground got rockier. My little flats kept coming off my feet, and after the fourth or fifth time, I gave up and threw them in the bushes. That was a mistake. Ten minutes later, my feet were so cold that they were burning with pain. I had to do something, or I wouldn't be able to continue walking on them, and I'd get frostbite. Ahead, a steep drop-off looked impossible to navigate, but when I reached it, I was able to pick my way around the side. At the bottom of the drop, a boulder provided cover from above. I sank down in its hollow and examined my feet. They were a mess—red, swollen, blistered, and bleeding. Cutting pieces from the trash bag, I taped them on for makeshift shoes. I cut a neck hole in the second bag and pulled it over my clothes for warmth. A shaft of morning sunlight filtered through the trees. In the quiet that enveloped me here, I felt hysteria building. If I thought about Connor, about whether he was dead or alive, I'd break down. I had to keep going.

I got to my feet, listening intently. The sounds were those native to the woods—trees creaking, leaves rustling in the wind, the warble of birds. Kovacs and Juliet must have discovered by now that I was gone. I had to assume that they'd set out after me and were gaining on me. I took a deep breath, gathering my strength. The air smelled of pine and wet leaves. And then I saw it—straight ahead, a slash of blue paint on the bark of a tree. A blaze. I'd found the trail at last.

For the next hour, I managed the steep descent down the side of Baldwin Mountain. Recent rain had left the exposed trail slippery and muddy, with patches of snow glittering in the hollows. I skidded and fell more than once, then struggled to my feet and went on. Drained and panting, I thought the ordeal would never end. But then I spotted the trailhead, and my spirits lifted. I came to the edge of the woods. The parking lot was ahead just through these last trees, the road on the other side of it. The sun broke through and glinted off something. Something metallic. Shit. A car, waiting there. I stopped short and pulled behind the trunk of a tree. A black car.

The Suburban.

Kovacs stood beside it, a pair of binoculars raised to his eyes. As I watched, he swept the woods, then stopped.

He'd seen me.

I backtracked, breaking into a run, bushwhacking parallel to the road in the hope that I could find another route out. The thick brush slowed me down. I could hear him behind me. To my left, a car sped by. The road was right there. I turned downhill, running, and began to skid, falling, making the last few yards on my butt. The pavement was straight ahead. I jumped up and stumbled out into the road, gasping for breath.

It was a quiet, two-lane road. I knew it well. And no surprise in the late morning, it was empty of traffic.

I broke into a run. I knew exactly where I was. About a mile from here was the ski resort. Early November—it wouldn't be open yet. Still, there might be someone there, someone who could help. There might be a phone. I hoped to God there was, because the police station was at least five miles in the opposite direction.

I panted, running full out, my feet in their plastic wrap exploding with pain. I looked over my shoulder. Nobody there. Where had he gone? Was Juliet with him? A minute later, I checked again, and had my answer. The Suburban was barreling toward me. At the same moment, a truck rounded the bend, coming from the other direction. I ran into the road, waving my arms frantically. The driver slammed on the brakes.

A youngish guy with a baseball cap rolled down the window.

"Are you crazy? I could've killed you."

"Help! I'm a waitress at the Baldwin Grill. That guy in the Suburban kidnapped me, and I escaped. He's after me."

He looked through the windshield. The Suburban slowed down as it approached. Kovacs was watching us. The driver took a second to weigh what to do. A crazy woman wearing a plastic bag—you don't just let her in your truck.

"*Please.* I'm begging you."

The terror in my voice was unmistakable.

"Get in," he said.

I ran around and jumped up into the truck, and he floored it.

"I'll take you to the police station."

"Yes. Thank you. Thank you so much."

"Shit," he said, eyes on the rearview mirror. "He's turning around. He's gonna follow us. Here. Call nine-one-one."

He tossed me his phone. I dialed the cops, telling them where we were, what was happening, describing the truck and the Suburban. The dispatcher said she'd send a patrol car right away.

The truck sped along the windy road, fishtailing around curves, the Suburban close behind. With several miles still to go to the police station, we heard a loud metallic clang.

"That asswipe dinged my truck," the driver said. "You want to shoot back, I got a gun in the rack. Can't do it while I'm driving."

Just then, we heard the sirens. Suddenly the road was full of police vehicles. The driver skidded off the road, onto the narrow shoulder.

"Get down," he said.

I threw myself to the floor, hunkering into the footwell. Outside the truck, shots rang out. I covered my ears with my hands, cowering.

The shots died down, and the driver raised his head. He was pulling himself up onto the seat when a second round of shots broke the silence. The windshield exploded, raining chunks of blue-green glass over us. I ducked, arms over my head. The next time I looked up, the driver's face was covered in blood.

"Oh, my God. Are you hit?"

"I didn't feel anything."

He put his hand to his head. It came away bloody. "Shit. It must be a graze."

"I am *so* sorry to put you through this."

"I been shot at before. Deployed a couple times. Don't expect it around here, though."

After that, we stayed on the floor for what felt like forever. Silence reigned. We waited.

"Are they all dead?" I whispered.

In the distance, more sirens shrieked, moving closer by the second. We heard cars pulling up, doors slamming, voices shouting. We stayed down. They were going car to car. From the radios, we could tell it was cops.

"Stay down till they tell us, or they might shoot," the driver said.

I nodded.

"I'm Tabitha, by the way."

"Alex."

"Thank you for saving me, Alex. I owe you big-time."

"Happy to help. You can pay for the windshield, though."

"You got it."

Eventually, someone came to the driver's-side door of the truck. It was a cop, in uniform.

"You folks the ones that called this in?"

"She did," Alex said. "Says the guy in the Suburban kidnapped her."

"Yeah, we got him. Are you Tabitha Ford?" the officer asked.

"Yes. How did you know?"

"Police down on Long Island had an APB out on that vehicle. We were specifically told to look for you."

"What about my husband? Is he all right?"

"I'm sorry, I don't know anything about that."

"Was there anyone in the Suburban other than the driver?"

"A woman."

"Officer, please. My husband was shot. I'm so scared. He'd lost a lot of blood. If he wasn't at the hospital—if he's not in the Suburban—I know where he might be. Can you look for him?"

I gave the cop the address of the ski house.

"We'll send someone right over there," he said. "You all sit tight and wait for the paramedics."

He strode away. Eventually, they took us from the truck and put us in an ambulance. The flashing lights of the emergency vehicles hurt my eyes. I didn't see that officer again. I asked everyone I encountered what had happened to Connor, but nobody could give me an answer.

42

The ambulance transported me to the nearest hospital, which happened to be the same one where I used to work years earlier. Being wheeled into the familiar lobby felt surreal, like my life as Mrs. Ford had been a dream. Or more accurately, a nightmare. Strange and wonderful things had happened, but terrible things also. And I waited, knowing that the most terrible of all was about to descend on me and change my life forever. I expected bad news about Connor. The delay did not bode well.

They bandaged my cuts and contusions, diagnosed me with a concussion, and held me for hours for observation. They did an ultrasound and told me the baby was fine. Seeing her on the screen, all I could think was *Where is her father?*

They told me to wait in the treatment room until the nurse came with my discharge papers. I was climbing the walls, cooped up there with no phone and no information, not knowing the fate of the man I loved. I asked every nurse who walked by about the police investigation, whether they knew if anyone else had been brought in. Nobody did.

As soon as my papers were signed, I got up and walked the halls until I found someone who remembered me from when I'd worked here. Kelsey was an administrative assistant in the emergency department. She searched admissions records and told me there was no indication that Connor had been brought in for treatment. The fact that he wasn't yet hospitalized made me more afraid than ever. Given his condition, he'd been in urgent need of medical attention. Yet they hadn't brought him here, to the nearest hospital. In the recesses of my brain, I'd already known that they hadn't gotten him to a doctor. The Suburban had left and then returned to the ski house in less time than it would take to get here. I'd been blocking that knowledge, but it flooded in now, along with the consciousness of what it must mean—that Connor had died in the car on the way to the hospital. I sat very still and focused my heart and mind on praying for that not to be true. But reality seeped in. I knew it was hopeless, and knowing that, I felt numb with despair.

"Tabitha, you look awful. Can I call someone for you?" Kelsey asked.

I asked her to track down the phone number for the police department back in Southampton, then borrowed her phone, called, and explained who I was. The dispatcher told me that Hagerty and Pardo were on their way to New Hampshire now, because of my case. She connected me to Hagerty's cell phone.

"I'm glad to hear you're okay," Hagerty said. "We were worried."

"Forget about me. Where's my husband? Tell me, I need to know."

"He's not with you?"

"With *me*? No. He got shot. He was in bad shape. I gave one of the local cops an address where he might be. Please, do you know if they found him?"

"I don't understand. I was told you were brought in with an injured male who was treated and released."

"But that wasn't Connor. I ran from Kovacs and Juliet, and a guy named Alex picked me up—"

"Wait, you're saying Connor Ford was shot and seriously wounded?"

"Yes. You don't *know* that?"

"No. Last night, we received an alarm that your bracelet had been deactivated, and around the same time there was a call about shots fired at Windswept."

"Yes, like I said, Connor was shot."

"We responded immediately and found blood in your bedroom, but we assumed it was yours. The housekeeper said she witnessed you and Ford get pushed into that Suburban at gunpoint by Kovacs. We've been very worried about you, Tabitha."

"How did you find me?"

"The housekeeper got the plate number, and we put out an APB. You're saying the assistant was involved, too? I got the text you sent with the photo of her birth certificate, but I didn't understand the relevance."

"It's complicated. Everything is explained on the recording from the ankle bracelet."

"I haven't had a chance to listen to that yet. It's being downloaded as we speak by a technician at the DA's office. Can you fill me in?"

"There's no time to explain. Just—Juliet killed Nina, okay? Kovacs was involved somehow. I don't really know how, exactly. But Connor is innocent. Juliet shot him. And I'm afraid he's dead. Please, Detective. Please. Do something."

I broke into sobs.

"Okay, now I understand," Hagerty said. "Listen. Hang up. I'll find out whatever I can and get back to you ASAP at the number you're calling from."

As I sat in the chair beside Kelsey's desk, crying hysterically, a familiar figure marched down the hall toward me. It was Liz, my manager from the restaurant, with her arms outstretched and a concerned look on her face. I stepped into her comforting embrace.

"Alex called me, and I rushed right over. What the hell happened?" she said.

"Alex?"

"The guy who picked you up in his truck, escaping from *kidnappers* apparently? He's my husband's cousin. What the hell is going on, Tabitha?"

I tried to talk through my sobs, but it was just too hard.

"Never mind, you can explain later. What can I do to help?"

I managed to get out that Connor had been shot, and I was waiting to hear if he'd survived. I had to wait by Kelsey's desk, because I didn't have my phone, and the detective was going to call me back on hers.

"I'll stay with you for as long as you need me," Liz said. "Let's text him my number instead, so we're not stuck waiting in this hallway."

After that, Liz brought me to the cafeteria and made me drink some herbal tea and eat something. It felt like a lifetime, but only fifteen minutes passed before Hagerty called Liz's cell. The recording from last night had been downloaded and reviewed by the DA. They now understood I'd been telling the truth all along.

"We're sorry for the inconvenience," Hagerty said. "Your charges are being dismissed."

I huffed in disbelief. "You're sorry for the—Jesus. My husband was shot. Would that even have happened if—"

I dropped my head into my hands, crying again, my breath coming in harsh sobs. Liz took the phone. I couldn't tell from her end of the conversation what was happening. She hung up after a couple of minutes.

"They're on the way here right now. We're supposed to meet them in five minutes in a conference room in the basement."

"I never want to see those cops again."

"You need to be strong, hon. I think they have news."

Her eyes were veiled with worry. It was bad.

I leaned on Liz all the way to the elevator, down four floors and one long, sterile corridor. Hagerty and Pardo were already there, waiting for me in a small conference room with buzzing lights, along with another man in plain clothes who had the look of a cop about him. I knew what was coming. I could see it in their eyes. The truth was, I'd known for hours. I couldn't forget what I'd seen—the deathly pallor on Connor's face, the blood soaking the back of the Suburban, Juliet's horrified expression when she checked his pulse. I knew in my heart that he couldn't survive all that. Yet, I'd been hoping. Praying. Pretending none of it was real.

"I'm sorry, Tabitha," Hagerty said, and his choirboy face looked crumpled and sad. "The local PD recovered a body from the ski house—"

I collapsed into the nearest chair, shaking all over.

"—and we believe it's your husband."

My body felt cold as ice. I stared back and forth between them, everyone in that awful room, for whom this was just another day on the job. I'd thought I'd known what was coming. How it would feel. I'd had no idea. It felt like the world had stopped. Like there would be no tomorrow. All I could do was tremble and beg.

"No, please. You must be wrong. It's not true."

But I knew it was.

"This is Detective Martinez. He'll take it from here," Hagerty said.

"Ma'am, my condolences," Martinez said. He was middle-aged, balding, with a sober expression. "It appears that the cause of death was a gunshot wound to the abdomen. The morgue is right down the hall. I have to ask you to identify your husband's body."

I dropped my head into my hands. "No, no, no," I whispered, but words couldn't make this nightmare go away.

"I understand this is very difficult," Martinez said. "But until he's identified, we can't proceed with the autopsy, and we can't release the body. He'll just stay in the morgue."

"Tabitha. Come on, sweetie, I know you're strong," Liz said.

I nodded blindly, my eyes full of tears, and reached for her hands. She helped me to my feet, and I followed Martinez from the room on shaky legs. The walk of twenty feet seemed endless, and I knew I would live it many times over in my dreams. We reached a pair of closed metal doors. The detective typed a code into a keypad on the wall, and I heard a lock disengage. We stepped into a refrigerated space no larger than a doctor's waiting room, and I gasped. There were no lockers for the bodies, like on TV. Just several steel gurneys and a smell of death and chemicals in the air. Two of the gurneys held bodies, covered by sheets. A pair of bare white feet protruded from the sheet of the gurney on the left.

His toe had stopped bleeding, at least.

"It's him," I said in a small voice. "I know because he was shot in the foot last night."

The detective stepped to the head of Connor's gurney and prepared to lift the sheet. "I'm sorry but we can't rely on that for the ID."

"Yes, I understand. Go ahead. I want to see him."

The breath left my body as he pulled the sheet aside.

Connor looked like himself, his perfect features so familiar, his dark lashes lying against his pale cheeks. He was just tired, I told myself, and pallid, and lying very still. I stepped up beside him and reached for his face, desperate to touch him again, as if my caress could awaken him from this terrible sleep. The detective stopped my hand.

"No contact."

"*Please.*"

"I'm sorry, ma'am. His body is evidence in the homicide investigation."

I doubled over in my grief, my hands on my stomach. It was just beginning to sink in that this baby would never know her father.

"He was shot protecting me. I want that known."

"Of course. We'd like to get your perspective, as soon as you're ready to be interviewed. Your husband's, uh—your *husband* will be released to you after the autopsy. I'm going to cover him again, okay?"

I nodded wordlessly.

"I'm sorry, but I need to ask one more favor. We have a second victim here, a female, who was found deceased from a gunshot wound in the passenger seat of the Suburban. The circumstances of her death are under investigation. We've tentatively identified her as Juliet Davis, though I understand that may be an alias. If you could—"

"Yes. Show me."

He pulled the sheet aside.

"That's her," I said. It gave me no pleasure that Juliet had lost her life. It wouldn't bring Connor back.

"What happened to Steve Kovacs?"

"Shot in a firefight with our officers. In surgery. Not expected to make it."

We returned to the conference room. I collapsed into a chair. Someone brought me a glass of water. The detectives and Liz talked around me, but I had trouble understanding what they were saying. Eventually, it was agreed I'd go home with Liz and return tomorrow for a full debriefing, after I'd had a chance to rest.

Somebody lent me a coat, a red puffer jacket from the lost and found. I followed Liz out to the parking lot. It was starting to snow in sharp, icy crystals that stung my cheeks and made me cold deep in the bone. She cleared a box of tissues and a stuffed animal off the passenger seat of her minivan and threw them in the back. I sank down and breathed deeply. I'd ridden in Liz's car a few times before. It still smelled like Goldfish crackers and sports equipment.

Life went on for some people, but mine would never be the same. Being with Connor was a dream that I never quite believed in. And now it was over, before it had really begun.

Liz started the car and turned up the heat. Just then, the baby gave me a hard kick, and I remembered that I wasn't alone. That I had her. And that part of him would live on in her. My hand flew to my midsection. The wonder of the moment must have shined in my eyes, because Liz turned to me with a sad smile.

"When are you due?" she asked.

43

One year later

Some things are too good to be true. Connor was like that. He was fireworks against the night sky—spectacular and beautiful and gone much too soon. Yet, he'd left me a legacy that would last.

My daughter slept in the baby carrier, snuggled against my chest, as I walked into the conference room and shook hands with my lawyer.

"I'm so glad you brought her. Can I see?"

I turned sideways so Meg's face was visible. Her thumb was in her mouth, her sooty lashes forming perfect half-moons against the velvet of her cheeks.

"Beautiful," she said.

"She has her daddy's eyes."

"I remember when we first met, and you told me you were expecting."

"Ugh, in that jail cell? I'd rather not think about it."

"You've been through a lot, Tabitha. I know you don't have the appetite for a fight, but you can still change your mind. It's a lot to give up for her. Are you sure?"

I'd come to my lawyer's office today to sign a settlement agreement. At the time of his death, Connor was the legal heir to Nina Levitt's fortune, and as Connor's heir, I'd stepped into that position. But the estate was still subject to the lawsuit by Nina's sister, Kara Baxter, who'd argued in court that Connor shouldn't inherit because he was responsible for Nina's death. I knew that was a lie. And I couldn't allow his name to be publicly sullied. So, I'd hired Suzanne Cohen again, to prove Connor's innocence in court for all the world to see. With the recording from that awful night, we had the evidence to win the case outright. Kara Baxter's lawyers knew that. They'd begged us to settle for half the estate. But that just didn't feel right to me. I saw no reason why I should get half of Nina's vast fortune. Not only didn't I know Nina, but I'd slept with the poor woman's husband. I felt guilty about that to this day, so how could I take her money? But neither did I see why Kara should get it. The two of them had been estranged for decades, and Kara had willfully lied about Connor and me, smearing us in the press and setting off our troubles.

I had my lawyer propose a deal where Nina's fortune went to charity, except that Kara would get five million in exchange for dropping the lawsuit and making a public statement acknowledging Connor's innocence. That seemed like a fair price to pay for my daughter to grow up knowing that her father had been a good man. Financially, we would be fine. We already were. Connor had three million dollars in life insurance from his executive position at Levitt Global, paid in full, so I knew that our future was secure.

"We have everything we could ever need. Let's do this," I said.

I signed the papers. Five million would be wired to Kara Baxter. Another five million was held aside as a settlement to Gloria for the pain and suffering she'd endured at the hands of Edward Levitt. The remainder was allocated to the Nina Levitt Foundation, dedicated to education and the arts.

Now, I had to go on with the difficult task of rebuilding my life, if only for my daughter's sake. I'd bought a house in Lakeside, about ten minutes from the restaurant. The house was modest, but the neighborhood was excellent, with wonderful schools for when Meg was older. I had a new Toyota RAV4 hybrid that got good safety ratings. And I was in the process of buying the Baldwin Grill, which had been put up for sale by its owners and might otherwise have shut down. Liz would continue to manage the restaurant, and Matt would bartend. But the chef had left, and I'd hired Liz's husband's cousin to replace him—the guy in the truck who'd rescued me that awful day. Alex owned an organic farm and had been to culinary school. He had a vision of turning the place into a farm-to-table destination, and I was interested in being part of that.

By giving up any claim to Nina Levitt's fortune, I'd put that strange, glittering, awful time behind me. I was making a life that felt right, except for one awful, yawning absence. Connor had died to protect me and our daughter. I wasn't sure I'd ever get over him, or even that I wanted to. If I did, it wouldn't happen for a long time. For now, I sometimes felt his presence around me, and saw him when I looked into my daughter's eyes. He was a good man. Not a perfect man, but he loved me. And I loved him, dearly. Our daughter is the legacy of that.

1. *The Wife Who Knew Too Much* opens with Nina's diary entry warning that Connor is planning to kill her to be with another woman, followed by the news report of her death. Did you ever question whether Nina was telling the truth in her diary? If you believed her, how did that affect your reaction to the other characters as the book unfolded? Were you able to keep an open mind about the cause of Nina's death, and who the guilty party (or parties) might be?

2. Tabitha first met Connor when she worked as a pool girl at his grandmother's country club. Years later, they found each other again when he walked into the restaurant where she was working as a waitress. How did the wealth and class differences between them influence their relationship? How did it constrain her behavior throughout the book?

3. Tabitha grew up in difficult circumstances, not just financially but also emotionally. What scars does she carry from her dysfunctional childhood? How does her past influence her actions in the present?

4. Nina's chapters reveal harrowing details about her relationship with her first husband, the real-estate tycoon Edward Levitt. What effect did that marriage have on Nina? Did you sympathize with her or judge her for staying with him? What role did Nina's marriage to Edward play in her later behavior toward Connor? What role did it play in the circumstances that led to her death?

5. What effect does the Levitt fortune have on various characters in the book? Discuss this with respect to Nina, Connor, Tabitha, and Juliet.

ST. MARTIN'S GRIFFIN

6. What did you think of Connor as a character? Did he have a moral compass, or was he motivated solely by vanity and greed? What was the source of his appeal to Tabitha? To Nina? Did you like him? Did your view of him change over the course of the novel?

7. The theme of trust within marriage is present throughout *The Wife Who Knew Too Much*. How does trust (or the lack of it) affect Nina and Connor's marriage? How does it affect Tabitha and Connor's marriage? What role does lack of trust play in advancing the plot?

8. The book follows Tabitha as she navigates two very different worlds—working as a waitress in New Hampshire, and enjoying vast wealth as Connor's wife in the Hamptons. How well or poorly does Tabitha deal with the change in her circumstances? In which setting does she really belong? How did the two contrasting settings affect your feelings about Tabitha as a character?

9. Were you happy with where Tabitha ended up and the choices she made at the end of the novel? Why or why not?

10. Did you see the ending coming? If yes, when did you start to figure it out? If no, what did you think was going to happen?

Nina Subin

A graduate of Harvard University and Stanford Law School, MICHELE CAMPBELL worked at a prestigious Manhattan law firm before spending eight years fighting crime as a federal prosecutor in New York City.